ABIDING HOPE

"I ain't changin' my name. I ain't gonna marry you. I'll wear what I want to wear. I'll . . . I'll go naked afore I wear your dang-blamed clothes."

No-Account furiously tried to unbutton her dress. A button popped off revealing the too-large chemise beneath. Her barely concealed breasts nearly bounced free in rhythm with her agitated breathing.

"Confound it," Mike said while he clasped the front of her partially open dress. It brought her closer. "Stop this instant," he growled down at her. She froze.

They stood toe to toe, her eyes wide open, lips slightly apart.

No-Account had the strangest feeling. Thunderation, she wanted to be mad as hell and she couldn't say another word. She licked her lips.

Almost violently he thrust her away. While he paced, she stood, silent and confused. "Let me make this clear." The words, soft with a threat, tumbled from his lips. "You can pick a name, or I'll pick one for you. Hope, I think."

TEMPTED
MONICA ROBERTS

LOVE SPELL BOOKS NEW YORK CITY

LOVE SPELL®

December 1999

Published by

Dorchester Publishing Co., Inc.
276 Fifth Avenue
New York, NY 10001

ISBN 0-505-52353-1

Printed in the United States of America.

Thanks to my husband, Bob, for believing in me, and to all of my children—especially Heidi, who unlocked my computer and proofread my work.

Thanks to members of Central PA Romance Writers who listened and counseled—and to Ginny Aiken, who predicted my book would be published.

And finally, thanks to Chris Keeslar and Dorchester Publishing, who nudged a new writer in the right direction, and to my agent, Jennifer Jackson, who stepped in when I most needed her.

Chapter One

Coldbottom, California
Gold Rush, 1853

"Hey, Preacher," yelled Dead-Eye Stiles. "Waitin' for a wife, are ya?"

Shaky Jake Bradley laughed deep in his chest, then spewed chaw. "Got the itch, huh?"

The gathered men laughed and pummeled each other.

Standing away from the crowd awaiting the stagecoach, Rev. Michael Mulgrew folded his arms.

Excitement and curiosity brought out a crowd every time a group of mail-order brides arrived. This time, however, the future wife of "Preacher Perfect" would be aboard the stage. That fact had provided fodder for speculation among the news-hungry residents of Coldbottom—and for more than twenty miles around town.

Mike refused to let their jibes ruin this day for him.

Trouble was, he did have the itch. Celibacy in a boom-town could wear a man down.

"Say there, Parson, I'll bet you're in a hurry to get *this* wedding day over," crowed a fellow nearby. Mike kept his expression bland—not an easy thing to do, considering he had a bellyful of butterflies.

That particular remark scraped away some of Mike's confidence. His life proceeded according to a preplanned schedule, and only after a long, fervent prayer did he act on any one of his daily, weekly, or yearly to-do lists. Those lists provided him with a sense of control. And tomorrow he could strike out the words *Find wife* on his life plan checklist.

The few women who lived in Coldbottom were either married or of questionable morals. Since he had little time to search for—or court—a suitable prospect, Mike had decided to put his faith to work; he'd placed a newspaper advertisement.

"Mike," yelled a wiry old man from the front of the crowd, "are you getting a wife 'cause you're tired of cleaning that parsonage you built?" It was Shy Boggs, and he continued, telling a group of newer arrivals, "Parson is odd. He washes his dishes, clothes, and even his person—every day. Hell, he even combs his hair before going to work his claim."

Bart Stoker rubbed his crotch. "When's the nuptials? I'm hankerin' ta share my bed as soon as my gal steps off that stagecoach."

"Eh, Mike," said Frenchy Fortier, waggling his finger, "You no cheat, live in sin."

"Preacher Perfect, your life's gonna be hell now," said a miner Mike didn't recognize.

The remarks raised his ire, but he didn't let it show. Even tempered, clean and tidy, Mike considered himself a fine catch for some lucky woman, no matter what this mob thought.

There was, however, one major detail that caused him some concern—and a man of twenty-seven couldn't just up and ask another what to do with a woman in bed, could he?

He shifted, jamming his fists in his pockets. *Don't think about it. It's all planned.*

With determination, Mike turned his thoughts to the more promising aspects of matrimony. A sweet, smiling woman at his side would ease his loneliness. While he tended his animals, she'd put bacon to sizzling and biscuits to baking . . . why, he could just about smell them. She'd mend and hum. Mike himself preferred whistling, but not in a woman.

Ziganya Kalmenos came toward him, her bold stride setting her bracelets jingling. The woman occasionally worked the crowds of men who awaited the stage. Today she held a burning cheroot between her teeth. The Gypsy had always made him feel uneasy, so he moved a few paces back to let her pass. She paused before him.

"There is much change in your future," she began, but behind her, her husky toddler of a grandson wandered out into the dusty street. It was only through the grace of heaven that Mike was able to dive after the boy in time to save him from passing carriage. He handed the child to Ziganya.

The old woman hugged the child to her, admonishing and comforting him while he sobbed into her shoulder. "You. I give you for free what others pay for. You will have surprises, but you will find your dream only after much discord."

"Pure superstition," he said, having done his good deed and not wanting to encourage her godless ways. He looked dismissively into the distance.

Ziganya blew smoke from her cheroot with a laugh. "Our paths will cross again. It is destiny." She carried the boy into the waiting crowd.

"Here they come," yelled Bart Stoker. In the distance a cloud of dust signaled the arrival of the stagecoach.

Mike stood alone. The other prospective grooms had grouped together, turned out in clothes that had been freshly laundered down to their long johns. Some spit on their hands and tried to slick down their wiry beards.

The circle of onlookers grew by the minute, and Mike knew himself to be the subject of much of their curiosity. Today every man and woman would see—and judge—Mike's life partner.

He'd taken a chance when he'd sent off the advertisement; the townspeople knew it. Risk unsettled him. However, in the ensuing weeks he had prayed with such fervor that he felt confident God would send him the perfect bride, a true soul mate.

No-Account Savage shaded her eyes to see ahead, but the dust raised by the stagecoach hampered her view. She took in the wilderness of California from her seat in an open wagon that clattered behind the mail coach. In this town she would put down roots, in this place of scrub grass and pine and snowy mountain peaks. She knew right off that this was where she belonged.

At the crack of the whip, the wagon surged forward. "We're almost there," she shouted, her violet eyes shining with excitement.

"Thank God for that," said the man who sat nearest her. He held a bandanna to his face when she bounced near.

"I'll tell my preacher husband you said that. He'll be mighty pleased ta know you're a prayin' man."

"You sure he sent for *you*?"

"Yep. Even gave me extry money for food, but I saved him some." She leaned forward, coins in her extended palm.

"Get back where you belong," he said, turning away to draw in a lungful of dusty air.

12

While her fellow passengers had complained constantly about the rocky ride, No-Account herself hadn't minded any part of the long journey. She'd seen much worse, and the future looked bright. She looked forward to *belonging* somewhere.

A smile tilted her lips at the memory of the fellow who'd crawled back to sit beside her a few days out of Kansas, asking, "I hear you're a gal."

"O' course I am," she'd replied. "Ain't you got eyes?"

"I got me some pretty-smelling soap I could use on you. Know what I mean?" He'd placed his hand on her dirty chest, leaning into her in preparation to nuzzling her neck. There he'd had the full impact of her daily dose of wild garlic. At the same time, No-Account had whipped out her knife and pressed it between his legs. "Get your hands off me, 'less ya want ta lose your pisser."

He'd moved. Fast. After that no one had bothered her.

She looked over at the man who slept soundly beside her, childlike and trusting. No-Account wasn't ready for others to know that the man was her brother, Slow. Their traveling companions had tagged him as witless, treating him badly. But Slow neither minded nor understood when others belittled him, so it had been only once that she'd had to step in to champion him, when a mean-looking loner had up and spit in Slow's face for no reason at all. Without hesitation, she'd aimed her gun directly between his eyes. "Mister, you better say your prayers, or tell him you're powerful sorry."

"You ain't going to shoot me, girlie. Never met a female any good with a shootin' iron."

At that, No-Account had sent his hat flying into the dust of the trail, where it had rolled off to the side.

Jaw hanging, he'd squinted at her, then turned to Slow. With a great struggle he said, "Beggin' your pardon."

Slow had smiled, wiping the heavy phlegm from his cheek. " 'Tain't no never mind," was all he'd said.

13

At the post stops, while the others ate indoors, No-Account had bought food for her and Slow to share, and they'd usually eaten alone under a tree. Until she met her husband, she intended to keep her brother's presence entirely to herself.

Sure was a mystery why folks picked on Slow, Ma's last-born child. Every place they had lived he'd suffered at the hands of those who considered themselves better.

When No-Account had became old enough to mind how things were for him, she'd made herself his care-taker. Where No-Account went, Slow tagged along. She hoped the parson had a kindly way with simple folk like Slow.

Despite the commotion in the wagon, Slow slept on. Her brother embraced life with childlike joy, trusting in No-Account's decisions. She scowled as she recalled that Pa had taken a switch to him regularly until No-Account had stepped in with a switch of her own. Swishing the hickory stick, she had circled Pa while Slow had gotten away. No-Account had wanted to throw a scare into Pa, and it had worked. He'd left them alone after that. Pa gave meaning to the words *shiftless coward.*

Though Parson Mulgrew had sent her a ticket, No-Account had stayed until she and Slow had worked long and hard to buy Slow's passage to California.

The wagon surged again, this time waking her brother. "What's happenin'?" he asked.

Two more cracks split the air as the driver shouted, "Yahoo! We're leaving that stage *behind,* boys."

No-Account leaned forward, thrilled to be in the thick of the action. "Looks like we're havin' a race," she shouted to Slow.

The men in the wagon held on to their hats as the wagon passed the stagecoach.

"I'm hungry, Sis," Slow complained close to her ear.

14

She reached into her bulky sack and withdrew a dried apple and a piece of jerky. "This'll have ta do. Now you remember ta keep to the back when I get off, then follow along behind. Mind now, not too close."

"I'm scared. What if your new husband don't like me?"

The noise had escalated, so No-Account just patted his hand. "Come on. Let's have us some fun!" she shouted. She rose to her feet, waving her hat with one hand while holding the side rope with the other. A brave front usually worked to soothe Slow's fear, and she needed a bit of courage herself right now.

Slow joined her, pocketing the apple for later. He stomped his feet and shouted with glee through the last quarter mile.

The wagon came to an abrupt stop where the crowd had gathered, and No-Account and Slow were thrown off balance, falling back down into the wagon bed.

So here we are, No-Account observed as travel-weary men climbed out and onto the dusty main street. She hung back, leaning her elbows on the wagon rail. "There must be a hunnert tents on that hill," she said to Slow.

"Looks like a big prayer meetin'." His eyes widened. "Maybe one tent belongs ta your preacher."

She nodded, looking the men over, wondering if her parson was among them. Most of them had beards, like the men back home. No-Account wasn't partial to hair growing on a man's face. Though some said you weren't a man unless you had it, in her experience facial hair didn't measure a man on the inside.

Her eyes scanned the clusters of men shaking hands, slapping backs. The folks here seemed friendly enough. What would a preacher look like here in gold country?

"Slow, you go over there by that horse rail. That way you won't be noticed. Follow where I go, though."

The stage driver, Ben, leaped from his seat after setting the brake. "Step up and meet your ladies, boys." He

15

opened the door with a flourish, placing a step for the ladies to leave the coach.

At each stop, No-Account had heard her female companions discuss their hopes and fears, so she watched with interest as Cornelia Roundtree, then Florine Berefort stepped out onto the dusty ground in their traveling dresses. She sniffed and rubbed a sleeve across her nose. No-Account preferred the freedom of her britches.

Cornelia had expressed her doubts constantly, though No-Account wondered why a body would worry over something she had chosen to do with her own life.

Two men came forward to claim the ladies. Cornelia looked relieved when her man bowed before her. With a small dip of her head, she offered her arm. He said something No-Account couldn't hear, but she saw Cornelia smile.

Florine's man, however, marched right up to her, grabbed her by the shoulders, and planted a lusty kiss on her lips.

Shocked, she stumbled back from him. No-Account didn't hear what Florine said from where she stood, but her words set the crowd to laughing uproariously.

Leaning against the wall of the mercantile, Mike observed the mating ritual. He grinned as the chastised Frenchy Fortier mumbled, "*Oui, mademoiselle,*" and took Florine's arm.

He thought them well matched. She might even civilize the former squaw man.

When the next passenger alighted, a murmur ran through the crowd. Delicate as a flower, wearing a simple gray dress trimmed with violet ribbons, she was everything Mike expected in a bride, right down to the demure straw bonnet tied under her chin. Now, that's a fine woman.

"Preacher's wife for sure," Bart Stoker said, nearby.

16

Mike started forward. God had answered his prayers, as usual. Yet he hesitated when he saw the driver direct Harvey Ketchum to her bags. Harvey worked for the hotel, and Mike wondered why she wanted to room there. Morals, he decided. The woman had morals.

Again he started in her direction. He would assure her of the safety of his home. But she passed right by him, leaving the scent of lily of the valley in her wake.

Every man respectfully tipped his hat. When she was out of earshot, Ben warned, "Don't none of you tomcats go getting ideas. That's *Mrs*. Pearl Damian. Poor thing is a brand-new widow. She's not for you, Parson."

"Ah . . . " Mike's gaze lingered on Mrs. Damian's retreating figure, but to establish an unruffled air, he quickly turned his attention to the three women who'd come out into the sunshine from the stage.

"Bart Stoker," called Ben. Bart wiped his hands on his pants and gave one last pat to his beard before he stepped forward to claim the arm of a woman Ben called Ada Crump. Ada, a tall woman, stood erect, her bountiful bosom at just about Bart's eye level, prompting bawdy jokes from the crowd. Bart actually blushed.

Next, Barney Coachman and Vince O'Malley were introduced to twin sisters, Daisy and Dahlia Hinkle, a pair as thin as grass and plain of face.

Someone in the back yelled, "Sure hope they can cook, 'cause it don't appear they eat regular-like."

"We cook." The one who spoke sent a withering glare in the direction of the remark.

While he nervously tried to slick down a stubborn cowlick at his crown, Barney asked, "Which is which?"

A guffaw rang out. "That there's a good question, Barney. All they need is broomsticks."

One woman paled, while the other pursed her lips and looked at the crowd. "Then I'd suggest you be more careful what you say around us."

17

Laughter erupted.

"Damn good sport you are," said Barney. "You must be my Daisy."

She smiled. "Indeed, yes. This is my sister Dahlia. She's to be Mr. O'Malley's wife."

Vince came forward. "Howdy do, Miss Dahlia. Don't be afraid, 'cause I promise I'll be good to you."

Mike felt the crowd's interest shift back to him, but Ben slammed the stage door. "Mr. Arendt?" he began. "My bride . . . where is she?"

Ben shifted from foot to foot. "Well, Reverend, there's no easy way to say this. Over there is Miss No-Account Savage." He pointed to an ill-kempt figure in the wagon behind the stage.

With horrible clarity, Mike suddenly realized the filthy youth was not an adventure-seeking boy. If he could believe the driver, under all that grime beat the heart of the woman he was to call *wife* for the rest of his days.

"That's *her?*"

"Yep, that's her."

With a smile on her face, the person in question sprang over the side of the wagon to swagger toward Mike. The crowd grew silent, falling back when she passed near.

Mike offered a prayer for deliverance, but no California earthquake came to remove the awful sight.

She stopped in front of Mike and shifted her rucksack, leaving her hand free to pump his. "Howdy. You must be my preacher. I'm No-Account."

Thunderstruck, Mike gaped at her. He noticed that silence, a rare thing in Coldbottom, had overtaken the assembly. With another prayer, this one that he might be swallowed up where he stood, Mike dug out a handkerchief to wipe his hand.

"Impossible. I'm waiting for a Miss N. A. Sage. I have her letter right here." Finished with his handkerchief, he put it away to take a letter from his shirt pocket.

To the side, Mike saw Ben shake his head.

No-Account looked at the letter. "That's me, but the damn fool what writ it must o' gotten my name wrong."

Mike almost gagged from the stench that wafted from her. His dreams of a perfectly run household and sweet words of affection toppled like trees in an avalanche. He became aware that the gathering now viewed his misfortune with amusement. Chuckles and low rumbles reached his ears. They were laughing at *him*.

Confound it! This didn't fit into his life plan at all. It just didn't fit.

"Parson?" the girl asked. "You look kind o' green. If you got a bilious stomach, I got my yerbs here. Hell, my yerbs been known ta bring back a half-dead mule."

When she bent to open her sack, fumes rose from it like a fetid fog. Flies swarmed.

"No, don't!" Mike stepped back, tugging his left ear.

She straightened. "I'm only gettin' my yerbs."

Mike stabbed at the letter with his finger. "Here. This is from Miss Sage, an orphan and one of fourteen children. It also says she's a 'cheerful and pleasant young lady.' "

No-Account lifted a delicate eyebrow at odds with the rest of her person. "He said that? Well, ain't that nice. I am Miss No-Account Savage what's on that paper. You want me ta name all my kin?"

"You come from Kansas?"

"No, sir. We lived in the hills way east. Hard country. And once Ma was gone, we moved on. We went to Kansas City, but it's too big. I knew right off it were too crowded for me. California looks like a place where a gal can stretch out her arms without bumpin' into another body."

Mike became aware that he and this urchin were the center of attention, and the crowd was avidly taking in every word. To save face, he looked at the letter and said the kindest thing he could think of. "You have a very good way with a letter, miss."

"Pshaw! A nice man at the newspaper writ it for me." She took off her hat to fan her face. "It's hot in this here sun."

The sudden movement sent her pungent odor to his nostrils, causing him to back away.

"There's got to be a mistake. You're not—" He stopped.

"I ain't a city gal. I thought you wanted a strong wife who'd stick by you. That man said he'd write it nice an' proper—just what I told him—iffen I'd leave right away. I cain't think how he got my name wrong. 'Tween us, I think he might o' been grievin'. His eyes was a-cryin' mighty fierce."

Mike sympathized. His own eyes had begun to tear. Dear God, what could he do? Get them both away from the growing crowd. After that, he would let the Lord determine his fate.

He realized that No-Account had boldly taken stock of him from head to toe when she announced, "I ain't never seen a man so purty. You're a big one, too. How's the weather up there?" She let out a husky, decidedly female laugh. Violet eyes sparkled through dusty lashes. She was brown dirt and dust from head to toe. He hoped it would wash off.

Grabbing her sack, she commented, "You ain't got a funny bone in you, I reckon. Where's your livin' tent, Parson?"

"Living tent," he mumbled. "Tent? What tent?"

"You have a place ta pile my bones at night, don't you?" She nodded at the jumble of tents in the distance.

"No. I mean . . . I have to find someplace for you to stay." He should have arranged for accommodations before this. A wife's arrival hadn't seemed real until now—*wife* was just a word on a list. And clearly he had qualms about taking this vagabond bride home.

She interrupted his thoughts. "Lookee here, if you're Parson Mike Mulgrew, I'm yourn." Her voice took on a decided edge. "We're gettin' hitched, ain't we? So I'll follow along ta your place. 'N stop lookin' at me like I'm Old Nick."

Mortified, and without a word, Mike marched toward his home. Maybe the two-mile walk would clear his head.

Someone yelled, "Hey, Mike, don't scratch that itch till you're sure you won't catch something."

Harry the barkeep, who rarely ventured out of his establishment, called out, "What about the weddings, Reverend? It might take you a while to clean up that bride of yours."

Though the catcalls and wisecracks urged him to run for cover, Mike did have a duty to perform. He hesitated long enough to say, "The weddings will be tomorrow, noon, at the church." He strode away from his humiliation, hoping he might lose the little savage. But she dogged his footsteps like a faithful hound.

Meanwhile, word spread about Preacher Perfect's imperfect wife. Money changed hands as wagers flew. Preacher Perfect wouldn't marry this one. No sirree!

Chapter Two

With her bulky sack against her chest, No-Account had to run to keep up with Mike's long strides. *He sure is testy,* she thought. *I wonder if he ever smiles. Now that would be a sight to see.*

She'd been stunned by the beauty of the man. His hair was black and shiny as raven's wings, and he had eyes the deep color of evergreens in shade. Why he wanted a wife like her was a real flamboozler. Stopping to wipe perspiration from her face, she put down her sack and called to him, "Wait up there, will you?"

He merely threw a scowl over his shoulder.

"Where's the church?" she asked.

"At my place."

"Do you always walk so all-fired fast?"

"Do you always ask so many questions?" he fired back, though he did slow his pace.

No-Account picked up her sack again. "How are the marryin' folk goin' to get to your place 'n the church?

Them ladies aren't fond o' walkin' in the sun, I can tell you right now."

"I usually rent a rig."

To her surprise they passed the tent town and a few rough buildings. She felt it her duty to ask, "Where we goin'? You live out in the wild?"

"No," he barked. "My house is—"

She hauled up short. "You got a *house?*"

When he didn't answer, she held her pack close and ran to catch up with him. *A house? Gawd almighty, a house.* The unexpected bit of news thrilled her.

"Hey, slow down. I'm losin' my things. There goes my hat."

He huffed, "I'll buy you a new one."

"It was a durned nice hat." She slammed into him when he stopped abruptly. Breathing hard, she retreated from his solid back. No-Account's belly clenched at the contact and she got all tingly. What the heck was wrong with her? she wondered. They covered another mile or more before he finally stopped beside a stream that rumbled into a creek.

Using her sleeve, she again wiped sweat from her forehead. Over Mike's shoulder she caught a glimpse of white, then went around him to get a better look.

Her steps slowed, then stopped. Before her lay a vision. A house. Vines of morning glories curled to the porch roof, their blossoms half-closed in the midday sun.

"Ain't it handsome," she whispered. "Whose is it?"

"Mine."

No-Account dropped her sack where she stood. "Damn. Real winders. An' it's painted. Kinda shines in the sun."

The sight drew her forward. "You got a rockin' chair on the porch." With a glance toward Mike, she trailed a finger over the short handrail anchored beside the steps.

Eyes glistening, face soft under layers of dust, she remarked, "Oh, my. I never owned nothin' so grand."

"Miss . . . Savage, you said?"

"Sure did, but then I don't rightly know." She scratched her matted hair. "In the hills we was called 'the Savages' from first I reckoned. Folks kinda left us to ourselves. 'Cept fer Pa. All they wanted from him was moonshine."

Her cumbersome pack lay in the grass. Mike bent to move it.

"Hold up there."

Mike looked up, then reared back. "Now what?" he demanded.

He hadn't expected her to pull a gun on him, she knew, but a gal had to stake her claim early. "*Nobody* touches my sack. I got my personals in there."

He stepped over the bundle, his neck corded in anger.

Cocked gun in hand, No-Account bounded onto the porch to try the rocking chair. It creaked in rhythm to her furiously pumping feet. "Whooeee! Ain't never seen nothin' go damn beauteous."

"That does it! I don't know if I should wash your mouth out with soap or dump you in the creek." He looked ready to kill her.

"What you gettin' your balls all knotted up fer? 'Sides, I ain't gettin' in no creek. Why, I might get pumoney." Jutting her chin, No-Account put the gun on a nearby keg and looked him straight in the eye. She liked looking people in the eye. It made them come around to her way of thinking. With her gun close at hand, she thought she presented a frightening sight.

The preacher loomed over her, palms together, index fingers touching his lips.

She leaned forward to peer at him. "Your eyes looked green afore. Now they're near black."

His voice seductively soft, he said, "You want to see the inside of my house?"

She nodded.

"Then you'll have to clean up." He reached for her.

"Nope." She came off the chair and tried to cut around him.

He grabbed a fistful of sleeve, but nearly lost his grip when she spouted a stream of profanity at the top of her lungs. To her amazement, he lifted her and threw her over his shoulder. No-Account pounded her fists on his back. He didn't flinch, but tossed her into the water where, outraged, she fought to stand. Finding a foothold, she came up spluttering.

No one got away with mishandling No-Account Savage. Mad enough to take on a pack of wolves, she charged him. "You low-down . . . " Her words died when he shoved her back into the icy creek.

No-Account blew water from her mouth, then ran her forearm over her eyes to clear them. What she saw rendered her speechless, an unusual occurrence for No-Account Savage.

A furious Mike had placed his wet shirt over a bush to dry. Tan, muscled arms bunched as he vigorously rubbed his hands through his hair. No man had a right to have a chest like that. And arms like stovepipes. Hell, no wonder he'd thrown her in the creek. The preacher had expected a wife with regular looks. Being that handsome, he'd gotten the short straw.

He reached under a rock and sent a bar of soap sailing toward her. "Don't come out of the water until you're clean."

She caught the soap, but let it slip from her hand. "So there. Now whatcha gonna do?"

He sat on a rock and folded his arms. "I'm going to sit here until you find that soap and wash."

"You're tryin' to kill me," she wailed.

Sudden movement drew her attention to the trees behind Mike. Uh-oh, that had to be Slow. He must have followed them, as they'd planned. She hoped he wouldn't try to rescue her again. Trouble always followed her brother's efforts at protection. The last thing she needed right now was his untimely appearance. Things were bad enough.

Deciding that a little cooperation might go a long way, she splashed around until she found the soap and rubbed it on her arms. After a good dunking, she asked, "That good enough for you?"

"There's a lot more of you that needs washing, and don't forget your hair. *Especially* the hair," he said.

"You're plain mean. Cain't you see I'm froze near ta death?"

He neither yielded nor replied.

No-Account *never* gave in. But damn, she wanted to see the inside of that house. People cleaned up, but she'd never washed a thing in her life. Where to start? With a shiver she set to doing what would get her where she most wanted to be, inside that house.

Yanking a thong from her hair, she tossed it aside. The greasy, dun-colored mass tumbled to her waist. Rubbing with vigor, she drew the soap through her hair to the ends. When she bobbed down to rinse, bubbles pooled around her, bright strands of copper fanning out.

"I'm gettin' out now," she called.

"You're going to wash again, and wash those clothes too."

"I ain't takin' my clothes off. It ain't decent."

"You *will* wash those clothes. If you want privacy I'll go sit on the porch."

She invoked all the demons she could think of, blasting him to hell and back. Eventually she turned her back and stripped. "No sense tryin' ta milk a dead cow," she muttered.

* * *

Mike's dream in shreds, he paced the porch with his hands clasped behind his back. After his third rotation, he stopped. "She's made me the laughingstock of the area." He resumed pacing. "Surely there's been a mistake." He stopped again when his eyes caught the wet sheen of her back between snakes of hair.

Mike's distaste warred with his conscience. "What am I going to do?" With his shoulder against a post, he observed that even from this distance her curves were unmistakably female. Her slender waist flared to a very feminine bottom. Not looking away, he went to his water pump to slake his thirst. In his imagination he saw himself licking the runnels of water from her skin.

Mike shook himself. Had God sent this wildcat to Coldbottom to be his wife tomorrow? "Send me a sign, Lord."

No-Account shouted, "I'm done now."

Lost in thought, he barely heard her. There had to be some way to salvage his self-respect.

This time her throaty voice echoed all over the valley. "I said I'm *done!*"

Resigned, he took a towel from a peg inside the door. It occurred to him as he trod the path that she might have lice.

Probably because he'd had other things on his mind, he hadn't seen her tug her wet clothing on. Goose bumps covered her from her neck to the three buttons of her dripping, show-every-curve shirt.

Compressing his lips, he handed her the towel.

She took the fluffy length and wrapped it shawl-like around her shoulders, coming straight toward him out of the water.

The croak that replaced his voice when he could finally speak forced him to cough and try again. "Miss Savage, you're supposed to dry yourself with that. It's a towel."

28

"The sun's out real warm today. It'll dry me fine." She went to the rock he'd sat on earlier, and stretched out, her hands propping her upper body in a distractingly seductive posture.

Mike hesitated. Was she really that innocent, to pose herself before him, or was she just wanton?

"Your soap is there on that shale," she said.

"When you're dry I'll check your hair."

"Why?"

"To see if you have lice."

"I'm cleaner 'n a new baby. 'Sides, I never get lice." No Account straightened, squaring her shoulders. "It's the garlic."

"Garlic?"

"Iffen you eat garlic ever' day, you won't get bugs."

Her show of pride weakened his intent, yet he couldn't relent. He cocked his head meaningfully toward the house.

Stormy violet eyes showed her opinion of his demands before she rearranged herself to present her head.

The odor she carried hadn't dissipated. It was garlic, all right. It wafted strong and true on the breeze. He knew she would carry the odor for a few days.

He picked at the knots in her hair with a comb while breathing through his mouth. "Confound it, don't eat any more garlic."

She turned her head to look at him, causing the comb to become caught in the tangle he'd been working on. "Ouch!"

"Maybe if I start at the bottom . . . but you'll have to sit still." His knuckles brushed against the skin of her neck where he drew the comb through. Her hair crackled as it dried, coming alive in his hands. For the first time in his life, Mike forgot his surroundings, forgot time, forgot everything except the thundering of his heart. He even forgot to comb.

29

"Parson?"

Coming back to "the here and the now," as his mother used to say when he went into his daydreams, he abruptly released her hair. "I don't see any lice. Can you finish it yourself?"

She yanked the comb loose. "It don't make sense to unmess what's goin' ta get messed again. You got a horse comb?"

"In the barn."

"That'll work the knots out."

Though deeply troubled by his boyhood habit of drifting off, he had started up the path without argument to get what she'd asked for when something hit him between the shoulder blades with a loud *thwack*.

"What the . . . ?" he said. Turning just in time to duck, he saw her haul back and lob another rock his way. It snapped a twig where he'd been standing. The little vixen was throwing rocks at him. Shaking his finger at her, he said with a growl, "Stop that at once, young lady!"

"Cain't make me," she shouted, firing another missile.

"Thunderation, someone could get hurt, No-Account." With a lunge, he nearly had her. A rock flew over his shoulder, and she dove into the edge of the forest. Mike landed in an unpreacherlike heap on the ground. No-Account was gone, so he brushed himself off, drew on his almost dry shirt, and strode to the barn to get the currycomb.

He banged a fist against an empty stall. "Well, I sure did it this time. Not only did I send for the world's most erratic lunatic"—he grabbed the pitchfork to muck out the barn— "but she's been here less than three hours and acts like a fishwife." Dragging the soiled hay out the door, he continued, "It's likely she'll murder me in my sleep with that gun of hers."

With angry stabs he soon had more than enough hay in the stalls. Calmer, he leaned on the handle of the pitchfork. "All right, Lord, I'll leave it up to you. Do I keep her or send her away?" Dust motes dancing in rays of sunshine were his only answer.

After a time, Mike became aware that his stomach rumbled. He realized that his "fiancée" probably hadn't eaten all day. It was time to move forward, to continue as if this day were like any other. He cleaned the pitchfork with care, hung it in precise alignment on the wall and then stuffed the curry comb into his pocket.

Not foolish enough to walk into an ambush, Mike called out from the broad door, "No-Account?" Confound it, where was his authority? That pathetic call had no backbone. He tried again. "*No-Account.*" Much better.

"What?" Over near the corner of the house, she stepped out where he could see her. "I'm dry now, an' I washed my neck. Can we go in the house, or are you goin' ta make me— Whatcha lookin' at now?"

What he saw had him sucking in his breath. Heavily lashed violet eyes stared at him from a heart-shaped face. Her clothes, drying at an alarming rate, were shrinking, revealing her tanned and fit body. A halo of fire created by her loose, tangled mane now billowed around her from head to waist.

"Are you still mad?"

Mike didn't know if he was in heaven or hell. Blood pounded in his ears, so he barely heard her.

Her eyes widened. "You *are* mad. Folks always get overset when I'm funnin'."

Her shrinking pants riveted his gaze. She had such long legs, he thought, nicely balanced with a generous bosom. How long had it been since he had noticed a woman's figure?

Mike called a halt to his galloping imagination. "Let's go inside. I'm hungry." That was no lie, but he would be unable to satisfy this sudden burst of physical hunger. He wondered how he could be so attracted to this untamed girl who wouldn't fit into his perfectly ordered life.

31

Stopping at the pump, he primed it, then stuck his head under the gushing water. There, cold water would settle his heated thoughts.

No-Account watched. "You got water near the house," she said in awe. "Don't make me do that, though. I believe I've had all the waterin' a body can stand."

"I needed to cool off."

She tossed the towel onto the porch, paying no attention to the tight-lipped look Mike threw her way. Picking it up, he went inside, slamming the door.

No-Account stood back to savor the sight before her. Mine, she thought, her covetous gaze taking in every detail.

When she approached the door, she found the brass latch solid and sun-warmed. The hinges, well fitted, gave no groan of protest at being swung open.

In the dim room, she waited for her eyes to adjust. Mike was tossing wood into the stove; then he started a small fire in the fireplace.

No-Account Savage closed her eyes and inhaled. She had found a home. Here was warmth. Here was welcome. Here . . . in *her* house.

"You live here, all cozy 'n tight from the weather," she remarked. "My, oh, my."

"Yes, I built it to withstand storms of all kinds."

With a half smile at that comment, she shook her head, taking in the beauty that surrounded her.

The table had four chairs—none of them broken. She went to a chair and pulled it away from the table. "Can I sit in it?"

Mike raised an eyebrow. "Yes," he said, "and here's the comb."

"I got ta thank you for lettin' me." She settled herself in the chair he usually occupied.

"Letting you what?"

32

"Sit in your chair—and use the horse comb." A button popped off her shirt while she worked it through her hair. "Damn shirt is tight. Mighty itchy, too."

Preacher Mulgrew swallowed hard, then ran outside. Again No-Account heard a resounding splash that sounded as if Mike had jumped into the creek. "Why, that man is washing again. Mighty unnatural." She shook her head.

Deciding to look the place over until he came back, she put the comb aside. "Lordy, I never saw the like," she said softly. Real beeswax candles, ten on a shelf near the mantel, and a lantern hung by the door. Palms flat on the table, she pushed herself up to explore, but the softness of the washed wood against her clean hands drew her attention.

"Looks like it's new. I wonder if he got it for me." That he might have done something just for her had her wishing she could be more like regular women.

No-Account found she liked the feel of her hair as it swept her back and shoulders. Clean felt all right.

"An honest-to-God house."

A fire glowed in the wood cookstove. Across the room, another oak rocking chair occupied a spot near the large fireplace that was filling that corner with warmth. "This winter's goin' ta be snug. I cain't wait ta tell Slow."

A cheery yellow cabinet stood next to a window, begging for a closer look. A gentle nudge at the latch opened it.

Sacks and jars lined the shelves; the aroma of coffee wafted to her nose. "I'll be havin' some o' that." There were corn and beans, beets and preserves lined up perfectly. To No-Account they were more beautiful than sparkling rings and ear bobs.

The outside door opened. "Parson, you're a lucky man ta have all this bounty."

He sloshed absently across the floor to the fireplace, where he gripped the mantel.

"Ya got real crockery. I ain't never et off none." She ran her fingers over a bowl. When she closed the cabinet, she saw Slow squatting outside the window. No-Account flapped a hand to warn him out of sight. He must be hungry. She sure was.

"Can we eat some of what's in there?"

Mike scowled at her. "You tracked up the floor."

Hands on hips, she answered, "I did not. You done it yourself."

"Impossible. I never track in the house."

She pointed at his wet shoes, then gestured to the door. A clear trail led to where he stood.

With a shake of his head, Mike went for a large frying pan. With a loud bang, he slammed it on the stove, causing the metal lids to rattle.

Life had suddenly careened out of control. Diving into icy water headfirst without bothering to remove his shoes and clothing . . . that was not like him at all.

There was no getting around it. Since No-Account Savage had arrived, all his plans had been destroyed. Gone were his peace of mind and sense of order.

From his position at the stove, he could see her move to the fireplace, her glorious hair swinging, catching on wool that now barely covered her decently. He tried to concentrate on cooking, gripping the cold handle of the frying pan that anchored him to the sensible part of his world. Every move she made treated his nose to a mixture of freshly washed woman and that confounded garlic she used.

She walked to where he stood. "What are you puttin' in there?"

His stomach churning, he tried to force himself to a calmness he had lost sometime in the last few hours. Worrying his ear, he asked, "Do you like ham?"

"Here now, ease up on that ear or you might need a poultice. An' I'll eat anythin' you got."

Mike walked away from her and took a deep breath to clear his head. He crouched at the trapdoor beside the table.

No-Account rushed over. "Knock me over an' kick my butt. It's a hidey-hole." She peered into the darkness below while Mike lit another lantern and descended the ladder.

Rather than correcting her foul language, he replied through gritted teeth, "It's a cold cellar."

Her eyes locked on to the ham and vegetables he brought from below.

"Would you close it for me?" he asked.

She looked from him to the hole. "A cold cellar. My house has a cold cellar. . . . What's a cold cellar?" She closed the door with something akin to reverence.

From her reaction he knew she'd been more deprived than he'd thought. His anger abated somewhat. "It's a place to store food so it won't spoil." His voice strong, he added, "And remember, it's not *your* house."

Peevish, his mother would have called him. She'd used that very word to describe his father.

"Whatcha doin' now?"

"I'm preparing our dinner."

"In the house? Oh, happy day. Can we eat in here too?"

Guilt-ridden, Mike reached for his ear, but dropped his hand. Heaven knew what kind of poultice she'd use. And without asking, he was sure that she had no place to go should he recant. It was a sobering thought.

After setting the ham to cook, he chose a knife from a wooden case and whacked at the vegetables with a vengeance.

"Parson, go easy there; you might hurt yourself."

Anger flared within him. How dare she tell him what to do!

Adjusting his stance, he brought the knife down on his thumb. Blood welled, spilling onto the table.

No-Account immediately took his hand and put the bloody digit into her mouth, sucking on it until he forgot the pain of the cut. But something else stirred within him. It started somewhere in his gut and radiated to other places he didn't want to think about.

"Stop it," he said in a snarl, pulling his hand away from the gates of hell.

No-Account spit the blood into the fireplace, where it sizzled. She stepped back, letting his wounded hand drop. "Fix it yourself then." With a toss of her fiery locks she sat down hard in the rocking chair, folding her arms.

He thought back to something his brother Lucas, the best-looking of his brothers, had once said; "You're too serious, Mike. Get out and spark some girls."

His younger brother Connor, the sibling always one step ahead of a shotgun, had added, "Maybe he doesn't know what his sparking tools are for."

Today those tools were making their purpose clearly felt. A glance at the window showed that the glow of twilight had given way to dusk. No-Account Savage would sleep in *his* bed, while he bunked down in the loft. By morning, his spotless reputation would be destroyed.

Chapter Three

Blood clung to her lips. His blood. Anger, as red as that blood, filled him, so that when he spoke he resorted to a snarl. "Don't you *ever* do that again. You can't . . . shouldn't . . . " What could he say? Her brazen conduct appalled him. Mike's dripping finger left a ruby trail to the pantry, where he fumbled for his cleansing alcohol.

"Every durn fool knows you got ta suck the poison out."

At the dry sink, Mike opened the bottle and poured a little onto his bleeding finger. It stung. *Good*. He needed a little penance right now.

No-Account left her chair to join him. "That smells like liquor. You're not one o' them preachers that drinks, are you?"

"No, I do not drink," he said. Inwardly he scolded himself for his surly attitude. In an attempt at civility, he cleared his throat. "This is for cuts," he explained. "Could you bandage my finger for me?" He replaced the corked bottle and took a roll of white gauze from the shelf.

While she worked, No-Account observed, "I recollect Ma took a swig now 'n then for medicinal. But I ain't ever seen a body pour it out like that.

"Don't go drinkin' it, though. Smells like Pa's best, 'n that don't say much for it. If you get a cold or somethin' sits bad in your gut, I got my own medicinals." She beamed with pride. "There. All knotted up. It won't come off neither."

Her smile made him long for home. Not Boston, but a home of his own, here in California.

"How 'bout I use the knife? Set yourself down 'n hold your hand above your shoulder."

Feeling a bit foolish, Mike raised his hand like a schoolboy.

"You're a city man, ain't you? You hold it up, the bleedin' stops," she explained. "Back in the hills we use sugar or honey for cuts.

"Granny Tilton showed me how to make a biscuit starter for the poisoned blood. You lay some on the sore 'n it works in no time."

Mike listened with interest. "Did your grandmother live with you?"

"Oh, she weren't *my* granny. I never had one. A few years back we come to be livin' in Hog's Holler. When we all moved to a new place, I looked for paths through the woods. I like ta find a little place where I can be by myself sometimes. You can find real good hidey-holes that way.

"One day I come up on her. I tromped right through her tansy patch. She blistered me up an' down, told me how she grew yerbs 'n other things for curin' sick folks. After that I tailed her all over them mountains ever' day. She took a shine ta me 'n my brother, Slow, 'n taught me ever'thin' she knew. Now I got my yerbs with me wherever I go."

"You have a brother named *Slow?*" Mike went to the stove to turn the ham.

No-Account looked up. "You got somethin' against brothers?" Her voice took on an edge.

"I have four brothers. It's just—your names . . . his name . . . *Slow?*"

"Here, let me put these in there." She carried the vegetables to the stove, where she poured them into the frying pan. "You mind if I have a bit o' carrot?"

Mike nodded assent. Why had this unschooled, rough mountain girl answered his ad for a bride? "Miss Savage, I think you cheated me," he said.

"Parson Mulgrew, I don't cheat nobody."

"You are not what I advertised for."

No-Account drew herself up as tall as her tiny frame would allow. He noticed she didn't stand as high as his shoulder.

"You got what you asked for."

"I asked for a *proper* wife."

No-Account perched on the wood bin to yank off her boot. From inside she retrieved a square of oilcloth. Limping back to where he stood, she unwrapped the soiled packet, then shoved a scrap of newspaper under his nose.

"I cain't read, but I put it ta mind permanent-like." She cleared her throat and spit into the corner.

Mike towered over her. "I told you not to do that again!" The veins in his neck and temples stood out.

"I cain't take off my boots in the house?" Her violet eyes showed her confusion.

"Of course you can take off your boots." He struggled for a calm he didn't feel. "I meant no spitting." Mike could barely utter the words. Had this girl lived in biblical times, he was certain she would have been one of Pharaoh's plagues.

"Spittin'? You're blastin' at me 'cause I spit? Ever'one got ta spit a time or two." Her eyes took him in from head to toe. "You don't spit?"

"It's not polite."

"Whatcha do when ya got catarrh?"

"I . . . Never mind. You did a nice job of changing the subject."

"No, sir, I did not. Preachin' at me for spittin' were your idea." She handed him the bit of paper, then quoted:

" 'Wanted: Woman of high moral cracker and gentle demeanor, ta marry preacher in California Territory.' Them's your very words on that paper."

A headache began in Mike's neck and shoulders. "What made you think you qualify?"

She limp-stomped to the wood box to put her worn boot back on. "I might not read or write, but I know how ta ask questions. There's lots o' folks in Kansas with book learnin'.

" 'Cracker' means you don't snivel 'n fuss when bad luck comes your way. Trouble knocked on my door plenty, 'n I'm here ta tell you I can still smile. So I got 'cracker.'

"I'm gentle as a baby lamb in a field of spring grass. I fixed your finger 'n never hurt you, did I?

"I near forgot me somethin'. Cracker has another meanin'. I don't steal." Her hands were suddenly of immense interest to her. "Not usually, anyhow," she mumbled.

Mike looked at her hands, too. He imagined how those strong, purposeful hands would feel rubbing out his headache.

She didn't *usually* steal? His head snapped up.

But she wasn't finished. "Ya can forget demeanor, though. I won't be mean ta any o' God's creatures. It ain't fittin'."

Her pack lay in a corner, where she had placed it earlier. "I gotta take care of somethin'," she said when she squatted to open the offensive bundle.

Mike's curiosity sharpened. What is in there? he wondered. A dried apple rolled out, followed by a tin plate that clattered against the floorboards. Something long filled the sack from bottom to top. A long gun? No, it couldn't be. A woman would never carry one. She didn't secure the top, so when she pushed the sack back, a Bible tumbled out. When she shoved the Bible back, it bumped against something that created a resonant tone.

The tin plate in hand, she asked, "Is it done yet?"

At his nod, she heaped a large portion onto the plate and ran for the door. "I'll be right back. I gotta feed some critters I saw."

No-Account had leaped out the door before he could object.

Dinner sat on the warmer. Mike waited. He considered himself a reasonable man, though his temper had flared often in his youth. Today he had found himself close to that abyss. He had wanted a soothing wife. There was nothing calming about No-Account Savage. He sighed.

Taking out his pocket watch every few minutes, Mike began to pace, mentally planning how best to admonish her about promptness, especially at meals. Six in the morning, noon, and six-thirty for the evening meal. Regularity satisfied Mike. How long could it take for her to put a plate out for critters?

Mike had never liked the way his mother served meals whenever she'd gotten around to it, sometimes early, sometimes late, a constant stream of Mulgrews wandering in to take from a simmering pot whenever it suited them.

At five past seven, Hope returned. Mike decided to overlook her tardiness—this time. He liked his meals peaceful, not contentious. Oh, how his jaw ached with the desire to reprimand her.

41

Nevertheless, he pulled a chair out for her. "Are the *critters* happy?" he asked. Darn, he'd been snide. Downright snide. Mike did not like arrogance in any form, and here he had slipped into it, an old habit. His mother had often told him to come off his perch and live like the rest of the family.

"Iffen they could talk they'd be most beholden ta you."

She sat on her hands, waiting—looking at him expectantly.

Mike was pleased to see that she waited for the blessing. He folded his hands.

She didn't move.

Maybe she didn't know to fold her hands. Here, indeed, was a soul in need of his guidance. Mike cleared his throat and began a prayer filled with much praise, thanks, blessing, and petition.

Suddenly she jumped up, shouting, "Tarnation, I know you don't want me here, but are you tryin' ta starve me?"

Startled, Mike said a hasty "Amen."

No-Account remained seated on her hands, looking at him from beneath lowered lids. His thoughts strayed. How firm her bottom would feel in his hands. Those legs of hers . . . *Stop it.*

"What are we waitin' for?"

His eyebrows came together. "Help yourself."

"Man gets his first."

"Miss Savage, I don't know where you got that bit of information, but that's not how it's done."

"It ain't?"

"Is that why you're sitting on your hands?"

"Yes, 'tis. Pa always whomped any woman or child who put a tooth ta food 'fore him. That was when Ma was still home and had somethin' ta cook. If we got us a squirrel or two, she'd boil it down. Didn't go far, though. Pa got most o' it."

42

Mike was liking Pa less with each revelation. "Well, I'm not your pa. Take what you want."

A startling transformation took place before his eyes. In fact, he wouldn't have believed it if he hadn't seen it for himself. Once freed, her hands were everywhere at once.

Mike gaped while she tore bread from the loaf, then tipped the serving dish into her china plate. Next she reached into her boot to bring out her knife, with which she cut and speared a large serving of the meat.

Dismayed that she stuffed her mouth with her hands, he was more worried that she might choke, since she barely chewed. She also gulped, smacked her lips, wiped her face with the sleeve of her shirt, and collected a size-able meal of drops and crumbs in her cleavage. That observation caused his tongue to flick across his upper lip. Mike had lost his appetite for food, but found himself craving something much more satisfying.

No-Account pushed her plate away and belched with vigor.

"Them was good eats. If you can cook like that, whatcha want a wife for?"

"Because it's time." Mike poured coffee into their cups.

"Time?"

He opened a drawer in the table and withdrew a small notebook, eager to share his method for order. "I've found my life moves along easiest if I follow a list." With pride he held up a book. "My goals are listed in here." Opening it, he moved his finger to each line as he recited, "I've come to California, built a house, church, and barn, furnished the house, bought a cow and some chickens. I'm right here: 'Find wife.' " Satisfied, he sat back and handed No-Account the little book.

"You're joshin' me. Ya cain't just plan life."

43

"Sure you can. I've proved it."

"Folks ain't natured that way. What if you broke a leg or your cow died?" She picked up the little book, tracing her finger down the unchecked portion of the list. "Bein' as I cain't read, I'll guess this says, 'Have baby boy. Have baby girl. Build bigger church. Add room ta house—' "

He snatched the book from her, impatient that she didn't understand. "Why?" he asked.

"Why what?"

With resentment, he spit his words with stark clarity. "Why me? Surely there were others. Why did you pick on me? Or was I the only one stupid enough to send a ticket?"

He regretted the words instantly. They were cruel words.

For a moment her cocky attitude disappeared, leaving the room unnaturally quiet. She leaned across the table, her face so close he could see silver streaks flash in her eyes. "You know what? I think you're horn-mad at me for messin' up your list. I ain't what you planned for."

Shame silenced him.

She moved to the fireplace, "I don't seem to fit in anyone's life plan. My real ma 'n pa left me 'side a road. Then along come the Savages 'n their brood. Ma just stuck me in with the others. That's how I got my name. Pa didn't want another hungry youngun, so he called me No-Account." She returned to her seat.

Nobody had ever wanted her. The impact of those words hit home. *Nobody.* He had his life plan, while she'd just adapted to whatever fate threw at her.

"Pa got liquored up all the time. Made him mean. Ma said it was a weakness. Bein' as he made moonshine ta sell, he was inclined ta taste more than he should. He beat Ma, 'n ever'one he could lay his hands or a switch on.

"Ma took off one night. Took a couple o' the younguns

with her. The older boys was gone as soon as they could light out.

"Pa sold off three o' the girls. Not that they wasn't glad to leave."

When she finished, the ticking of the mantel clock punctuated the silence. Finally Mike spoke. "Why didn't your mother take you when she left?"

"When we saw Pa was spoilin', me 'n Slow hid. Ma had to git whilst she could. There weren't time ta look for us. With Pa, you had ta stand up 'n move when you could."

"Did you try to find her?"

"Could of. But Slow needed me, 'n Ma most-like had her hands full puttin' down roots.

"We was all right 'till some months ago. How long is a year?"

"Twelve months."

"Is that right? I cain't figure time.

"Ta get on with my tale, Pa heard screamin' near his still one night. He didn't like folks knowin' where he hid his makin's."

"So someone took his moonshine and he blamed you?"

"Nope. Feller from town heard I was a girl 'n decided he'd try me. I knew what he wanted, 'n I ain't ready for that. I bit his nose off." She folded her arms with a grin.

"You bit off his *nose?*"

"You think *I* did the screamin'? After that I knew I was marked. Pa weren't too smart, but he knew a dollar when he saw one.

"I lit out, headin' west. One day I heard a gal talkin' 'bout gettin' a man out o' the newspaper. If you think you seen ugly, why, I'm here tellin' you she were harder on the eyes than yestereve's cat-kill. But damn, someone sent for her. That settled it for me. I decided I'd like to try California myself."

45

"Let me guess. You took that clipping from the next newspaper you saw."

"I ain't hasty less it's important ta save my butt. Kansas has plenty of livestock ta care for, 'n I got a job so I could think things over some. The owner of that stock-yard read the news ta them who wanted ta hear it ever' Thursday. When he read your piece, I got a good feelin' 'bout it. It's important ta pay attention ta feelin's."

Mike pushed himself up from the table so fast that his chair crashed to the floor. *You sure did it this time, Mulgrew.* This homeless waif expected to become his wife. God had answered his prayers, and he didn't want to accept the gift.

"I'll see if I have something for you to wear. There are some clothes in the loft." He righted his chair.

"You got extry clothes? What for?"

"Sometimes people give me things to use for those less fortunate."

"You mean *poor* folks? I cain't take from poor folks. What's wrong with what I got on?"

"It's too tight." Another button popped as he spoke and Mike's face flamed.

"Damn, it looks like I'm gettin' more fresh air than a body needs." Her husky laughter chased him up the loft stairs. He fumbled with the latch of a large chest. When he had it open, he tore into the neatly folded stacks of apparel. Keeping order in the trunk didn't occur to him. He dug, yanked, threw back, and dug again. Something silky caressed his hand, reminding him of her wild, heavy tresses.

"I've got to get control," he said with a groan, looking at the rock-hard ridge between his legs. Mike Mulgrew thought he'd mastered his body years ago. Maybe he needed a wife more than he had realized. He'd expected a simple wife and a marriage of convenience, yet he found himself lusting after this brash woman. Folding his hands, he asked, "Please, Father, help me." After a time the pressure eased.

He grabbed a handful of womanly garments without care for size or style. When he went back to the kitchen, he dropped the pile on the table. "I'm going to the barn," he said.

No-Account looked at the swinging door. "He sure lit out o' here fast," she said to herself, pawing through the pile.

The jumble of wearables didn't offer anything No-Account recognized as a dress. One Christmas Granny Tilton had made a warm wool dress for No-Account, but when Pa had seen it, he'd sold it right off.

She decided to take care of a few domestic matters before she changed. Gathering the leavings of their meal, she piled a plate high, then placed it on the porch: She believed she had a duty to care for animals, which made it all right when she brought them down for food.

"Here you are, little ones. No-Account is here to stay, and I never forget my friends." She crouched, waiting inside the open door. Not long after she settled down to watch, a fox slunk out of the twilit brush. It looked, sniffed, then dug into the feast.

No-Account backed deeper into the house, still watching as another fox joined the first. A small black face appeared next, a long white stripe training on the ground after it. A single candle and a small fire in the fireplace illuminated the scene.

Leaving the door open and taking care not to frighten the animals, she turned her attention back to the heap of clothing. "Ain't much here, but it might be all he had. Either that, or for a prayin' man he sure wants me to dress sparse." That thought cheered her, since she wanted to please him. Up till now she'd done only what pleased her—and Slow, of course. Pleasing someone else would be a nice change.

She slipped into a pair of drawers that had a row of ruffles just below her knees. "This shirt won't cover much either," she said, buttoning a lacy, armless piece of frill. For the first time in her life, No-Account Savage felt at ease. The fire warmed her back, tempting her closer. She sat Indian fashion on the hearth rug.

Gathering her hair over one shoulder, she tied it with a ribbon she removed from an item she'd cast aside.

The tight dried wool she'd been wearing had left her itchy. After scratching her arms and legs, she looked around for a way to scratch her back. A tree trunk would do, but she didn't want to leave the comfort of the cozy fire. The edge of the yellow cabinet looked promising.

Mike had finally cooled off, and he now walked the path from the barn, where he'd tended his livestock. He carried a pail of fresh milk.

Resigned that No-Account must spend the night, he knew the arrangement would be fodder for the townfolk's wagging tongues and sly glances.

Closer to the house, he sensed that something wasn't right. When he rounded the corner, he stopped. The door hung open, revealing No-Account, eyes closed, with her back against the yellow pantry, sliding up and down. She moaned in sheer obscene pleasure and . . . confound it, she was wearing only underwear. Anger exploded within him. "No, no, no," he shouted, running toward her—straight into a tangle of hissing, barking, and the strong smell of skunk.

He shrieked and No-Account straightened. Hands on hips, she advanced to the porch. "What kind o' damn fool are you?" she demanded. "You don't come 'tween a polecat 'n his vittles."

They stood inches apart. Awareness tingled through

Mike, while the air reeked of skunk and crackled with tension.

"Look what you done. Scared them away, ever' last one." Her breasts nearly bounced from the gaping front of the camisole as she vented her anger.

Mike huffed in indignation, his only defense. "That was a skunk. And . . . and other wild. . . . you gave them our food." His voice had an unusually high pitch, even to his own ears.

Narrowing his eyes, he brought his tone down a few notches to a menacing bass. "You already fed the animals. You were late for dinner because of it."

She ignored him to go on with her own lecture. "Yep, 'n some foxes, 'n a cub, too." Arms akimbo, she went inside, leaving Mike to view her gently swinging bloomer-clad hips and legs. Would he ever stop thinking of her legs?

"Everything stinks like skunk. I think it got on my boot." Mike stormed after her, kicking the door shut. He set the milk pail on the dry sink.

"Well, take off the dadburned boot."

"Are you crazy? The whole *house* stinks!"

"We didn't eat all the food. I wanted to share. Them's God's critters too. You ought to be ashamed."

She tapped a bare foot, like a princess impatient with a servant. He kept his eyes lowered. Her bosom would no doubt pop into view at any moment. Taking a deep breath, he sat down to collect his thoughts, but she continued her tongue-lashing and left him no peace. With as much steadiness as he could manage he asked, "Why aren't you dressed?"

Her arms flung wide. "I'm wearin' what you gave me. Leastwise, I'm wearin' *some* o' what you gave me."

Her discarded clothing lay in a heap next to a smaller pile near the fireplace. He lit a lantern. Under closer scrutiny, he saw that he'd grabbed an assortment of garments. Among them were a man's nightshirt, stockings, a petticoat and what she wore now. No dress.

Rather than admit his mistake he remarked, "You should have changed in the bedroom." Mike knew he'd lost this battle. Looking at her scantily clad body, he felt his confounded flesh begin to respond once again.

"Damn. What the hell's a bedroom?" With those words, she snatched his attention back.

"Miss Savage, please stop using those words." Mike rubbed throbbing temples. It seemed he'd had a headache since he'd claimed her.

"I don't know what words you're talkin' 'bout."

"You swear too much, and cuss, too, I might add. I will *not* have swearing in my house."

"If you keep callin' me 'Miss Savage,' you'll think it's rainin' cuss words," she threatened. "I want to see what a bedroom looks like."

Mike's shoulders slumped. He led the way to a door at the back of the large main room.

When he opened that door, No-Account squeezed herself under his arm and stood there, her hair barely touching his muscled arm.

"Oh." The whispered word tamped his lust when her garlicky breath assaulted his nostrils.

She moved farther into the room. "I thought you was throwin' me out," she whispered. "A room for sleepin'. I never seen such."

Enchanted, she went to the bed. "Can I touch it?"

Incapable of speech, he nodded.

"It's soft." No-Account sank into the mattress. An oil lamp with a flowered glass shade sat in the exact center of the bedside table. "Whatcha need a lamp in your sleepin' room for?"

"I always read before I go to sleep."

"Wish I could read."

He nodded.

"You don't want to spoil your eyes. The lamp should be closer to the bed." She moved it.

Mike's hands throbbed with the urge to replace it dead center, yet the sight of her on his bed conjured up a host of more pressing thoughts.

"I think you must be right special blessed, Parson. Ain't many folks has a house with a sleepin' room."

At that moment, Mike wanted to give her every comfort, every thing of beauty he had ever seen . . . and fall into that bed with her softness under him.

I've got to get away from her, he told himself. "I'll look in the trunk again." He fled the room.

No-Account watched him disappear into the loft, then bounced on the bed. "A place for sleepin'. I wonder what this is." Her arms wrapped around a plump square of fluff. It held Mike's freshness. With pure joy, she tossed it in the air, caught it, and hugged it to her. Mike's scent pleased her.

The mirror over the dresser beckoned. She'd seen few mirrors in her lifetime. They were bewitched, some of her family had said. *Look in a mirror, the devil takes your soul.* But No-Account feared nothing. She put the pillow aside to stand before the mirror. With one finger she touched her reflection. "I look mighty fine." She ran her fingers through her tumbled mass of hair.

"No-Account?" Mike stood at the open door. "I found a dress. It looks to be about the right size."

"Here, you can have these," she said, her fingers finding the tie on her pantaloons.

"Don't take them off." His voice tight, he explained, "That's the underwear."

"It don't look like any I seen." She took the dress. "Which way does it go?"

He closed his eyes and took a breath. "The buttons go in front. I'll show you."

51

He puddled the dress on the floor. "Step into the middle." He pulled the dress up to her shoulders. "There."

"Hold on a time. The long johns is all bunched up." No-Account raised the skirt to tug everything into place.

She had little skill with buttons, and after three false starts, Mike had no choice but to offer assistance. His bandaged finger seemed to hamper his efforts, and he appeared to be keeping his concentration on the buttons.

To No-Account, the heat from his fingers traced a fiery path on her flesh, while the room became overwarm. She inhaled, letting the breath flow from her lungs. Something was wrong with her breathing apparatus. Maybe she needed a sniff of eucalyptus and a little something for her erratic heartbeat.

She reached to lift her hair so it wouldn't be in Mike's way and their fingers touched. Heat lightning ran from her fingers straight to her heart.

Mike stepped back. "I'll try to get some of the skunk smell cleaned up."

She went to fetch her knife, putting it in her boot, then went to the kitchen. "I'm goin' out," she announced.

"You can't go out in the dark alone."

"I gotta piss." No-Account stormed out the door, leaving a red-faced Mike.

Slow needed a warm place to sleep, and she knew he wouldn't use their blanket or look for a place to bed down unless she settled him in. What had he been doing all this time?

Before disappearing into the woods, she turned to look back. Lantern light beamed from the windows. She wanted this. All of it. House, barn, church, animals. And the parson wouldn't be too hard to take either, she decided.

She would do what she'd never done before: apologize. For the mess only, of course. That would bring the preacher around. For him, No-Account Savage would eat crow.

Chapter Four

"Slow." She whispered his name.

A sliver of moonlight helped some in her search to find him. The air reeked of skunk. "He must be a city man to come up on a polecat that way." She chuckled, remembering the look on Mike's face. "Lordy, he 'bout pitched a fit."

"Sis." Slow ran into her arms. "I'm cold."

"Hush, baby." Her arms only partially encircled him. Built like a blacksmith, he towered over her. "You're shiverin'. Where's our blanket?"

"I stuck it under a rock near the barn, Sis."

"Let's go get it. Where is the barn? Ya know how I get all turned around when it's dark."

"Foller me." Thoughts didn't come easily to Slow, but he had an unerring sense of direction.

She fell in behind him. The clearing lay to their left, the barn a dark shadow ahead. Suddenly she touched his arm. Soft whistling accompanied by the crunch of boots on dirt announced that someone was coming their way.

The two hunkered close to the ground, a habit they'd adopted so they could hide anywhere.

Mike strode right by them, an arc of lantern light marking his passage. When he entered the barn, the two let out a sigh.

No-Account continued to hold her brother's sleeve. Only when they heard Mike speaking softly to his animals did she release her grasp. "Is the blanket far?" she whispered.

"Naw." Slow retrieved the blanket. They had bought it from an Indian for two bits, and Slow treasured it. "I took good care o' it. Here's my pack."

"If I ain't with you 'n it turns cold, it's all right to wrap that blanket tight 'round your shoulders," she explained. "What's in the barn?"

"There's a cow 'n some chickens."

"Did you count the chickens?"

"They was six." His voice rose. "That means he got eggs 'n milk, don't it, Sis?"

"Shhh . . . " Slow tended to get worked up about food. "Let's go out o' his hearin'."

Slow led the way deeper into the woods. When she judged they were far enough away, she settled beneath a tree. "I swiped a piece of bread for— Your pack's movin'. What's in there?"

Slow wrung his hands, a bad sign.

"Did you steal somethin' from the parson?"

"I found me a kitty in the barn."

"Now that man is goin' to miss a kitty. Probably got it writ in his book. Take it out of your pack."

Slow reluctantly undid his sack. With gentle hands, he withdrew a tiny lump of fur.

"Slow, that's a *baby* kitty. It's goin' to miss its mama."

"But Sis, I left the others."

"You have ta put it back, else it'll starve." Her eyebrows rose. "I just thought me a thought. We could tuck

54

you up in a corner o' the barn. 'Less he locks it, o' course."

"I still gotta hide? I guess he don't want me." Slow spoke with resignation.

"I ain't got around to tellin' him just yet. Slow, maybe I was wrong and he don't want *me*." No-Account didn't like to be wrong. "He sent for someone who could do him proud. I don't think I'm the someone he expected."

"Why did he throw ya in the creek? I was scared he would drown ya. Did ya know he jumped in, too?"

"Strange as strange, ain't it? You'd best get used to the idea, 'cause if he does keep us, we'll be dipped regular-like."

They heard the barn door slam, then Mike whistling his way in their direction. She looked at her brother and put her finger to her lips.

To her dismay, Mike didn't veer toward the path. He stopped a few feet away. The next sound was a rustling, then that of a stream of liquid hitting the ground.

The two clamped their hands to their mouths to hold back their giggles.

When Mike finished and continued toward the house, Slow whispered, "He were piddlin'."

"Yep. I guess everybody has to." No-Account giggled again.

As soon as she heard Mike close the house door, she hurried to the barn to check the latch. It was unlocked. With a sigh of relief, she swung the door open.

"Parson's a trustin' man for sure. Do you recollect the layout? Is there a nice corner where you can hide under the hay?"

"I'll be warm this night." Slow held the kitten to his chest and did a little dance of joy.

"No-Account? No-Account, where are you?" Mike's shout broke the night quiet.

"Uh-oh. Mind now, find that kitty's mama 'n put it back."

*   *   *

Mike waited on the porch, looking at his watch. He felt a wave of relief when she appeared. "Where've you been?"

A copper eyebrow rose. She looked at his watch. "You cain't hurry nature."

"The woods are sometimes dangerous. I was worried."

"You worried? 'Bout me?"

"Of course I did."

"Nobody ever worried 'bout me in my life. I can take care o' myself. There was plenty of wild wood in the hills."

He slipped his watch back into his pocket. "You're covered with leaves and burrs." His fingers tingled with awareness when he plucked debris from her shoulders. Crickets sang their night song. Somewhere an owl hooted. "Maybe you should shake your dress."

She opened the first two buttons.

"What are you doing?" he demanded.

"I'm trying' to take off my dress. You said to shake it."

"Confound it. I didn't mean . . . Just brush yourself off and come inside."

He held the door for her.

"Parson, you got a extry blanket I can use?"

"In the bottom drawer of the chest."

"I'm plain out tired. Would it trouble you if I bunk in the loft?"

It would trouble him a great deal. Merely having her in the house would trouble him a great deal. Tomorrow he would find another place for her to stay. He must. For now he offered the only solution available. "I'm sleeping in the loft. You take the bedroom."

"I don't know how ta sleep on a bed."

When Mike reached to pick a leaf from her hair, she recoiled. So, she was used to ducking. He hid his anger for her in busyness, removing cups from the cabinet.

He brought a pan from the stove to pour the steaming

liquid for them both. "I've made hot chocolate. It'll warm you while we talk."

Her fingers brushed his when she accepted her cup. "Could I sit in the rocker?" Not waiting for an answer, she settled herself before the fire while Mike took a chair at the table.

No-Account sipped from the cup, careful not to burn herself. She looked up with a smile. "It's sweet."

"It's milk with sugar and chocolate shavings."

"You're givin' me sugar? Pa never let us have sugar. What's choclit shavin's?" She took another sip.

"Chocolate is a bean . . . like coffee. My parents keep me supplied."

"You got folks that send you sweets 'n real coffee?"

"All the time."

She clutched the cup, her knuckles white.

"Something is worrying you, isn't it?"

"I expect you need some explainin'. I saw right off you didn't get what you paid for. I'm askin' you not to send me back." She looked up. "I'll get a job to pay back your passage money."

Mike tipped his chair, crossed his ankles on the hearth edge, and inhaled deeply. He smelled wood smoke and chocolate and No-Account. It occurred to him that some of her offensive odor had lessened. His heartbeat accelerated.

"No," he began with a sigh. "We'll marry. I don't make promises lightly. Besides, after tonight we won't have a choice. People will talk." *That's right, Mike, he thought, you just made a commitment! To an ill-bred rapscallion whom you barely know.*

"There's always a choice. I'd be willin' to work for you. Folks will find somethin' else to talk 'bout. It would shame you worse bein' stuck for the rest o' your life with a gal who cain't read nor write."

It was his chance to weasel out, but he didn't take it. Instead he said, "You can learn. Right now I'd like to know more about you. How far from Kansas did you live?"

"You'd teach me to read?"

He nodded. *Another commitment.* He dragged his attention back to her recitation of her life in the East.

"Way east, but we moved around. There were so many hills, folks had ta piss with one leg higher than the other."

Mike, in midsip, choked at her frank description.

"Are ya all right?" At his nod, she went on. "We was dirt-poor. Now 'n then someone might slip Ma some food for us when Pa weren't around." She got up to stir the embers. "Mighty fine fireplace."

"Are you the youngest?"

"Ma didn't birth no more babies after Slow."

"Your brother."

No-Account nodded. "Slow was slow bein' born. Pa named him. He named all o' us. Oak and Ivy were twins, named because Pa got poison from them plants. He couldn't tell one tree from another. Ma told me once that Doc told Pa he had to stop humpin' on her."

Mike coughed into his hand to cover his shock. "Your Pa did what the doctor said?"

"Had to. Doc threatened ta bust up his still if he got any more babies on Ma. Said he had ways o' keepin' track o' Pa."

"How old are you?"

"How would I know?"

"I saw a Bible in your sack. Your mother probably wrote the year you were found."

"You looked? Then's *my* things in there. I never said you could look." No-Account slid a glance at the corner where she had placed her sack.

"It fell out when you got your plate. I wouldn't intrude on your privacy."

"Oh, I'm sorry—and whilst I'm sorryin', I won't give your food to the critters again. That skunk did have a powerful smell, didn't he? I don't know who was more surprised, him or you." She laughed her husky laugh, and was pleased when Mike joined in.

"I was." His mouth lifted on the left in a half smile, revealing a dimple. "So your ma didn't keep a list of birthdays."

"You know, Parson, folks don't all live by lists. I never saw Ma lick a pencil—not that there was any around." She paused. I been thinkin' on this some. You might be mad as hell, but I won't lie. Mostly 'cause I want you to know I won't do what ain't square if you hire me on.

"There was this teacher come to the mountain. He liked Pa's corn liquor, 'n offered to read to us in trade. I heard them stories 'n I wanted ta learn readin'.

"In no time he had the old schoolhouse fixed up. The first day o' learnin', I come to the schoolyard. He lined ever'one up so they could pass by his desk. He had a book where he marked names 'n things. Come to my turn he asked for a penny. I never owned a penny, so he took me outside 'n told me it cost a penny a week to go to school. Can you imagine that?

"He told me ta come over after the payin' ones left. He said we'd make a trade. That first night I learned to count to a hunnert. When it come time for readin', he said I'd have to pay up 'fore he could teach me more. Hell, I reckon I didn't want readin' bad as I thought. When he said what he wanted, I pricked him in the balls with my knife, then run out o' there lickety-split. I took the book, though. It's the only thing I ever stole. Honest."

Mike didn't comment, so she went on. "When I got home 'n looked at it, 'n saw it was a Bible, I knew I did somethin' powerful wrong, so I hid it."

Mike's jaw had tightened as she told her story. Suddenly his left cheek dimpled, and the corners of his mouth turned up. A rumbling started in his chest, and when it reached his throat, he doubled over, braying like a mule.

Startled, No-Account ran to him and whacked him on the back with her fist. As he crashed to the floor with his chair, his head hit the edge of the table.

He lay perfectly still. No-Account ran in circles around him. "Oh, crap—oh, my—hell n' blast. I kilt him. Sweet Jesus, I didn't mean to kill him." She knelt beside him and used a finger to open one eye. It blinked. "Hallelujah! You ain't dead!"

Mike touched his head and winced. "No, I'm not. But you're dangerous. Why did you do that?" He pulled himself up, then righted the chair.

"I thought you was takin' a fit or somethin'."

"I was laughing." He gingerly touched the wound on his head. There was very little blood.

"How was I to know? You don't seem a laughin' man. I'll put honey on the cut if you have some."

"On the shelf above the stove. Why honey?"

"Sit yourself down, Preacher, 'n I'll have you right in no time." She dipped her finger in the honey jar, then dabbed gently at his injury.

He bit his lower lip at the pressure she applied.

"You're goin' to have a nice bump there, Parson."

"Since you've bled me twice in one day, I think you can call me Mike. Honey really works?"

"Maybe I don't have book learnin', but No-Account Savage is a damn good healer."

"I have to do something about that name. Maybe a good night's sleep will clear my head."

No-Account retrieved something from her sack. "If we're beddin' down, I got to take care o' somethin'. I'll be back after I clean my teeth and piddle."

"You clean your teeth?"

"O' course. Ma had some yanked. Granny Tilton said that if she'd cleaned them, she could have kept them. Want me to show you how? I have lots o' ground mint mixed with saleratus."

"No, thanks, I have my own tooth powder." He watched her duck into the trees outside. He laughed again when he took their cups to the basin. This woman was amazing.

No-Account lay in bed, arms rigid, unable to sleep. The stove kept the room comfortably warm, but she had been awake for a long time, sure she'd fall out. She flung the pillow across the room. Mike had told her it was for her head. Sleeping in a tree was easier than this. At least one could hook a foot over a branch.

In the next room Mike whistled softly. She'd never heard the tune, but it soothed her. After a while she heard him go outside, his footsteps soft across the porch. When he returned he climbed to the loft. Tired as she was, she lay there listening to the night.

Mike, too, lay awake on the hard floor. He felt like a fisherman trying to reel in a bigger fish than he'd expected. Sending her back was out of the question. He wouldn't set her loose in the wilds of California either. As strong-minded as she was, he suspected she wouldn't go anyway. The only thing left was marriage. He had pledged to marry her.

He tossed and rolled. A man of God with a blood-and-thunder wife would cause talk for miles around. As it was, they were already compromised. Spending the night in the same house would seal their fate.

Mike began the Lord's Prayer. He needed to get his mind off No-Account.

Gradually his thoughts slowed, allowing him to drift to sleep. From far off, he heard the padding of bare feet, then a plop. Half-asleep, he caught No-Account's scent as she curled into her blanket next to him. Thinking it a dream, he slept.

* * *

Mike woke slowly, snuggling closer to the warmth pressed against him. Sleep-drugged, he felt a sensation under his chin like warm silk. Something tangled in his chest hair. Still half-asleep, he opened his eyes to find No-Account curled in a ball against him, her fingers resting there. He pulled her closer to nuzzle her soft tresses. Such a wonderful dream. The color of her hair in the hazy morning light gave the illusion of fire. The flame of it was everywhere. Copper locks tangled under his shoulder, caught in his night's growth of beard.

No-Account moaned in her sleep and snuggled closer.

He tucked his face into the fragrance of her soft shoulder, moving his lips back and forth over the fabric of her dress. It was a dream, after all, so it wouldn't matter. His hand trailed down her back to her tiny waist. She moved, bringing one leg over his.

That woke him.

He rolled away, fast, and he felt her hair release him. *Good.* She hadn't woken up. Mike's control had never slipped this far. He hurried from the house.

Moments later he stepped out of his clothes to plunge into the creek, allowing the icy water to cool his ardor.

While swimming and diving, he wondered why he had this reaction to No-Account. He had mastered his body years ago, was always able to clear his mind of lustful thoughts. This, though, was different. The horrid smell of her when she had arrived should have been enough to eternally disgust him. But it hadn't.

Mike's family would laugh themselves silly if they knew. Mike, the levelheaded Mulgrew. Though he had never admitted it until now, they were an embarrassment to him, especially his parents—the way they argued, touched, and kissed in public always made him squirm.

Back and forth he swam. He hadn't realized he'd been ashamed of his family and their antics.

Tempted

A gunshot split the morning quiet. Birds flew overhead. Mike stopped swimming and his feet hit bottom. His heart pounding, he came out of the water running. It had been a mistake to leave No-Account alone. She needed his protection.

Tearing toward the house, he hopped over roots and stones. A branch grazed his arm. He broke through the brush surrounding the house. "What happened?"

No-Account looked up from where she sat in the yard, a bright smile lighting her eyes. "Mornin'. Why, Parson, you're naked."

Mike looked down, then dove for a bush. Crouching, he could just barely see over the top of his cover. "Confound it! What in blazes are you doing? Get into the house before you get hurt."

"I ain't gonna get hurt. What made ya think that'?"

"Didn't you hear that shot?"

"That was me. I bagged us some breakfast." She held a dead animal aloft.

Furious, and still breathing hard, Mike tore into her. "Last night you were feeding them, giving *me* a lesson on God's bounty. Today you've killed a perfectly harmless . . . What is it, anyway?"

"You don't need to yell at me. I figured I'd show you how good I'd be a fetchin' food. 'Sides, didn't you know it's all right to take them for food?" She peered at him. "I expect you been in that water again. You're all wet. Folks die from overwaterin', you know. You'd best get dressed."

Mike pressed his lips together, jutting out his chin. "Stay right where you are. We have to talk."

"I'll start cookin' this—"

"No!" he shouted.

"I swear, you're the most changeable man I ever met." He looked back to see if she did as he asked. She sat in the dust in the wrinkled dress.

* * *

When he returned she had the carcass skewered on a stick. "You have a damn nice behind, Parson," she remarked.

"How . . . ?" He blushed, tugging at his ear. Striving for a calm he didn't feel, he squatted beside her. Maybe what he had to say could wait. "That's a nice fat one. I'll take care of breakfast while you wash up." He took the animal from her. "You've got a little blood on your dress."

No-Account looked down. Her hands were bloody as well. "There's no way to collect food 'less you're willin' to get dirty. Why are you so all-fired set on me washin'?"

Mike smiled crookedly. "You can wash, or I can throw you in again."

That sent her running for the creek. He turned to the house when he heard her hit the water. She had jumped in fully dressed. He knew it without seeing, and vowed to give more precise directions in the future.

Her voice bounced off the hills with the epithets she shouted. Just before he closed the door behind him, he heard her say something about rather being in hell, where at least a body could get warm. He found himself smiling again. She had a way about her that lightened his mood. She had managed to change him—in one day. Strangely, he didn't mind.

No-Account soaped her hair, then her arms. She inhaled the scents around her. Pine and grass. Soap and sunshine. Morning smells were best because of the dew.

She ducked to rinse before coming out of the water. While the sun warmed and dried her, she thought about her future.

In the beginning No-Account had chosen to go west because she'd reasoned Pa wouldn't risk his hide to follow them, him being the lily-livered coward he was. Everything scared him, from Indians to his own shadow.

Marriage hadn't had a place in her plans. What No-

Account knew of marriage consisted of the bare facts of harsh sex and total submission on the woman's part. If she was smart, a wife could make herself scarce most of the time.

No, her thoughts had been simple. Life in the mountains was hard, cold, and mean. She'd figured, how much worse could California be?

Leaving the shacks and shanties behind, she and Slow had found that most folks could have a kinder life. If she worked and saved, she could earn enough to live with a full stomach and a roof over her head.

But No-Account had had a particular reason to leave. She carried with her the memory of the day Pa had sold her oldest sister, Feather. Ma had begged and Feather had cried, while Pa'd tied a rope to Feather's wrist and handed the end to the man who had given Pa a considerable amount of money for her.

Still a child, No-Account had followed, hoping to cut her sister loose. At sunset the man who'd taken Feather had tied her hands above her head and done terrible things to her. No-Account had watched, tears streaking her cheeks. When he'd gone to sleep, No-Account had crept out of the woods to free her sister, but it had been too late.

She had buried her sister and returned to the family shack determined to keep out of Pa's way. Pa had gone right out and bought the makings for a fresh batch of 'shine.

From that day No-Account had learned to use her knife with great skill. She'd kept that knife strapped to her waist, with slit in her trousers that allowed easy access. Later she'd acquired a second knife to fit in a sheath in her boot.

A few summers later she'd gone to the nearest town to buy a gun. Firearms were costly, but No-Account had taken small jobs until she'd had enough cash to purchase a Texas revolver. The day she walked into the general store and asked to try one, the owner was so put off by her appearance that he wouldn't let her sight it outside the door. If he'd known her to be a female he probably wouldn't have let her look at it at all.

A rifle had caught her eye, but she hadn't had enough money. That would have to wait, and No-Account had a great deal of patience.

She had actually gotten the long gun she had from a dead man she'd stumbled over in the woods. From all appearances he'd simply fallen on his rifle. She'd dug a hole to bury him, taking the rifle, bullets, and powder as fair payment.

It had taken a while for her to figure out how to load and shoot, but she'd soon acquired dead-center accuracy. She now felt secure with her arsenal.

Looking around her now, the morning sun drying her, she thought how truly fortunate she had been. She'd gotten to California, where she had plenty of food and a warm place to sleep—and no need to use her arsenal. Next she planned to own that house, with fresh water at the pump, a cold cellar, and a rain barrel that sat just off the porch.

"Pssst."

She looked around. "Slow?"

"I'm in the trees. When do we eat? He already got the eggs."

"He didn't see you, did he?"

"Naw, I heard him in the water 'n got out o' there. I found me a watchin' place in the crook of a tree yonder."

"I'll bring your breakfast soon as I can. He says we're goin' ta Coldbottom, but I'm stayin' here. He just don't know it yet. Were you warm enough in the barn?"

"Warm as warm. I'm a little itchy from the hay."

"While me 'n him eat, get washed in the stream. That'll take away some o' the itch."

"Aw, Sis." He hung his head. "You're gettin' like him."

"Once you get used to it, washin' ain't bad. Now, go on. I'll leave your breakfast under the porch steps."

She started back to the house. Noticing how the sun glinted off the church bell, she decided to have a look inside.

Open doors welcomed her. Was God in there? He had never seemed to be in any of the revival tents with the shouting and singing. Maybe he preferred a more permanent place.

Looking around, she ducked inside.

Rows of plank seats lined each side of the aisle, and sun streamed through the windows, bathing the inside with a golden glow.

She inhaled the scents of beeswax and pine boards. "It smells special-like." The whispered words sounded loud in the empty church.

The Good Book rested on the preaching platform. There were so many candles. She tiptoed down the aisle to get a closer look. "Real wax," she said in awe. She touched a wooden cross that hung on the wall.

A piano stood to one side. No-Account loved music. She dared to plink a few keys. "My, oh, my." Settling herself on the bench, she folded her hands in her lap.

"Howdy. My name's No-Account." She waited a moment. "I need some help. You see, I got to take care o' Slow, 'n I don't want to pass my troubles on to Preacher. He's a good man 'n all—stubborn as a mule, though.

"I guess you know I didn't play him fair. A man advertises for a wife, he got a right to expect someone who knows wifin'. Damn—ummm . . . beg pardon. See, I cain't be a wife 'cause I ain't much for doin' what I'm told. An' you'd know better 'n anybody he don't want me." She paused.

"That sure is a mighty fine house. You done yourself proud when you made the parson.

67

"He's probably lookin' at his timepiece, so I better go. I'd be obliged if you aimed me in the right direction. Thank you kindly."

Mike had been looking for her when he heard her voice coming from the church. Drawing near, he hadn't heard all of her simple plea, but he'd heard enough. *Confound it, I can't send her away.*

A rustle of clothing alerted him that she neared the door. He hurried back down the path. It would be better if she didn't know he'd been there.

"Ah, you were in church," he said when she came through the doors.

"I should have asked your leave to go in there."

"You may pray anytime you like. Breakfast is ready."

"I'm real peckish. You ain't goin' to pray all mornin', are you?"

He held the door for her and didn't answer, but he kept grace agreeably short.

Mike had prepared a larger than usual meal. She'd been so hungry last evening, and he didn't want her to think she had to sneak and hide outside to eat her fill.

No-Account's eyes widened. "Biscuits 'n gravy, eggs, sausage, potatoes. Do ya eat like this ever' day?"

"You had a real appetite yesterday. I don't want you to be hungry."

She dove into the food.

"Ahem." Mike cleared his throat, but she didn't stop. "Miss . . . No-Account, use the knife and fork."

"Why?"

"Eating with your hands isn't ladylike."

"I ain't a lady."

"Try."

Wishing to please him, she wiped her hands on her dress.

"Use the napkin. Right there by your plate."

"What the hell do you want me to do with it?"

Mike gave a low groan. "Place it on your lap. It catches droppings. You can dab grease from your mouth."

She watched to see how he held his fork, and brought a bit of egg to his lips. His mouth fascinated her.

Everything drifted into a haze as she focused on how his lips took that bite of food. Beautiful lips. White teeth. There were creases at the corners of his mouth. A deep dimple scored his left cheek. Yes, he'd be right easy to curl up to on cold nights.

"No-Account?" he said. "Will you try?"

Startled, she rubbed her neck and shoulder. A shiver ran up her spine when she realized that she had been damp in just that very place when she'd awakened. Had he been nibbling on her?

She picked up her fork. "I'll try. It don't look too hard." Actually her heart was in her throat, and she doubted she could swallow a bite. She tried. Lord knew she tried. In the end it wasn't her heart that kept her from eating her fill; it was the table tin—the knife and fork, as he had called them. The most she could spear and eat were potatoes and meat. Since Mike broke pieces of biscuit off to dip in the gravy, she followed his lead.

Mike pushed his plate away. "After we wash, we'll get started. I want to give us enough time."

"I'll stay here."

"You need some dresses. You can't sleep in your day dress."

No-Account noticed how abruptly he stopped. She rubbed her shoulder again. "You're turnin' all pink. Is it 'cause I put my blanket next to yourn? I was fearful o' fallin' out o' that dang bed. 'Sides, it don't seem natural for folks to sleep alone. We *was* dressed, after all. Least-ways, I was. It ain't a shameful thing for a man ta sleep without his shirt." She remembered the feel of his solid chest under her fingertips.

Mike changed the subject. "You shouldn't go in the water with your clothes on."

"You mean take them off? Outside in the mornin' light? Preacher, I think that knock on the head last night must've done addled your senses. You were naked this morning, but I recollect you been in the creek wearin' duds a time or two."

Mike hurried to the sink with the dishes. "Never mind. If I'm going to perform the weddings on time, we have to leave soon." He put the dishes down and pulled out his watch.

No-Account was learning to hate that timepiece. She took her own dishes over. After she put them down, she folded her arms and tapped her foot.

Hip against the sink, Mike took on the look of a patient teacher. "Obviously you have something to say?"

"I ain't goin'."

"We have to get you outfitted, and I have to find a place for you to stay. I can't just go in and buy a dress for you. They have to measure and do . . . whatever they do."

"I like what I'm wearin'." No-Account thrust out her chin.

"I plan to have you settled in a room this afternoon. You'll go with me, or I'll know the reason why." While he spoke, he approached until he towered over her.

Disliking the advantage his position gave him, she moved closer in challenge, even if she did have to tilt her head to look at him.

He went to the door. "Be ready in half an hour."

"See? I cain't go. Don't know a half hour."

"See that clock on the wall? When it chimes, you come outside."

"So that's what that thing is? Might have known you'd

have another timepiece. That noise it makes, is that chimes?"

"Yes." There was a solid thud when he closed the door behind him.

"I ain't goin'!" she shouted.

Chapter Five

When Mike disappeared to the barn, No-Account stuck a biscuit into her mouth. She gathered the leavings for Slow, stuffing them into the sagging top of her dress.

The lumpy outline of food in her bodice caused her to smile. "The gal who owned this must've been top-heavy," she mumbled.

Outside, the smell of skunk still hung in the air. Slow stood at the edge of a thicket. "I'm here," he said.

"Hush up. You have to keep cover," she said when she joined him.

"Sis, ya got growed on top."

"That's your food." She led him deep into the underbrush. "You oughtn't come in the open like that."

"He be downstream."

Shaking her head, she reminded him, "There might be other folks about. I got biscuits 'n bacon. Where's your dish?"

"In my shirt," he said with a sheepish look.

"How many times do I have ta tell you to put it in your sack with your other things?" She delved into her dress and piled the contents onto his plate. "Slow, you got to find a better place to keep that. One o' these days it's goin' ta slide down your britches. Folks will look at ya queer-like."

"Ain't no place else if I want it close by."

While he dug into his food, No-Account picked at crumbs that stuck to the inside of her dress.

"Uh-oh. There's grease on my dress." She rubbed at it but it didn't help, which meant she'd have to explain. That man didn't miss much.

Slow spoke around a mouthful of food. "Eggs 'n all. He must be well set, Sis."

They sat on a rock while he ate. No-Account liked to see her brother happy. He ate the last biscuit after rubbing his plate clean with it. "Them was the best eats I ever chomped on. Cooked 'n ever'thin'." A bit of food flew from his overstuffed mouth as he spoke.

No-Account bit her lower lip, remembering the times they'd made do with raw fish, or eggs that slid down their throats still warm from the hen. She put the memory away.

"We got to make another plan. He's aimin' to set me up with someone. By the look o' things he ain't takin' no for an answer." Covering her concern for her brother with brashness, she continued. "You recall how to get to town? Course you do. You always find your way real fine."

With the tin dish on his lap, Slow asked, "I smelled coffee. Be there any left?"

"It's real-as-real coffee. Don't taste like chicory. I'll get it for you." She got to her feet and ran for the house, returning with the pot.

While he drank enthusiastically from the spout, No-Account gave careful instructions. "Try to get a job at the livery. You're good with animals. Maybe they'll let you sleep there. I have to put off tellin' him he got two o' us, though. That man don't take to change at all. Don't worry yourself none. He'll come around, 'n we'll all be a family."

"How can ya tell?"

"He has a gentleness under all that starch. It's in his eyes." She went to retrieve the bundle of clothes she'd hidden under the porch.

"Here, put these on." A desire to protect Slow's dignity had driven her to take them from the trunk in the loft. No-Account didn't consider that thieving.

Most people judged others by how they looked. She knew why they'd been shunned all the way across the country. Even Parson couldn't wait to change her. She was determined Slow would look tolerable when he asked for a job, no matter what she had to do.

Slow preened as he dressed. "I'm gonna look grand. Ya got any shoes?" As an afterthought he said, "It be bad ta steal, Sis. Did ya?"

She helped him button the shirt, then handed him the shoes. "It don't make no never mind if I go to hell for takin' these. I'm probably goin' there on account o' that Bible anyhow." She stepped back. "Ya look real handsome. Them pants are a little short in the leg, though."

Slow's eyes sparkled. He loved new things.

"Settle down on this rock. I borrowed the preacher's shavin' soap, so I can shave you easy." She unsheathed her knife, and he sat still while she shaved his stubble.

Mike's whistling alerted her to his return. "I have ta get back. I'll try ta let you know where I'm stayin'." She grabbed the coffeepot and lit out for the house.

No-Account found Mike seated at the table, paper before him, pen in hand. He looked up. "You must have been hungry."

After the brightness outside she had to squint to see

him. "I been hungry all my life." She didn't try to hide the pot. He deserved *some* honesty.

He corked the ink bottle and put his paper and pen aside. "Put the coffeepot in the dry sink and come over here."

"You're put out with me, ain't ya? I was outside, so I didn't hear the chime."

Propping his elbows on the table, Mike replied with a question of his own. "When did you eat last? I mean aside from supper last night."

"I eat somethin' ever' day."

"Like what?"

No-Account searched her mind for something other than the truth. She skirted the issue. "You saw how good I can shoot game."

Arms folded, Mike continued to stare at her. She wondered if he knew she had walked around the truth.

"What did you do to your dress?"

She looked down. "I . . . umm . . . I wiped my plate with it." First she'd swiped food; then she'd put a lie on top. Yep, she was headed straight to the devil. "I guess I cain't go with ya then. Since I don't have another dress."

"We're going to Coldbottom. You need some clothes that fit. That dress just will have to do for now."

He turned the inkwell around and around. "Before we leave I'd like to discuss a few things with you. Some changes."

"What kind o' changes?" No-Account smelled an ambush. She directed a wary glare at him.

Mike took it as a challenge. "You *will* go with me."

She folded her arms and stood firm. "An' what's next, your worship?"

Mike smiled, giving her the full impact of that dimple of his.

Something about his grin made No-Account's knees weak. She tilted her head. "Are you funnin' me?"

"I'm smiling because my mother always called my father 'your worship' when he laid down the law." Mike tugged his ear, then ran his hand over his face to fix his features into their comfortable, preacherlike lines.

"Did he beat her?"

"Certainly not."

"You ain't told me much 'bout you. Why did you turn ta preachin'?"

"I wanted to do something to bring joy into people's lives. My father and brothers liked shipbuilding. For me it held no appeal, so I became a minister."

"Do you like workin' for the Lord?"

He hesitated. "I think that's why I came to California. There were plenty of clergy in Massachusetts and the Eastern states. I'd heard California needed everything."

"So you came here with your lists and started right off preachin'."

"Not exactly . . . I really never fit in. Not at home, not among my family—not here."

No-Account sat opposite him. "Now that's a pure sorrow. You didn't fit in with your own kin? You said you had a ma and pa. How many brothers and sisters?"

"I have four brothers and two sisters."

"Don't ya like your brothers?"

"Brothers can be a curse. But I do like them. In fact, I love them."

"So you came here ta find your promise."

"Promise?"

"Your promise in your life. Are you happy?" She picked up a dry pen and made looping motions with it over a sheet of Mike's paper.

"I wish I could tell you I've found happiness, but the people here seem put off by me."

"You are a pretty off-puttin' man with your washin' 'n prayin'. You're all stiff, like a sapling that won't bend. Don't worry; I'll help you fix all that."

77

"Maybe you could."

"I can. An' I'm glad you like your brothers."

He picked up his pen, tapping the dry point on the table. "You can't run around with your hair flying wild. Put it up out of sight."

"And how am I supposed to do that, seein' as I lost my hat 'n you took away my holdin' leather?"

He put the pen down to take a clean handkerchief from his pocket, then folded it several times to make a length of soft cotton. He went behind her to tie the wild mane at her nape. "This will do for now. Didn't you have a ribbon last evening?"

"Must've got snagged by a bush."

Silky strands clung to his hands as he tied them in place. Mike Mulgrew couldn't find his voice, nor could he control his hands when they cupped the base of her neck, stroking outward to rest on her soft shoulders.

"Mike?"

To cover his lapse, he went back to the table. This time he didn't sit. "We have to pick a name for you. Do you have any preferences? If not, I have several in mind." He picked up the sheet of paper upon which he had been writing, now folding and unfolding it. He didn't look at her. He'd chosen the names with care. They were digni-fied names, proper for the wife of a minister. "How does 'Hannah' feel?"

Silence.

He looked up just in time to duck the stove lid coming his way. It crashed against the wall behind him. No-Account grabbed another. He dodged it.

"I'll tell ya how 'Hannah' feels, ya miserable high-toned . . . " She shot a barrage of words at him, unladylike words.

He crouched left when the salt tin narrowly missed his ear. No-Account grabbed, then flung the coffeepot. With a lunge he put himself between her and the cupboard, where she was headed for more ammunition.

"Stop it!" He dove at her, his hands spanning her waist.

"I ain't changin' my name. I ain't gonna marry you. I'll wear what I want to wear. I'll . . . I'll go naked afore I wear your dadblamed clothes."

No-Account furiously tried to unbutton the dress. A button popped off, revealing the too-large chemise beneath. Her barely concealed breasts nearly bounced free in rhythm with her agitated breathing.

"Confound it," Mike said while he clasped the front of the partially open dress. It brought her closer. "Stop this instant," he said down at her with a growl. She froze.

They stood toe-to-toe, her eyes wide open, lips slightly apart.

No-Account had the strangest feeling. Thunderation, she wanted to be mad as hell, and she couldn't say another word. She licked her lips.

Almost violently he thrust her away. While he paced, she stood silent and confused. "Let me make this clear." The words, soft with a threat, tumbled from his lips. "You can pick a name, or I'll pick one for you."

Waiting for the words to sink in, he added a cowardly argument. "I sent for a respectable bride and you cheated me. Therefore, you'll learn to look, act, and speak with propriety. And you'll have a *real* name."

She wanted to be mad as hell, but he had her. Raising her chin, she ambled toward the door, where she had to pass him. Stopping a few feet away from him, she spit on the floor right next to his shoe. "You cain't *make* me respectable. Hell, I don't even know what respectable is."

He cleared his throat and gritted his teeth. The glistening glob of spittle gleamed at him. "No cussing. No swearing. No more spitting in the house."

No-Account strode around him. She stopped at the door. "Anythin' else?"

"We're leaving now." He flipped open his watch. "That will give me an hour to find a room for you. You can't live here without our being legally married."

"I ain't marryin' you, so why does it matter?"

"I bought a wife. We'll be married as soon as a circulating preacher comes through. Hopefully by then you'll be at least half-civilized."

Her back straight, she asked, "What name you got for me?"

"Pick one, if you like."

She lifted the corner of her sleeve and blew her nose, not bothering to turn around. "You call it."

"Hope, I think. I like it. There's a certain . . . promise about the name."

Hope. What could she do?

No-Account went outside. From the porch she could almost see the crude road that led to Coldbottom. In her lifetime she'd experienced every sort of mockery, yet nothing cut like Mike's words. Why should she care what he thought? She stepped off the porch. Mouth dry, she went to the pump, primed it as he had done. Imagine. Water just outside the door. No-Account drank from the dipper. The liquid slid down her parched throat. She hung the tin ladle on its nail, then cupped her hands to splash her face.

She made her decision with the water drying on her face. No-Account Savage was no more. In her place stood a woman named Hope. This new person possessed the grit and determination of the old. But she, Hope, would use every talent she possessed to please Mike Mulgrew.

This house would be hers, though she didn't expect to marry the preacher. Still, before the snow fell, she would convince him that she'd make a mighty good partner. He would know about Slow by then and have to accept him into the household.

When she heard Mike step onto the porch, she cleared her throat loudly, then spit—farther than she'd ever done—for the last time. She plastered a smile on her face and turned to him. Poor man just didn't know what was good for him. He was a handsome man, and smart, but he needed direction. She was the person to show him the way.

Mike was beaten before he began. As he walked the dusty road with Hope, he worried about the wagging tongues they would confront in Coldbottom. Hope's compliance troubled him, too. He'd expected more rebellion, yet she trudged along with him like an obedient servant. And she chattered—continually.

"Where we goin' first?"

"You'll go to the mercantile, where Mrs. Allgood will find a few things for you to wear."

"I want ta see all the buildin's. Kansas City has lots o' them. You ever been ta Kansas?"

"No." He had noticed that when she was excited or angry her accent became more pronounced.

"You got here without passin' through Kansas?"

"I came by boat."

She broke away from him. "Lookee over here. You can see way down. It's a water foam."

"It's called a gorge." Mike kept walking. He hated this stretch of road. It dropped off sharply to the left.

Ever since he'd climbed that tree when he was eight, he avoided heights. He had wanted to impress his friends and be like his brothers. Instead he had become paralyzed with fear. The branch had started to crack and he'd begun to cry—

"Gorge." She leaned over to get a better view.

"Get back here. We don't have time for that. And you might fall in."

Since he kept walking, she ran to catch up. But she wasn't finished. "Does Coldbottom have a livery?"

"Of sorts."

"You know who owns it?" She trotted to keep up with his long strides.

Mike stopped and frowned at her. "No, I don't." He walked on. Actually he knew only a few of the permanent citizens of Coldbottom, though he had lived in the city until he'd built his house. He'd mostly kept to himself, though. He knew a few names, but nothing of the lives of those whom he wanted as his flock. Hope had a way of making a man question his actions.

"I got ta warn you. I might get my ass kicked out o' the mercantile."

"Don't say 'ass'."

"What should I say instead o' ass?"

"Hope . . . just leave out the cuss words." Looking her over, Mike wondered how many things had been denied her because of her upbringing. Even now, the dirty, wrinkled dress gave her a far from acceptable appearance.

"There it is," she shouted. "There's Coldbottom. I want to see it all."

"We don't have time for that today. You can look around when you live here."

"You don't want folks ta see me with you."

Mike turned to look at her, a denial on his lips. Truth hammered at him. Ashamed? He *was* ashamed of her, as he'd been of his parents. The stunning realization pushed him to walk faster.

But she wasn't finished. Trotting to his side, she inquired, "Parson, if you really want us ta marry, why cain't we do it with the other folks?"

Broad shoulders slumped. "Do you never stop prattling?"

"What's prattling?"

Mike closed his eyes. "Please. No more. All you do is talk, talk, talk." He turned away, walking well ahead of her.

She pressed her lips together. He wanted quiet; he'd get quiet. Meanwhile she intended to do as she pleased.

They'd reached the store. At least he had.

He opened the door, waiting for her to enter, but she looked up when the tinkle of the bell caught her attention. She tapped it a few times with her finger, her eyes shining.

All the bustle of the busy store ceased. Two old men looked up from their game of checkers. Someone whispered audibly, "Parson's going to find out how it feels to sleep with a wildcat." Bawdy laughter erupted.

"What's that you said?" No-Account sauntered in their direction.

Thaddeus Allgood hurried over. "Morning, miss, Parson. Fine day for a wedding. Can I help you?"

"Thaddeus." Mike nodded. "Miss Hope Savage here seems to have, er . . . lost her belongings. Could Mrs. Allgood outfit her?"

Alberta Allgood emerged from the back room as if she'd just been waiting to be summoned. "Good morning, Parson Mulgrew. This must be your new bride." She cast an appraising eye over Hope.

"Howdy. *I* don't need a damn thing. Ask him."

"Hee-hoo! That gal's got spirit, Parson," hooted one of the checker players.

Mike rubbed his face with his handkerchief. "She needs some dresses, a coat, hat, sunbonnet, shoes, and maybe some galoshes."

"What do I need all that for? What's galoshes?"

"They're overshoes for wet weather. It can get pretty muddy here," commented Thaddeus.

"She'll need unmentionables and nightdresses. Whatever ladies wear. Handkerchiefs." Mike fiddled with a pile of yarn. He was clearly out of his depth.

"Wait just a dadblamed minute here. A body cain't wear all that. An' stop talkin' like I ain't here. Howdy, Mrs. Allgood. I'm No-Acc—"

Mike had a coughing fit and she stopped talking to whack him on the back. "Now where was I?"

"You were about to tell Mrs. Allgood your name, *Hope*."

Thaddeus exchanged glances with his wife, who said, "Hope. What a pretty name. I'm Alberta to all my friends."

"You got a nice store here," said Hope.

Thaddeus puffed out his chest. "Best one for fifty miles."

Alberta took Hope's arm, leading her through curtains that shielded the inner sanctum of the back room.

"Wait," called Mike.

Alberta looked at him over her shoulder. "Something else, Parson?"

"Do you think you could teach her to do up her hair?"

"Such thick hair," Alberta commented. "How would you like to wear it, Hope?"

"I don't rightly know. There's so much o' it."

"Don't you worry. You'll be the prettiest bride of them all. I'll have her ready at noon, Parson."

Mike didn't like Alberta's assumptions. Especially since Hope neither looked or acted like the mail-order angel he'd been expecting. Unfortunately, this angel needed coaching. He turned to leave, knowing that when his wedding *did* take place, everything would be perfect, including Hope—right down to her dress and behavior. "She doesn't have to be ready. We won't wed today," he said before opening the door.

Alberta Allgood's mouth snapped shut. She actually glared at him. Then she gave him her opinion. "Mike Mulgrew, you of all people aren't going to marry this

84

poor girl? She spent the night under your roof. Tsk, for shame."

The room shuddered, causing a few things to fall from the shelves. "You got some thunder with not a cloud in sight," remarked Hope.

Mike grabbed her, hauling her against him to stand in the doorway. Another shudder rocked them.

"Earthquake!" someone shouted.

"Mike, let me go. What's an earthquake?"

Dust began to settle and Mike released her. "The next time you hear that kind of rumble, I want you to take cover, Hope. Sometimes the ground opens up and swallows everything nearby."

"Oh, well, thank you. You're the first person ever wanted ta keep me safe." She kissed his chin.

Now all of Coldbottom would think they'd shared a bed. Mike tried not to look guilty when Hope disappeared behind the curtain with Alberta.

He couldn't say she'd lied, not with the hot memory of waking with her curled against him. Distracted, he missed the first step and nearly fell.

As he righted himself he could see the old men through the window, chuckling and wagging their heads.

He tried the boardinghouses first, then the hotels, all three. There wasn't a room to be found in all of Coldbottom. Mike stopped at the building that held the sheriff's, bank, and post offices.

Sheriff Stably often knew what few others did. Mike looked in. "Oliver?"

Stably looked up from the newspaper. "Mike! I understand congratulations are in order."

"I can't find a room where she can stay till the circuit preacher comes around."

"There aren't any rooms. Thought you knew that.

Every time a stage comes into town the rooms are at a premium."

What happens to those who can't find rooms?" Mike asked.

Oliver cocked his head. "Lizzy can always fit another lady in at her place."

Mike's jaw tightened. "You mean she gives them a home and they pay for their keep?"

"Lizzy runs a business."

"What am I going to do?"

"I'll marry you two if you want."

"I want a preacher."

"Suit yourself. If you need me, just send word."

Crestfallen, Mike rose to walk from the office. He glanced to where Hettie Elger worked sorting mail and knew the news would be all over town.

Outside, he looked up the hill. Miss Lizzy's Establishment For Gentlemen overlooked Coldbottom. Mike shook his head. He couldn't allow *that*.

Crossing the street, he went to the livery. While he walked he prayed. *God, give me an answer. What should I do?* Nothing changed. He knew not to expect an immediate answer.

Shouts came from the back of the livery, sounding much like a fight. Mike almost turned away until he heard someone say, "Hold him down."

Mike looked around into the side yard.

"Naw. Please don't hit me ag'in."

Three men were taking turns hammering a giant who whimpered while he tried to cover his face with his arms. One of them kicked at his knees. He crumpled to the ground with a moan. "Aw, naw, don't hit me no more."

"Here. Stop that," Mike shouted.

They ignored him.

"Hey, boys. Want to see me piss on him?"

The downed man struggled while another attacker kicked him again.

The man unbuttoned his pants at the same time Mike went into a black rage the likes of which he hadn't experienced in years. With a howl he dove at them.

Chapter Six

One fist grabbed a shirtfront while the other smashed into the face above it. Mike fought like three men, and he had the advantage of surprise. The bullies scattered like frightened birds.

The downed man cried, "I hurt. They hurt me."

Mike went to where he huddled in the dirt. "Here. Let me see." With his handkerchief Mike wiped the filth and blood away. A small cut on the man's cheek seemed to be the only visible sign of injury, but Mike had seen the vicious kick that downed him.

"I jist asked fer a job." He tried to brush dirt off his shirt. "Aw, naw, my new duds is all ripped. Dang."

"I'll take you home. Where do you live?" Mike helped him to his feet.

"Ain't got no home. I wanted ta live in the stable 'n take care o' the horses 'n wagons."

"Tell me your name."

"I cain't say my name. Leastways not fer now. Where's my hat?"

Mike spotted it. "I'll get it."

"It's all spoilt." The man wept when he tried to put it on.

"Here, I'll fix it up a little." Mike pushed the crown up and ran his fist around the inside to reshape it. "Don't you have a mother or father nearby?"

"Nope. They be gone."

Mike knew the man couldn't stay in this miserable place for long without falling victim to every kind of villain. "I could use a hired hand. Would you like to work for me? You'll remember who you are in no time."

Slow looked closely at Mike. "You be the parson, ain't ya?"

"Reverend Mike Mulgrew."

"I never seen a parson what could fight like that."

Mike had fought like that before, though not in years. Losing his temper had shaken him. The attack had reawakened the lion that Mike had never quite put to sleep.

"Let's get a wagon. I'm late." And conscience-stricken, he thought. "Could we call you Daniel until you remember your name?"

"That's a real name like other folks has."

Mike wondered at that comment. It reminded him of No-Account.

Losing his temper troubled him. Everything that had happened since yesterday made him uneasy. He thought he'd left his temper and temptation in Seaforth.

In the past when No-Account had ventured into a store, the proprietor watched her closely. Here at Allgood's, after being measured, she found herself urged from one item of clothing to another.

"Here's the prettiest nightgown you'll ever see, Hope. Mike'll forget he's a preacher when he sees it." Alberta draped tissue-soft cotton flannel over Hope's head, lifting her hair free to cascade over one shoulder.

"Is that me?" The image in the mirror took her breath away.

"It sure is. Save that gown for your wedding night."

"But there ain't much to it. I might as well be naked."

Alberta removed the gown, adding it to the growing pile of clothing. "I have just the thing for you to wear this afternoon for the weddings."

"But he says I ain't goin'. I wonder where he's puttin' me up. Is it been a hour yet?"

With practiced hands Alberta smoothed a soft petticoat before she slipped a lavender frock over Hope's head. Alberta clucked her tongue. "You'll be right there with him. Wait and see.

"Sit down and I'll show you how to do your hair." Alberta eyed the clock. "Parson isn't back yet, though I wonder what kept him. He's usually prompt."

"That won't set right with him. He does everythin' by that damn time-teller. Oops, I forgot. He won't let me say 'damn.' "

"Mark my words. There'll be a lot of changes in Preacher Perfect's life now that you're part of it."

Thaddeus piled the clothing in a wooden chest while Alberta showed Hope how to twist and knot her hair.

Someone shouted from the door, "Here he comes."

"Just in time," said Alberta. "What do you think?"

Hope had her doubts about getting the hairpins right, but for now she liked what she saw. Alberta had made it all seem so easy. "You made me look like a real lady," she said in awe. "I look like I *could* go to the weddin's, don't I?"

Alberta grinned. "Let's go see what *he* has to say."

Outside, a noisy crowd finished decorating Mike's newly rented wagon with ribbons and a few wildflowers. Five brides lined one side, while the grooms occupied the other.

Slow climbed into the wagon, where he plopped next to Frenchy. "Howdy."

The Frenchman returned his greeting while Mike climbed into the driver's seat.

"Wait up, Parson. Here's your Hope, all prettied up and ready to go," shouted Alberta over the general confusion.

Mike halted. Hope rushed into the sunshine, a vision in lavender calico.

"That's Hope?"

"Close your mouth, Parson. You're gaping. Of course it is." Alberta glowed with pride.

Everyone within looking distance took in Hope's appearance. From her neatly bound hair to the modest bottom of her skirt, she looked born to be the wife of a parson.

"I gotta hand it to you, Mike, she sure cleaned up nice," commented Vince O'Malley.

The wagon had already moved into the street.

Mike's hands fisted on the reins he held, making the horses restive.

"I ain't never seen a weddin' my whole life," Hope claimed.

Thaddeus came out carrying the trunk. "We decided to give Hope a wedding present. You said she lost her belongings. She can keep her clothes in here until you have time to get a chifforobe. Then it'll make a nice blanket chest." As an afterthought he added with a wink, "Or you can use it to store baby clothes."

Frustration and something like fear overtook Mike when he saw that trunk. He couldn't look at Hope, with her eager violet eyes.

"Ain't that nice, Mike? Thank you for everything." Hope spoke for him. Then she added, "I want to see these nice folks married. You can bring me back later."

Mike hated to be wrong, and he muttered, "I couldn't get a room for you."

"You mean I'm stayin' with ya?"

"We'll let you know if we hear of something else," said Thaddeus.

"Do *you* have an extra room?" Mike was hopeful.

Alberta shook her head.

It all added up to real trouble for Mike. He knew it. Hope had a strange effect on his emotions. Losing his temper was evidence that his self-control was slipping. He'd be doing a lot of praying. Visions of him wearing out his trouser knees swam before him.

Hope circled the wagon, exchanging greetings with the excited brides. "You got a wagon, 'n someone to bring it back." She nodded at Daniel. "Howdy."

When she hoisted herself onto the wagon-bed, everyone got a long look at her stocking-clad legs—above the knee. Mike dragged his gaze away from the dainty lilac and lace garter. He'd have to talk to her about propriety, but the image of long, shapely legs had already gotten to him.

The women carried on pleasant chatter, while the men just stared.

Mike was sure every last man who'd seen her sprawl into the wagon now lusted after her. He was stumped about why the women were in Hope's thrall.

He moved over, leaving the other side of the driver's seat vacant. "Sit here, Hope." Mike did not want those men to get too close.

She hauled a leg over the seat and plunked her dainty self beside him. "Who's the extry feller?"

"This is my new hand. Daniel, this is Hope Savage."

Slow smiled up at her. "New names 'n all. Ya got a nice fella here."

"I'd say you're right."

The return trip by wagon took less time than the walk to town, and Hope Savage held court. She turned around in her seat to engage in animated conversation with the other passengers.

Guilt about losing his temper earlier besieged Mike, yet he knew those ruffians who'd been beating on Daniel wouldn't have listened to reason. Add to that the randy way he felt around Hope and his mistrust of every man who set eyes on her, and he found himself confronted by moral choices he had never expected to make. His life was suddenly complicated, and Mike didn't like it.

His introspection was interrupted by Hope's shout. "There it is, everybody. Home." She stood up when Mike pulled the wagon into the yard.

Though the men were familiar with Mike's spread, the women they would marry expressed their approval at one of the few real homes they'd seen since their arrival.

Mike pulled up, handing the reins to Daniel. "See that creek? You can water the horses there, Daniel. After you finish, would you clean up a little?"

"Shucks, I knowed that were comin'." He led the horses away.

Inside the church, Mike instructed the couples on the seriousness of the step they were about to take. Hope watched from the piano bench while he performed the age-old ceremony. It pleased him that she listened attentively to every word.

"And will you promise to love, honor, and obey until death?" he asked of the ladies. "Please answer, 'I will.' "

"I wi—" they chorused.

"Hell's bells!" Hope jumped up, shattering the peace in the little church.

All eyes were upon her. "Why do the gals have ta obey 'n the menfolk just cherish? It ain't right."

"Doggone it, Hope, you stay out of this." Mike clenched his jaw and tugged his ear.

"I heard 'bout this 'obey.' Don't it mean they got to do everythin' they're told?"

"Well, yes. That's how it's done."

"Do you gals want to fetch 'n pick up 'n every other thing they can think of?"

Dahlia and Daisy looked at each other, then at their "almost" husbands. They took a little step back.

Ada, Florine, and Cornelia gathered in a close circle, whispering. Several times they looked toward their anxions soon-to-be mates.

Cornelia stepped forward. "Is the marriage legal yet, Parson?"

"Almost. I have to pronounce you man and wife."

Vince, Barney, Bart, and Zeke moved to take their brides by the arm. They were eager to finish, but their "almost" wives stood fast.

Hope looked at Mike. "Well, it pure galls me. I think it ought to be they both say 'obey,' or they both say 'cherish.' Um, what's cherish?"

Amused, Frenchy asked, *"Oui.* Why is it so, Mike?" He loved a good fight, and he surely saw one coming between the parson and his lady.

Mike took a few steps toward Hope until they were toe-to-toe again. "Hope, go to the house."

"We ain't married, so I don't have to."

Mike's eyes were almost black. A lively breeze drifted through the open windows, ruffling his hair. He'd once been told that he had the menacing look of a pirate when he was riled. "We can remedy that. Frenchy, you can witness *our* marriage."

Hope glared at him. "I ain't sayin' that word to nobody. Come on, gals. Let's go in the house. Mike has some nice fresh milk." She led the women down the aisle. The men stood frozen with shock as they left.

Mike slammed his prayer book down and strode after them. But when he mounted the porch, he heard Hope slip the bar into place. He banged on the door. "Come out of there. All of you!"

From his place behind the frustrated parson, Frenchy said, "Eh, Mike, you want we break down the door?" His voice bubbled with mirth, irking Mike.

"Hope, be reasonable. They can't take back their vows!" Having lost his temper once this day, he made a heroic effort to control himself.

Bang! The rifle shot had them all ducking for cover. Overhead, a hole in the porch roof rained debris over them.

Mike poked his head from the corner of the porch where he'd taken shelter to see Hope standing at the open window near the door, rifle in hand—the one he kept over the door for emergencies.

"She a crazy woman, Mike. You no want to marry that one," Frenchy shouted from where the other men huddled. They'd run a considerable distance to hide behind a tree.

"Maybe we ought to do what they want," Zeke called to Mike.

"I saved my money for this day. I ain't anxious to spend another winter alone," said Barney.

"If we don't lay down the law now, they'll have us over a barrel." Vince O'Malley's tone belied his blustering words.

Zeke disagreed. "We can put the cards on the table later. Let's get hitched and take 'em home."

The argument continued while Mike sat on the top step of his porch, shaking his head in disbelief.

Inside, the ladies found chairs for themselves. Hope busied herself pouring milk. While they sipped, Hope gave her opinions on the world of men. "I never met one feller could do what a gal can. Some gals—like me, naturally— can shoot a tail feather off a duck without grazin' his skin. I can catch a fish 'n drive a rig, too."

"Can you cook?" asked Ada.

"Well, I kin put meat 'n such on a spit. Or boil things in a pot. That's what I don't understand. Mike can cook 'n sew 'n everythin'. He don't need a wife. Now I'm wonderin' what kind o' obeyin' he wants."

She set her cup on the table with a dull thud. "Men go off like little boys when they want to have a good time; then they expect us to take care of every little thing while we have little ones hangin' on to our teats."

Dahlia gasped at the wicked word; then someone giggled.

"She's right, you know," said Daisy. "We're supposed to let them have at us every hour of the day or night. If we get a baby in us they don't care, long as they get their vittles. We need some rules, ladies."

Heads nodded in agreement.

Hope continued her observations. "They go off to do their 'manly work,' shakin' a pan for hours, come home, hump on us, then go to sleep. Nary a word o' thanks do they say." Hope postured like a man looking to bed his wife. When she dropped her head, closed her eyes, and gave a loud snore, she had them laughing uproariously.

When they settled down they took a vote. *No*, they agreed. The vows, as they stood, wouldn't do.

Cornelia, the most adventurous, peeked out the side window. "Zeke. Stand out there where I can see you."

"You wantin' to talk?"

"Well, I thought we could make a little agreement. I'm not happy with that damp tent. I expected a house. Or at least a cabin."

"Now, Cornelia, be reasonable. I got work to do."

"I'm not asking you to build one today. It doesn't have to be fancy either. I'm thinking you might work on it evenings and Sundays."

"Can't work on Sunday. Right, Parson?" Zeke looked hopefully at Mike, who banged his fist repeatedly on a porch post.

Shy Ada Crump squeaked, "Leave the parson out of this. Gentlemen, we have some rules." The women clustered around her near the open window.

Hope stepped to the front. "Do any o' you have a dwellin'? Other than a tent, o' course."

General mumbling and shifting confirmed her suspicions. They'd done nothing to prepare for families. She continued. "They got a right to want a home. They'll work at your side. Right, gals?"

"We'll carry half the load," said Ada. "Bart, I don't take kindly to a stubborn man."

Bart stomped forward. "We're miners. If I build a house, I can't go to the next strike."

"That's another thing," said Florine. "We want to stay put."

"Y'all hear that, fellers?" asked Hope.

Frenchy sauntered up the porch steps to stand next to Bart. "*Chérie*," he said to Florine. "I am a trapper. I hunt, sometimes for months." He gestured with open palms, indicating he had no control over his situation.

Hope stepped in when Florine began to stammer. "I seen lots o' muskrat 'n squirrel since I got here. Maybe it's time you settled down. I know what travelin' life is like. What you can get there, you can get here," she said.

Florine and the others nodded agreement.

"Enough!" shouted Mike. After two bold strides, he confronted Hope through the open window. "Hope, this isn't any of your business. Let them out of there."

"Shame on you. They deserve better," she countered. "Hell, I ain't got half their learnin'. Cain't tell the front from the back o' a dress. Fact is, I don't like dresses a' tall." She picked at the collar of her dress, which she'd unbuttoned earlier for a little more breathing room. "I'm wonderin' just what you have in mind for me."

His eyes wandered to where her fingers rested. "This isn't about you and me."

"Yes, sir, 'tis. It's about all gals."

The sun was low in the sky. Word would travel about his balking wife. Weary to his very bones, Mike had a rebellion to quell. But how?

The five hopeful husbands huddled to confer. Barney Coachman, elected spokesman, came forward. "Parson?"

Mike turned blazing eyes on him. Through clenched teeth he barked, "What?"

"We decided we'll do what they ask if they'll come home with us."

Mike looked at each man. Some didn't meet his eyes. "You *all* agree?"

Every one of them nodded.

"No one wants to back out?" he asked.

"Let's get it over," said Bart.

Excited, the five women moved to the door in unison.

"Wait!" shouted Hope. Leaning out the open window, she waved her purloined Bible. "Make them swear on this first."

Chapter Seven

Everyone looked at Mike. What did they want from him? he wondered. He thought of murder. He counted to ten, then went on to twenty. "Hope," he gritted out, "this is a domestic problem. Put that Bible away."

"I heard it said that swearin' on the Bible seals a mighty important promise—though I know you don't take kindly to swearin'."

"Hope, they made their wedding vows. That's all that's necessary."

Vince came forward. "Daisy, will you unbar the door? It's getting late and I sure would like to tuck into that stew you made. Yes sir, boys, she's a fine cook."

Daisy twittered; then she slid the bar free before Hope could interfere again. Dahlia followed her sister. One by one the men helped their women back into the rented buckboard.

"Say the words, Parson," Zeke said, eager to leave.

They'd been married—and they now they also had a great tale to tell about Preacher Perfect's bride.

Mike had barely sealed the marriages before they were off in a cloud of dust. Hope, who had come outside to watch, chased the wagon to the road, shouting her good wishes. "I like weddin's. I surely do," she commented while retracing her steps.

When the wagon disappeared, Mike sat under a tree. He'd failed to have his own marriage witnessed. It wasn't like him to forget something that had to do with his life plan. *Something that would sully his reputation.* Oh, he thought, what difference would it make if she stayed another night? They were already compromised, and he hadn't even touched her. His conscience reminded him that he certainly had wanted to.

Hope passed him to go inside. "You comin' in?"

The door swung in the afternoon breeze. Remembering how he'd been barred from his own house earlier, he stepped inside before she could slide the bolt again. Her snap decisions and misunderstandings confused him.

She sat on a chair, rubbing the rifle with a soft cloth. "This shotgun needs to be oiled," she remarked.

"Hope, why did you lock the door earlier?"

"Truth is, I thought if you caught me you might beat me. You cain't whomp me till we're hitched."

The remark shook him.

He saw her eyes drift to his clenched hands. Relaxing them, he went to where she sat. "Hope, I will not beat you. We can talk our differences out."

"Never?"

Her Bible lay on the table beside her. Mike put his hand on it. "I swear."

Hope put her gun aside, the only sounds those of birds nesting for the night and the call of crickets. "You just made my heart sing." At his puzzled expression, she took his hand. "My heart sings when I'm happy."

The corner of his mouth lifted in that smile of his.

She went on, still holding his hand. "I like you, Mike." *Giving Daniel a job . . . that showed me you're a gentle man.*

He squeezed her hand and rose, taking her with him, their hands still joined. "Then why did you worry I'd harm you?"

"Because that's the way most men are back in the mountains."

He drew her into the circle of his arms. Something was happening to him—inside him. He wanted to protect her. Always

Instead, he released her hand. "I'll fix some supper. Maybe it will take care of this headache. I think some food might help."

Gathering food did nothing to keep the memory of the previous night away. *Heavenly father, please keep her in the bedroom.* He knew he was praying for something he didn't truly want, but this time the Lord answered him swiftly. Daniel. The new hand would sleep beside him in the loft.

When Mike returned to the kitchen, Hope came out of the bedroom carrying a small leather bag and a pewter cup.

"Put them things down. I'm goin' to fix your ache."

With practiced fingers she crumbled some leaves into the cup. She poured steaming water from the kettle onto the leaves. "Here, drink this."

He hadn't the energy to fight her.

"I'm going to rub your head." Surprisingly strong fingers raked slowly through his hair with gentle pressure. While he sipped at the not unpleasant concoction, he could feel his tension abating. She moved to his neck and shoulders, kneading, pressing, stroking.

"Mike, what's a vow?"

Why couldn't she keep quiet? His headache had become bearable, and he had begun to feel the intimacy of the massage. If he tilted his head back their lips would be inches apart. Didn't she know she shouldn't get so close to a man? He had to find a way to separate them.

"You can sit down while I explain."

She ran her fingers through his hair one more time. "I'll sit if you finish the tea."

She sat, not in the rocker, but next to him at the table.

"A vow is a sacred promise." He drained the cup and went to the stove, putting some distance between them.

"What's that have to do with cussin' over the Bible?"

"Cussing. You thought . . . " Mike rubbed his face, then tugged his ear. "Swearing has different meanings. See the brown book on the shelf? It's a dictionary. Inside are thousands of words with all their meanings."

Hope went to get the book. Holding it carefully with both hands, she brought it to the table. "Can you teach me all o' them?" She turned the pages with reverence.

"Would you like to start this evening?"

"Glory, yes." She put the book aside. "Are you goin' to let the new feller eat with us? He looks like he needs a lot o' eats."

"Certainly. Would you tell him to come in?"

"I like his name. Daniel. You're a good man, Parson. I sure could have done worse pickin' a husband."

The softness of her voice, and her words of praise, made Mike feel he'd captured a rare prize.

She stood in the doorway, her hand on the latch. "Why'd you name me Hope?"

"I always liked it."

"I'll tell him to come in after I take myself to the woods. I'm fit ta bust."

"By all means. Go to the woods."

She stood at the edge of the surrounding greenery. *Maybe now is the time to tell him about Slow. He just vowed not to hurt me.*

Slow stepped out of his hiding place so fast she nearly ran into him. "Sis, is he goin' to feed me?"

"Sure as day follows night. He sent me to get you for supper."

Daniel nearly knocked her over to get to the house.

"Slow, wait up. Ya got yourself a fine job. 'N a real nice name, too. They wouldn't hire you at the livery?"

"Sis, they beat me. Like folks done afore." Slow lowered his head. "One o' them wanted ta piss on me. The preacher come by 'n lit into them."

"*My* preacher?"

"The very one. There was three o' them, 'n he whipped them all. Then he said he'd give me a job."

She recognized adoration in his voice. It irked Hope. Until now she had been his champion.

"Guess he didn't like your name either, givin' you a new one like he did," she said sourly.

"Ya told me not ta tell my name, so I made like I didn't remember. He said I'm Daniel, that quick. I'd be obliged if ya called me that, too. He sure is a nice man."

"Who pissed on you? I'll find him 'n slip some castor oil in his drinkin' cup." Hope wanted to restore her place in her brother's eyes.

Daniel wasn't interested. "Can I go eat now?"

"Go on in. An' don't forget my name's Hope. Whilst we eat, I'll ask if you can stay in the barn. You washed didn't you? If you don't, well, he does have a bad side."

"I wish I didn't have ta keep washin'. That water is cold," mumbled Daniel.

Gloating, Hope replied, "In his house ya gotta be clean to get any food." She smelled his shirt and decided he was passable. "You'll do. Go on in. I'll be along."

She climbed a rocky outcropping so she could view Mike's land. Those buildings were surely his. Even the barn was tidy. It looked like Mike, big and sturdy. Never

105

in her imaginings had she dreamed of such. Satisfied, she climbed down, heading for the door. A beautiful door on a beautiful house, and she would live there.

She pondered the last few days. She had answered Mike's advertisement to put distance between herself and Pa, and she certainly didn't fit in with the other mail-order brides. But on that trip across the country she'd found she liked being free. The closer they got to California, the more she realized marriage might put a stop to that freedom. That bothered her.

Mike's look of disgust at the first sight of his bride had actually pleased her. Talking him out of the wedding would be simple enough, and she could get a job to pay back her passage money.

But the house changed her mind. She had to have it. Hell, if it took marriage she'd tie herself to him, though she was damned sure she wouldn't do what she was told.

The man was all-fired set in his ways, though. There'd have to be changes, sure as spring, if she became Mrs. Michael Mulgrew. She would bring him around to the right way of thinking.

"Hope?" Mike's soft voice broke her reverie. "Aren't you coming in?"

"I'm comin'." She headed for the porch.

"We're having ham again," he told her. "There wasn't time for anything else." He caught the scent of the yellow soap she'd washed with. Closing his eyes, he willed himself to calm down. After all, it was plain yellow soap.

She stopped halfway to the table. "We're havin' meat two days straight? We had bacon this mornin', you know. Don't you put by for lean times?"

The look of concern in her eyes wrung Mike's heart. "You won't be hungry again," he said. "I keep the pantry well stocked."

"I jist love ham," said Daniel, 'N look, sweet taters an' beans. It's the grandest supper ever."

Mike made the prayer short. Hope flashed him a grateful smile.

Daniel dove into the food with both hands. Mike held his tongue. He had the impression it had been a long time between meals for his new hired hand.

Hope surprised Mike by picking up her napkin to wipe her hands. "Here, Daniel, Parson likes to use these things." She helped him wipe his hands, then inexpertly cut his meat. "Do you think you can do it?"

"Yes, ma'am, I'll sure try."

Her kindness moved Mike. She displayed an almost motherly manner that led him to think of a row of rosy faces seated at the table—their children. He swallowed some unchewed food that stuck in his throat. Their children?

Hope looked up from her plate. "Parson? Ain't you hungry?"

Glad to put a stop to his thoughts, he attempted to eat.

But confound it, he noticed that when he dabbed at his mouth, Hope did the same. Was she trying to please him? The idea set his senses to rioting. He ate, though he tasted nothing.

She had opened the three top buttons of her dress. He saw two peas drop from her fork into that hallowed place. When she reached into her bodice, Mike heard a roar in his head and wondered if either of the other two could hear it.

Mike shook his head to clear it. "Daniel, you can sleep in the loft with me while you're here." He spoke to the man, but his eyes addressed the woman.

Wide-eyed, Hope asked, "Where am I beddin' tonight?"

Mike stiffened. "You'll take the bedroom, and you *will* stay there." He thought he sounded overly harsh.

"I get to stay here? Oh, happy day!" She took some of their plates to the sink.

In the hours since they'd left Coldbottom her hair had slowly slipped free of its pins, so that tendrils framed her face. Mike couldn't look at her without feeling a burning need to loosen the entire mass.

"You'll have the bed again. This time you'll stay there."

"What's a bed?" Daniel looked from Hope to Mike.

"For sleepin'. And it's softer than moss. You can have the bed, Daniel," she offered.

"No," said Mike.

Hope deposited more dirty plates on the sideboard with a decided clank. "I don't like the bed."

"Get used to it."

Daniel dove under the table, drawing the attention of the quarreling couple.

"Now look what you done. You scared him," Hope scolded. "Talk soft 'n come off that high horse."

Mike went to the table and squatted next to Daniel. "What's wrong?"

"You're goin' ta hit us, ain't ya?"

"No, she's stubborn. I need to make myself clear to her."

"She sure does try a man," said Daniel.

Hope soaped up a rag and scrubbed the table harder than necessary.

At Mike's invitation, Daniel went to climb the ladder to investigate his new quarters.

Mike couldn't take his eyes off Hope's gently swaying hips as she cleared the table. His brain seemed to have lost the ability to focus on anything else, so he forced himself to turn to the soiled dinnerware.

"Parson, I'm obliged to you, but if you don't mind, I'd rather sleep on the floor. How 'bout in here by the fire?"

Mike scrubbed at the dishes with vigor. "You'll sleep like a lady, in a proper bed."

"Damn it! I told you. I ain't a lady. I been sleepin' on the floor or the ground all my life."

"Hope, I really wish you'd clean up your language."

"If ya show me where my lang-age is I'll sure try." She inspected her hands and pushed the lavender sleeves up, apparently looking for the spot he wanted her to clean. The wet cloth in her hand released drops of moisture to run from her wrist to her forearm. She had come to where he stood at the dry sink and leaned against it with her hip.

Mike slammed a bowl down. A chip flew from its edge to the floor.

"Ya broke it. Best be careful with your crockery, Parson. You're blessed ta have it. Cain't you show me where my lang-age is without losin' your temper?"

Frustrated, Mike faced her. "You use too many . . . " He searched his mind for a phrase she would understand. "Too many cuss words." He sighed resignedly, then chuckled at his choice of words.

Daniel's face appeared at the opening above their heads. "It's big up here. We can all sleep on the floor."

"Come down, Daniel. We're having a treat." Mike opened one of several packages he had bought from Thaddeus.

Daniel scrambled down the ladder while Mike unwrapped a brown package to reveal a pound cake.

Hope's mouth fell open. "It's a whole cake. A whole damn cake . . . sorry. Did you ever see the like?" She sat at the table, chin in hands, just looking at the mouthwatering sweet. "It's vanilla. I can smell vanilla."

Daniel hauled himself up short. "What do we gotta do ta get a bit?"

Mike laid the knife aside. "You don't have to earn it."

109

"Beggin' yer pardon, Parson, but I want ta earn my keep." Daniel's eyes showed his sincerity.

"You'll start tomorrow. There's plenty of work to be done."

"I do believe you're the best person I ever met."

Hope stood up, almost knocking over her chair. "I ain't eatin' your cake."

Daniel looked at Mike. "Can I have her piece?"

"I think you have something on your mind, Hope. Do you want to tell me about it?"

"You want him to like you better than me."

"I do?"

"And you laughed at me 'cause I didn't know what lang-age meant. I saw you laugh."

Mike sliced the cake. He put the first piece on Hope's plate. "I wasn't laughing at you."

"You were. I ain't sittin' here another minute. Come on, Daniel." She went out the door. A few seconds later she returned for her sack. "You comin'?"

"Naw, I don't want ta leave. He got cake there. Preacher, don't let her take me away."

"Hope, you can't leave in the dark." Mike placed the knife on the table.

"Hell's fire, I'm goin' to the woods. What's gotten into you both? Daniel, get over here." She grabbed Daniel's hand.

They had barely cleared the porch when Mike grabbed her waist. "Where are you taking him?"

"I told you, I'm goin' to the woods. You must be hard o' hearin'."

Daniel broke free to go back inside.

"Why are you taking your sack—and Daniel?"

"You want me clean 'fore I get in that hellfire bed o' yourn. I expect you want him clean, too. My things are in here." She shook the sack. Something inside twanged and she clasped it to her, muting the noise.

110

"You weren't leaving, then?"

"You think we're goin' to sleep outside when it's makin' ta rain? You must be daft." The first drops lightly spattered them. "Daniel, get yourself out here now. You can eat the cake later."

"Make her promise ta let me have my eats, Parson."

"Tarnation, Sl—Daniel! You can eat it whilst the rain falls. Right now we have to tend to our outdoor needs."

Mike watched them duck into the woods. He took the basin to the pump and filled it. "Confound it, that woman is exasperating." They didn't have to wash in the creek when he had a well and two rain barrels to draw water from, but how would they know?

Mike washed while thinking of the twists and turns of this day. And that sack of hers—something about it gnawed at him.

He wouldn't pry, but when they were married she might feel secure enough to enlighten him.

Hope certainly had a gentle way with Daniel. Mike had felt a keen stab of anxiety when he thought they might leave. For the first time the house felt like home, even with all the recent hassles. He washed his face. A glance at his image in the small shaving mirror above the dry sink had surprise widening his eyes. He was smiling. If he thought he had trouble by the tail, why was he smiling? "Because this is not just a house anymore. It's a home." The words came in a whisper of disbelief.

Taking the chipped plate, he filled it with supper scraps for Hope's woodland friends. When he put it under the porch, he hoped his actions would please her.

When Hope and Daniel returned, the kitchen smelled of freshly brewed coffee. She wanted the cake Mike had set out, but wouldn't ask for it. Instead she said, "Rain's goin' to last. Maybe all night."

"I have something to show the two of you." He opened

the bottom of the sink and pulled out two containers. "They're chamber pots. Let me explain."

When he'd finished, Daniel said, "Ya don't have ta go out in the rain?" Already seated at the table, he dug into his treat.

She'd forgive Mike this time, she thought. "I think I might eat that cake now." She took her plate and cup to the rocking chair, which was fast becoming *her* rocking chair.

Mike enthusiastically explained to Daniel his plan for an outhouse.

Daniel signed. "That's the grandest thing I ever heard." Hope felt left out. Daniel used to admire her. Now his loyalty had shifted to the preacher.

"Daniel," she said, "don't jam your mouth so full. Watch me."

Daniel meekly obeyed.

Hope took her fork and cut a tiny piece to place on her tongue. She didn't want to do this wrong, but the preacher was looking at her mighty strangely. Three bites, and he hadn't taken his eyes off her.

Daniel interrupted her thoughts. "Lookee here. I can do it, too." He lifted a bite to his mouth.

Mike nodded. "You certainly can."

Daniel finished his second cup of coffee and rose from his chair. "Can I go up now? I want to turn in early."

Mike went with him. Hope heard them moving around. Soon after, she heard their muted voices.

The least she could do was wash the cups and plates. Mike was an accommodating man. She liked that, but when he became quarrelsome, it got her back up.

"You're good to him," Mike said when he came back.

"So are you, and I thank you for it. Though come to think on it, it's your job."

Mike smiled. "I guess it is."

"When is Sabbath?"

"Tomorrow. We'll have services; then I thought we'd have a picnic. I'll try to find a room for you on Monday. We shouldn't clutter the Lord's day."

"A picnic. Never heard of it."

"We'll take a basket of food and find a pretty place to eat in the woods."

"I'm guessin' that Daniel will like it fine. He likes anythin' that has cats." She giggled, and Mike joined in her merriment. She liked the way his eyes crinkled at the corners. Along with that dimple in his cheek, it set her insides to warming.

Hope shied away from that thought. "I could do without churchin', you know. You ain't gonna get longwinded like them tent preachers, are you?"

"I try not to. Otherwise the few people who do come will leave in the middle of things."

"Folks don't come?"

"Not many. Those who do, come for the gold I give them."

"You give them gold? I thought churches *got* money."

"That's the way it's supposed to work, but I give what I can from my own mining."

"You're a preacher and you pay folks to come? So you work a job, too?"

"I have investments, but I don't like to dig too deeply into them."

"I don't understand that. Maybe you can explain it sometime. What were you talkin' ta Daniel 'bout?"

"He didn't know any prayers, so I taught him a small one."

"That's all?" Satisfied that her brother hadn't revealed their secret, she went to pull the dictionary off the shelf. "Could you take some time so's I can learn to read?" She turned the pages with care.

The rest of the evening Mike showed her simple words. Her eyes sparkled when she recognized *can* and *boy*.

113

* * *

Hope closed the bedroom door. From the chest the All-goods had given her, she removed her new clothes. "I don't know how I'm goin' ta wear all them," she said on a sigh.

Next she opened her sack. She removed everything from it. Her gun, her oilcloth-covered shot, and her bag of medicine and herbs. Most everything would go into the chest under the clothing. But she didn't know where to put her fiddle, and the rifle was too long for storing with her other things. She decided to put them under the bed until she could find a better place.

At the very bottom she found her moccasins, a gift for having saved an old Indian's son on the trip to California. She had never worn the moccasins, fearful of getting them dirty, but now she'd use them in the house.

She replaced all the clothing, putting the moccasins near the bed. After she'd changed from dress to night-gown, she loosened her hair and climbed into bed.

"I don't know how anybody can get a night's rest with all this." Every time she lay down, the gown bunched up and her hair tangled around her.

When Mike knocked, she grumbled. "Whatcha want now?"

He opened the door, but seemed unprepared for the sight of her. She looked down. Her hair was in disarray, and the soft nightdress was above her knees. It covered her primly, she thought, but Mike seemed funny about that sort of thing. He tugged at his ear.

"Well?" she asked.

"I'm sorry, I . . . " He paused. He went to the stove, stoking the fire, though it didn't need tending. "I thought I'd help you with the stove."

"Do you think I cain't take care of a fire?"

He closed his eyes. "I bought this for you. It was in my parcels." Hope peered at what he held, but as the only light came from the stove, she couldn't make it out.

114

"What is it?"

"It's a hairbrush . . . to get the tangles out."

"Afore I go to sleep? Hell, I got enough troubles just gettin' myself settled. How do folks sleep in all this get-up? I guess I'll learn, won't I?" She smiled.

The preacher backed to the door, then moved closer again. Violet eyes gazed into green. He reached out to caress her cheek with his left hand, to run his thumb along her lips. Then he tipped his head and brought it close to hers. She wasn't sure what he wanted—what she wanted.

Lightning split the sky, startling them both. Mike's face hardened. He dropped the brush on the bed and tore out of the room.

"It's rainin' out there," she called after him, a little disappointed.

She snuggled down under the blankets, holding the brush with both hands. For a while she'd felt special. Hope would have to think about that.

She tried again to get settled but it was no use. Finally she sat up and threw off the gown. Cozy in just the comforter, she slept.

Mike was soaked through when he returned to the house. The steady rain had become a downpour, and lightning flickered in the distance. The fireplace burned low.

He put another log on the fire, then removed his wet clothing. He was fully naked when he remembered he'd put the towel in the laundry basket; it was now damp and musty.

The heavy towels he preferred came from Boston by mail. He kept them safe in his wardrobe—in the bedroom.

The door was ajar. He must not have closed it fully when he'd fled. Maybe he could just slip in, retrieve a towel, and slip out.

He crept to the door. Good, she was asleep. With a

deep breath he slid into the room, opening the door just enough to allow his body entrance.

The slap of his bare feet on the wooden floor sounded louder than the rolling thunder to him. Grateful that he'd put the chest near the door, he cautiously slid a drawer open. He could tell by the feel that he had trousers and a shirt in his grip, so he pulled them out. In the lower drawer he felt rough linen. He tugged gently.

Something cold pressed against his back. "Drop them duds, mister, or you're a dead man."

Chapter Eight

Hope had a gun on him. Without turning he said, "Don't shoot. It's me."

"Mike? Why are you sneakin' around your own house? You're naked, you know."

"Of course I know." Wrapping the towel around his waist, he faced her. The shirt and pants slipped from his grasp, but he held the towel firmly. She stood so close he could smell her scent. It was soft, feminine, and new to him, but he felt he had known it forever. He peered into the low-lit gloom. "You're not wearing your night-gown." The words fell from his lips on a slow whispered breath.

She lowered the gun. "Well, no. The dang thing rucked up 'tween my legs. There was too much o' it. Did you ever try to wear one o' them things?"

Mike stood like stone, unable to comprehend her lack of modesty. "But . . . but . . . you refused to take off your clothes to bathe."

117

" 'Tisn't smart to get naked outside." She went to tuck the gun under the pillow. "You'll get lung fever."

He couldn't look away when she bent over to tuck the pistol away. In profile he saw flared hips, a nipped waist, and small breasts that seemed made to fit in his hand. The way his body reacted to her, he could have kept the towel hanging where it was without holding on to it.

Hope climbed onto the bed, pulling the quilt into her lap. "You're lookin' fit to bust somethin'."

Turning his back to her, he fumbled to retrieve dry pants. His blood seemed to bubble along his veins, making his efforts awkward. *God help me. She's not a bony scarecrow. She's all soft, candlelit female.*

"You know, you're a mighty fine-lookin' man. You got the best hind end I ever saw."

He straightened, feeling his face flush. She was so direct. What should he say? He fumbled his trouser buttons closed and turned around and moved closer. In his whole life Mike Mulgrew had never seen an undressed woman, and he liked what he saw.

"Mike, you're beginnin' to worry me."

"You're not afraid of me, are you?"

"Course not. You're a preacher and a gentleman. Not like Pa 'n his kind."

" 'Sides, even though you got a real fine marriage tickler, you're suckin' in them balls so tight they could get caught in your throat." She laughed at her outrageous joke, but he hardly registered her words.

There was a husky intimacy in her laugh. He longed to stroke her shoulder, slide her hair between his fingers. No more than a yard separated them. He needed to touch her desperately enough that his fingers burned.

Hope shifted off the bed.

Thunder cracked sharp and close. Rain pelted the

house. Somewhere a tree branch slapped against the roof, in unison with the beating of his heart.

He raised his hand to cup the back of her neck; her pulse beat beneath his thumb.

Hope extended her index finger to trace the dimple in his cheek. "You know this little hole? Did you know it comes from a angel kiss 'fore you were born? It means you're special."

Mike took her hand in his. Lowering his head, he opened her palm so he could feel the pulse point at her wrist. He breathed in the scent of glycerine and rose water.

They stood like that until Mike lowered his head to taste each fingertip, at first tentative, unsure. But when Hope moved into his arms, when their bodies touched, his body reacted on its own.

Hope leaned back her head, baring her neck for him. His lips opened, and his tongue tasted her there, following along until it came to her ear.

Thunder and lightning sliced the silence when she turned her face to meet his lips. Inside of Mike a ferocious storm filled his being, as wild as that raging outside.

He adjusted himself to feel the length of her body, lowering his hands to press her hips against his. The kiss deepened until he needed to taste her, to trace his mouth along her shoulder and down to the rosy tip of her breast.

Hope whispered his name while she stroked her fingers through his hair. Lightening split the air again.

This time Mike dragged himself away. "I have to leave, Hope. I don't want to, but I must."

"You can stay if you want. The bed's big enough, and I don't take up much room at all."

He inhaled her fragrance. "I can't." Somewhere nearby a tree crashed to the ground. The storm within Mike eclipsed the one around them. He was close, so very close, and he could not do what he desperately wanted.

119

Why? Moral decency? Or was it that little bit of fear that she might know him to be unskilled as a lover? She might laugh at his ineptness.

"Good night, Hope." He hurried from the room.

Outside, as he leaned against the cool support of the door, Lightning flashed, illuminating his cast-off clothing.

"Hope?" he called out.

"Hmm?"

"I forgot my shirt. May I come in?"

"O' course."

Eyes averted, he rushed back into the room, scooped up his shirt, and ran out as if Lucifer himself chased him.

There'd be little sleep for him tonight.

Hope rolled onto her side when she awoke. Seeing the sun, she marveled that she'd slept so well. Snuggling down for an extra minute, she thought of the previous evening. Mike had gotten to something deep inside her. The thought frightened her a little, so she put it out of her mind.

No-Account Savage would soon be living in this house on a permanent basis, and the thought thrilled her. But the passion of last evening welled up to take over her heart. She closed her eyes, wondering if this was what love felt like. Daniel was the only person she'd ever loved. Last night with Mike . . . Never had she felt like that.

I'm gonna show Mike how much help I'll be.

Her feet touched wood when she got up. Cool, clean wood, not dirt. She wiggled her toes.

Though it was early, she heard voices and laughter. Mike had said that everyone went to town to replenish their stores on Sunday. She wanted to run out and give a big "Howdy" to the passing folks, but she had work to do. She dressed quickly and slipped into her moccasins.

In the kitchen she found plenty of tinder and wood in the wood bin. Hope set to work. She stuffed as much wood as she could into the stove. After lighting it, she took the coffeepot to the pump.

The stove had heated nicely, so she judged it ready for cooking. It didn't take long to find the bacon and fill a skillet.

Back in the bedroom, Hope tucked her hair up as close as she could by rolling her braid around, then stabbing pins here and there.

On the porch she touched a morning glory. "My very own house." *Mike Mulgrew, you'll come around once you get used to things.* They could build a little house for Daniel, too.

With ground mint in her pocket, she went down the path.

"Sis?"

She turned. "Mornin', Daniel. Did you like the loft?"

"Best sleep I ever did have. Sis, ya remember the time we found that old buffalo hide that we rolled up in ever' night one winter?"

"Sure do. Was the warmest winter we ever had. Too bad Pa found it. He sold it so quick, I didn't have time to steal it back."

"Well, I was that warm, Sis."

"I liked it when you called me ma'am yestereve. It was good thinkin'. You wash up whilst I clean my teeth."

Daniel scratched his head.

"Ya got lice?"

He ducked away when she tried to inspect his hair. "Let me be."

Satisfied, she let him go.

"Is he cookin'? I need eats."

"I'm cookin'. Is he goin' to be surprised."

"Ah . . . ma'am, ya ain't never cooked for-real cookin'!"

"I watched him yesterday. We'll have a fine hot breakfast in no time.

121

"Howdy," she called to four men who passed nearby.

"How do, Mrs. Mike."

Hope recognized Vince O'Malley. "How's Mrs. Daisy?"

"Just fine, ma'am. Ya know she brought flour all the way across Kentucky? Don't that beat all? We had biscuits last evening."

"You all can have a drink at our well. Mike's got a pump rigged over it. Are you comin' to church today?"

The four looked away, and Vince dug at a rock with the toe of his boot. "Daisy's expecting me back. You see, we got a tent pitched near our claim. Being newly wed 'n all, well, I don't like to leave her alone."

"I see." She cocked an eyebrow. "An' y'all, will we see you in church?"

"Thank you for the invite, but we got a lot to do on Sunday. You understand."

Hope did understand. She opened her mouth to give them a scolding when a shout bounced off the surrounding hills.

"Fire! Fire!"

"It's Mike! We're comin', Mike," she shouted. They all pounded through the trees toward the sound of Mike's voice.

Hope stopped at the clearing, unable to move. Everyone ran toward the house. Stunned, she stood looking at the black smoke that poured from the kitchen. Mike ran from the pump to the house with a bucket, water sloshing over the sides.

"Find every bucket you can," someone shouted.

"I know where there's buckets." Daniel took off and was back before Mike staggered from the house.

Hope suddenly bounded forward. "Damn! My house is on fire! I gotta get my things." She ran past the line of laboring men to the porch.

"Mike, do somethin'!"

Mike dragged her back. "Stay outside."

Hope wailed, "My house. Save my house."

Minutes later, though it seemed like hours, someone said, "I think we got it."

Mike looked inside, Hope close behind. Acrid smoke hit her, burning her eyes.

"Stay out!" Mike commanded.

"But my things! I got to get the bacon 'n coffee. 'Taint right to waste 'em."

The air began to clear. Daniel and the others crowded at the open door.

"Tough luck," said Barney, "but everything looks all right except for being smoke blackened. Stove is all burned to hell. Beg pardon, Mrs. Mike. I forgot you were here."

Mike's head snapped up. He looked from the stove to Hope. "Your bacon and coffee. *Your bacon and coffee?*" he roared.

She backed up. "What ya yellin' for? I heard ya." She thrust her jaw forward.

"*You* were cooking *bacon and coffee?*" His words dragged out soft and low. He tugged at his ear. A muscle jerked under his eye while he clenched and unclenched his fists.

A little at a time the smoke cleared. Mike threw more water on the still-overheated stove. It sizzled.

"Daniel, please get another bucket of water in case the fire starts again." The others backed onto the porch. A fight was brewing and they didn't want to miss it.

"Look!" Mike pointed at the blackened stove and charred floor. "Damn it, Hope, look what you did with your damned cooking!" He shouted the words, and the stovepipe belched a puff of black soot as if in agreement.

The men clustered together. Barney remarked, "She done vexed the parson."

Hope, however, moved closer to Mike and tried to look him in the eye. "You said not ta cuss."

123

"What the hell are you talking about?"

She stomped to the door. "Didn't he just cuss?" she asked the onlookers.

They nodded in unison.

"There. You cussed. Now how can you expect these fine men to come to your church iffen you talk like that? You said no cussin' in this house." Hope stabbed her finger toward the floor for emphasis.

Mike's face flamed. He opened and closed his mouth twice, then strode to the door, pushing through the crowd. "Where ya goin'? We gotta clean this up," she shouted.

He kept walking, past the trees, and apparently into the creek, judging from the splash that followed.

"I swear, that man picks the dangedest times to jump in that creek." Hands on her hips, she looked around. "Thank you kindly. Would you men like some bread and jam? I think there's a pail of buttermilk, too. I gotta talk ta Mike about his wrong-naturedness. Just sit yourselves on the porch 'n I'll bring you some eats."

In the distance they could hear Mike shouting while he swam. "Her bacon! Her coffee! Her house!" The words echoed over each other like shingles on a roof.

When Mike finally returned, he found her holding court. The crowd had grown. All of Coldbottom seemed to be here to witness his lapse. The perfect preacher had sworn. In his own house. In front of everyone.

Hope looked up as Mike returned. "Come have some eats, Mike. Look, we got lots o' folks come ta visit."

Mike did not smile. Suddenly a flurry of activity had all her guests hastening to leave.

"Where are you goin'?" she asked the departing mob. Barney took over as spokesman. "Thank you kindly for inviting us to eat, Mrs. Mike, but we outstayed our welcome."

"*Mrs. Mike?*" Mike leaned his head against the porch frame. "She's not Mrs. Mike."

Hope stood. "Don't pay no mind to him. He's a bit overset. Y'all come back for church. What time do you want them, Mike?"

Mike pursed his lips.

"After the noonin' hour, I think," she said. "That should give these folks time to take care o' their business, 'n we can get spruced up."

Taking a deep breath, Mike turned to face the group. "If you hadn't passed by when you did, the house might have burned to the ground. Thank you." His words were directed to the original four who'd rushed to put out the fire. "I'm sorry for my unfortunate language. The fire . . . I just wasn't myself."

Hope couldn't believe her ears. He'd thanked them . . . even apologized. She moved to his side and took his hand. He looked down at their joined hands. "Service will be at two o'clock." She said. "Please join us."

They lit out of there as though they were being chased by a mountain lion.

"You sorried yourself to them, Mike. You did yourself proud."

He slipped his hand from hers. "There were eight men here. Now all Coldbottom will get an earful!"

She saw Daniel in the corner of her vision, fear in his eyes. "Daniel, go feed the cow. She needs milkin', too," she said.

"But what if ya need me?"

Wanting to ease his mind, she said, "We'll clean up here. There's a lot of water to get off the floor."

Satisfied, her brother loped off toward the barn. To Mike she said, "You got anythin' to say, I'd appreciate it if you wait till he's out o' hearin'." She followed Mike into the house.

"What did you think you were doing?" he demanded.

"Don't get tetchy with me, Mike Mulgrew. I was doin' a deed to help you."

"Help? Thank goodness you weren't trying to destroy me." He threw his hands in the air. The pungent smell of burned food filled the air. "You said you don't cook. What is *this?*" He put the skillet under her nose.

She pushed it aside. "I'm learnin'. Nothin's that damagefied it cain't be fixed." She looked at the blackened meat. "An' that's bacon."

"Nothing's damaged?" He stood back and swept an arc with his arm, indicating the blackened area around the stove.

"I can have it clean in no time. My whole life I found lots o' stuff folks threw out. After I was done with them they looked new." She paused. "Oh, and 'bout the cookin'. I'll do better next time."

"Next time? What do you mean, next time?" He towered over her, his eyes blazing.

"Why, next time I make vittles."

"There won't *be* a next time. Not until you learn to cook," he shouted.

"I been patient with you up to now, Mike, but you're puttin' me in a fury. Comes a time when you gotta get on with things. So simmer down or I might make you sleep in the barn." Hope tapped her bare foot.

"*You* might make *me* . . . " He gasped.

"For a parson you sure are a hard, unforgivin' man." She picked up the burned pot and skillet. "I'm goin' yonder ta rub these with silt. Might do you some good ta have some food. There's a heel o' bread left, 'n you might find a bit o' jam, too."

She rubbed the burned tin and iron while muttering, "He should be gettin' down ta kiss my feet." Her anger spurred her to scrub harder, faster. She couldn't help it

126

that the stove had flamed up. Heck, you had to make a few mistakes to learn. Plain bad luck had caused the ruin of the food, but he had more in that cellar. She rubbed and grumbled for over an hour before the tin and iron shined again.

Mike looked up when she entered the kitchen. There was no part of Hope Savage untouched by grit and mud.

"You've ruined your dress," he barked.

"You are the unthankfulest man I ever met. Here's your cookin' pot. Could you at least show me how ta make coffee? I missed that today."

Mike reared back. "Coffee? I've spent the last hour removing firewood from the stove and you want coffee?"

"What are you fussin' for? The house is all right."

He tried to speak calmly. "Hope, go back down to the water, take off your clothes, and take a bath." *There. That should be precise enough.* "You'll need to wash your hair again."

"What? Look at my hands. They're already wrinkled from the water."

"You can't go to church dressed in dirty clothes. I'll get another dress from your trunk and bring it down to you; then I'll bathe, too."

She stepped out onto the porch, turned to face him, and said, "Damn! Hellfire! . . . You hear that? I'm not cussin' in the house." She swore all the way to the creek.

Mike sighed. Then he chuckled. He looked at the pile of firewood he'd taken out of the stove and he laughed. Oh, how he laughed, in great whoops. In the bedroom he leaned against the dresser, where he stopped to catch his breath. When was the last time he had laughed so hard? He had to admit, it lightened his heart.

He looked around the room, which held subtle traces of Hope's essence, and he smiled. Whistling softly, he went to the wardrobe where he had hung her dresses, choosing one of yellow with russet flowers, a perfect match for her hair. In the chest he found a chemise, petticoats, pantalets, and stockings. He stopped. He stopped. He had to fight temptation. Here was an opportunity he'd been waiting for. Her sack lay in a heap, empty. Somewhere in this room were her personals. "Don't even think it, Mulgrew. If she wants you to know what they are, she'll show you herself."

Mike grabbed his pastoral garb and headed outside to bathe himself.

Daniel stood just off the porch. "I cain't let ya go down there, Parson."

"Why not, Daniel?"

"I won't let ya hurt ma'am."

"I won't, but you might think about protecting *me*." He couldn't supress his laughter at Daniel's puzzled look.

At two o'clock, Mike Mulgrew strode into his church and stopped dead. Maybe twenty rough prospectors occupied the last three benches on each side. Hope and Daniel sat in front, with five women directly behind them.

He coughed, then cleared his throat while feeling in his pocket to see if he had enough nuggets to go around.

Hope stood. Everyone did the same.

Mike walked to the piano. "Good afternoon. Welcome. Let us begin with number fifteen, 'Amazing Grace.' " He lifted his hands to the keyboard, but wasn't quick enough.

Hope had come to stand beside him, facing the congregation. With her hands folded at her waist, she began the hymn. Some of the assembly tried to sing with her.

Mike took his hands from the keyboard, his face frozen in disbelief. Those who had begun the hymn with her dropped off one at a time until Hope alone sang loud and clear. Her voice, Mike thought, could be compared only with the sound of a rusty saw caught on a knot.

Hope stopped. "Come on now. Don't be shy. Mike, are you goin' to plink that piany or just sit there?"

Mike flexed his fingers, then played and sang as loud as possible, trying to drown her out.

One of the miners chuckled. He lowered his face when Hope looked in his direction.

Mike played a final chord, not continuing to the end of the hymn. His face reddened. The giggles and a low rumble in someone's throat that sounded suspiciously like laughter halted him. There was no point in continuing. This was another story to reach far into the gold fields. People here lived for gossip. Mike felt whipped.

Hope's rebellion at the weddings, and her actions this morning, were juicy bits for everyone to digest and laugh at. Worse, the parson had cursed and raised his voice. No, Mike realized, he had shouted. Word of Hope's tuneless singing had now sealed his fate, pulling his reputation down a notch or two. Was he doomed to be a laughing-stock? No more hymns today. He closed the piano and rose from the stool, keeping his face as bland as possible. He had to give the sermon, but secretly he prayed for deliverance.

People oughtn't laugh in church, thought Hope. Folks around here needed more music. But it beat all how Mike went on and on with the lesson.

At last he finished. "Daniel, would you please come forward and pass the plate?"

Daniel watched open-mouthed as Mike dug into his pockets and counted out nuggets, one for each person. He placed them on the plate.

Hope jumped to her feet and went to stand by Mike. "Don't you give them folks your gold," she whispered.

"I want them to come back next week. They certainly aren't going to come back unless they get paid."

"Daniel. Give me that gold."

129

Hope put the gold into the pocket of her dress. "There. Now take the plate." She handed it back to Daniel.

"Stay out of it, Hope. I want them back." Mike's whisper became louder.

"I'll give you back your gold when they're gone."

"I didn't mean the gold. I want these *people* back next week."

The men in back crept forward one by one. Some had cupped an ear.

Hope's voice raised a little. "Seems to me folks should come to hear the word 'cause it makes them feel better. You do ramble on, Mike. I'll help you fix that, though. You got to learn when to say 'Amen.' " She paused. "We need another song, too. Want me to start one?"

Mike rubbed his forehead. "Can we discuss this later? Daniel, take the plate. Hope, put the gold back."

"No," she said in open rebellion. There was no need for the congregation to strain to hear that. The two were nearly shouting.

Bewildered, Daniel gave up on passing the plate and plopped into the first pew.

"Hope," Mike threatened.

Her lips pressed together, her foot tapping with impatience. "No."

"Sit down then."

"Iffin ya ask me nice."

Mike clenched his fists and bit out the words. "Please, Hope, *sit down.*"

Chapter Nine

It was then Hope noticed that those in back had moved forward. The congregation had taken all in.

"Hope," Mike hissed, "everyone is watching. Don't create a scandal."

"Well, all right, but I don't like you tellin' me what to do in front o' these nice folks." Her words were less than quiet, but she did sit.

"We'll have the closing prayer," Mike announced. "I apologize for the disturbance." Then he rambled on for another ten minutes.

Hope couldn't take it anymore. She stood and said, "*Amen!* Y'all can go now. Thanks for comin'."

Mike clamped his mouth shut. The audience waited, wanting to see this out so they could spread the news.

Pearl Damian alone rose to leave, and Hope hurried to catch up with her.

"Miss Pearl, would you like to stop over for a glass o' buttermilk?" She sneezed and wiped her nose on her

131

sleeve. "I need some advice." Hope liked the widow for her kindness on the journey to California.

"I'd be happy to have a glass of buttermilk with you," the woman said softly. "But I'm not sure I have any advice you need."

"Believe me, you do." Hope took her arm.

Mike watched them leave. The ladies always felt it necessary to offer praise for his sermon. The men couldn't leave fast enough.

He sat in the first pew, then realized he had taken Hope's seat. Confound it, she left her imprint on everything.

Words tumbled from his lips. "What do You want me to do? I came all this way to get away from the wild Mulgrew reputation. I trusted You to find me a helpmate, someone I could raise a family with. I can't marry *her*." He stopped. "Still, she makes me feel . . . well, You know." Mike looked at the cross, wishing an answer would come.

"She's destroyed my peace. Nothing falls into place anymore, yet I can't send her away. She seems to stir up trouble wherever she goes."

Hope sat across from her guest. "Thank you for comin'."

Pearl smiled. "Thank you for inviting me. What kind of help do you need?"

Hope leaned forward. "You know he got me from the newspaper?"

"There's no shame in that. Are you happy?"

"I purely am. But Mike ain't. He sent for a wife 'n got me. I come out willin' to do it, but knew right off he didn't fancy me."

Pearl set down her buttermilk, then took a handkerchief from her bag to dab at her mouth.

"See? I didn't even know ta carry one o' those with me.

132

You are a real lady, Miss Pearl, right down to your nose duster. That's why I want to ask you somethin' special."

Pearl smiled. "Go on."

"Miss Pearl, it took toil just gettin' here. When I saw this"—she arched her arm to indicate the pleasant room—"I wanted it bad, 'n I can tell he ain't inclined to keep me."

"It's a lovely home. Has he said he wanted to send you back?"

"Not exactly. But I think it crossed his mind."

"How can *I* help?"

"I want to be like you. Talk purty, look nice all the time, say what's right. I know I ain't good at any o' those things. I guess you know I near burnt the house down tryin' to cook today." She studied her toe.

"I heard. When do you want to start?"

"You mean you'll help me? Would tomorrow be too soon?"

"Bring your reticule. Put your comb and pins into it so we can do your hair."

"What's a reticule?"

Pearl showed Hope her bag, then drew the strings to display the inside.

"I thought it was for carryin' eucalyptus." She saw a few coins, some hairpins, and a comb. Hope pointed to a small mirror. "You got a little lookin' glass to carry around. Ain't you worried the devil will get you?"

"It's not evil. Sometimes you'll need to freshen up." Pearl handed it to her. "Would you like to have it?"

"I cain't take anythin' so fine. It's all different colors on the back," she said as she ran her fingers over the piece.

"It's mother-of-pearl. Keep it. It'll be a friendship gift." Pearl closed Hope's hand over the mirror and held it there.

"I never had a friend. Just kin. I'll remember you every

133

day when I look at the back. Pearl, just like your name. Thank you."

"You're welcome."

"This whole thing is 'bout Mike. What that man needs ain't a wife. I tell you true, he can do all them wife things hisself. 'Cept havin' a baby, naturally." She gave her low, throaty laugh and slapped her thigh. "He'd probably do that too, if he could, but he'd need to get his man parts out o' the way—'n they're considerable!"

Pearl smiled. "You are a rare person, Hope."

"What Mike needs is a partner. I aim to be that partner," she continued. "Trouble is, these nice duds don't make me useful. He made it clear he didn't want me shootin' meat. Hell, he got a whole cellar full o' salted meat. He's stocked on everythin'."

"Mike seems the sort who likes to be well stocked."

"You sure are right on that. He got his life on a list."

"Really?"

"Yep. Trouble is, I ain't on anyone's list. I always did for myself. What I want is to be so folks don't fun on him or shame him on my account. I want Mike to see I can do somethin' 'sides burn down the house," She pointed to the blackened stove, then continued. "He goes out to his claim early, 'n I'm goin' ta have the livelong day to make myself useful. He took on a feller for seein' ta the animals, 'n I don't fault him for that." Hope whispered, "Mike don't know what's good for him, but I aim to bring him 'round to my way o' thinkin'."

"I understand he hired that young man who traveled with us."

Hope became suddenly wary. "He's the very one. Name o' Daniel." She sighed, worriedly. "Pearl, I have a question. Is it right to keep secrets?"

Pearl took a delicate sip. "A woman has to keep some secrets." She smiled. "When you come tomorrow, wear gloves."

"Tomorrow . . . I'm goin' to start bein' a lady." Hope leaped from her chair to hug Pearl. "Thank you for not laughin' at me. You're my first friend, and I'm pleased to say it."

Pearl returned the hug. "I'm at the Goldworth Hotel. Come about ten."

Hope lowered her head. "I don't know how to read that timepiece, and Mike puts so much store in it."

"We'll put that on *our* list." Pearl chuckled.

Hope stood at the door while her friend walked down the path. She suddenly had a thought. "Pearl," she yelled. "Could you help me figure out how to put on these duds? I'm partial to pants, but he's a contrary man, and I don't understand these at all."

"I'll promise you'll be a worthy partner for Mike."

After Pearl left, Hope set to scrubbing the stove. This time she put on a pair of Mike's old work clothes, not wanting to catch hell about dirtying another dress. *I'll get ever' bit o' black off your stove, Mr. Preacher Perfect. Then I'm goin' to learn to work for you. Whilst I'm at it I think I just might get you a wife. If I'm not right, maybe she is. O' course Daniel 'n me will live here. We'll even help you build a nice new place for yourself 'n Pearl.*

Mike was outside chopping wood while Hope was making plans for the rest of his life. He definitely needed wood after the morning fiasco. Besides, it calmed him to swing the ax and watch the dried logs split clean.

"Parson?"

Mike looked up. It was a warm October day, and his shirt was wet with perspiration. "Yes, Daniel."

"I can do the choppin' for ya. It bein' Sunday 'n all I don't like ta see ya workin'. God won't notice me."

Mike sat on a log. "Daniel, sometimes a man's got to calm himself. But you're right. This isn't work for Sunday." He wiped his brow. "God notices you, Daniel, and don't think otherwise. We'll just leave it, and tomorrow you can split enough for a cord."

"It's her, ain't it? She does give a man fits."

Mike nodded.

Daniel reached into his pocket and withdrew a small turtle. "Lookee what I found. I'm goin' ta keep him for a pet."

Mike held out his hand for the turtle, making a mental note to buy a change of clothes for Daniel. "That's a nice one. Look at the marks on his shell."

"Yep. I never saw such afore. I thought I might make a cage for him."

"He's a wild creature, Daniel," Mike said gently. You wouldn't want to keep him away from the water. Let's go make a rock dam on the edge of the stream. The water isn't so deep there."

Mike partially constructed a small aquarium. When they had nearly finished, he wiped his hands on the grass. "There you are. Do you think you can finish the job?"

"I got me a pet an' I'm makin' him a fine home. Thank ya, Mike."

Mike whistled a tune while he walked up the porch steps. Though he'd built the house over a year ago, he'd always before come here at the end of each day with an empty feeling. The morning glories were something he had put in to please his expected wife. Nothing had changed, yet everything had changed. The house was a home now, warm and welcoming.

The stove shone in the dim interior of the front room. The floor and wall around it were clean as well.

"Hope?"

There was no reply, so he went to knock on the bedroom door.

"Hope?" He opened the door to look inside. He needed to talk to her, but he wasn't sure what he wanted to talk about.

He noticed that the chest lid lay open. She'd piled things inside. It wouldn't hurt to put things in order, and if he found anything . . . well, that couldn't be helped.

"What do you think you're doin' with my things?"

"Hope." He jumped like a schoolboy caught reading a dime novel. "I was looking for you."

"In there?"

Mike rubbed his forehead. "Are you hungry?"

"Yeah, my backbone's been shakin' hands with my stomach for a spell. And I'll bet Daniel's hungry." She looked at him. "Are you goin' to put my things down?" she asked.

He let the garments slip from his hands. "Let's go into the front room. You must have worked very hard. It looks beautiful." *Just like you.*

He wanted to discuss their future, or rather lack of it, but this was not the time. He noticed a cut on her palm. She had probably scraped her hands in her attempt to make things right. What kind of brute was he to make her ruin her hands?

Hope had stacked fresh wood next to the stove, and he angrily went through the routine of starting a fire. *Whang!* went the burner lid. *Crash!* The skillet followed.

"I don't know what crawled up your behind, Mike, but you cain't eat every meal in a upset. Your food will ball up in your gut."

He took a deep breath. This time he counted to thirty before turning from the confounded, almost like new stove. Honest violet eyes showed her caring nature. And then he saw something he hadn't noticed when she'd caught him folding her clothes. Though she'd worked hard, she'd combed her hair and washed herself clean. A damp spot at breast level revealed her female curves, alerting his body to the fact that she wore no undergarments.

"I'm just working out some anger. I might warn you, I have tried to keep it down for some years. Temper is hard

137

to leave behind." He forced himself to look away. "Go put on some underwear. Then find Daniel. He might be upstream with his new pet."

"I can't help you with the anger, but if you want to talk about it, that helps, and I'm good at listenin' ".

"Not now."

"All right, Mr. Preacher Man. But you better get off that high horse. Folks don't like to be looked down on." She spun and walked out the door with a parting shot. "If you didn't notice, the smoke took care o' the polecat smell. And everybody's good for somethin'—even me."

She was gone before Mike absorbed what she'd said.

Hope found Daniel. His turtle had gone into its shell, so her brother had used the time to catch a few fish.

Hope praised his skill and his pet, then said, "How 'bout you take them fish to Mike? You 'n him eat 'em."

"Where ya goin' Sis—I mean, ma'am?"

"It's a place like I had afore, back in the old days."

"He's goin' ta be mad."

"So was Pa. Difference is, Mike won't beat me."

"I'm powerful afraid, Sis. I had a dream last night. Pa came lookin' for us 'n he was powerful mad."

"Pa never put hisself out when Ma left. Why would he come for us? You're worryin' over nothin'."

"It looked like one o' them times when I get the sight."

"You've been right many a time, but it takes a heap of work ta get here. You know how Pa gets when he has a task."

"He hides with a jug."

"See? And I'll bet he's still drinkin'."

Daniel joined in her laughter as she walked away from the house. "What'll I tell him?" he asked.

"I need some soothin'. I'll be back by nightfall."

"I think he'll be put out," he called to her retreating back, but she kept walking.

* * *

Tempted

Hope went to the church for her fiddle. Mike hadn't complained about the rifle, but she wasn't ready to trust him enough to tell him about her music. Men were queer creatures. She'd soon have to hide it in her room so it wouldn't be ruined by the cold and damp. For the time being she had it hidden in the church. She moved a few heavy wooden boxes filled with candles to reach under a shelf filled with paint cans. The cans reminded her that Mike didn't have time to paint the church. She'd take care of that soon. Right now she needed music.

Deep in the woods she'd found a clearing surrounded by trees and heavy brush. The clearing itself blazed with fallen leaves and late-summer wildflowers.

Hope needed to deal with the chaotic changes in her life. In her heart she knew she was no good for Mike, yet she had begun to have feelings for him.

She sat on a fallen log, placed her instrument under her chin, and closed her eyes. Hope put all her emotions into her music. She'd watched many a fiddler until she could strike a tune. Today, she began with frenetic energy, the "twiddly" way she felt when Mike came near.

She gave herself up to the music. It helped put her feelings into perspective. Daniel needed a home and family, and Mike was patient and gentle with him.

She changed mood and tune until at last, when she put down her bow, she felt at peace. She lay on a carpet of leaves, where she fell asleep in the late-afternoon sun.

It was full dark when she opened her eyes. A half-moon and a million stars lit the sky. She picked up her fiddle. It was time to go home. *Home.* The word brought a contentment she'd never known.

"Where is she?" Mike demanded. "Go check the barn again."

Daniel shook his head. "She'll come back when she's ready. But I'll go if ya want."

139

Mike wondered how the boyish man could guess at Hope's habits. Daniel couldn't comprehend the dangers in these mountains after dark.

Again Mike called out for her, checking the perimeter of the property; then he made another trip to the creek. The thought of what could happen to her, alone in the wilderness, made his stomach churn. She could have drowned or run into a bear. He wondered if she had her rifle with her.

He checked the church again. Fear brought him to his knees in the dark church. "Please, Father, keep her safe. Bring her home."

Outside again, he followed the path to the house and nearly bumped into her when she stepped from the brush. A snake slithered from under a nearby rock, but he didn't see it. Relieved, but blinded by fury, he shouted, "Where have you—"

"Stop where you are, Mike," she said in a soft voice.

He continued toward her.

She sent her knife sailing right at him. It plunged into the ground next to his foot, impaling a rattler that had been coiled there.

"Damn! What do you have for brains? When a person tells you to stop, you stop." She retrieved her knife, tossing the dead snake into the bushes.

"I repeat, where have you been? I've been worried sick about you."

"I'd think you'd at least thank me kindly for savin' your hide 'fore lashin' me with that dad blamed tongue o' yourn."

"Where were you?"

She folded her arms in a stubborn stance.

"Hope, there are dangers out there in the night; the least of them are those that slither. If a drunken miner tried to take advantage of you—"

"That's why I take my pigsticker everywhere. I can take care o' myself, Mike."

They stood close enough that he could see the smoky violet of her eyes in the moonlight. He wanted to lash out at her for the anxiety she'd caused him, for being calm in the face of his irritation.

Instead, he finger-combed her hair. "I thought I'd lost you."

His lips found hers before he knew he'd moved. The kiss began as a frantic outlet for his fears. Hope moved her own lips lightly across his, her mouth slightly open. Her breath surrounded his senses with the sweet fragrance of the mint she used to clean her teeth.

Mike wanted to taste her fully. The kiss became soft, slow, seductive. They were wrapped together like trees that had intertwined after years of growing side by side.

"Parson?"

Mike barely heard. He wanted to smell and taste every secret piece of her.

"Parson! I see ya found her, an' ya ain't mad no more."

Mike forced his eyes open and stepped back. "Yes, Daniel. She's back."

"I told him not ta worry, ma'am."

"You were right." Hope's voice shook. Mike could see the vein in her neck throbbing in time with his own heartbeat.

"Let's go inside," he said. "Are you hungry?" He kept his arm around her so she was close to his side.

"I'm tired. I took some bread with me."

Mike accompanied her to the bedroom. "Please tell me when you go out." He leaned over her, bracing his hand against the door frame.

"Sometimes I don't know I'm goin' out. When I need time alone I go where I can be alone."

"I've got to teach you to write so you can leave a note."

141

"Do you think I can?" She gave him a brilliant smile, then retreated to the bedroom.

Mike looked into her eyes. "You have a beautiful smile."

"Good night, Mike."

She stood with her back against the door, trying to slow the rhythm of her heart. When Mike had kissed her she had felt she wanted to give him something more, something of value. She would tell him about Slow in the morning. It was a matter of trust now.

She took her clothes off and slipped into her nightgown, thinking about her plans for him. It was Pearl he needed. Pearl with her ladylike ways and her pretty face.

She had trouble falling asleep. Her thoughts skipped from here to there, always landing smack-dab on Mike. "I shouldn't have kissed him back." They were whispered words in the dark. "Must be because he's the first man I ever kissed."

She'd gone to the woods to find peace. Yet the minute Mike pulled her into his arms, the calmness she'd found had fled.

Maybe a cup of chocolate would help. She slipped into her moccasins and opened the door.

She'd assumed Mike would have gone to bed by now, but he sat at the table writing. "You're still awake," she said.

"I have things on my mind."

"Do you want some hot chocolate?" She opened the door to the cellar.

"That sounds like a good idea. Daniel is asleep. Do you think he'll wake up at the smell of chocolate?"

She laughed along with him as she descended the steps.

Seconds later she shouted, "Here! Get out o' my taters." Hope came bounding up the ladder.

"What's wrong?"

"Them damn critters is in our food," she said as she ran to the bedroom.

Mike stood at the fireplace. "Critters?"

Gun in hand, she went back to the cellar. Three shots rang out. "Ya damn spawn o' Satan, I got ya."

When she came up, she held three rats by the tails. "They was eatin' our supplies. Soon as I get rid of them, we can have our treat." She slipped off her moccasins to go outside. At the edge of the woods she flung them as calmly as anyone would discard dirty dishwater.

"There. Now we can have that chocolate."

Mike sat in a chair, elbows on his knees.

"Are you feelin' faint? Seein' rats does that to some folks."

He tugged at his ear. "No, I am not going to faint. Damn it, Hope, they could have bitten you."

Daniel came from the loft. "What's all the shootin?"

Hope looked to Mike. "See? He smelled the chocolate." She put milk on the stove and prepared the cups, hoping Mike would let it be. But he had only just begun. He went into a list of all the dangers she'd escaped this day. By the time he finished, his cup was empty, and he didn't even remember drinking from it. "I'm going to bed, but we'll have a talk in the morning."

"I don't know why we have to talk about rats."

"That's another thing. You let *me* take care of the predators."

Hope put her cup down. "I don't know what a predator is, but them was rats, 'n not one has ever got close enough to bite me. And I seen my share."

"You don't understand. Rats are a real problem in the mining camps, and they carry disease."

"You mean all them folks got rats? Even the folks in the tents?"

"Yes. Some of the prospectors gamble on who can shoot the most rats in a night."

Her eyebrows rose. "They do?" She sat down. "Who's the best shot?"

"Dead-Eye Stiles, I believe."

"What are the stakes?"

"I'm tired. Can't we talk tomorrow?"

She pushed him into a chair, massaging his shoulders. "Them muscles are like iron bars. You got to settle yourself or you'll wake up with a stiff neck." She paused. "What are the stakes for the most rats?"

"All kinds of things," he mumbled. "Money, gold, liquor, sometimes supplies and tools."

She continued to minister to him but said no more. Hope's mind chewed its way around another scheme. This one would do him proud.

Chapter Ten

"I got some good liquor yonder."

"I'll just bet you do." The bartender had taken the measure of the man who occupied a space at the end of the bar. He'd heard talk about the stranger. Pure mean through and through, they said.

"I'd sell it ta ya cheap."

"I buy pure Kentucky whiskey. Comes by stage. I'm not fond of seeing my customers puke up their guts."

Maybe ya can help me then. I'm lookin' fer my daughter. She run off in the middle o' the night with a tinker."

Wanting this bad apple to leave, the barkeep continued polishing the bar, until the vagrant slapped his filthy hand on the rag.

"Appears ya didn't hear me. I'm lookin' fer my gal."

"Women don't come in here much, except for the ones upstairs."

"I ain't told ya what she looks like yet. I know she went through here, an' I want ta know where she's

145

headed. Hain't leavin' till I know where I'm goin'. Right now I'm low on cash money. Got no place ta stay, 'n cain't work. Lumbago, ya know. That gal should of stayed ta take keer o' her pa."

"Most leave sooner or later. I guess you'll be leaving town soon," the barkeep said hopefully. The man was rumored to have a nasty temper and had started several fights. Last night he'd been met with a shotgun at Sally's whorehouse because he'd beaten one of her girls badly, and Sally's place would take on almost anybody.

"Not till I find someone who can give me her trail."

"What makes you think she was here?"

"I know it fer a fact. Feller she worked fer in Kansas told me after I knocked some sense into him."

"Tell me about it." He spoke so the troublemaker wouldn't notice him reaching for the gun he kept under the bar.

"Yep. Her 'n that boy hitched up with some others with gold fever." He cleared his throat and hawked on the floor.

Spittoons were spaced every three feet along the bar, but not wanting to rile the man, the bartender replied, "I haven't seen her. Any of you boys?" He indicated his regular customers.

They squirmed in their chairs and shook their heads.

"Well, you heard them. You'd best move on."

The man hauled his skinny form into a semiupright position. "You askin' me ta git? Me, Otis Savage?" When he bared his rotted teeth, he took on a feral look.

The bartender moved fast for a big man. "I'm *telling* you to leave."

Otis's eyes focused on the gun aimed at his midsection. Now Otis smiled. He began to back away. "That's a nice piece o' iron ya got, but I got no feud with ya. Shit, I'm just tryin' ta git my fam'ly together. Ya can pass the word that I'm stayin' till I find whar she went. She's a ugly one. Skinny, 'n wears men's clothes. That tinker is a big 'un, kind o' tetched." His last words trailed him as he passed through the swinging doors.

Otis stormed down the boardwalk mumbling, "You jist wait till I git my hands on you. I'm goin' ta wring that scrawny no-account neck o' yourn. Ma should of left ya by the trail, but yer too damn lucky ta die. Was then, are now. I need a grubstake."

Two women were chattering at the entrance to a store, and he swung his arms between them, knocking them to the ground.

A snarling dog ran after him, and he kicked it. "Git out o' my way, ya mangy cur."

"Mister," cried a voice. "Hey, mister."

Otis stopped to look around. His eyes found a dark shape huddled between buildings. "I know you?" He closed one eye, squinted with the other. To anybody else the man was a wretched piece of humanity. Otis recognized a kindred spirit.

The man's hands shook. "You got any whiskey?"

"I might. What ya got fer me?"

The two went behind the row of buildings, where the smell of dung was strongest. Neither noticed.

"This gal yer lookin' fer. I think I saw her once or twice. My head's jumbled up a bit. Might do ta have me a taste o' that corn. Sort o' smarten me up a bit."

"You see a boy, too?"

"Mebbe."

"Well, ya jist foller me. I got a whole batch ya can test."

In Coldbottom, the citizens were getting used to seeing Hope come and go every day. Each morning, clean and groomed, she walked to the hotel to spend several hours with the widow Damian.

147

She greeted everyone with a cheery "Howdy" when she passed them on the street, sometimes stopping to chat. Gentlemen and cowboys greeted "Mrs. Mike" with a tip of the hat. There was a great deal of curiosity and gossip about her, but Hope never bothered to inform them of her unmarried status.

The citizens liked her. True, right after her arrival rumors flew about her inadequacies—everybody knew Preacher Perfect had his work cut out for him. But she had changed.

This particular day Hope stopped at the mercantile. "Mornin', Alberta. I need two or three handkerchiefs."

Alberta immediately came to help her. "I thought I put some in with your things."

"I ruined a couple."

"How's Parson?"

"I never see him. He gets up before light and goes to work. I don't see him till nightfall. After he sees to my lessons he goes to bed."

"Those with claims near his are passing the word that he talks to himself while he works. Even swears, they say. I'm glad to put those rumors back at their faces. Here's your linen."

"Thank ya kindly, Alberta. It's how men get when they aren't used to a female livin' with them." She accepted her parcel and left with a wave of her hand.

Hope had earned respect slowly in Coldbottom. Several boisterous fellows had found themselves looking down the barrel of her gun when they'd made the mistake of touching or pinching her. "I'll thank you to keep your hands off me," she'd said on each occasion. She could draw her gun without so much as disturbing the set of her bonnet.

According to Pearl, it was necessary for a woman to wear a bonnet to keep the sun off her face, so Hope wore it grudgingly. She envied the men their wide-brimmed hats with no tie under the chin.

The day after that disastrous Sunday of the heated public argument, Hope had walked to Coldbottom after Mike had gone to work. She had never been apprehensive about anything in her life, handling each problem as it arose. That day she wiped sweaty palms on her skirt before knocking.

"Am I too early?" she asked.

Pearl invited her in. The room, though small, had a desk, a chair, and a dry sink, along with the bed. "Sit down, Hope, and take off your bonnet."

"Nice place. I never saw a hotel 'fore yours. I want to thank you for bein' so damn nice to me."

Pearl nodded. "You're welcome."

"Now I got that out o' the way . . . " Hope hiked up her skirts and sat on the bed Indian fashion. "Would ya look at that? I cain't keep these stockin's from slidin' down."

"Do you have garters?"

"I don't know. This mornin' he pitched a fit 'cause I was wearin' a petticoat for breakfast. He told me he wanted me ta wear them; then he changed his mind."

Pearl smiled, "That's easily fixed. Mike has found a rare gem in you."

"He don't think so. I cain't even wash clothes. Last week I mixed some water with lye soap 'n set the shirts 'n long johns ta soak. When I took them out o' the water in the afternoon, they fell apart. I buried them, but he'll miss them sure as spring brings rain.

"He don't like the way I eat or comb my hair either. I guess you know I ain't allowed to cook. After one little fire! Don't that beat all?

"He frets over little things. Says I need to clean up my lang-age, but I clean myself all over. Where is it, anyway?"

"Language means the way we speak. Ladies don't swear, and I imagine that's what he means."

"Well, he did say no cussin' in the house."

"Let's get started then."

From ten until noon, Hope learned deportment, after which they walked to Della's Kitchen for a box lunch. Until Hope mastered her table manners they ate in Pearl's room. Within a week Pearl had thought it time to dine in the hotel dining room. Hope was on her way to becoming a proper lady. Late in the afternoon, she strolled home after buying three plates of supper from Della's.

Mike worked late, giving her time to teach Daniel what she'd learned each day. Daniel didn't like using a fork and knife, but he either did what she said or she would give him plain bread—without jam.

Each night when Mike came home he took his plate off the warming shelf, ate, and sat right down to listen to Hope list the spelling words he had left on the table in the morning. Then he looked over her penmanship.

Several times, Hope found herself longing for this time with Mike. She found herself looking at his hands . . . strong, sure, and beautiful. He had tasted her fingers. Now she wanted to taste his.

If their shoulders touched, her heart seemed to roll over in her chest.

Sometimes she felt him watching her. When she glanced up, he closed his eyes as though he listened to her reading, but he didn't notice when she missed an entire line.

In November Pearl's house was finished. Hope and Daniel helped her move in. The next day Hope had her first cooking lesson. It relieved her nagging conscience, because she'd been running up quite a sum of debt at Della's.

On her way home several weeks later, Hope saw a young girl writhing in the pains of childbirth. She lay in the street, near a few men, who joked at her plight. Hope edged her way near. "Where is the midwife?" she asked.

"Ain't none would help *her.* She ain't decent," said one fellow.

Kneeling in the dust beside the girl, she took her hand. "Where's your ma, honey?"

"I don't have one," she wailed.

Hope looked up at the now silent men. "Anybody know her name or where she came from?"

"She's a goddamn whore from Lizzy's."

Hope understood immediately, though it made her angry. "She's nearly a baby herself. What's your name?"

"They call me Sherry, but my real name is Patricia." She gasped as another pain gripped her.

"Lizzy threw her out for being careless."

Ignoring the youth who spoke, Hope asked, "What were you careless with?"

"I got a baby in my belly. But nobody told me how to keep it out." The last words ended in a wail as another pain took her.

Holding the girl's hand, Hope said, "Two of you men pick her up real careful 'n take her to Pearl Damian's house."

There wasn't a sound. Someone coughed. A few walked away.

"You're a sorry bunch! Could be one of you is about to be a pappy." Squaring her shoulders she repeated, "Now take her to Pearl's."

They were backing away fast.

Fumbling with her reticule, Hope said, "So that's how you want it?" She withdrew her gun, aiming it at the two closest men.

"I'm sure none of you gentlemen wants me to get a wrong idea about your character. And I know you are all aware I can handle this shooting iron. Take her to Pearl's, and someone go for that doctor I keep hearing about."

"Doc's drunk."

"Is that so? Well, since I have my weapon aimed at

something you value"—she waved the gun between two of the men—"I'd suggest you pick her up and carry her to Pearl's nice and gentle-like." It amazed her that she could act so calm when she was spitting mad.

Hope kept her gun on them until they'd delivered the girl to Pearl's keeping. As soon as they put Patricia down the men ran out.

Privately she vowed to find a way to keep her gun easily available. The pocket of her dress slowed her draw, and the reticule was impossible.

Pearl held the girl's hand while Hope prepared for the birth. A baby boy came into the world with a lusty squall. Pearl handed him to his mother. "Do you have a name for him?"

Patricia nuzzled his downy head. "I like the name Tom."

Hope gently cleaned Patricia while Pearl cleaned and wrapped Tom.

When both mother and baby fell asleep, Hope said, "I got some business to take care of. Can you keep her here for a time?"

"You know I will. Where are you going?"

"I'm headed to Allgood's; then I'm going to see Miss Lizzy. After that I'm going to introduce myself to that doctor."

"Be careful."

At the door, Hope turned. "I owe you another one. Someday I'll return your favors." She grinned. "Did you notice I got all the words right?"

"Mike would be proud of you."

"If he ever notices."

"Mrs. Mike." Thaddeus Allgood hurried to meet her. "Is your husband needing supplies?"

"No, sir. He's at work. Could I buy something without him along?"

"Absolutely. What do you need?"

She placed her reticule on the counter to withdraw her gun. "I'd like to see a holster for my gun."

The marathon checker game stopped. Thaddeus seemed frozen in place.

"Do you have any?" She kept her voice pleasant and soft.

His mouth worked a few times until he was able to reply. "Yes. Yes, I have several." He moved to where he kept leather goods. "I'm not sure we have one to fit you."

She touched each of the five holsters he'd placed before her. "I'll try this one." When Hope buckled it, she tested her draw to see if it would suit. "It flaps up when I draw."

"That's because it should be tied to your . . . um . . . " He tried again. "Men tie those strings around their pants leg."

"I surely do miss my pants. But how's a lady to protect herself if she cain . . . uh, can't strap on a gun?"

Hettie Elger, Coldbottom's leading gossip, appeared at Hope's elbow. "Mrs. Mulgrew—it is Mrs. Mulgrew, isn't it?"

Hope tilted her head and decided not to appease Hettie's curiosity. "Do you have a suggestion?"

"It's the husband's duty to protect his wife."

"Is that so? How's he supposed to do that and work at the same time?"

"A *lady* doesn't go where there's danger. You must use good sense, my dear."

"Good sense," replied Hope. "I always spit in the eye o' good sense." She slipped back to her old ways to shock Hettie. By the look on the woman's face, she knew she'd succeeded.

Hettie huffed to the door. "Well, I never . . . "

Smiling, Hope said, "I'll bet you ain't," then turned to examine the rest of the holsters. "My dress gets in the

153

way every time," she said after trying them all. "The buckle's too big."

"I have something you might like," Thaddeus told her. He pulled a small box from the shelf behind him. "These just came in the other day, straight from Philadelphia." He opened the box.

Hope drew in a breath. "It's a baby gun! Will it shoot?"

"This gun is called a derringer. Ladies like them because they can hide them. It's good for close range."

"Where do they hide them?"

He leaned forward to whisper, "Sometimes in the garter, or in the . . . " He cleared his throat to continue. "In the bosom."

Hope's eyes widened. She picked it up to sight along the barrel. "Got a good heft to it. I'll take a box of balls too. Would you mark it under Mike's name?"

Thaddeus Allgood rubbed his hands together. "Let me wrap it for you."

"Thank you kindly, but I like the feel of it." She opened the top of her sedate bodice and stuck it in there right before Thaddeus's eyes.

Alberta came from the back room as Hope stowed it.

"Mr. Allgood! Did I just see what I thought I saw?"

"Alberta, Mike's gone all day. She needs protection."

"Oh, I don't need this at home. It's for going places— and right now I'm going to Lizzy's whorehouse. Too bad Hettie left, though. I know she'd like to send this bit of gossip around first."

She heard pandemonium break loose at the same time the bell jingled above her, signaling her exit.

Hope strode up the hill to Lizzy's. She was curious about the house, and had wondered what the inside would be like. She knew she wouldn't get beyond the front parlor, if that, but she was going to have a talk with Lizzy. She knocked at the door.

"Who is it?" someone shouted from inside. "We're closed till evening."

"I'm here to talk to Lizzy. Name of Hope Savage."

An irate woman with flaming red hair opened the door.

Hope looked her up and down. "I can see right through that dress. It's about the prettiest one I ever saw."

The woman moved her cheroot from her mouth to her hand. "Who the hell is Hope Savage?"

"I'd like to see Miss Lizzy, please. I got business with her."

"Come on in and set yourself down. Are you looking for work?"

The front hall was a marvel of white and black decor. Pegs for hats lined the wall on both sides, with a sign above.

"No, I'm looking to strike a bargain. Could you find her for me, please?"

"You've found her. Come on in."

Hope followed her into a dazzling room. The chairs were red plush, and carved wooden tables held gold and crystal decanters of whiskey. On the walls were framed pictures of naked women. The room smelled of flowers and spice. Taking a seat on one of the stuffed chairs, Hope remarked, "Where are the flowers? They smell mighty nice."

"We don't have flowers. It's perfume. From Paris. What's your business with me?"

Hope wasn't ready yet. She loved to experience new things slowly. "Where's Paris?"

"France."

"I never heard tell about France. Maybe someday you can tell me about it. Right now I want to clear my mind about something, and if I stay too long, Mike might walk in and find me gone."

"So you're Mike Mulgrew's mail-order bride."

Hope nodded.

"Don't try to reform me. I never met a preacher I liked, and that goes for your husband."

"No, ma'am. I don't tell folks what to do. One of your ladies—Sherry, she said her name was—that little girl was in a terrible state, about to give birth in the street." Hope paused for effect. "Don't you worry, though. She's with Pearl Damian, and you couldn't hope for anyone better to care for her. It troubles me some that folks are mud-smearing your good name, though." Hope, aware that not many people liked to be cast in a bad light, hoped to appeal to Lizzy's vanity.

"Oh?"

"There were some men saying you put her out because she was carrying. Now that I've met you, I know you wouldn't do a thing like that. She's too young to know how to frolic without birthing."

"Hope Savage"—Lizzy took a long drag from her cheroot—"I'm on to your game. You're a sly one, and I like you. Do you want me to take the girl back?"

"It wouldn't be seemly to have a mother working here with a baby near. Could you give her another sort of job . . . cooking or cleaning? She's young and strong."

"I have a cook, but you're right. The housekeeper is always complaining about the workload. I'll try her out, but only after she's on her feet again."

"You're a kind soul, Miss Lizzy. You won't be sorry." Hope rose and walked with Lizzy to the front hall. "Do you know anything about Doc McBride?"

Lizzy nodded. I'll give you a little advice about Doc. He's the handsomest man in California, but he's no good to anyone because he's rarely sober."

"Is he one of your regulars?"

Lizzy shook her head.

"What's that sign say?" Hope asked, pointing to the sign she'd seen when she first came in.

"It's for the men. They get rowdy at times. It says, 'Hang guns here.' "

"I can't read yet, so I ask your forgiveness for not hanging my irons up."

"You carry a gun?"

Hope opened her bag to show Lizzy her pistol. As she drew the strings she remarked, "I couldn't get it out of there fast enough. A holster would be nice if Mike would let me wear pants, but he won't—so I bought this." She pulled the tiny revolver from between her breasts.

"You're a smart girl, Hope Savage. Keep those handy. There's a lot of riffraff in Coldbottom. Why didn't you tell me right away that you were Mrs. Mulgrew?"

Hope stood in the open doorway. "Because I'm not."

Lizzy laughed. She had a large, gusty laugh that Hope could hear even after the door closed.

Hope knocked on Dr. Matthew McBride's door four times before hearing a shouted curse. When the door opened, she stepped back. Though Mike was a big man, Dr. McBride was bigger. He seemed to take up the entire entrance.

He squinted at the bright light. "Who are you?" he demanded.

"You're the doctor? You're filthy *and* you're drunk."

"Damn right."

"Well, you're a sorry excuse." She stepped over the sill, causing him to move back to let her pass. "I'm Hope Savage."

He pressed his fingers to his temple. "Do I know you?"

"You know the parson? He sent for me."

"I try to avoid any preacher I can, but I remember he sent for a bride. What do you want?"

"I'm not here for Mike. When you sober up, could you go to Pearl Damian's house? There's a young girl there

157

who just had a baby. I wanted you to look in on her, make sure she doesn't get childbed fever. "No, I changed my mind. You're not clean"—she looked around the house—"and I doubt you'll be sober anytime soon."

Doc went to the cold stove and poured thick, cold coffee into a dirty cup. "If I had my way," he said, "I'd drink myself to death."

"Sounds like you need inner healing. Nobody but you can do that."

"I don't want to hear about church."

"Who's talking about that?" Hope asked. She went to the door. Before opening it she looked him over thoroughly. "Were you a churchgoing man before?"

"Before what?"

"Before someone closed up your insides."

Doc didn't reply, but his eyes clouded. I'll look in on the girl and check the baby." He held the door open for her.

"Lizzy told me you were the best-looking man around. . . . Well, you could be. There's a saying in the hills. 'Handsome is as handsome does.' " She stepped outside. "Try to clean yourself up before you go to Pearl's, and don't go till you're sober." She turned her back and walked away. She saw the colors of trouble around the man, and some powerful deep hurt.

Mike had his own problems. Lustful thoughts intruded in his thoughts day and night. He slept little and rose early, working until he could barely see his way through the darkness with his lantern. Hard as he worked, Mike was haunted by that kiss.

Every Sunday, Hope disappeared into the woods and didn't return until late afternoon. It didn't bother him, he supposed, for attendance at services had increased weekly, and each man and woman came to him afterward, asking him to convey greetings to Mrs. Mike.

That name infuriated him with its inaccuracy, but each

day she stayed on, it became more difficult to explain why they weren't married.

He wondered if she spent her time in the woods with Daniel. They seemed comfortable with each other, often talking and laughing together. Mike felt left out, though he wouldn't admit it even to himself.

While he ate, he could hear them talking, while the porch rocking chair squeaked and the last crickets of Indian summer chirped. It smacked of romance.

Deep inside he envied Daniel because the man could be around Hope all day. Daniel seemed to know her habits. Mike frequently took a dip in the November-chilled creek to cool his anger. The rein he held on his temper slipped a bit each day, but it didn't crack.

Not until one rainy evening in late November when he came back to something that shocked and infuriated him.

One evening after Mike had gone for his nightly wash, Hope was clearing the table when a biscuit fell off a dinner plate with a *thunk*. Daniel playfully threw it at her.

Through the window, Mike saw her laugh and throw it back at him. Before long peas, carrots, and more biscuits flew back and forth, the two dodging behind chairs. They giggled and bombarded each other.

Mike opened the door in a fury, then stood there. A vein throbbed in his neck while a muscle in his jaw worked.

Hope and Daniel sat back on their haunches.

"What in God's name are you doing?"

Chapter Eleven

Still smiling, Hope brushed loose tendrils from her face. "Good evening, Mike." She stood to brush off her apron.

"Are you two hell-bent on wasting our supplies?" he shouted.

"It's raining pretty lively out there, Mike. You might want to close the door."

"I demand an explanation for this . . . this mess! This waste!"

"We were having fun. Want to play?" She had a biscuit in her hand, which she casually flung at him. It landed next to his foot, bouncing several times.

Mike folded his arms and cocked an eyebrow.

Daniel had stopped laughing. "Come on, Mike, them biscuits ma'am made are like rocks anyhow. Cain't put a tooth in 'em."

"Who made them?" The house vibrated with his bellow.

Hope raised her hand and waggled two clean, neatly

161

manicured fingers. "I'm not so good at biscuit baking yet, but I'll get better."

He strode to where she stood. "I forbade you to cook. You nearly burned down the house." His finger pointed emphatically at the floor.

"That's an ex ... adur ... ation. I got it right that time," she said, smiling from ear to ear. "Anyway, it was just a small fire. The stove still works, and I painted the whole wall behind it."

Mike rocked back and forth on his feet. "You didn't paint. I'd have known."

"You've been working so hard, you wouldn't have noticed if I was feeding the chickens in the house. Which I'm not. Now sit yourself down while I get you a plate. You're scaring your hireling." She nodded to Daniel, who seemed to be trying to disappear.

Mike drew a deep breath. "Daniel, go feed the stock."

"They been fed."

"Then milk the cow."

"She been milked."

"I want to have a private word with Hope."

"Why didn't ya say so?"

Hope put Mike's dinner, a steaming bowl of chicken stew, at his place. "If you take the biscuits and soak them some, they're not too bad."

"I want an explanation, Hope."

"Your food is getting cold. We can talk after you eat."

She took a steaming kettle from the stove to fill the oak bucket.

Mike tasted the fragrant stew. It wasn't just meat and potatoes. Carrots and some greens flavored it, too. "Where'd you get the chicken?"

"Sometimes the Allgoods get a wagonload of fresh supplies—flour and such. You're on the list for some. I ordered more chickens and buffalo meat." She got on her knees to scrub. "Uh, I did order a rooster. That way we can have fresh chicken meat. Once they've mated and all."

"We have a rooster?"

"See? You didn't notice." She moved to another messy spot.

"What are you doing?" he asked.

"We made a mess. I'm cleaning it."

"Get up."

She ignored him and continued to scrub the floor.

"I said, get up." He emphasized each word.

"Eat your supper."

He opened his mouth to reply, but he *was* hungry, and the food tasted good.

When he finished, he sat back in his chair. "Who the hell taught you all this?"

She squeezed the rag into the bucket. "You're swearing."

He abandoned his bowl to take the bucket away. "Don't muddy the waters on me, Miss Savage."

Her eyes sparked lavender fire. She got up, then stood nose to chest not a foot from him. "You said no swearin' in the house."

"Answer the question."

Hope turned, skirts swinging, and ran onto the porch, leaving the door open. Standing there, she shouted into the increasing rain. "Mike Mulgrew is a no-good, god-damn, pissant man. He's a quibblin', carpin' old crank. Mike Mulgrew farts flowers dead. Preacher Perfect is a mud-ass who sucks up his balls so they choke him." She continued with worse profanity until her voice echoed satisfactorily off the mountains.

Mike watched in stunned silence. She *had* changed, and he hadn't noticed. She cooked, and from the look of things did the cleaning, too, now that he looked around. He had been so consumed with staying away that he'd forgotten the everyday necessities. When had he last washed clothes? She might have taken them to the wash-house in Coldbottom, but how could she know of such luxuries? She'd likely done the work herself.

He ladled himself another portion of the stew. This time he ate leaning against the pantry. Gone was the uncouth ragamuffin. Hope was well groomed, from her thick braid to the moccasins on her feet.

She finished washing the floor, and took the bucket of dirty water outside to empty it into the pouring rain. Back inside she hung the bucket on its peg with the easy grace of a practiced housewife.

"Hope?"

She faced him.

"Have you been doing all this?" He let his glance swing around the room.

"If you didn't notice the cooking, it must be tolerable."

"It has been." After finishing his coffee, he went to the stove for more. "The coffee's good, too."

"I'm glad you like the supper." She poured water from a kettle into the tin pan to wash his dishes.

Uncertain how to deal with her, he picked up a towel and joined her. "You've done a good job."

She dried her hands on her apron and half turned to face him. "I want you to hire me on, Mike. Now you know I can learn."

"Is that what this is all about? You want me to *hire* you?"

"Well, not for cash money. First I want to pay you back for the passage money; then I'd work for room and board . . . and I'd like to continue my lessons." Mike's thoughts went in another direction. He would like to learn a few things along with her.

She was speaking again, and he forced himself to concentrate. "I would like to learn numbers. I know Thaddeus wouldn't cheat me, but I'd still like to add and do other number things. All I can do now is count to a hundred."

Her speech had changed. He liked the sound of her

voice, soft, with a slow drawl. It slid up his spine and tickled his imagination. He remembered that hot kiss. The almost . . . in the bedroom . . .

"I know you aren't happy about our frolic tonight. But there's something in the Bible that says forgive, forgive, forgive. You'd know the part better than I would."

"Frolic?" He left the table to take his dishes to the sink. This close he could see the freckles on her nose. He had almost forgotten them. How could he not notice the way she had filled out?

"What we did with the food. Didn't you ever have fun? That's what frolic is."

"Not in a long time. Maybe too long." He stretched the towel. "Hope, who taught you the cooking, how to clean, and your language? Everything's different."

Hope's eyes softened. "You finally noticed. You've given me my letters and words. That's the most important thing anyone ever gave me. For the rest, Pearl's giving me what she considers polish. I didn't want to shame you."

Mike flung the dish towel down, touched her neat braid and, closing his eyes, swallowed visibly. His voice rough, he said, "*I* should feel shame." He looked at his shoes. "The reason I became a minister . . . I was ashamed of my family, because they 'frolic.' I wanted to be better than they are. I sent for you because I didn't want to put myself out. You see, I've been doing some thinking of my own." His hand rested on the back of her neck.

"Don't you know folks in town hold you in high regard?"

"They dislike me. You said you never fit in well, neither did I."

"Oh, but you're wrong. They talk about how you went looking for little Stuart Soams when he was lost in the snow. He was about frozen to death when you found him. They say you held him in your arms in his bed to keep him from losing his fingers and toes. His mother comes to church every Sunday, and she takes a beating for it every Sunday evening.

"I met Mr. Witendaly one day, and he showed me how you patched him together after a fall at his claim. Mike, they like you. Some poke fun, but they're wanting to look special, like boys that show off. Even Doc admires you." She raised her hand to brush back a lock of hair.

"Doc? He doesn't know what he's saying most of the time."

"Sometimes he does. But he has a deep hurt, and he's hiding it under whiskey." She quieted. "You have a hurt, too, I think, and you hide it in the Bible. You want to give something special away. That's why you pay folks to come each Sunday when they could be buying their supplies."

"Oh, Hope, I have no secret hurt. Just too much pride for one man."

"You are worthier than you think, Mike."

He moved back a step, not wanting to make a very foolish mistake. Mike realized he wanted her with a longing he had never known. He needed to examine his feelings, make some decisions, look at his lists.

Hope moved closer, taking his callused hands into her own. "Preacher Perfect, we all have weaknesses, but you take yourself much too seriously."

His breath hitched in his throat when she stood on her toes to plant a light kiss on his lips.

All Mike's plans to keep distance between them fled. He didn't need his lists to know that he had to take her in his arms. When he did she came willingly, eyes misty, lips glistening. Her scent engulfed him, fruit, flour, coffee beans, and her own unique perfume. When he dipped his head to kiss her, he breathed her name into her parted lips.

She relaxed in his arms, now returning the kiss. Each of them slid their lips together, slanting, sucking, biting.

Mike ran one hand down to cup the softness of her bottom, while the other sought her prim pinned-up braid. He tugged and pulled her wonderful mass of hair out of its sedate bun.

Hairpins scattered. The warm smoothness of her skin felt cool to his hot touch. He kept her tight against him with one arm, but that wasn't necessary because she had wrapped her legs around his waist, giving him better access to her mouth—that soft, silky mouth.

Trailing kisses from her lips to her ear, he felt her change position, allowing him better access to her neck.

She responded, tilting her head back with a soft and very feminine moan. His rigidity rested against her private place, and she began to move against him.

"Mike." She kissed his ear and neck until he took her lips again. His fingers reached for the buttons of her shirtwaist. She helped him, exposing her shoulder to his wandering mouth. Hope gasped when he sucked her nipple through the fabric of her dress. She moved her hips frantically.

Mike became aware of a thunderous sound in his ears. It took a while to realize that it was someone pounding at the door.

"Parson! Open up!"

Hope spoke into his neck. "Sounds like someone wants you mighty bad, Mike. I'd like to do this again sometime. It made my insides tickle all the way up in my throat." She finger-combed her hair back over her shoulders and rearranged her clothing.

Mike's breath came in gasps. He could not get himself under control. "Hope, my Hope." Slowly he slid her down until her feet touched the floor.

The banging and shouting continued. "Mrs. Mike. Are you home?"

"We're coming," she called while she quickly braided her hair.

Mike picked up the towel. Holding it close to his belt, he opened the door. It was Hector Samuels.

"Parson. We need . . . There you are, Mrs. Mike. Old Jeb Landry got in a knife fight with that mean Ravenaugh boy. Jeb needs tendin', and Doc McBride is drunker than hell."

Mike was frozen in place while Hope sprang into action at Samuels's words. Hector stood on the porch, his clothes dripping. The rain fell with typical California frenzy. It was the kind of rain that rolled down the hills and buried gold claims, tents, and people.

"I'll get my bag," she said.

"Hope, you can't go in this. This is more than a little storm. The mud is on the move. You could be buried alive." Mike followed her into the bedroom, where she filled a grain sack with small leather bags from her trunk.

"I won't let her go," he said to Hector, who still stood in the open doorway.

"Someone needs a healer, Mike. I've got to go." With calm precision, she checked her sack, making sure she had everything necessary.

"You could slip in the mud. I'll go for you." Mike's voice had risen along with his anxiety. He sensed he had been on the brink of discovering something wonderful, and that he might lose it.

She brushed past him and sat to exchange her moccasins for a heavy pair of shoes and her boots. "You can't go for me. You don't know anything about healing."

"Healing. Healing? What do you mean, healing?"

"I told you about my calling." She looked up at him, her eyes flashing with determination.

Hector scraped thick mud from his shoes. "Parson, if Mrs. Mike can't fix Jeb, he'll be needing your services.

168

Right now she's the only one in Coldbottom who can try to put him together again."

"Well?" She looked at Mike expectantly.

"All right. But I'm going with you. I already know you won't change your mind, and the way those gullies run you could be caught in the current and drowned." He reached for his own boots, knowing action would help him forget the ache in his loins.

Hope gave him a glorious smile when he helped her into her slicker.

"You're all right, Parson," Hector said as he led them off the porch and into the driving rain.

"I'm comin', too." The shout came from Mike's left as Daniel joined them. "Where we goin'?"

"Someone has to stay here and look after the house. The animals need tending to. Do you think you can handle all that, Daniel?"

"But who'll take care o' her?"

"I will. Don't worry."

Daniel looked at Hope, who grasped his hand and nodded. That was enough reassurance for him.

Hector guided them with his lantern while rain slashed into their faces. Their slickers were inadequate in the downpour. Along the way, Mike lifted Hope and carried her whenever the mud began to tug at his own feet or the runnels were like driving streams.

The trip took twice as long as usual, and when at last they came to tent town, Hector led them through the labyrinth to Jeb.

A group of miners hovered outside. When they caught sight of Hector's lantern bobbing toward them, they parted to make a path. Someone pulled the tent flap aside, and the three entered.

A Mexican woman rocked back and forth, wailing

169

over the inert Jeb. Water dripped from above, and the rain pounded with a deafening peal. The smell of blood, thick and metallic, hit Mike's nostrils.

Hope went to the woman. Whispering in her ear, she put her arms around her. The woman countinued to wail, but moved away; Hope smiled at her in encouragement.

The stench overwhelmed Mike, but Hope seemed unaware of anything but her patient. She lifted the tattered wool blanket from the man.

He saw her lips move close to Jeb's ear. Was she talking to him? Outside, the rain continued its assault on the small tent.

Mike stood beside her when she exposed Jeb's bloody chest.

"Mike," she shouted over the din of the rain. "I need hot water. Get someone to bring it right away."

"I'll go. But where will I find hot water at this hour?"

"I need you to help me. Send Hector and one other person to Hester Copley's boardinghouse. She always has a pot or two simmering."

Mike turned to convey her message, but Hector was already on his way. "Tell your missus not to worry," Hector called over his shoulder.

Kneeling beside Hope, Mike said, "This is insane, Hope. He's lost too much blood."

"Don't you dare say that. It turns the healing sour." She opened her sack, from which she withdrew a packet wrapped in oiled paper. While she transferred broad leaves from it to the worst wounds, she called out, "I need more light. Get a lantern or two. Mike, I need your handkerchief and shirt. There don't seem to be any clean rags here."

Mike removed his slicker and jacket so that he could take off his shirt. "Do you want me to tear the shirt?"

Hope nodded.

There was a small disturbance at the entrance. Someone handed in two lanterns. The illumination intensified the gruesome scene. Jeb's woman continued to wail.

Mike handed Hope a length of his torn shirt.

"Where's the handkerchief? I need it now."

"I think it's in my coat." He took the square of pristine cloth from the soaking, muddy coat. "Here."

Hope bunched it in her hands, then breathed into it before placing it directly on Jeb's face.

"Mike, can your preachering get her to quit her cater-wauling?"

Mike crab-walked to Jeb's woman. With one eye on Hope, he looked around to find a seat. There was no chair or stool. There wasn't much of anything in the tent. For the first time he really saw the poverty of his people. It humbled him.

The woman was filthy, and her smell made bile rise in his throat. He tried to see past the dirt, asked for guidance.

She held a string of beads, and crossed herself several times. Mike knew what he had to do. Putting his fastidiousness aside, he enfolded her in his arms and spoke to her in hushed tones, easing her distress.

Hope's messengers returned, bearing steaming kettles. They respectfully removed their hats when they carried in the water.

She washed Jeb's wounds. The comfrey packs had stayed the bleeding, but some of the deeper cuts required stitching. Jeb breathed peacefully now, probably due to the amount of alcohol he had consumed prior to the row.

Though Hope herself had never minded dirt of any kind, Granny Tilton had always insisted that she use clean herbs and bandages, that the needle be sharp, and that the thread be white silk.

Jeb began to shiver as she tied off the last stitch. It was not a good sign.

"Mike." Hope rose on unsteady legs. She'd been kneeling for hours.

Mike left the quieted woman, saw Hope sway. He caught her to him. "What can I do?"

"He appears to be taking a fever. We have to get him out of here. I want him moved on that cot to Doc McBride's. If the doc isn't sober yet, I'll sit with Jeb myself."

"You need to rest."

"I have to stay until he's some better."

"I'll take you to Doc's." He covered Jeb with his slicker, then helped Hope into hers. She took her bag outside. "I need two men to take him to Doc's. Carry him on the cot."

Hector again came forward.

"I'll go ahead and wait for you there. Be careful not to jiggle him."

In the glow of lantern light a wet face demanded, "Is he goin' ta die? He owes me plenty."

"Only the Almighty knows that. Maybe you'd better say your prayers, Dead-Eye."

"Thanks." She patted each man on the shoulder. "I'll go ahead and wait for you there. Be careful not to jiggle him."

They nodded.

She concentrated on putting one foot before the other, trying not to let them see her weariness. Each step was a struggle. The relentless rain lashed at them.

She looked up in relief when Mike shouted, "I'll go rouse Doc."

Doc's house was a tiny two-room wood structure. Though he hadn't responded to Mike's shouts, the door was unlocked.

Mike lit a lantern.

"Doc. Doc?" Hope pushed open the bedroom door. "Well, he's not going to be any help." An empty bottle had fallen from the man's hand onto the floor. Doc snored peacefully.

"He looks younger in his sleep," she remarked. There was nowhere to put her slicker, so she cast it into a corner.

"Mike, help me put him on the floor."

"Who? Doc?"

"Since he's in no position ta . . . to object, we're putting Jeb in Doc's bed." She took Doc's feet and waited for Mike to lift his shoulders.

The door slammed against the wall, heralding Jeb's arrival. The two helpers carried Jeb in, stamping their feet. One sneezed.

Even when they put him on the floor, Doc never moved.

"Mike, do you think you can lift Jeb onto the bed easy-like?"

Though the other man had gotten out of there as soon as he could, Hector stood near the door. "I'll help you, Parson," he offered.

"Thank you. After that, you can leave us, Hector. This is the watching time." Hope needed to draw some strength for the night. "I think I'll rest by the fire. It's going to be a long night."

A plush green chair had caught her eye when she'd entered. It faced the fireplace. Hope sank onto it.

After they moved Jeb, Hector said, "Are you sure you won't be needing me anymore, missus?"

"A load of prayers might help. Now go get some rest. And take the cot back to Manuelita."

When they were gone, Mike knelt before Hope to pull off her boots.

"I'll take them off. . . . " The rest went unspoken when Mike began to massage her icy feet.

"Oh, my, that feels mighty fine. This chair is fluffy as a pile of pine."

"You knew her name," Mike said. "You know all of them."

She was always so tired after a healing. This one had

taken more out of her than most, so she let herself drift while Mike brought warmth back to her feet.

The chime of the wall clock roused her from her doze. She started to rise.

Mike gently pushed her back onto the chair. "You sleep a little, my Hope. I'll keep watch."

"Thank you, Mike," she said. "Could you heat water for some tea?"

He went to the stove, where earlier he had started a small fire and put a kettle to boil. Soon he carried a cup to her, along with a jar of tea leaves.

"Would you bring my bag?" she asked.

She took a pinch from three separate packets and put them into the cup, which she filled halfway with hot water. "Help me spoon this into him."

She murmured in a strange tongue while trying to get Jeb to swallow. Afterward Hope dropped tea leaves into their own cups.

"We're drained out. This will bring us back." They sipped in contented silence. Mike wondered how much more about his mail-order bride he didn't know.

As the gray dawn broke, Doc stirred, then sat upright. "What the hell?"

"Morning Doc," Hope said. "I'll wager you have a sour stomach and a ripping ache in the head."

Doc got to his knees, then fell backward. "What're you doing here, Mulgrew? Am I dying? Sure do feel like it."

"We brought you a patient, Doc, but you were indisposed." Hope loved that word. She smiled at Mike when he raised his eyebrow.

Hope had dropped bits from other pouches into some strong tea. "Here, drink this so you can take care of Jeb Landry."

Doc drank the liquid, then got off the floor. "What's he doing in my blasted bed?"

"He was in pain. You weren't." Mike's answer dripped with derision.

Doc rubbed his eyes while struggling to his feet. "What's wrong with him? Have you been making your hokum again, Hope?"

Anger flared in Mike's eyes. Hope saw and understood. Though himself confused by her ability, Mike didn't like anyone doubting her. She felt a jerk in the area of her heart. An explanation would be required when they got home, she knew. *Home,* she thought. *Do I really have a home?*

"Come have a look, Doc." She lifted the blanket from her sleeping patient.

"What the devil happened to him?"

"Knife fight. He lost a lot of blood, and took some fever."

Doc leaned in to get a better view. "Good stitching." He touched one of the deeper wounds.

"Get your hands off him till they're washed!" Hope said with a snarl.

"Listen, girlie, I got a medical degree."

Mike stepped between Doc and Jeb's still unconscious body. "Maybe so, but he's Hope's patient until she releases him to you. Wash up. You stink."

Doc's eyes widened.

Hope was amazed. Mike had a gun leveled at Doc's midsection.

Chapter Twelve

Mike held the gun with two white-knuckled hands.

"Whoa, Parson, don't get careless. I'll wash." Doc shook his head and retreated to the kitchen.

Hope finally found her voice. "You sure do like to surprise a body. Scared me about to death—not to mention Doc."

"He wasn't cooperating, Hope, and you're tired. I don't have the patience for an argument." Mike put the gun in his pocket.

She sat back in the green chair, lips pursed. "Oh, my," she said. So Mike packed a gun and wasn't as vulnerable as she'd thought. Hope touched her own gun through the fabric of her dress. He'd pitch a fit if he found it.

Doc came back into the bedroom. "May I take a look at the patient now?"

He'd run a damp comb through his hair, though it was untamable with curls, and Hope smelled fresh soap. Even with the stubble of a beard, Doc was a handsome man.

"I'm glad you put your iron away, Mike." Doc's blue-bonnet eyes sparkled with humor.

Hope didn't miss the look the two men exchanged, like two dogs after the same bone. "Would you make me some coffee, Mike?" she asked. "You make delicious coffee."

"I could use some myself," he said. When he went to the kitchen, he left the door open.

"What did you treat Jeb with, Mrs. Mike?"

"I sure wish folks would quit calling me that. I am not anybody's missus. It kind of gets to him, too."

A kettle banged in the adjoining room.

Doc's eyebrows rose while he examined the still-sleeping man. "You did a good job of putting old Jeb back together."

"I only have my herbs, and mountain know-how. You call it hokum, Doc, but it does me just right." She looked pleased. "It's important to clean the cuts. Then I packed them with comfrey to stop the bleeding. He'd have been all right after I sewed him up, but that tent was filthy, and bone-chillingly cold."

"The fever seems to have abated. Could you show me what you used?"

Mike came back carrying three steaming cups to find Hope displaying the contents of her bag. "Poppy leaves for the pain, and angelica to stop putrefacation. What do you use?"

"Most doctors use laudanum. It's pretty much the same thing. Where did you get the poppies?"

"I took some seeds from my old patch back home. I have some to plant, and I keep some ground for numbing pain."

"You've done a good job, Hope."

"Are you feeling well enough to take care of him, Doc?"

"Call me Matthew, since we're colleagues. I feel better than I have in a long time."

Mike didn't like this conversation one bit. While the

coffee cooled, he felt himself becoming tense. "Are you two going to drink this coffee?" he demanded.

"Which one has sugar?"

He tapped the cup closest to Hope's right hand. "We'd better leave soon, Hope. It's going to take us a while to get back in this storm." He pulled out his pocket watch, checked it, then snapped it closed.

That brought an impatient, for his ears only, "Damn timepiece!"

"Take my horse back," Doc offered.

Hope beamed at him. "Why, thank you, Matthew."

Mike gritted his teeth. He could have sworn she'd batted her eyes. The two of them carried on like old friends, and Mike was secretly glad when Hope considered Dr. Matthew McBride recovered enough to care for Jeb. That meant they could leave.

Hope was pushing her feet into her galoshes when Mike said, "McBride, stay off the liquor. She can't cover for you all the time."

Doc didn't reply. He led them to his stabled horse.

Mike climbed on, then reached for Hope. Matthew also reached to help her, but she surprised them when she climbed into the saddle on her own.

Mike smiled triumphantly when she settled her bottom close to him, her head under his chin. He wrapped his arms around her, taking the reins. His hat tipped forward against the pelting rain. "Doc?" he said.

Doc looked up but couldn't see Mike's eyes.

Mike pulled a pouch from his pocket, then tossed it to Matthew. "Find someone to take Jeb's woman home to Mexico if she wants to go."

"I'll do that." Turning to Hope, Matthew spoke again. "Would you walk out with me one day soon?"

Mike kicked the horse just a little harder than he should have, causing the animal to bolt away before Hope could reply.

*   *   *

Destruction lay everywhere. They passed a pile of lumber that looked as though it might once have been a dwelling. It slid along in the relentless mud. Picks, shovels, cans, all stuck out of the ooze in odd places.

Mike held Hope plastered against him, their bodies joined from her head to her rump. Sharing the saddle led to thoughts she wanted to shy away from. It was Pearl and Mike who belonged together. She'd forgotten for a bit, this healing had reminded her. She herself would always be No-Account Savage. She had a new name, and all the girl trappings, but she was still the same inside.

Confused by her feelings, and tired, she wanted to turn, to put her lips against Mike's neck and inhale, to breathe in Mike's own scent of soap and hay and musky man.

The horse plodded along, mud sucking at its hooves. When they neared Mike's land, Hope asked, "Do you think it might have taken the house?"

"We'll see in a few minutes. I thought I'd built it far enough from the water."

Hope peered through the driving rain when they rounded the last bend. "It's still here!" she cried.

Mike pulled the horse up near the porch. He dismounted and lifted her from the saddle. When her feet hit the ground she went limp, leaning against him for support.

Daniel flung the door open, allowing it to bang against the side of the house. "You got back! I was fretful, ya been gone so long. I done what ya said, Mike, kept the house warm and all the animals is cared for."

Mike carried Hope into the house, where he deposited her in the bedroom.

"Get out of those wet clothes. I'll fix a hot bath.

They were both soaked through. He grabbed a change of clothes for himself and hesitated before he left the room to take one last look at her.

Exhausted, Hope began to unbutton the dress she'd worn for the last two days. Mike wanted to tuck her in. He remembered the morning in the loft, when he'd awoken with her close beside him. "Hope," he said.

Hope looked up. "I know. I ruined another dress."

"That doesn't matter." His voice low, he went on. "There's a lot of courage in you, Hope. You're more than I bargained for."

He went to where she stood, bedraggled and wet, tipped her chin with his forefinger to place a quick kiss on her lips, and left the room.

In the other room, he turned to his hired man. "Let's heat some water, Daniel. Get the tin tub from the porch."

"I kept water a-boilin' the whole time ya was gone, an' the rain barrels is full."

Mike clapped him on the back. "Thanks."

"Was it a bad one, Mike?"

"Yes. How could you tell?"

"She's always like this after a big healin'."

Daniel knew her better than he himself did. It hurt to admit it. He had just begun peeling away the layers that defined his future wife. When had he begun to think of her as his wife?

He washed and dressed, only half listening to Daniel's report on the state of the property.

Hope should have been tired. She let the dress drop to her feet. Was Mike proud of her; or embarrassed that he had kissed her? Her heart fluttered. Such a little kiss—not like the man-woman kiss of the other day—yet still she'd lost track of the time.

"Lordy, I need to eat or something." Throwing a flannel gown over her head, she went to the kitchen, where she watched the two men.

There, Daniel talked nonstop to a shirtless Mike. Chest bare, he had lathered his face. She watched him draw the

181

razor along his dimpled cheek. A bit of soap dropped to the hair on his chest, drawing her eyes to follow its path. Black, curly swirls offset that blob of white. He was all muscle and sinew, and she recalled how he had wrapped her safely against him.

Lips parted, she watched him dip the razor in the basin. The movements seemed slow to her, her vision magnified, making every whisker visible. Intensified senses brought the scent of shaving soap to her. Hope felt feverish. The desire to retreat behind the door warred with her desire to watch him to the finish.

"Here's ma'am. She can finish shavin' ya. I about got the tub half-filled. You're goin' ta get a bath *inside* the house, ma'am."

Mike half turned, his razor stopped in midpath, and he nicked himself.

Daniel happily went for a chair and brought it to the dry sink. "Sit down, Parson; it'll be the best shave ya ever had."

Hope drifted forward to take the razor from him. She expected resistance, but Mike gave her none.

"You cut yourself," she remarked. A tiny trickle of blood claimed her attention. "Do you have a clean kerchief?"

His eyes caught hers. "The towel's clean."

Hope dipped a corner of the towel in water and dabbed at the wound, mentally chiding herself for her inability to speak. No-Account Savage always had something to say about everything. Maybe she was more Hope than she thought.

She draped the towel over his shoulder, then tipped his head back. He kept his eyes on hers. The first slow stroke from jaw to throat was more a caress; the rasping against his beard indicated more than just a shave.

Wipe the razor, she thought; now shave. She instructed herself with each stroke, memorizing his face. Here was a little mole, there a tiny scar, and that dimple . . .

Suddenly she put the razor by the basin. "I can't do any more, Mike. I'm too . . . tired." *And Pearl's the lady for you.* She dampened the towel to wipe his face. Slowly and easily she ran the towel under his chin, then down lower to wipe away the still-soapy dollop on his chest. Why couldn't she stop and leave things alone . . . leave Mike to Pearl?

Mike didn't know when he'd stopped breathing, but when she stepped away, he gasped for air, then ran his hand across his chin. "Thanks," was all he could say.

"You need something on that cut. Did you want me—"

"No."

"Don't she do a right tolerable shave?" crowed Daniel.

"She does indeed." When she'd wiped his chest, he'd become aware that he was shirtless, and now he reached for the clean one he'd brought into the room.

"It's your turn now," he said. "Go get in the tub and relax. We'll eat when you're finished."

"Bathing in the kitchen? I couldn't."

Mike hung a towel over the rocking chair. "We'll go to the loft."

Hope watched them go before lifting the flannel gown to toss it aside. "We've been wet for hours and he wants me to get wet again," she said to herself.

Bracing herself, Hope lowered her right foot into the tub, and sighed when she felt the warm water. She climbed in, leaning back. *Hope Savage, you never had it so fine.* After relaxing for a few minutes, she got down to the business of washing. If her growling stomach was any indication, she knew Mike had to be as hungry as she.

Dried and dressed, she called the men. Her brother asked, "Was it too warm for ya?"

"You should try it," she replied. "It's the best thing I ever did."

"Then we can eat. Mike said so."

183

She sent Daniel for a slab of bacon.

When he disappeared from view, Hope said, "I know you have things to say, but I'd appreciate it if you'd hold off on the hell-raising till he's asleep."

He turned to answer her, but the words wouldn't come. In the flannel nightgown, she appeared angelic and fragile.

"Things will keep until tomorrow. We all need a good rest."

She took her place in the rocking chair and sat back, closing her eyes and letting Mike do the cooking. After their simple meal, Daniel went to the barn for his evening chores.

Hope sat sipping her second cup of chocolate. "Are you having church tomorrow?"

The question jarred Mike. He looked up from the dishpan. "I'd forgotten tomorrow's Sunday." Rain lashed at the house, and he peered out the window. "I don't think anyone could make it out here."

"I invited Pearl Damian for supper. She might try to come."

"She's a sensible lady. I don't think she would chance it."

Elbows on the table, chin in her hands, she observed, "I don't believe she ever came up against hard weather. Maybe I'll hotfoot it to her place and—"

"You will *not!*"

Her back straightened. "And how do you plan to stop me?"

"Be reasonable, Hope. You're tired. Hell, I'm tired."

Her lips curved into a smile. "You must be. You just swore, and for a change I agree with you."

When they all retired for bed, Mike didn't fall asleep right away. He had visions of Hope in that filthy tent, doing for Jeb to the best of her ability, a skill he had not believed she had, though she told him that first day. It got under his skin that the people of Coldbottom knew her and loved her.

He, the shepherd of his flock, had failed in his duty. While he'd kept his distance, expecting them all to come to him, Hope had gone about ministering to the downtrodden.

They all woke the next day to the sound of rain pounding down with relentless fury. Mike went to the kitchen to build up the fire in the stove. After cleaning the fireplace and restarting the fire, he put coffee to brew and read his sermon.

Hope came from the bedroom fully dressed, though her face still bore the flush of sleep and her hair hung in a loose braid over one shoulder.

Her appearance unsettled him, so he put his sermon aside to get her a cup of coffee. "Good morning," he said.

"Morning. I purely love coffee in the morning. In my whole life I never had but chicory or mint tea. We made it when Pa wasn't around. I hope that wherever Ma put her shoes down she has a good supply of coffee."

Struck by her deprivation and her simple wish, Mike vowed she would never know want again. "Are you hungry?"

"I can wait. We've got to clear the air."

Mike sat opposite her, refilling his own cup. "You did an admirable job yesterday." He thought it downright heroic, under the circumstances.

"Are you vexed with me?"

"At first. Hope, how did they know to come to you when Doc was drunk?"

"I didn't mean for anyone to find out. Folks thought like Doc said, that it's hokum. But things changed a bit when I saw that poor girl birthing in the street and no one helping her."

"Who . . . ?"

185

"Hold on. I'll get to all that. Her name's Patricia. Lizzy made her fancy it up. They called her Sherry."

"Lizzy? Don't tell me you've been consorting with those . . . those . . . " His hands flat on the table, he leaned in toward her.

"I'll get to her, Mike."

"That woman. She's a . . . that house . . . "

"Can't you say the words? It's a whorehouse, Mike. Now settle down and let me finish. They all came west for a better life. Like me."

That hit Mike like a slap in the face. He sat back in his chair. "Tell me about it."

"Patricia's Pa sold her. Like mine sold my sisters. The man got gold fever and brought her out here. When he ran out of luck he sold her to Lizzy so he could move on to the next stake." Hope grimaced. "I told you how I found her. After she had baby Tom I took myself up that hill and struck a bargain with Lizzy."

At that moment, Daniel came from the loft. "What's for breakfast?"

Hope went to the stove and busied herself making oatmeal and another pot of coffee. She and Daniel chatted comfortably while Mike stewed. He wanted to hear the story out, but things kept getting in the way.

When he and Hope had finished chatting, Daniel put on his slicker and headed for the barn, then hustled right back in. "Mike, the creek is comin' too close ta the house. What are we goin' ta do?"

Mike hurried to the porch with Hope close behind.

"Do somethin', Mike. It might take away our house," she cried.

Mike grabbed his boots and slicker to follow Daniel. Hope ran to the bedroom to find her canvas pants. She'd bought them against Alberta Allgood's advice.

Right now she needed something she could work in, and those blasted skirts were always in the way.

Tempted

Outside, the deluge continued, swelling the creek well over its banks, crawling through the brush and trees. No stranger to floods, she knew their power. Once she had watched Pa's lean-to and his still get washed away, but nothing she valued had been inside. Here she not only prized the house, but her fiddle and firearms and even her moccasins were threatened.

"Confound it, God. How about a little help here?" She ran back inside for her Colt. On the way out she grabbed a shovel from the porch.

When she joined the men, they had dragged two fallen trees to the edge of the clearing, trying to make a mudbank.

One of the logs broke away and rolled downhill, collapsing their dam. "It ain't workin'," she shouted.

Mike looked around. "Hope, get inside. Daniel, let's try to find a better way."

The water advanced a few more inches. "Damn it!" she shouted to the sky, then smiled. "I guess You want us to do the damming." She ran to the barn, where the men were loading bales of hay onto a small work wagon.

"Leave off that. I got a plan," she said.

Mike looked up. "There's no time."

"Just hear me out. There's a place where the creek narrows a little way. It curves away from the mountain and comes inland. I think we can dig it out and make it go over the edge of the hill."

"A shunt! I think I know where you mean. Let's go!" He nodded at her in silent approval.

She hurried after them; then the three worked furiously against the encroaching water. Hope's back ached by the time they were finished hours later, but when the water gushed over the hill, she shouted, "Hallelujah!"

"Thank God," Mike said, and cast his shovel aside to shake Daniel's hand. In his exuberance, he grabbed Hope and whirled her around. "We did it, thanks to you," he shouted. Lightning shot through him where they touched and he released her quickly.

Mike tried to keep himself busy. Anything to keep away the memory of Hope in those pants. Despite his tired shoulders and back he had to put a damper on his desire. That woman did maddening things to his heart.

She'd changed into a dress to let the pants dry, but while she read her lesson from the Bible, those same pants hung on a rope line Mike had strung over the fireplace. All he had to do was look up, and there they were—a testament to his carnal thoughts. And that was what those thoughts, were—purely carnal. It couldn't be love. What was with him lately? He hadn't been thinking straight for some time.

He wondered how he had missed the changes in her. The graceful way she now brought her cup to her lips, shaping them to sip.

Daniel finished eating his dinner and yawned. "I'm goin' ta take care of the stock. That cow ain't been milked yet today. Is it all right if I turn in then?"

"You're entitled to a good night, Daniel. You just go get comfortable and I'll do the evening chores."

"I am plumb tuckered." At a signal from Hope, he added, "Thank ya."

When he was out earshot, Hope said softly, "You're wonderful with him." She carried her dishes to the sink.

Mike felt as though she'd given him a mountain of gold.

He had missed so much of her metamorphosis while he had absented himself from the house. She was still No-Account, who flew in where no one else dared, but in many ways she really had become Hope, too. No-Account's courage and spirit had brought her here against terrible odds. Though she didn't care about appearances,

188

Hope had tried to accommodate herself to his idea of womanly ideals.

He had tried to cast off his past—mostly the shackles of his own mischievous family: parents he saw as too affectionate, brothers who wanted only to roam and womanize, and sisters who attracted too many admirers with their outrageous behavior. Mike had wanted to be better.

Still, Hope was like his family, yet not like them. She was a rare puzzle he wanted to solve and he had to admit that this house wouldn't be the same without her. True, she couldn't carry a tune as he had hoped his wife would, but she had other talents. He shifted uncomfortably in his chair, remembering what he'd felt less than two nights ago, when Doc and Hope had been working together. It came again. . . . *Do I love her?*

"Mike? Are you sleeping?" Hope leaned over him, her braid falling into his lap and interrupting his pondering.

"No, lost in thought." He coiled the rope of her braid around his arm, pulling her closer. "Are you going to bed?"

"Lordy, no. I've had much more wearying days." She looked into his eyes. "What were you thinking about?"

"You."

"Me? I'm just the bride you sent for by mistake."

"Maybe it wasn't a mistake." He pulled her into his lap.

"No? Well, you know all about me." Hope said, picking at a blister on her palm. "Do you like Daniel?" She asked, looking up at him expectantly.

"I wonder who he is. It's been a couple of months and nobody's come looking for him."

"Do you like him?"

"I do. He's a hard worker, but I like the man himself." Seeing Hope's pleased expression, Mike continued. "And you? Do you like him?" He tried to keep jealousy from his voice.

"He's company when you're not home." She paused. "Why don't you get some sleep, Mike? No telling what tomorrow will bring."

"What about you? Aren't you tired? If it weren't for you, we'd probably be washed out by now. You worked as hard as we did." Instinctively he reached for her hand, turning it palm up. It was raw. "You never complain."

"Whining doesn't get things done."

He held on to her hand.

"I have salve for those sores. Would you like me to put some on your hands?" She took his hands in hers. "Too bad about Dr. McBride," she continued with a yawn, "A real fine-looking man like him losing his soul in a bottle."

"McBride? You think he's good-looking?" Mike couldn't fathom why he felt jealous of every man she spent time with. But this was different, she'd said Doc was good-looking.

There was a sudden rumble. Hope cocked her head. "Is that another earthquake? It sounds like thunder."

Mike pointed to the books, jostling on their shelf. "When it shakes like that it's a small quake."

"Oh," she said with another yawn. "I'm pretty tired, Mike. I guess you can tell me tomorrow what work still has to be done." She walked to the fireplace, where she felt her trousers to see if they were dry.

"I don't want you to wear those anymore."

"A body can't work in a dress, Mike. Did you ever see those women prospectors in a dress?"

"Women?" Mike raised an eyebrow.

"There are four, and they all wear canvas pants."

It was surprising news for Mike. He had never seen a woman in the gold fields . . . but if they dressed like men . . .

"Where did you buy them?"

"At the mercantile. I'm sorry if I shamed you, but I'm glad I bought them. I'd have ruined another dress working out there today. They'll be dry by morning, and I'll put them away until I need them again."

Not if I have anything to say about it. The picture of Hope wearing those pants would haunt his dreams tonight. Before she closed the bedroom door he said, "Get rid of them. They aren't proper for a lady."

"No." She closed the door with a defiant click.

Chapter Thirteen

"Mike Mulgrew, where'd you put my work clothes?" She'd come out of her bedroom to put them away, but the pants were missing. "I want them back and I want them now." She climbed the ladder to the loft.

He wasn't there. "Dadblast him." The trunk caught her eye. She smiled maliciously. "He hid them in there." But she came away disappointed.

She rushed outside into a perfect sunny morning, and her toes sank into thick mud. "Confound it! Without my work clothes this dress will be spoiled, too." She looked about. "Preacher Perfect, where the hell are you? You get home with my pants right now." The words echoed off the sodden mountains.

She banged back into the house. The coffeepot and a plate sat on the warmer. Breakfast. "Well, I need to fill my belly before I start. Where could those pants be? I'll bet he turned tail so we wouldn't have a fight. I never saw a man who so didn't like a good argument."

She scrubbed her plate, then went to the bedroom, where she removed her petticoats. After rummaging in her trunk, she pulled out a hide belt she found. With it secured around her waist, she reached between her legs to grasp the back hem and pulled it through, tying it to the front of the belt. Her legs were exposed, but she didn't care. There was planting and harvesting to do, and she would blister his ears later for taking her duds. No use in complaining now, when there was work to be done.

She stopped at the church to see if the damp had damaged her fiddle. A few soft strokes with the bow reassured her. Replacing it, she went to check on her plants.

Because her family had moved around so much, Hope had learned to seek the most protected spots for planting her herbs. Her little patch, though battered, had survived the weather. She set to work, cutting a few plants back, and collecting seeds from others.

Mike was walking home when he heard twigs snap nearby. He followed the sound. A woman was on her knees in the mud. She had her back to him. "Hope?"

She moved quickly to the side in a crouch. In mere seconds he found himself the target of her gun. He put his hands up and stepped back. "Where in blazes did you get that? Ah, Hope. Your legs are bare again."

"You should give a warning when you come up on someone. I nearly shot you." She put the gun back inside her bulging sack. "What did you do with my work clothes? The weather here isn't decent enough for working my garden every day in a dress, Mike. That's why I have my skirt hiked up."

"Are you finished here? We have some discussions that have been postponed long enough."

"I know. We could have had it out this morning if you hadn't bolted like a shy filly." Hope hoisted her sack over her shoulder and started in the direction of the house.

Mike took the sack from her as they walked. "I didn't bolt. There were a few funerals this morning."

"Oh. I mistook you then. Jeb still with the living?"

"I stopped by his tent. Manuelita took the money and went back to her people, and Jeb is healing nicely."

"That pleases me," she said.

"So that's your herb garden."

"Yes, 'tis. With all this rain and more to come, I had to work today. The mud makes it difficult."

"You can plant closer to the house. Right beside the porch, if you like."

"I'm pleased you offered." They were passing the church when she said, "Mike, could you go ahead? Just put my sack on the porch. I have a few words for the Almighty."

He was about to refuse when he realized she had a right to some privacy. "I'll start some coffee."

Taking her shoes off, Hope left them by the door, walking barefoot down the center aisle, where she sat in the first pew.

"It's me again," she said. "I'm surprised Mike let me come in, especially with my legs showing.

"I'd like to thank you kindly for saving the house. Glory, I never saw so much wet! We beat it, though didn't we?"

She waited. "Could You calm Mike down a little when I tell him about my doctoring? I know I told him before, but he thought it was something I did only in the mountains back home, and he's like most folks who don't understand things that can't be explained."

She turned her hands over in her lap. The blisters were nearly gone, with just a bit of pink to show where they'd been. Her herbs had helped. "Thanks for letting Jeb pull through. I don't know about Doc though. I'm wondering if he's going to make it. But I have to leave that up to You."

Finished, she went for her shoes. When she had them almost buttoned she looked up. "I'd appreciate it if you'd help me find my pants." She paused, then added, "You won't let him find out about Friday nights, will You? I'll tell him when the time seems right, and he's going to need time to choke down learning about my doctoring. Heck, I've been avoiding the subject for too long now. I've got to tell him Daniel is my brother, too. I wonder how that's going to sit."

Mike heard her enter. When he came from the bedroom, buttoning a clean shirt, he saw her bending over to take off her shoes. Though the dress now covered her legs, he couldn't help picturing the bare flesh he'd seen so recently. They had so much to talk about.

At his look, she folded her arms, her legs wide apart. "One dress got ruined the other day. I'm trying to save this one."

"It's not proper. Your legs were *bare,*" he spluttered.

"They wouldn't be if I had my things."

"*Sit down!*"

Hope shrugged, retiring to her rocking chair. She sat in a manner that left no doubt that she regarded it as hers. "Well? You got something to say, get it over with."

Mike clenched and unclenched his hands, tugged his ear, then cleared his throat several times.

Not intimidated, Hope glared at him obstinately. "Well? Get it over with. And don't think you can stop me from tying up my skirt. Women do dirty work sometimes, and men shouldn't keep us from dressing for that work. Who said women can't wear pants?"

"Hope," he began, then walked outside. He came back in raking his fingers through his hair. "Hope, why can't you be like every other female? You're always so contrary."

"If you'd be reasonable, I'd be more agreeable."

He sat down opposite her. "All right. I'll listen."

"That's hard to believe!"

"Hope . . . " he began in a growl.

"For now we don't have to talk about what I wear or don't wear. But you have to hear me out about something else—my healing." She peered at him cautiously. "It started with Patricia, a girl who got a bad deal and had to work for Lizzy. She's the one I was telling you about the other day. When her belly swelled, Lizzy put her out. She lived the summer in an old shack. When it came her time, she went looking for help. Doc was drunk.

"That's when I first saw her. She lay in the dirt. Some of Coldbottom's male citizens watched her, joshing like they were at a tent show." Hope had spoken slowly so she wouldn't slip up in her speech. It was important to sound the way Mike wanted especially when she was broaching a topic with which she knew he'd be uncomfortable.

Appalled, Mike asked, "Weren't any women around?"

"Watching through their windows."

"That still doesn't answer how you know Lizzy."

"Give me time to get to that. I made them take Patricia to Pearl's to have the baby." Her face brightened. "She had a boy. Have you ever been at a birthing?"

Mike had his hands folded between his knees. "Hope, finish your story."

"Guess not. Men aren't privileged that way. Too bad. After Tom was born I took myself to the whorehouse to have a word or two with Lizzy. She agreed to let Patricia help with the cleaning when she's back on her feet."

Mike got up to pace, his hands clasped behind his back. "That still doesn't explain to me why Hector Samuels came for *you* when Doc was out cold."

"There's more comes before Jeb. I'll tell it all in good time." She left the rocker. "Right now I'm going to have a bite of cake. You want one, too?"

"Anything," he answered. "This doesn't make any sense. You can't step in for a medical doctor."

She put coffee and a plate of cake at his place at the table and sat facing him. "Even when he's dead drunk? You know, I never met him until that night with Patricia. Word around Coldbottom had it he would more likely kill someone than cure them."

Mike stared at her. "You don't know him?"

"I may come from poverty, but I don't look for trouble, and Doc seemed to be trouble. Though he seems like a nice enough fellow. He must have something gnawing at him pretty bad."

Mike choked on his coffee. When he was able to reply he said, "You were filthy when you came here. You refused to wash, yet I saw you make sure that everything that touched Jeb, heck, every*body* who touched Jeb, was clean. And what was that blowing in my handkerchief all about?"

She took a bite out of her own food. "Mmm, that cake's good. There you go, putting the wagon before the horse again. A few days after the birthing, I was looking for mushrooms and came upon an old man sitting near his claim. Just sitting. I said a 'howdy-do' but he didn't even look at me. I thought he was tetched till I saw his hands. All knotted up they were, and when I took a closer look, I saw he was bent every which-a-way." She stopped and looked at him pointedly. "This damp is hard on people, but mustard poultices and a syrup made with angelica had him moving around in a few days." Mike sat, stonefaced.

"Then flux started in tent town and Doc wouldn't go. He was sober that time. I dosed the sick with plantain juice. Seems everybody told somebody, and before long I was taking up Doc's slack." She took another bite of cake and looked right into Mike's eyes.

He stared back. "You went where Doc wouldn't go?"

"I thought you knew. Haven't you been to Allgood's to pay? I bought a hundred little bottles."

"Allgood's? Bottles?"

"The pants came from there, too. Mike, be reasonable. How would *you* like to work in a dress?"

He opened his mouth with another argument, but closed it. After a moment, merriment showed in his eyes and he laughed out loud at the thought of himself in a dress.

When he recovered himself he said, "Hope, you really should try to conform. You can't go here and there. It's dangerous. I need to know you're safe."

"Why? I've always taken care of myself. You saw that I'm good with this knife." She reached under her skirt to remove the instrument, and she placed it on the table. "I don't go anywhere without my guns."

"*Guns?* You have more than one?"

"The one you saw today, I take wherever I go." She removed the revolver from her pocket and placed it near the knife. "Then there's my long gun. I keep it in my trunk. Want me to get it?"

"No. You realize you have a whole arsenal?" His voice had become high-pitched again.

"I have more."

"*More?*" he roared.

"I'm showing you I'm prepared, so I'm not in danger."

She had unbuttoned the first four buttons of her bodice. Now she pulled the derringer from there to place it on the table next to her revolver. She hadn't taken her eyes off his, waiting for him to blow up. She didn't have to wait long.

Mike slammed his hands on the table and stood up. "Where did you get those?" he shouted. "You can't go running around with firearms hidden on you—especially there." He pointed at her bosom.

"Who says? I got them both fair and square." She withheld the information that he'd be getting a bill for the derringer. She didn't think he needed to hear about that yet. "Are you going to make me stop healing?"

"I don't know. This is too much. I can't think."

"Some folks think it's witchery. That's why I tried to keep it secret."

"Ah, Hope. Whatever am I going to do with you?" He went to the table and pulled his papers from the drawer. Looking through his lists, he wrote something down.

She worried a fingernail. "If you're making a list for me, I won't follow one."

"I'm making a note to pay at the mercantile. I used to do that weekly, but since you came my schedule is wrecked." He folded his hands. "You might as well go on. I assume there is more to your story."

"I told you about Granny Tilton. Pa stayed at Hog's Holler longer than most places. I learned all my healing from her. At first I just helped with her plants and followed her around when she visited sick folk, but one day a man come in shaking. He was all yellow. Granny sat him down for some dandelion wine. I told her not to give it to him. 'Whatcha seein', child?' she says to me.

" 'He got red glowin' from his head.' She put the wine back and made a potion. Told me to give it to him, but she said I had to wash my hands first. I didn't want to, but I did."

"You saw red. What difference did that make?"

"Dandelion would have finished him. That color I see around folks is something Granny couldn't see, the spirit of the person. It tells me what they need."

Mike snorted. "What color is my spirit?"

"I don't rightly know. You're like a rainbow, different colors. They change, like your eyes. You're not sickly, though."

His eyes met hers. He saw honesty and truth and courage there, but this superstitious nonsense went against everything he thought he'd known. "I'm going out to clear my head."

200

She followed him to the porch. "Where are you going?"

He didn't answer. Crashing through the bushes, he shouted, "Stay away from Lizzy's."

It was all superstition. It had to be. What of the white cloth over Jeb's face? Probably more "hokum," as Doc said. Mike went back to check on the bypass. He saw Daniel by the barn; the man joined him and they secured it against winter.

When he entered the house that evening, Hope's skirts properly covered her legs. Supper was cooking, and Doc McBride had come calling.

"Here's Mike now, Matthew. We have a visitor for supper, Mike." Hope actually glowed.

"Doc," Mike said and nodded. He was caught off guard when the man rose. Mike was tall at over six feet, but Doc had inches on him. Sober, neatly dressed, and with his hair combed, he truly was a handsome man. "What brings you out this way?"

"Just a neighborly visit to thank Hope. Jeb's walking around now, and ornery as ever." He extended his hand to Mike.

Mike turned as if not noticing and went to the dry sink to wash. He sluiced water through his hair to give him time to digest this new element.

"Daniel will be here any minute." Hope said. "He's our hireling and purely loves to eat. Sit yourself right here, Matthew."

Doc took the place indicated, while Hope put platters of pork chops, fried potatoes, beans, and biscuits on the table.

When Daniel came in, he craned his neck. "Who's that?"

"Daniel, this is Matthew McBride. He's the doctor in Coldbottom."

201

"Howdy."

Mike took his usual seat at the end of the table. "You really didn't have to come all this way to bring news of Jeb. I checked him out for myself this morning. You wasted a trip." His eyes glowed green, raking Doc up and down.

Hope slammed a plate before Mike, trying to catch his eye.

"It's never a wasted trip to visit with a pretty lady," said Doc. "I think it's time for me to get out more."

Mike's gut told him it was more than a friendly visit. It seemed Doc McBride was courting Mike's woman, and she loved every minute of it.

Hope had developed more social graces than he realized. She knew when to pass the food, and that the guest was served first. She carried on a positively lively conversation.

He was arrested in his observations when she tapped him on the hand. "Matthew is from your Massachusetts, Mike."

He heard the tautness in her voice, and forced himself to respond. "Boston?"

"My family is inland. I studied in Boston, though. Hope, you're an excellent cook. These are the best biscuits I've had since I left home."

Mike choked on his coffee, while Daniel responded with glee, "You're gettin' it right, ma'am."

Hope beamed. "I'm just learning."

Mike sat in stony silence for the rest of the meal. When Hope began to clear the dishes, he took out his watch.

"Hmm, nearly seven o'clock. Don't you need to get back, Doc?"

Giving him a furious look, Hope swiped the crumbs she was wiping off of the table into Mike's lap.

But instead of responding in kind to Mike's rudeness, Doc just smiled. "The road is pretty clear now, and I brought a lantern. I'll stay to help with the dishes."

He was making Mike look like an inconsiderate boor—but Mike didn't care. "I can help. You'd best get along. Oh, and take your horse. That's why you really came, isn't it?"

Doc raised his eyebrows. "Among other reasons."

Hope put a pot down. Hard.

"I'll wash," said Mike. "Hope, get off your feet." He was way out on a limb now. No need to look at her to know Hope would blow up the minute their guest departed. If she waited

"Matthew, you'll have to forgive Mike. I think my biscuits don't agree with him. He has a delicate stomach." She took the towel from him. "We really thank you for the use of your horse."

"I think I understand, Hope. I wonder if you'd come out with me next Sunday? I'll rent a rig for a little ride. That is, if it's all right with Mike."

"He's not my pa. I'm inviting Pearl Damian for Sunday."

Mike intruded. "You asked her to come yesterday," he said sourly.

"You said yourself that nobody with a lick of sense would venture out in that storm. I'm asking her for *next* Sunday to make up for it." She gave him a look he didn't recognize. "You'll like Miss Pearl."

Mike clattered the pewter forks and knives, but it didn't prevent him from hearing McBride assure Hope that if they left in the morning, they'd be back in plenty of time for supper.

"We have services in the morning," Mike remarked.

Doc parried. "Is that so? I understood Hope doesn't attend."

"That's going to change."

"Just a dang minute here. I'll make up my own mind. If

I want to ride out with Matthew, then nobody can stop me. I'll walk you to the barn, Doc. That's a dandy horse you have."

Mike wondered if Matthew would try to kiss her. And would she let him? He didn't want anyone kissing Hope—or looking at her legs—but himself. Then why hadn't he done something about marrying her? *I could slip into town for Sheriff Stably tomorrow, and then Matthew would have to sniff around somewhere else.*

When Hope came in, she lit into him. "What bit you in the ass? You call yourself a man of God and act like you're better than everyone. No wonder nobody wants to come to church."

"You don't know what you're talking about." He had dried his hands and now advanced on her.

Daniel, who had been finishing off the fried potatoes, came to stand between them. "Just 'cause you're mad, don't take it out on ma'am. I liked Doc, too."

"I won't hurt your precious *ma'am. She's* attacking me."

"You ruined my first supper company, and *he* liked my biscuits."

Daniel went to the door. "I'm goin' out with the chickens. At least I can figure them out."

Neither Hope nor Mike noticed.

"I hope he chokes on your biscuits," Mike continued.

"You're being bullheaded 'bout something, and I won't talk to you till you can talk peaceable." She followed Daniel out, slamming the door so hard that it didn't settle into the latch, but swung in the breeze.

She stalked down the path. Who was he to order her around? "After I went to the trouble of learning to cook, he still doesn't appreciate me." She sat on a log and exchanged her moccasins for the shoes she'd picked up on her way out.

Entertaining Matthew was not her idea of a good time,

but Pearl had said men liked pleasant talk. She'd hoped Mike would enjoy the company. "I ain't no sweet talker," she mumbled. "Mike could have at least helped out with the visiting." Her face hurt from all that smiling. "But no, he took out that dad blasted timepiece of his. Some day I'm goin' ta stomp on that thing. Who cares what time it is? When it's dark you go to bed, and sleep till it's light."

In her agitation, she failed to mark her path, walking pell-mell through the dark woods. When she finally simmered down she knew she was lost. The deep woods surrounded her in blackness where the light of the moon did not penetrate. She looked for a nice spot to sleep. Fallen pine branches had made a bed for her many a time.

Mike was frantic. He'd spent the night looking for Hope and had fallen asleep with his back against the door. He woke when Daniel tried to get in.

"Daniel, she's still out there. Maybe we should go look for her."

Daniel didn't seem overly concerned. "She can take care o' herself. I'm gettin' bread and jam. Want any?"

"She might need help. She could have been attacked by a mountain lion. Or some unprincipled rogue might have taken her away. I wonder if she had her guns with her."

"What's a uh . . . un . . . what you said?"

"Never mind. What if she's lost?"

Daniel looked up from his task and scratched his chest. "Well, you're right there. She cain't find her way around a room with the lantern burnin'."

"How do you know that?"

"I just know."

"That woman can get into more scrapes than any single female I've ever known. She needs a husband to keep her safe from herself."

"She don't want marriage no more. You was right when you said she cheated you."

"How did you know about that?"

"I got ears. 'Sides, she tells me things."

"What does she want? Passage?"

"Naw. She wants the house."

"This house?" Mike reared back in surprise.

"Yep."

That hit him hard. She didn't want *him* at all, but craved the confounded house. His eyes narrowed. Doc had a house, too.

Daniel shook his shoulder to get his attention. "I'd like some coffee. Then ya can tell me what work ya got planned for today."

When Mike realized he had no plans, he made a fist and slammed it against his thigh. His life had become a series of uncontrolled events. "We'll look for her."

"She'll come back now it's daylight. Might wander around some, but she always comes back."

"What can I do?" Mike didn't direct his question to Daniel, but the man looked up from his coffee.

"You still got her pants?"

"Why do you ask?"

"I think she'd be more agreeable to ya if she had 'em back. She were real proud o' them, and don't like to work in dresses."

"Hmmm . . ."

"I'll go feed the stock; then I'll go on up to the claim. You comin'?"

Mike stared out the window. "I'm going to wait a while." Hope wouldn't run away, he realized, she wasn't that type of person. She faced the obstacles in her life. In taking away one of her possessions, he had become an obstacle. She'd be back.

Mike went to the bedroom and dug to the very bottom of the drawer where he kept his own pants. He lifted hers out and placed them on the bed.

Chapter Fourteen

Otis Savage was going to die. It was all that thankless No-Account's fault. She always had put him through hell.

Crossing the Rio Grande had taken several weeks. He'd possessed nothing of value to trade for passage, and the old horse he'd stolen wouldn't go near the water. He'd finally attached himself to a man who agreed to take him to the other side if he'd help him build a raft. For the first time in his life, Otis had had to work to get what he wanted. It put a man out to have to lash boards together.

At last they'd set out on their wobbly craft, the current sweeping them along. Otis had closed his eyes and hugged a log like a long-lost lover. When he'd felt a bump, he'd raised his head to see what new danger had found him. But it was that they'd arrived.

Over the next two weeks he'd stolen and sold just enough to buy a horse that had seen better years. Then he'd set about latching himself onto another fellow, who needed a guide.

On the way through the Guadalupe Pass, they'd come upon a band of Indians. There were no more than ten, and they'd sat their horses, neither attacking nor retreating. Indians were Otis's worst nightmare, and they'd been just a mesa away. He'd hidden behind a rock while his traveling companion shouted dares and curses, shooting randomly in the air.

One of the band had approached to negotiate a trade. Otis had hidden while his cohort haggled with the Indians. For guns and rifles they were told they could buy safe passage. The Indian who'd done the talking told them their greatest threat would be through the pass itself, where bandits had many strongholds.

They'd given up their firearms, grateful for the protection, but awoke the next morning to find they'd been swindled. The Indians had taken not only their weapons, but their horses as well.

Throughout the next several days, forced to walk, they'd hidden at every noise. Otis had woken this morning to the creaking of wagons. "Hey! Sam. There's folks movin' through," he'd said.

Sam had ventured forward for a look. Four wagons ambled along. "Looks like families," said Otis. "Let's follow them."

"Why can't we hitch a ride? My feet are about wore out."

Otis had shaken his head. "We ain't got no money. What's the matter with you?"

They'd talked the matter over while trailing along behind the wagons just out of sight. They'd agreed at last to sneak up on the company after they were asleep and steal their horses, and maybe a rifle or two. Otis had claimed they had a right. "We don't have nothin' 'cause it was took."

But he hadn't figured on a guard, and now Otis found

Thrill to the most sensual, adventure-filled Romances on the market today...

FROM  LOVE SPELL BOOKS

As a home subscriber to the Love Spell Romance Book Club, you'll enjoy the best in today's BRAND-NEW Time Travel, Futuristic, Legendary Lovers, Perfect Heroes and other genre romance fiction. For five years, Love Spell has brought you the award-winning, high-quality authors you know and love to read. Each Love Spell romance will sweep you away to a world of high adventure...and intimate romance. Discover for yourself all the passion and excitement millions of readers thrill to each and every month.

Save $5.00 Each Time You Buy!

Every other month, the Love Spell Romance Book Club brings you four brand-new titles from Love Spell Books. EACH PACKAGE WILL SAVE YOU AT LEAST $5.00 FROM THE BOOKSTORE PRICE! And you'll never miss a new title with our convenient home delivery service.

Here's how we do it: Each package will carry a FREE 10-DAY EXAMINATION privilege. At the end of that time, if you decide to keep your books, simply pay the low invoice price of $17.96, no shipping or handling charges added. HOME DELIVERY IS ALWAYS FREE. With today's top romance novels selling for $5.99 and higher, our price SAVES YOU AT LEAST $5.00 with each shipment.

AND YOUR FIRST TWO-BOOK SHIP-MENT IS TOTALLY FREE!

IT'S A BARGAIN YOU CAN'T BEAT! A SUPER $11.48 Value!

Love Spell  A Division of Dorchester Publishing Co., Inc.

Get Two Books Totally
FREE —
An $11.48 Value!

▼ Tear Here and Mail Your FREE Book Card Today! ▼

PLEASE RUSH
MY TWO FREE
BOOKS TO ME
RIGHT AWAY!

Love Spell Romance Book Club
P.O. Box 6613
Edison, NJ 08818-6613

AFFIX
STAMP
HERE

himself looking down the barrel of a gun. Yes, he was definitely going to die.

"Hey, Cog, get yourself over here. I just caught us a horse thief," the man behind the gun called.

Cog hurried over, carrying a shuttered lantern. "Anyone with you?" he asked.

True to his nature, Otis Savage showed his yellow streak. "Don't shoot me. The feller I'm with took my money an' made me come along ta steal horses for him." He pointed to the place where Sam hid, waiting for his signal.

"Bring him in," ordered Cog. He doused the lantern.

Otis didn't have much choice with a gun at his head, so he gave a muted clap.

"That's your signal?" asked Cog.

"I conjured that myself," Otis bragged.

"We could hear that six miles away."

"It's just a little snap, like a twig."

"In case you didn't notice, there aren't many twigs around."

That was true. Otis lost his confidence. "Here he comes. But ya better let me go. He'll kill me sure." He felt the rifle press harder.

"What makes you think we won't save him the trouble? You're a low-down horse thief."

"I'm tellin' ya, he made me."

"Shhh," whispered the leader.

"Where are you?" whispered Sam. "It's too blamed dark."

"Over here." Otis's voice cracked with fear.

Someone lit the lantern, and the prospective horse thief was surrounded. Three men and four boys, all well armed, closed ranks, so there was no place to run. Their women and children stayed in the wagons.

"You a horse thief?" the man holding the gun asked Sam. "This man says you are."

"I'm tellin' ya, he made me help him. I'm on your side," whined Otis.

Sam looked at him as if he were mad. "Why, you no good liar!"

"We'll sort this out come morning. You look like you could stand a little rest."

"Tie him to a wagon wheel," ordered Cog, pointing to Otis.

"I cain't sleep sittin' up-like. Don't let *him* near me," Otis said, looking fearfully at his former partner.

"Don't worry. He won't get to you. And you can't sneak away."

Throughout the night he heard the shouts of his previous partner echoing off the rocks. When they released him he asked, "What'd ya do with him?" Cog led him to the edge of a cliff, where they had sent Sam down on a rope.

After that, Otis thought he'd travel in style in one of the wagons, but soon found he'd be expected to shoulder some of the work, including replacing a broken axle. *It's that No-Account's fault, he thought. She'll pay for this.*

They released him in Tucson with a few coins, and things got better when he found someone who remembered seeing Slow. Four days later he was on his way to Coldbottom.

Hope came home close to noon. After she got her bearings she realized how far she'd wandered from home. Daniel and Mike were probably working on the claim.

She went to the bedroom for a change of clothing, and she found her pants. Hugging them to her, she felt a glow inside her. Mike had apologized. Maybe not in words, but she understood his gesture. "I'll do him proud and be the best preacher's wife he ever saw." Mike was a kind, thoughtful man, and she wanted to keep him for herself. She looked into the mirror and sighed at what she saw.

"No, Pearl is for him. I'm just an uneducated mountain girl."

Mike's claim had to be rebuilt, and he hoped the weather would hold until they finished. The work had helped take his mind off Hope. She'd be at home when they finished their day. He'd never prayed for his own gain, but this morning he'd prayed as he'd never prayed before—for her safekeeping.

"Here comes Mrs. Mike," shouted Barney from his stake, which was nearby.

Mike looked up. Hope came up the hill looking like an angel in a yellow linsey-woolsey dress. She carried a basket with her.

"Good day, gentlemen," she called.

Mike threw his shovel aside and went to meet her. "You're back." He took the basket from her. "What's this?"

"I fixed a picnic. We never had one."

Daniel came running. "Ma'am. I told him you'd be back."

"She brought lunch, Daniel. We can save the jerky for another day."

The three of them sat on a blanket she'd brought. Pearl had shown her how to pack a picnic when they'd been getting the box lunches she said. She told them how she'd spent the night, but Mike barely heard a word she said. Oh, how he wanted this woman who made every day an adventure!

When Daniel finished he said, "I'm goin' back to work on that last piece, Mike. Then we'll be ready for winter."

"I'm going to walk with Hope. I'll be along."

When he turned back to Hope, she had repacked the basket. "Do you feel like taking a little stroll?"

"If you tell me what it is, I'll try it."

Mike chuckled. "It means a walk."

She took his arm. "Thank you. I do believe I could use a walk."

"I want you to be happy. Sometimes I'm not very good at showing it." He looked over at her, a little anxious.

"You showed me—and I appreciate your trust."

He knew to what she was referring. "It took a while, but I realized those pants meant a lot to you."

"You might think about going home soon. Those clouds yonder look like a real storm is brewing."

"They do look ominous."

Suddenly the ground beneath them trembled. Daniel had finished shoring up the claim and looked around. "What's happenin', Mike?"

Someone shouted, "Earthquake!" Then the mountain split in two.

"Mike! Look out!" Those were the last words Hope spoke before he saw her slide past him over a ledge. When the dust cleared there was a large shelf of rock a foot away from where Mike and Daniel stood.

"Where is she? Hope! Answer me."

"She's down below on the next ledge," Barney shouted from where he stood.

"Hope," Mike lay down to see over the edge of the mountain. His heart sank as he looked down to where she lay far below. Backing up, he shook his head. No! he thought. He went to look again, despite his vertigo. He had to conquer his fear. "Hope!" he shouted.

There was no movement at all. Her stillness frightened him more than the nausea he experienced.

"She be daid." Daniel whimpered, wringing his hands.

"Hope, answer me!"

Four men joined them on the ledge.

Mike backed away. He couldn't save her. He feared heights more than he feared God. Thoughts of being stranded, crying in that tree all those years ago, held him captive. "Someone bring her out," he begged.

"Not me," said Barney's partner. "I'm too young to die."

Mike looked at each impassive face.

"I'll go, Mike," said Daniel. He had tears in his eyes.

Mike looked down, and swallowing, he made a decision. "I'll need you up here to pull her up. I'm going down." Mike found a coil of rope that hadn't been completely buried in the quake and sudden slide. "Could I borrow your mule?" he asked.

The owner of the animal, a man named Dubb, who was Barney's partner, spit out a chaw. "What's it worth to ya?"

Stunned, Mike said, "There's a woman down there. We've got to help her."

"I ain't gotta do a lick in this world that don't suit me." He turned away.

"Twenty dollars." Mike's voice was rough with anger.

Dubb patted the mule's back. "Good strong mule like this is worth more. I might lose it."

"Fifty."

Dubb raised his eyes to the sky, but Mike heard a moan from below. "Forget the mule. I'm going down there. Daniel, you hold the rope while I climb down."

Daniel wiped his eyes. "That shelf slants in, Mike. Ain't no place ta put yer feet."

Mike made a sling from his shirt. "When I tell you, pull her up. Then throw the rope back down for me." His hands shook as he tied the rope around his waist, and he prayed as he'd never prayed before. Fear had to be put aside. Hope needed him.

"Hold on there," said the newly interested mule owner, "I didn't say yes or no, yet."

"Make up your damn mind."

"Ya got the fifty on ya?"

"No. I'll get it for you later. Come on, Daniel, we can't waste time."

"All right." He led his mule over. "I want my money, though."

Mike took the end of the rope from Daniel and tied it around the mule with a bitter thank-you to the man. Grasping the rope, Mike went over the edge. Inch by inch, his feet dangling, they let him down. He gritted out the Lord's Prayer, so he could concentrate more on the descent than that his arms felt as if they would come out of their sockets.

Now he could see Hope more clearly on the shelf, close to the edge. She saw him coming and got to her knees. She was alive!

"Stay where you are. Don't get up," he shouted.

She crumpled. "I hurt my arm."

"Don't worry; we'll get you out." Sweat slicked his hands, rolled into his eyes. The sun gave way to clouds while he descended.

At last his feet touched the shelf. His stomach clenched. The rain had washed away this side of the mountain though he'd thought he'd built his claim far enough away from the edge. He hadn't figured on this quake.

"Get back," he shouted to the others. "It's pretty unstable up there. Daniel, move the mule away from the edge."

Hope tried to rise.

"Be still, my love. Which arm did you injure?"

"I think it's just twisted."

Mike ran his hand along her left arm. There were no breaks, but her forearm was at an odd angle.

A drop of rain touched his head, then another. He tied his shirt sling into a seat, fixing it around her like a swing, then tied it to the rope. "Can you hold on with just one arm?"

Hope nodded.

Though he knew she was in pain, she bore it without a sound.

He gave the order to pull her up. The rain had picked

up, and more of the underside of the ledge above crumbled from the weight of the straining rope.

Above him, Daniel lay flat, arms extended to help guide the rope.

"It's breakin' off, Mike," he called.

"She's almost there. Can you see her yet?"

"I got her," Daniel shouted as he pulled her over the edge. "Sis, are ya all right?"

"I have a twisted arm. Don't cry, Slow." She wiped his tears when he lifted her from the sling. "Go get Mike. That whole side is going to break."

Daniel lay flat again, ready to throw the rope, when he felt it go slack. He looked behind him.

"What did ya untie the rope for?"

"I only lent my mule for one. For him I want fifty more."

"Throw it down." Mike called into the increasing downpour. "Is something wrong?"

The rope appeared from above. Hope's clear voice came to him over the sound of the rain. "There's nothing wrong. Come on up, Mike."

He secured himself, and with a quick prayer he began his climb. Arms aching, hands raw, he kept his eyes up, his own fear forgotten in his anxiety for Hope. A remarkable scene met him when Daniel brought him over the top.

Hope lay in the mud her gun aimed at Barney's partner. Slowly she returned the weapon to her pocket. "Now you can take your darn mule, and don't expect Mike to pay you."

"But I helped get you up like he asked."

"You ain't . . . aren't too smart. How'd you expect to get paid if you left him down there?"

Mike looked him over, figuring out what had happened. "Get out of here, or I might fire that gun for her." Turning his attention to Hope, he wrapped his shirt

215

around her shoulders to protect her, then lifted her. "Let's go, Daniel."

"Is she goin' ta be all right?"

"I'll be fine, Daniel." Her voice was weak. Though she wanted to demand Mike put her down, she liked the feeling of being carried. In her entire life Hope couldn't remember a time when anybody had carried her. Not once. Ma, Pa, her sisters—nobody. She fell asleep like that, cradled close to his heart.

Hope awoke when Mike lowered her onto the bed. She lay atop an old horse blanket. "Where . . . ?"

"Do you think you can get out of those muddy clothes and into a nightgown? I sent Daniel for Doc."

"We don't need Matthew. All you have to do is give it a yank. The bones are twisted." Hope swayed when she stood. "Oh, my. I need my sack."

"You need to get out of those clothes and get to bed."

"I am not going to bed for a little twist."

"Well, at least get out of those wet clothes. Pile them on the blanket and I'll take the whole mess to the barn. Do you need my help?"

"I can undress myself."

It sounded as if Mike shut the door a little harder than necessary when he left the room. Hope soon realized she could have used his help.

It took a while to cover herself. She called for Mike, then dug in her bag for salve.

She had fashioned a toga of sorts to leave free her damaged arm. Mike had come, but stood immobile at the door.

"Come on over. Don't stand there gawkin'."

He obeyed, not taking his eyes off her.

"What you have to do is stand about there." She indicated where she meant with her good hand. "Now take hold of my hand and give it a hard pull, till you hear a snap."

"I can't do that. I might hurt you."

"Of course it'll hurt. But there's no sense paying Matthew for what we can fix ourselves."

Mike took her hand, raising it, but stopped when she winced.

Annoyed, Hope said, "Go on. Get it over with."

Hearing footsteps on the porch decided him. Doc wouldn't see Hope's bared arm and shoulder, or his own name wasn't Mike Mulgrew. He braced himself and gave a hard pull. A pop-crunch sounded; then the bones settled into place. Hope must have been holding her breath, because she let out a gusty sigh.

"Good," she said, lowering herself to the edge of the bed.

Mike closed the bedroom door before Daniel and Doc entered the front room. "How does it feel, my dear Hope?" he asked.

Her heart picked up its beat at the endearment before she answered. "Tolerable. It'll need to be tied against me for a couple of days. Go in the chest and get that hide belt I wear. That'll do it."

"Hope, you need to rest. You also need your face washed." This last he said with a smile.

"I might have known you'd think about that before anything else." She let out a throaty laugh. A knock at the door got his attention.

"Mike?" It was Matthew.

"Just a minute, Doc." He pulled back the quilt and lifted Hope into the center of the bed. Looping a shawl over her shoulder, he made sure that nothing more than elbow to fingertips was uncovered.

"What are you doing?"

"I won't have you exposed to him."

"He's a doctor. He's probably seen more body parts

217

than you can think about. I'll bet he's even pulled babies out."

Mike shook his head and opened the door. "Thanks for coming, McBride, but I took care of it."

"In that case, I definitely want to have a look."

The last thing Hope needed right now was a fight. "The bones were twisted, Matthew."

Doc pulled a chair to the side of the bed and ran practiced fingers over the length of Hope's forearm. She winced.

"You're hurting her; leave off it, Doc." Mike's hand tugged the blanket back into place before Doc could reveal any more of her arm.

"It'll be a little sore for a couple of days, Hope. I'll give you some laudanum for the pain." He opened his leather bag to withdraw a small bottle.

"I don't need it. I got my own, but I surely would like to see your doctor satchel."

He placed it beside her and used his arm to lever her into a sitting position so she could inspect it.

"Don't sit up, Hope," warned Mike.

Doc and Hope looked at him. Doc said, "You're being overprotective, Mike." He went back to showing her his bag.

Hope liked the way it opened, leaving the contents in full view. The equipment, too, took her fancy. "This is a darn sight better than my sack. What's *this* for?" she asked, pulling out a dangling thing.

"It's called a stethoscope. Here." He put an end to his chest and beckoned her to put her ear to the other end. "You can hear my heartbeat."

Her eyes lit up. "I can! Mike, I can hear it! You try."

Mike grudgingly leaned his ear to the instrument. "Well, I'll be. You actually *have* a heart."

"Mike Mulgrew, you apologize to Matthew right this minute! That was a mean thing to say."

"Never mind, I'm used to remarks like that, though they're usually about my drinking." Doc put the stethoscope away, closing his bag.

"Parson should know better."

Mike moved away. "She's right. Sorry, Doc."

"Where's Daniel?" Hope asked.

"Praying at the church. He's afraid you're going to die."

Apparently satisfied, Matthew stood. "I'd better get back to town. Every time it rains someone needs a doctor." He took out a handkerchief and wiped his forehead.

"Mike, go make Doc some coffee and something to eat. Come to think of it, I'm hungry, too. And call outside for Daniel. He'll hear you."

When Mike looked about to object, Hope admonished him. "We all need nourishment. It would be unkind to turn Matthew out without offering him something. He had come all the way out here in the rain." The preacher nodded and went out into the front room.

When Hope heard the door to the cold cellar open, she whispered, "Matthew, are you craving the drink?"

"A little. But I won't go back to it. I swear I won't, Hope."

"See my sack on the writing table over there? Bring it here."

He did, then propped her up again while she awkwardly sifted through the contents. "This dadblasted arm holder is getting in my way." She pulled out a small cloth sack. "Here it is. You got a piece of paper I can put powders in?"

Matthew pulled a tiny envelope from his pocket. "Will this do? It's what I use to dispense pills."

"It surely will. Beats folding paper around powders. You put a few grains of this on your tongue when the craving gets bad. It tastes vile, so you might want to have something to eat soon as you take it."

He dipped a fingertip into the powder and tasted it. He made a face. "You're right; it's bitter. Here, let me tighten that for you." He reached around her to readjust the sling.

Mike came in with a tray at that precise moment. "The food is . . . " He stopped. "Get your damn hands off her."

Chapter Fifteen

Doc looked over his shoulder. "Something wrong, Parson?"

"You're practically crawling into bed with her."

"I adjusted the sling." Matthew slid his right hand down her arm, lingering at the elbow.

"Is it necessary to get that close?" Mike moved the lamp and put the tray down with a clatter.

"You forget, Mulgrew, I'm a doctor."

"I don't care what you are, and she's not your patient. *I'm* taking care of her."

Hope followed the exchange with her eyes. "You two are like a couple of tomcats."

Doc stood up. "Are you telling me that I can't see to her well-being?"

"I'm telling you to keep your hands to yourself."

"I wouldn't treat her as anything less than a lady."

"She's not a lady."

Hope struggled to her knees, incensed. "Well, I'm trying to be. You sure ain't a gentleman, Mike Mulgrew."

Mike felt the sting of her chastisement. He had insulted her. The tension left his body. "You're right. I should think before I speak."

Doc, being closer, helped her back into a semireclining position.

Mike hurried to the other side of the bed, knocking away Matthew's hands in a show of plumping the pillows. "Go eat, Doc. Coffee and food are on the table."

Hope tried to swing her legs over the edge of the bed.

"Stay there," Mike said, putting the tray he had brought in on her lap.

"What's this?"

He tucked a napkin under her chin and handed her a quarter of the sandwich. "You haven't eaten in hours."

Her mouth fell open. "You want me to eat in the bed?"

"For a couple of days, until you can move your arm more freely."

"Get this dad blamed tray off me. I think you're plain brainsick."

"You're staying right there."

She'd managed to push the tray aside and sit up, her shawl dipping lower than Mike liked—at least with Matthew around. "I'm eatin' at the table." Hope struggled to get out of bed.

"You can't go in there like that. Daniel and Matthew will see you."

Her brows drew together in a frown. "What's that got to do with anything? They're standing right here."

Mike looked up. Daniel had backed out the door, while Matthew stood there smiling broadly.

"It's not ladylike to sit at the table in your nightclothes."

"You said I'm not a lady." Napkin still tucked under her chin, shawl dangling, she gave the appearance of a rumpled child. "And I ain't in nightclothes. It's a blanket, or didn't you notice?"

222

Mike caught the end of the wrap and retied it over her bosom, removing the napkin.

"Thank you," she said raising her chin a notch.

When she disappeared into the other room, Mike sat on the bed, his hands clamped between his legs. He didn't like this one bit. Not the way the blood thundered in his ears when he thought she'd been hurt, nor the way she'd felt so right when he'd carried her home. He could hear the clank of pewter and plates in the kitchen, yet he remained on the bed.

The taint of garlic no longer assaulted his nose when he held her near. Instead she carried the fragrance of flowers, sage and berries. Hope had worked hard beside him and Daniel, yet she was more woman than he'd ever encountered. Oh, yes, he'd noticed that. How could he not?

He liked the way she'd fallen asleep while he carried her home, her lashes spiked from the rain that continued to fall. A barely discernible bump at the bridge of her nose caused him to ache to kiss it.

Surely he wasn't falling in love with Hope. It was only when he was being silly that he prayed he could actually marry her. A clergyman needed a demure, quiet wife, one to keep his house and life orderly. Hope Savage would never be passive. It must be lust, he thought. He was much too sensible to fall in love.

He heard them laughing in the kitchen. Hope called out, "Mike, are you going to get in here and say the blessing? We're hungry."

"Show me the way, Father." He carried the tray back to the kitchen.

After Doc went home, Mike helped Hope to the rocking chair while he washed dishes.

Daniel brought a kitten to her from the barn. "I thought you'd like somethin' small to keep you company."

"You always know just what I need." She held it in her lap, singing a mountain song in her off-key voice. Hope fell asleep while Mike sat at the table.

Daniel played with the kitten near Hope's feet. This was too much like a family for comfort.

Mike cleared his throat. "What do you and she do in the woods on Sunday?" The question had been eating at him for some time.

"I cain't tell ya, Mike. She'd skin me alive."

Mike got up from the table to pace. "You know more about her than you're telling. Are you her lover?"

Not looking up from his carving, Daniel said, "*You* told her to keep away from the church, and we do."

Mike squatted next to him. "I'll bet you know what she does in Coldbottom."

"Yep."

"Does she go in every day?"

"Not anymore. Sometimes she eats with Mrs. Pearl."

Mike got up. This wasn't as easy as he'd thought. The usually talkative Daniel was keeping Hope's secrets. He decided to try another approach.

"You look after her?"

The block of wood began to take on the shape of a bird. Daniel seemed to think a long time before he answered. "She don't think she needs protectin', but I feel danger comin' her way."

"Is she afraid of something?"

"Naw. She ain't scared o' nothin'. Fact is, she don't believe me when I say Pa's comin' for her."

"Pa? You mean her no-good father?"

Daniel sneaked a glance at his dozing sister.

"Yep, *her* pa."

Hope turned her head and began to rock again. She'd heard the tail end of that conversation. She startled both of them when she spoke. "I told you, Pa's got no guts. He won't come this far. He wouldn't walk to the creek if he was dying of thirst. Seems to me you're asking the wrong person, Mike."

To her brother she said, "Why don't you take the kitty up to the loft? You won't mind, will you, Mike?"

Mike shook his head. "You can keep him in the house if you like. He might keep some of the rats out of the cellar." The happy Daniel scrambled up to the loft.

"Now, Parson, if you have questions, you can ask me. I reckon you were trying to trick the boy."

Mike had stopped his pacing and leaned against the fireplace. "You're right. What *do* you do all day Sunday?"

"I go to the woods."

"With Daniel."

"Most of the time. We get along, him and me."

"Do you love him?" Mike held his breath.

"The Bible says we should love all folks," she said. What was he getting at?

"He thinks he needs to protect you. How could he ever imagine your father is coming? That sounds like a close bond between two people."

"Don't know about bonds." Hope rose awkwardly to go to the cold-cellar door.

"What do you need? I'll get it."

"I'm wanting some chocolate milk before I go to bed." She sank into the rocking chair again.

Hurrying down from the loft, Daniel sat at the table with her.

"Did anybody ever tell you that you have a talent for knowing when there's food around?" Mike asked Daniel with a smile.

"Sis always did. I'll go to bed soon as I get my milk."

Mike looked up. "You just mentioned a sister. Do you remember something?"

Daniel opened his mouth to speak, but nothing came out.

"Looks like it just popped out of his head to me," offered Hope.

"It did, it surely did."

"Hope, how often do you go to Coldbottom?"

"Now and then." She noticed her boots beside the sink, where Mike liked to put them. "I told you I want my boots near the door." They had argued about the location of her boots nearly every day since the rain began. According to Mike, boots belonged near the sink, where they could be cleaned and dried. Hope preferred them near the door so she could get them in a hurry. She left the table, moving the boots to where she preferred.

"Hope, put them back."

"They're my boots, and I want them by the door."

"I nearly tripped over them the other day." He poured the milk into cups, added chocolate, and stirred the fragrant mixture.

When Hope sat again, Mike moved the boots back and continued his questions. "Daniel, what makes you think Hope's in danger?"

The change of subject surprised her.

"I sometimes got the sight."

"Mike, that wasn't fair. You're fuddlin' up his head."

"I want to hear more about this 'sight.' "

Daniel looked at her while chewing a piece of buttered corn bread.

Hope took a long sip from her cup. "Daniel can tell what's going to happen . . . sometimes. He got this dream some weeks back that my pa is coming to get me. Pa's scared of his shadow, and there's not a reason in the world for him to risk his neck coming across the country."

"How accurate is this 'sight'?" Mike wasn't about to believe any superstitious ideas, but he wanted to draw Daniel back into the conversation.

"When I get them dreams and feelin's, they almost always happen. Ain't that right, Si—uhm—ma'am?"

"To be fair, I've got to say yes. But Pa isn't like that. You just had a dream, Daniel."

"Did you know each other before coming to Coldbottom?"

"He sat next to me in the wagon."

"Then you knew his name?"

"His name is Daniel."

Mike saw the openmouthed look Daniel gave her. Maybe she wasn't lying, but he had a feeling she was withholding something. He decided to postpone his inquiry. It seemed the deeper he dug, the more the riddle of these two deepened.

He sighed. "Are you ready for bed, Hope? You look tired."

"I'm plumb wore out. Daniel, fetch my sack."

"He can go to bed. I'll take care of you."

Daniel climbed to the loft while Mike brought her bag. She found a small jar. "Here's some salve. Put some of it on my arm."

She loosened the shawl, exposing her arm. Mike's eyes fixed on that alabaster shoulder. A frightening thought leaped into his consciousness. This couldn't be merely a case of desire. Not when his heart accelerated just at the thought of touching her soft skin. Lust didn't explain his reaction to Doc and Daniel, either. "Well?" Her words broke into his thoughts.

"Show me where you want it." He dipped his finger into the pungent stuff. Though she didn't complain, he could tell it hurt. He'd have taken her pain away if he could.

When he had her tucked in, her arm set comfortably, Mike shoveled fuel into the potbelly; then he thought to ask, "Hope, do you have any idea of when your birthday is?"

227

"Birthday . . . ? Oh, you mean my borning time. Ma told me the leaves were turning when she found me, and I was real small. I don't know when, though."

"Can you figure in years about how long you've been with your family?"

"Ma counted from the time of her taking me in. She'd counted seven winters before she snuck off. She's been gone fourteen winters, but I don't know what that makes up to."

"You must be just twenty-one. We'll celebrate next September."

"Why? It's not as if a birthday's like the Fourth of July or Christmas. Anyhow, I don't like celebrations. Men came to Pa's still for Christmas celebrations, and many a family suffered for it. That's why I never wanted them."

"You never had Christmas?"

"I never did, though folks who had Christmas were kind to us. I recall getting knitted gloves from the church once. They kept my hands warm. Some of the children at that school I told you about got candy and such. One girl got a brand-new store-bought coat.

"When we were living in Hog's Holler, Pa and Ma went at each other real bad. Pa believed Christmas was for jollying. That year Ma dumped out all his moonshine. She paid for it hard."

Mike leaned his hip against the dresser, mentally comparing their lives.

He was amazed that Hope never felt deprived.

"There was one time at Granny Tilton's. She had a little pine tree stuck in an old wooden box, right there in the house. She let me help string cranberries for it; then we took bits of yarn and hung them all over that tree.

"Granny gave me an orange and a rag doll. Three licorice whips, too. She told me Christmas was for giving. I had a mind to tell Ma about that, but on the way home I decided to keep it to myself. I didn't want the others to take my treats or my doll. I ate the licorice whips first. When I ate the orange, why, that was the best thing in the world."

"Do you still have the doll?"

"It's in there." She pointed at the chest. "One of the button eyes is missing, so she don't look like much. I gave it a name, too. Baby Nell. Isn't that pretty?"

Mike felt tears sting his eyelids. She found true joy in things he had taken for granted. Every year the Mulgrews had a huge tree, and there were fine, store-bought toys and clothes. After church they sang carols. They dined on the fattest goose his mother could find.

"Oh, my sweet Hope. You've missed so much." He leaned over to kiss her cheek.

His lips drifted to her mouth, and again he felt that jolt of passion as her lips moved softly under his.

She offered her chin and neck, but Mike's cheek brushed the sling. Fearing to cause her pain, he backed away.

"Good night. If you need me in the night, I'll be sleeping outside your door."

"Mike, would you teach me a real prayer like you taught Daniel?"

He cocked his head then knelt at the side of the bed and took her hand. They said the Lord's Prayer together, sentence by sentence.

When they finished Hope added, "And God, thank you for helping Mike and me out of that hole."

Mike's eyes misted at the sweetness of her prayer. He lifted her hand to his lips to kiss her palm, then folded her fingers, like wrapping the kiss in her hand. "Goodnight, my Hope."

Her eyes shone in the lamplight.

Mike felt like he had touched the moon.

* * *

By Friday, Hope had read every book Mike owned, as well as her own Bible. She took the wrap off her arm and flexed it a few times.

"Shouldn't Matthew have a look at that arm before you try to use it?" Mike asked.

She picked up the dictionary. "I'm all fixed up. I've been lifting things every day. Muscles heal better if you work them."

He placed her food before her. "I've got a few errands to run today. Daniel will stay in case you need something."

Hope couldn't believe her luck. The day had dawned sunny and clear, and Mike would be gone for a while. She'd been anxious to practice her draw. If her arm could withstand the recoil of her gun, she would be in Coldbottom tonight. She had things to do.

Daniel sat on a stump while she fired, then fired again. "That's it. We're going to the rat shoot."

It had been six weeks since Hope had begun her crusade to bring people to Mike's church, though she'd been careful that he had never suspected a thing. She'd developed a sound plan. The mishap with her arm had cut into her practice time, but by that night she was ready.

She recalled that very first Friday when she'd walked into the saloon after ten o'clock, and the room had fallen silent. What was Preacher Perfect's wife doing in the saloon late at night? And wearing men's pants to boot?

Harry had taken it upon himself to question her. "Mrs. Mike. Lost your way?"

"Not if this is where I place a wager on the rat-shoot."

She'd heard snickers and one loud bark of laughter.

"I hear anyone can join in the fun," she'd said, her hand in her pocket, her gun cocked.

A fat man with a flat face and a big nose had stepped up to stand near her at the bar. "So, luv, ye're wantin' to sit in the dark with the rats, are ye? Well, ye can start in my tent. I got more rats than anyone, and a nice fat one special for you." He'd made an obscene gesture, not lost on Hope.

To her amusement, he hadn't been able to run fast enough when she shot a hole right between his feet without troubling to remove her gun from her pocket.

"As I was saying, I'd like to wager this nice Colt against getting the men I outshoot to attend church on Sunday."

The room had rumbled with jeers, speculation, and jovial remarks.

Hope had continued, "Who's in charge?"

Harry had pulled out a slate. "Anyone want to go against Mrs. Mike?"

Several men had stepped forward, and one asked if he could inspect the gun. Peering at it, he'd nodded. "Mighty fine firearm, missus. I'll go again' you."

That first night she'd shot thirty-seven rats, getting five new attendees for Sunday. Before she'd gone home, she'd reminded them that they were honor-bound to fulfill their bargain.

One fellow had laughed, and she'd hauled out her gun to send his hat flying. "Any of you who don't show up better keep your eyes open." It had been Dead-Eye Stiles, the best shot in town. He hadn't shot against her yet, because he wouldn't go against her until he saw what she could do. He still hadn't, in fact. Dead-Eye had an aversion to churches.

For each of six weeks Harry'd had a list of claims or homes that had been overrun with rats. Opponents had begun to know she would be there late on Fridays, and each man thought he could be the one to best her.

This was the seventh Friday, and she was glad she didn't have to miss it. She waited for Daniel to climb down from the loft. He appeared only when Mike began to snore.

Together they crept outside. When they entered the saloon, Harry greeted them. "Evening, Mrs. Mike." He handed her a long list. Each miner and prospector, knowing of her injury, believed that tonight he'd be the one to take home her Colt. Hope had no intention of losing.

"The rats must be trying to find a warm place for winter." Hope took the slate, her finger tapping each name.

"Maybe some human rats are looking to take advantage of an injured opponent," Harry said. He looked at each man who'd challenged Hope.

"I see you're at the top of the list, Dead-Eye, and you're putting up your best gold nugget," Hope said with a smile.

"You can't beat me tonight. I feel lucky."

"Well, then, we'd best be starting if we're going to finish before morning."

Hours later, she and Daniel walked the trail home. She smothered a yawn. "It puts a body out to shoot ninety-three of them pests. But I still got my gun." She patted her pocket. "And I have a nice-size nugget for Mike's collection on Sunday."

"You sure do, Sis. That one feller was real put out that he didn't beat ya. He be a mean one, I think."

"He about popped his brain when I picked off three with one shot. You recollect how many he got?"

"I counted seven. Even if he did say eight, you still got him by three."

"Put 'em up." A shadow stepped from the dense brush.

Startled, Hope stopped, then recovered herself. "Morning to you." She deliberately didn't raise her hands.

"I said put yer hands up!"

The man was waving his gun, and Hope realized at once just where she'd seen that particular piece earlier.

"Had a little more liquor, have you?" He had reeked of the stuff when they'd competed, and she had beaten him early in the night. "That's Mr. Stiles, isn't it? For goodness' sake, take that mask off your face."

Stiles reared back, spewing epithets. Finally he got down to business. "I aim to get me that nice Colt. You can give it over or I can shoot you for it."

"We already shot for it." Daniel was slowly moving sideways, while Hope moved back by inches.

"Give it over." He swayed a little.

"Hold on. My damn boot is untied." She squatted, slipping one hand into her boot.

Getting up, she was in a half crouch when she flicked her knife. Since Dead-Eye was obviously drunk, she aimed for his gun. That way he'd lose his hold and nobody would get hurt.

The knife hit as Hope had intended, but everything exploded in chaos.

Matthew McBride bounded from the brush to their right. "Drop it Stiles!"

Behind her, Mike came out shooting into the sky.

Stiles fell to the ground, his arms covering his head, cowering, just before Daniel jumped him.

"What the hell . . . " she yelled. "What's goin' on here?"

Mike reloaded, shouting, "That's what I want to know."

Chapter Sixteen

Recovering her senses, Hope demanded, "Matthew, what are you doing here? Daniel, get off that sneaky varmint." With a disgusted look at her rescuers, she retrieved her knife.

"None of you has a lick of sense. Why, you scared me half out of my wits. I could have hit someone else 'sides this here sore loser. Stiles, I have a mind to turn you over to the sheriff."

He reared back, bug-eyed, when she held her knife to his nose. "Just don't carve me up. I kinda favor my nose."

"Hmph. Get going then, and don't come back." She indicated the path, now visible in the early light.

Mike ranted and incoherently scolded her while waving his gun in her direction, his face red with fury. "He could have killed you. Or worse. He might have had accomplices. You put yourself in harm's way." He stopped to take a breath.

Hope calmly put her knife back into her boot. "Mike, if

you're going to use that gun for pointing, I'd be obliged if you'd empty it. You ever shoot anybody with that firearm?"

Mike looked at her as if she'd lost her sanity. "I know how to use it." He was indignant.

"On people?"

"Well no." He went mute and emptied the chamber.

Daniel said, "I only done what ya taught me. When you look up, I jump on 'im."

"You did fine, except you didn't look out for my knife. You could have been hurt."

"I couldn't see what ya were doin'. I thought ya had ta tie your shoes."

She fixed her eyes on Matthew. "Where'd *you* come from?"

"I had trouble sleeping, so I went for a walk. You passed me in the dark, and I thought you were going to a patient's."

"Where *were* you?" asked Mike. He stood so close she felt breathless. She could almost taste his lips on hers, his . . . But how was she going to explain where she'd been?

Hope sucked in her cheeks, looking up first at Mike, then at Doc. "Daniel, I'm sleepy. Let's get some shut-eye."

With her chin in the air, she found the path. Daniel hurried after her.

Mike and Matthew exchanged glances of disbelief. They'd been ignored.

Mike shouted, "Hope, you get back here. You owe me an explanation."

To drown out his shout of outrage, she began to sing a hymn.

When the men neared the house, she waited on the porch. Like a queen chastising her servants, she said, "I had private business. You ought to be ashamed of yourselves. Especially you, Parson. Now I'm going to bed." With a nod she went into the house.

Matthew broke the silence in her wake. "I need a drink."

"No. I think we both need a swim to cool off. She is the most irrational woman I've ever met." Mike reached inside for two of the three towels he now kept in the kitchen.

Matthew followed him down to the creek. They shed their clothes and plunged into the icy water simultaneously. "Is she always like that?" he asked when they broke the surface.

"Worse. She spouts off worse than my mother ever did." Mike dove again and came up blowing water. "You planning to court her?" They dove again, then went to dry ground. Mike handed one of the towels to Matthew. "She might drive you back to the bottle. There've been times over the last few months that I've thought about having a little something to soothe *my* nerves."

Silent until they'd dressed, they looked each other over and roared with laughter. Mike slapped Doc on the shoulder. "Let's have some coffee. From here on, I'm declaring she's not available."

"Is that so? You're not married yet."

Mike opened the door and motioned his rival in. "You think this morning was bad? Let me tell you about the skunk."

The next afternoon, Mike knew Hope had woken up when he saw her disappear into the church, then come out with something in her arms. She started off into the woods. He was about to follow her when a wagon pulled up. "Parson. I got my pardner here. He be daid."

Not recognizing the man, Mike said, "I don't recall seeing you at church."

"You ain't. Name's Ross Kostalnik. He be Old Dan."

The stench of death reached Mike's nose, alerting him that the corpse was putrefying.

"Smells like he's been dead for some time."

"Our claim is way up yonder. Mud got him two, maybe three days back."

"We'd better put him to rest now," said Mike. "Where do you want him buried?"

"In the boneyard. Ain't got money for a regular place."

Resigned to the fact that he wouldn't be able to catch up to Hope, Mike climbed onto the wagon. It would take half the day to get everything done. The boneyard lay just outside Coldbottom. It was parcel of land that had been stripped of its gold. "Potter's Field" was for those who didn't hit it big.

When they got there, Mike paid for the casket himself. He added a bit of gold dust to pay the grave diggers.

On the walk home Mike practiced what he would say to Hope. He'd also decided to get to the bottom of her disappearance last night. Where had she been until near dawn? Why had Dead-Eye Stiles come after her dead drunk?

His stomach growled. He hoped that she'd be fixing their evening meal.

Because he'd been so uncertain about marrying Hope, he'd allowed her to go along without restrictions. Most of her comings and goings had been without his knowledge. From now on, Hope Savage would go nowhere unless he accompanied her.

The circuit preacher should be along soon, too. He'd settle the matter of their marriage once and for all. No jailhouse union for him. The sheriff might be empowered to join people in wedlock, but Mike wanted his marriage blessed by a man of God. *I'll tell her tonight. That should settle it. If she'll have me.*

Hope wasn't at home. Mike's temper raised a notch as he peeled potatoes. Could she be with Daniel? That jacked up his temper again.

A short time later Daniel came in alone. "It's goin' ta be a cold one. Is supper ready?"

"Hope's not here. Do you know where she might be?"

"Naw. She just went off like she does sometimes."

"It's late, and she was out *last* night." Mike's words were clipped, his eyebrow raised.

"She's where she wants to be." Daniel dove into a plate of corn bread, slathering it with butter.

Mike looked at his watch every few minutes, making several trips to the porch to stare out into the coming darkness. By the time Daniel went to bed, Mike had gone beyond anger to worry. She could have fallen over another cliff. Maybe Stiles had come back for her.

At midnight, Mike got a blanket and fixed himself a place near the front door so he'd know when she came in.

Mike awakened to the savory aroma of sausage, blending with the pungent smell of fresh coffee.

He sat up, momentarily disoriented until he saw Hope's figure at the stove. "Where have you been this time?" he rumbled.

"I was working yestereve. Some things need planting by the light of the moon."

"You were gone all night again." Mike's voice had a rough edge.

"No, sir, I was not. I got home before the snow fell."

"Snow?" Mike peered through the window near the dry sink. "It's too early for snow."

Hope came to stand beside him. "I never liked snow because once it came to the mountains, we didn't get warm till spring. I like looking at it with the stove going and the fireplace blazing at my back."

There it was again. She had a special scent that drew him. He put his arm around her as they watched the still-falling snow. With his arm around her, Mike pulled her into his embrace to inhale more of it.

"I like your eyes, Mike, and I feel so safe with you."
Hope tilted her head back to look into those eyes. "Isn't
the snow pretty?"

Restraint fled. He lowered his lips to taste that little
bump on her nose. "Umm. I like your nose," he whispered, sliding his lips to her cheek. Hope folded into him
to return the kiss. When his tongue traced the outline of
her lips, she opened them to savor him.

They moved together, touching and kissing. Neither of
them heard the knock on the door, or the sound of it
opening.

"Well, I'll be darned. Is that my brother actually kissing a girl?"

Mike broke away, shocked. "Lucas? What are you
doing here?" He strode across the room to embrace his
brother. They pounded each other's backs.

"Who's the lovely lady, Mike?"

"My fiancée, Hope Savage. This is my brother, Lucas."
Mike said.

"How do you do," Hope said in her best ladylike way.

Lucas took her hand, kissing it at the wrist. "I'm
pleased you're joining the family, Hope."

"But I'm not."

Lucas raised an eyebrow, then changed the subject.

"Damn, I didn't know you lived this far out in the
sticks."

"Did I miss a letter?" Mike asked. "I didn't know you
were coming."

"I just decided to take a little trip in one of our new
ships. You know how I like to see the way they handle. A
lot of people want passage, comfortable passage, to gold
country, so I thought, why not visit my brother?"

Hope went to turn the sausages. "You're one of Mike's
brothers? Of course you are. You look just like him. Welcome."

Lucas put his tongue in his cheek. Mike's smile faded

when Lucas said, "Aren't you a soft, pretty sight. I'd like to get to know you, Miss Savage."

"Everybody calls me Hope."

Mike had clamped his mouth into a straight line, while Hope flushed with Lucas's compliment.

"Maybe you didn't hear me. This is my future wife, Hope." His eyes shot sparks.

Lucas folded his arms, feet wide apart, the stance of a man accustomed to the roll of a ship. "Do I sense trouble in paradise?"

"Not that I can't handle."

"Do you live nearby, Miss Savage?"

"I live right here, and I plan to stay. Mike is stubborn. Maybe you can convince him he needs a *proper* wife."

Lucas drew back, grinning. "Oh, you're *im*proper? This gets more interesting by the minute."

"Oh, I ain't— I mean, he sent for me, but doesn't know what to do with me."

"I've been telling him that for years." Humor flashed in Lucas's eyes with the hint at Mike's virginity.

Mike glared at him.

Daniel stamped the snow from his feet as he entered. He stood on the rug at the door, staring. "There's two o' you?"

"Sit down, Daniel; this is Mike's brother, Lucas. He's come for a visit." Hope busied herself placing plates on the table.

Everyone sat but Mike, who stood staring at the plates as if they held worms. Mike knew his brother's ways where women were concerned. Hope needed protection from the likes of Lucas and his honeyed tongue. Worse, even experienced married women worshiped at Lucas's feet. His brother had been the ruin of quite a few young ladies. He loved his brother, but this turn of events was not good at all.

"Mike?" Hope tipped her head to the side, then licked her lips.

Mike sat down at the table. "Are you here for long?" he asked his brother. The words held little welcome, as Mike intended.

"I might stay till spring, if you have room." Lucas tried to pass the platter of eggs, but neither Daniel nor Hope moved to take it. "Aren't you people going to eat?" he asked. "I'm starved."

Mike suddenly realized he hadn't said the blessing. Lucas wouldn't know that, however, because he didn't have a pious bone in his body. *Cool off, Mike. He's your brother.* When he merely said, "Bless this food, Amen," Hope's jaw dropped.

Still, although he was sure that Hope and Daniel couldn't believe their ears, they dug into their meals. Mike picked at his food, leaving the conversation to the others. Lucas would bear watching.

"You'd better hurry up and finish your eggs, Mike. I think we'll have a full church today. And don't forget, Pearl's coming for an early supper. Do you think Doc will still want to ride out?" Hope's eyes glittered with excitement.

Mike wanted to be the cause of her joy. He pushed his plate away. His right hand rubbed his temples. It seemed life continued to sidestep his plans.

"Are you feeling puny?" Hope went to his side to feel his forehead. "You seemed just dandy a little while ago."

His face became scarlet at the memory. "I forgot about church. Lucas, come with me. I have to prepare, and we have some catching up to do." He took his pocket watch out, looked at it, then snapped it shut. "Hope, you and Daniel come over in an hour."

"Are you really letting me go to church today?" Hope's eyes were wide with wonder.

Mike stopped with his hand on the door latch. "Of course you're going."

Lucas looked at him curiously.

"By cracky, Daniel, did you hear that? I gotta clean up and put on one of my Sunday meetin' dresses."

Was she dressing up for church, or for her ride with Matthew? Mike slammed the door on his way out.

True to his promise, Matthew didn't let the light snow keep him away. He showed up driving a closed carriage.

"You brought this just to take me for a ride?" Hope asked.

"A carriage fit for the finest lady in Coldbottom," Matthew responded.

Mike looked as though he had eaten something especially sour, while Daniel danced around, hoping to be asked to ride along.

They headed to the church.

Hope had been right about the crowd. The little church was packed. All eyes were on Hope as she sat between Matthew and Lucas.

The first hymn went well. Nobody could hear Hope over the large crowd. The sermon was a different matter. Mike stopped several times, as if he couldn't remember what he'd planned to say.

He caught a whispered, "Preacher Perfect done forgot his words." A few chortles came from the same direction. Once while playing a hymn, his hands drifted to his lap while he sat looking at the music. Though the larger-than-ever congregation continued singing, Hope raised her voice to cover Mike's lapse—which brought his attention back to the job at hand.

Afterward, an awkward silence fell when Hope picked up the collection plate. She brushed Mike's nuggets onto the lectern and personally took the plate around. When she returned it to him, real coins clanked against gold nuggets of various sizes. Hope took the large nugget she had won from Dead-Eye Stiles from her pocket and dropped it into the plate.

Mike's eyebrows rose. He tugged at his ear and cleared his throat. He seemed in shock.

Zeke Poteet broke the silence. "Parson, I got things ta do today. When can we leave?"

Seeing Mike's shock, Hope left her place between Matthew and Lucas. She stood beside him.

"Mike wants to thank you all for coming. We're much obliged for the alms."

He remained speechless, so she went on. "He's never been one to lack for words. A body could starve till he finishes praying over the food." There was a great deal of laughter at her little joke.

Mike's eyes were locked on the collection plate.

Hope knew he needed time to recover his wits. Leaving his side, she went to the supply room and returned with her precious fiddle. She said a silent prayer that he wouldn't take it away from her.

Necks craned. A fiddler . . . in Coldbottom? He was an awesome thought for music-starved miners.

"I'd like to play you a little song on my fiddle. We can't let you go out of here without a proper thank-you." She placed her instrument under her chin, launching into a rousing rendition of "Turkey in the Straw."

Glancing over, she saw Mike's eyes widen. Meanwhile, folks clapped in time with the music. Grabbing the nearest person, they swung about, stomping their feet in jig steps. They danced their way out of the church until only Mike, Matthew, Daniel, Lucas, and Pearl remained. Hope had slipped into another tune. She played with her eyes closed, composing as she went, putting her heart into the music, sending all she had to the man beside her.

Her eyes snapped open when Mike slammed the collection plate on the piano. "How dare you humiliate me! You turned reverence into a . . . a . . . revival."

She lowered the instrument, cradling it like an infant

while Mike stormed from the church. The other men followed, but Pearl stayed behind.

"I thought he'd been struck dumb." she said. "He didn't say anything. Hell, he didn't even move. Seems like he took leave of his senses." She went to put the instrument away.

Pearl followed her. Hope tenderly wrapped the fiddle in its old flannel blanket, then raised a hand to dash the tears from her cheeks.

"Hope, don't cry. He didn't mean it." Pearl embraced her, smoothing her hair.

"He might make me get rid of my fiddle. I shouldn't have let him know."

"He won't do that. His pride just got a bit bruised."

"Why did I do that, Pearl? I never told a soul 'cept my brother about that fiddle. It's the most wondrous thing I ever owned."

Wiping Hope's tears with her own handkerchief, Pearl said, "Well, I suspect that since all of the territory will know in a few days, you are about to become a most popular young woman. Your brother would be proud of what you did today."

"Daniel's proud about everything I do."

"Daniel? He's your brother?"

More tears flowed. She'd gone and let out the secret. "Mike don't . . . Sorry, I'm forgetting. Mike doesn't know about that, either. It's hard to tell how he'll take that bit of news."

Pearl patted her hand kindly. "That man isn't good with surprises, is he? You might keep that in mind when you marry him."

Silence descended upon the room. "Whatever do you mean? I'm not going to marry Mike. He doesn't want me. Not really. Sometimes I think he does, but then I go and do something stupid. That's why I brought you over." She looked at Pearl expectantly.

Pearl slanted her eyes at Hope. "Are you doing a little matchmaking?"

"You'd be better for him than me. I'm no wife for a preacher."

"Hope, I don't love him."

"That doesn't matter. He's a right fine gentleman. Handsome 'n smart. He smells good, too. In the morning he has some fierce whiskers, but he shaves them off right away. It's hard for him to figure out how to help folks. You could help him."

"You're the bride he sent for."

"Mike deserves better than a gal who has to ask someone to teach her how to dress and eat and such. I can't even talk right when I'm overset." She felt miserable. "I'm much obliged, Pearl, but I'll never fit with him the way he wants."

"And what does he want?"

"Someone nice and proper. Like you. Someone kind and gentle. Sure as summer comes every year."

Taking a seat beside Hope on a packing crate, Pearl folded her hands in her lap and lowered her eyes. "I won't marry again unless it's for love, Hope. My husband and I didn't love each other. There was respect, but very little joy." Pearl looked off into the distance. "We had an easy life. Some might call our marriage idyllic. We were rarely alone. There were parties and balls. When we weren't out we had friends over. Have you ever heard of New York City?"

"You lived *there?*" Hope's eyes shone with awe.

"We did. Stewart came from old money. My father made millions of dollars. Our marriage was an arrangement. I was thrilled to be getting into society. Furs, jewels, friends everywhere, and never a spare moment. But we never kissed." She looked sad. "After a few years with no children, I became restless. I had everything, yet I had nothing. Sometimes I'd watch a couple holding hands, or laughing together in the rain. Stewart and I never did that. I don't even remember the color of Stewart's eyes."

Hope put her hand on Pearl's arm, until the older woman continued. "When he was killed in a carriage accident I felt sad, but not because I'd lost a beloved husband, just a very dear friend. And I felt guilt because I didn't love him."

"You never kissed? Well, I'll tell you right now, Parson gives a right nice buss."

Pearl smiled. "Hope, I think you are in love with Mike. That's why you risked your music."

Chapter Seventeen

Hope got off the crate. "We'd better get over there and feed the men. I left the food cooking while we were gone."

The air outside felt fresh with the new-fallen snow. Their feet crunched along the path to the porch. "Do you love him?" Pearl asked.

"Hell, I don't know nothin' 'bout love. It's a magical word. I don't believe in magic. Folks marry, get babies, work hard, then die."

Pearl took her hand. "In my old world—New York—people married, had a baby or two, then spent the rest of their lives drifting in search of pleasure.

"Once I overheard one of the maids talking about the way her heart fluttered when a certain police policeman greeted her. After they married, she smiled all the time. He would come to the kitchen for lunch every day so they could be together.

"My best friend refused to marry a duke her father had

249

chosen for her. She had fallen in love with a circus clown. Since then, the circus has been her life—her husband and children her pride. She sends me letters filled with excitement. Her life is blessed with more contentment than I've ever known."

"You really never been kissed?" Hope asked while she traced a pattern in the snow with the toe of her boot.

"Oh, yes, I've been kissed. Stilted little kisses in pretense of love. But they weren't real, pulse-pounding, heart-leap-from-your-throat kisses." Silent for a moment, Pearl asked, "Is that how you feel when Mike kisses you?"

Hope had her hand on the latch, and she didn't answer.

"What you feel for your brother, the way you protect him, that's one kind of love." Pearl saw Hope's back stiffen.

"You won't tell about him, will you?" Her words were barely audible. "I've been trying, but things keep getting in the way."

"You know I won't."

"He likes Daniel, but I've waited too long. It's a kind of lie, and Mike hates lies." Hope opened the door to an amazing scene. "What are they doing in there?"

Matthew sat at the table, smiling, while Lucas dunked Mike's head in a bucket of water. He would yank him out, let him take a breath, then plunge him right back in. Water splattered the floor and walls. Daniel skipped around them with glee.

"What in the world?" said Pearl.

"Stop it! You're acting like a couple of scalawag boys," shouted Hope.

Matthew looked in their direction. He raised his coffee cup. "Good afternoon, ladies."

Lucas never looked up. Hope grabbed Daniel by the arm. "Daniel, get the hell up to the loft and behave yourself."

She whirled to face the brothers. "Stop it, I say. What are you trying to do?"

"You had enough, baby brother?" Lucas shouted when he yanked Mike's head out once more.

Mike blew water, shaking his head. "She's ruined me."

His head disappeared back into the bucket.

Hope reached into her pocket and fired her gun into the floor.

Stunned, Lucas let go of Mike.

Mike came out of the water.

Daniel peered from the loft.

Matthew stopped grinning.

Pearl began to place dishes on the table, though she'd stopped momentarily, smiled, and then went on with the job at hand.

"What in tarnation is goin' on here?" Hope asked. She pulled her gun out of her pocket.

"I'm trying to teach my brother a little tolerance."

"Mike, what in blazes is he talkin' about?"

Groping for a towel, Mike shouted, "Hope, I'm tired of your sneaky secrets. You go creeping out two nights in a row, one of which put you in grave danger, I might add. You give no explanation. *No explanation!* God knows what you've been doing."

"I most certainly did tell you. I was planting my medicinals."

"Moonlight planting. Ha! Nobody does that but witches."

"Lucas, why were you dunking him?" Hope asked. "He's not making any sense."

Mike pushed Lucas out of the way, his hair wet, and bristly from rubbing. He continued. "Then you have the nerve to turn my church into a revival tent. I won't have dance music in my church!" His voice gained volume with each word.

"It's God's church, not yourn. You only built it. A little while ago you weren't able to say a sensible word. Someone had to let them folks go home. You always have so much to say—a lot of it good—it plumb ached me to see you standin' there like a jackass."

Mike tossed the towel aside. "Where'd you get that violin, and how long have you been hiding it from me? In my own church. In *my* church!"

"It ain't *your* church. That's your trouble. You're so busy watching out for your reputation and looking down your nose at everybody, you lost sight of what a church is for."

Mike had his mouth open to argue, but closed it.

Hope took over again. "The fiddle's been with me since I was knee-high to a horse. Don't you try to take it from me. I'm goin' to hide it from you 'less you promise."

Pearl interrupted them. "Dinner's ready."

They stopped their argument to look at her. Daniel scrambled down from the loft to join Lucas and Matthew at the table.

"Promise you won't take my fiddle," Hope demanded.

Mike started for the door.

She grabbed her Bible. "Swear."

"What would I do with it?" Mike flung his hands into the air. "Put the Bible away. I promise."

Hope noticed the gun in her hand and moved to put it in her pocket. "Look at what you made me do to my dress. There's a hole in it."

"Nobody told you to go shooting that thing off in the house. Why do you have a gun in your pocket anyway?"

Hope flounced to the table, taking the chair that both Lucas and Matthew vied to hold for her.

Mike changed his direction to join them at the table. Daniel already had his hands folded, eyeing the meat and potatoes.

"You lead the prayer, Daniel. I'm not in a praying mood right now."

"Me? I can make the prayer?"

"Go on, Daniel; you remember it," Hope prompted.

"I got a better one. 'Tain't as long." Closing his eyes, Daniel said, "Bless the mountains, bless the trees, bless the food, and God bless me." He looked up, pride in his eyes. "Let's eat."

Lucas covered his mouth while Matthew took a gulp of coffee.

"You did fine, honey." Hope patted his hand, glaring at Mike, who looked like he might explode.

Throughout the meal, Lucas regaled them with stories of his voyage around the Cape. The subject interested Hope, who couldn't imagine being on the water for so many days. She had enjoyed the river crossings to California.

Mike sulked, barely touching his food.

When they finished, Matthew said to Hope, "Are you ready for that ride now?"

"You still want to take me out?" At Matthew's nod, she rose from the table. "Good. I need to get away from here for a time. Mike can clean up. Might give him time to think on his proud ways."

Matthew held Hope's coat for her. "Lucas, you clean the floor."

"I was planning to take Mrs. Damian for a walk," Lucas said as he handed Pearl into her coat, putting on his own while she tied her bonnet.

"You do that. I'm sure Mike prefers his own company anyway."

Mike didn't answer.

When the door slammed a second time, Mike looked out the window. Lucas and Pearl walked to the path, leaving two sets of footprints to mark their way.

253

His eyes were drawn to the rig, where Doc tucked blankets around Hope. Mike slammed the dish he carried down. A chip flew up, putting a small cut on his right wrist.

Daniel came from the loft. "I'm goin' to go play with the baby cats."

"Go on. I need to be alone."

He needed to be alone, all right. For the last few months his life had become one disaster after another.

Getting a wife hadn't been as simple as he'd planned. Instead of the idyllic life he'd hoped for, every little thing had become a problem to solve.

He wished he'd put her on the first stage out of Cold-bottom, as he had planned, rather than doing the right thing by giving her a home. It had all seemed so simple: put an advertisement in the paper and wait for the wife he expected.

But she'd walked in and gotten under his skin. That galled him. She had bored a hole right in his heart as sure as if she'd fired that doggone gun at it.

The last two days had been torture for him as he'd realized his feelings for her, and the impossibility of a marriage between them. He sighed as he began to scrub the floor, remembering his promise to her. "We *will* marry." She wouldn't be tamed, not in the manner of a conventional preacher's wife. *What am I going to do?* he wondered.

And then there was the little matter of Lucas. "The best lover of all the Mulgrews," they called him. He was smooth with the ladies.

In Seaforth, when Mike was eighteen, he'd fallen in love with a girl he'd thought suited him, a shy, quiet, raven-haired beauty. Unsure of himself, he'd spent many nights loving her from afar. Every man he knew had craved her attention.

Those black eyes danced when she laughed, and that

was what she'd done when Mike had kissed her, too. It had been a short, chaste kiss—his first ever. She'd laughed at him and told him to go to Lucas for kissing lessons. Mike had locked his heart that night and had never planned to open it . . . until Hope had come along with the key: joy. And the more he knew of her, the more he knew that for him Hope *was* joy.

Hope should have enjoyed the carriage ride. Doc turned west, where ice had fallen instead of snow. The trees had a make-believe look, limned by the late-afternoon sun.

Matthew McBride was her first gentleman caller. Considerate, he'd tucked blankets around them. Hot bricks wrapped in rugs warmed their feet.

They chatted about the differences between various methods of healing. Matthew leaned close when she spoke. Why couldn't Mike be this attentive?

The sun gave a fairyland beauty to the scene, yet she found herself wishing the ride would be over. What was she, No-Account Savage, doing in a pretty dress, riding out with a man of some consequence on a Sunday afternoon?

When they were silent, Hope thought about Pearl's words. *Love.* What was love anyway? She looked at Matthew, the square line of his clean-shaven, firm jaw. He had lips fuller than Mike's. His blond facial hair would leave no stubble in the morning. Hope looked at her gloved hands. Hands that ached to touch Mike's hair, or cheek lay in her lap. She had no desire to touch Matthew.

"There it is." Breaking into her thoughts, he said, "I wanted to share this with you. It's one of the most beautiful sights around here." He pulled the carriage to a stop overlooking a mountain stream and waterfall. His hands circled her waist to help her down, so that they might move closer. When she was on her feet before him, he tipped her chin with his finger, claiming her lips in a deep, questing kiss.

Hope tried to kiss him back. Where was the tingling that shot through her at Mike's kiss? Why didn't she want it to go on? Mike's kisses always left her wanting more. Was that what Pearl meant?

"It is a sight," she said, breaking away and looking out over the water. "How did you find it?"

He came up behind her, wrapping his arm around her shoulders. "I like to fish. There are fewer disturbances here than closer to the mines."

"That's a powerful stream to fish in."

"Farther up the mountain is a lake with some of the biggest trout in California. Do you fish?"

"Had to. Sometimes fish was all that went down my gullet for days. I don't like fishing much, though."

"Maybe you need a good rod. There are some fine ones at the mercantile."

"A knife does me right. I saw folks fish with those poles. Seemed a silly way to go at it. They didn't catch much either."

They watched the water gushing along. Hope wanted Matthew to take his arm away. She wanted to go home. Mike might understand about the fiddle if she explained she hadn't stolen it.

She pretended interest in the birds Matthew pointed out.

They seemed to be there forever before he looked at his watch. "Time to start back. It's not easy to find the way in the dark when you're this far out."

For a change she didn't want to break a timepiece.

Matthew sat next to her, tucking them in. The bricks had turned cold.

Searching for conversation, she said, "Mike has one of those watches. I don't much like them."

"As a doctor, I need it to check my patient's pulse."

"Pulse. Is that a doctor word?"

256

"Here." He took her wrist. "The blood creates a rhythm as it passes through here. Sometimes it's too slow or too fast, like after a run or a fright."

Hope placed her fingers on Matthew's pulse. "Why, it's like hearing a heartbeat."

"Exactly." The horses trod carefully back the way they'd come, while the cooling air froze the ground, aided by a chill wind.

The idea of timing a pulse was the first practical reason she'd heard for having a watch. She looked at it closely, questioning him about its use.

As they neared home, she became quiet, hoping the others were off somewhere so that she and Mike might have a quiet conversation. She wondered if he had escorted Pearl home.

Matthew kissed her again when he helped her down. She moved back a little. "Doc, I'm sorry, but I don't know how to kiss you back."

Matthew pulled her close. "It's Mike, isn't it?"

She didn't want to hurt his feelings. "Would you look at that? The house is dark."

Doc climbed back onto the carriage. "Good night, Hope. Thanks for trying." He tipped his hat as the carriage rattled away.

Mike wanted the dark. It suited his melancholy mood, as cleaning the kitchen had allowed him to vent his anger. Lucas and Daniel had returned to Coldbottom with Pearl.

While Mike knew his brother wanted to be alone with the comely window, Pearl had asked Daniel if he wanted to go with them. That was all the encouragement Daniel had needed. It occurred to Mike that Pearl Damian wasn't ready to be alone with the likes of his charming older brother. With Daniel along, Lucas would have to keep his distance.

He heard a carriage approach and went to the window.

257

Though he couldn't hear what the two said, Mike saw Matthew lift Hope down. She raised her hands to wrap Doc's scarf tighter around his neck.

Mike held his breath when Doc covered Hope's hands with his own, lowering his face to hers in a kiss, then wrapping his arms around her. Mike found he was capable of some very unchristian thoughts.

He seated himself so that, when Hope came inside, he could observe her entry without notice.

She looked around the room. "Is anybody home?" she called.

Mike heard the carriage leave. He watched her sit on the stool near the door to take off her boots. She sighed. Still wearing her coat, she slipped into her moccasins.

Mike caught the scents of spruce and pine and fresh snow. It took a moment to realize she carried some of Doc's scent, too.

He was overwhelmed by a powerful need to hold her, to kiss her until no trace of Doc remained. He fought it.

Hope hung her coat and woolen scarf on a peg, then went to the yellow cabinet, where she rubbed her spine up and down against the joined corner. The simple motion fed his desire.

"Why do you do that?" He spoke from his place beside the stove.

Hope jumped. "Mike? I wish you'd stop surprising me. I thought you took Pearl home." She sank into her chair.

"Lucas and Daniel did." He paused. "You haven't answered my question."

"Question? Oh, you mean scratching my back. It itches. Back home I scratched it on a tree trunk."

"Here, sit on the bench. I'll scratch it for you." That might appease his desire to touch her.

"I'd be obliged. Umm, that does feel good." She moved her shoulders to give him better access. "Mike, I'm sorry if I hurt your reputation."

"I'm sorry I embarrassed *you*. You're right. The church is for the people."

Mike noticed she seemed chilled despite her heavy dress. "Where did you go?"

"There's a gorge east of here. It's a pretty spot that Doc favors. Remember that first time you showed me the gorge on the way to Allgood's? You acted like it was too small to concern yourself with."

"I try to stay away from heights."

"You do? I knew someone back home who was afraid of high places."

"I am, too." It was hard to admit his weakness to this invincible woman. He wanted her to think him invincible, too.

"But you climbed down that cliff to get me. Why?"

"Because . . . " He wasn't willing to say it. "Did you enjoy the carriage ride?" He continued to run his hands over her back.

"I'd never been in a carriage. It's about as cold as riding a horse, except it does cut the breeze a little."

He exhaled slowly, then took in another breath and let it out. "Your hair is mussed."

"I think the wind took some of my pins."

He ran his fingers up the back of her neck into the silky mass, pretending to look for pins to remove. It tumbled down until it hung its full length.

Hope shivered.

"You're cold. Let's go over to the fireplace." Mike had to stop scratching her back. They needed to clear the air. "About church—"

"You can give me a scold if you want."

"You did what you thought best."

"Thank you for that." She turned to him, smiling. "You should have seen your face when you got that plate, all heavy and ajingle. You looked like there was a knife on it and you would be carved up for supper."

Mike chuckled. "I was surprised enough by the size of the crowd. When I saw that plate, I just couldn't think."

"You lost part of your sermon, too. And what happened to your piano playing?"

"You're what happened, Hope. I worried all night."

"I told you before, there's no reason to fear for me. Nobody ever did before. Although I like to pretend my real folks went back to find me after Ma and Pa took me away."

Mike felt tears form in his eyes. "Maybe they did. You might have fallen off a wagon, you know." He had trouble keeping his voice even. The necessity of holding her became unbearable.

Her face brightened. "I could have!"

Silence claimed the room for a time while the fire crackled. Outside the wind had picked up, and Mike gave in to his need, pulling her into his arms.

"Mike?"

"Hmm?"

She looked up. She barely came to his chest in her moccasins. Would she resist if he kissed her?

She came willingly, offering her lips, drawing closer to him. They tasted and teased until they were both breathless. Mike wanted—needed—to feel her against his arousal. With no thought of consequences, he carried her to the bedroom.

He placed her on the bed, but the room was too dark. He wanted to see her. Memories of the day he had watched her from the porch overcame his sense of propriety. Her face glowed when he joined her.

Touch. It was something he had never cared to do with any woman. He'd thought he was immune to desire. Hope's womanly fragrance surrounded him. She curled under him, her wonderful hair like a sunburst that ensnared him. Powerful desire locked out his conscience, so that he didn't know when or how he had removed his shirt—and hers.

They floated together, moving as in a tableau. She scraped her nails down his arms, and he lowered his face to kiss her shoulder. "Oh, my love," he whispered. He bared his teeth to slide them from her ear to her breast.

Hope rolled from under him, curling her fingers into his chest hair. On her knees, she leaned into him until they were breast to chest, and Mike groaned. He loved the softness of her skin, and moved to offer her access to his own neck, so that he could revel in the caress of her lips. She surprised him when she ran her tongue around his ear, then dipped inside.

They breathed in gasps. "I love you, Mike." She'd given him her heart with those whispered words. "Show me how a man loves a woman."

He had unfastened his belt, but the kitchen clock chimed and brought him back to the reality of what he was about to do.

"I'm sorry," he said in a gasp. "I didn't mean for this to happen. This isn't right."

"Course it's right," she whispered, coming to her knees to wrap her arms around him. "Men and women are natured this way. I just don't know how, and I need you to show me."

"No." He got off the bed. How could he leave her? How could he not?

"Where are you going?" She followed him.

Mike yanked the table drawer open. "Here, I found a book you didn't read in the attic." He ran into the bedroom for his shirt, tossing her blouse and chemise on top of the book. "Get dressed," he said softly.

"Mike, are you going to take my fiddle away?"

That stopped him. "I brought it into the house so the dampness wouldn't ruin it. It's in the bedroom. Would you play it for me sometime?"

A glorious smile lit her face. "Oh, yes. Where are you going?"

"To the barn."

Physical activity was what he needed. He'd milk the cow.

When he got there, he realized it hadn't been a good idea. Though Hope bore no resemblance to a bovine, his hands on the cow's udder brought everything into focus. And, Lord, his groin ached. Was there something wrong with him?

Leaving the cow, he grabbed a pitchfork and started shoveling hay like mad.

"Parson?"

Mike stood in a rain of hay. He looked up. "Daniel. I thought you and Lucas might stay in town."

"Ya got too much straw down. 'N Lady kicked over her bucket."

"I didn't finish milking her anyway. Where's Lucas?"

"He's helpin' ma'am ta read. She can read real fine out o' that book."

Lucas was with Hope. Mike tossed the pitchfork into a stack of hay on his way to the door. He wouldn't trust his brother for two minutes with any female.

"Parson, could we eat supper? I saw coffee 'n that's all. She be likin' that book too much to leave off it."

Mike left the barn and slammed into the kitchen. Hope and Lucas looked up. "Daniel says he's hungry, and so am I."

Hope had dressed and tied her hair back. Thank heaven for that. If Lucas had seen what he'd seen, well . . . there might be a rift in the Mulgrew family.

She looked up at him. "I'm not hungry. Thank you for the present, Mike. It's wonderful."

Mike hadn't looked at the title when he had found the book. He tilted his head to read the name.

The Taming of the Shrew. Good choice, Mulgrew, he thought. But he wanted to read it with her, not merely to put distance between his brother and Hope, but because he wanted to experience the book with her.

"Lucas." Mike nudged his brother aside. "Why don't you fix the meal. I'll help her."

"I can't cook."

"There's cold chicken downstairs." He gave a cocky grin when he took the place next to Hope.

Lucas put the chicken and some bread out. "You might want to put the book away. I wouldn't want to spill coffee on it."

Mike came off his chair. "Let her read if she wants to."

Lucas grinned.

Hope sighed and put the book aside while Mike washed up.

Though he was hungry, he couldn't eat. Hope kept looking at him, a soft look that he knew he returned. Though Lucas and Daniel carried on a conversation, he didn't hear a word.

Hope picked up the book as soon as she finished eating. Taking it to the rocking chair, she said, "I'm going to read before bed."

Mike looked at his brother. "Have you had enough of California, Lucas?"

"California has possibilities I'd like to explore." He flashed a wolfish grin.

"You'll have to find someplace else to stay then."

"According to Pearl, rooms are hard to come by in Coldbottom."

"Then maybe you can get a tent."

A loud thump drew their attention when Hope slammed the book to the floor. "What in the *hell* did you say?"

"There's no room here for him."

Daniel scooted away.

"He's your brother, for heaven's sake." She advanced on Mike, hands on her hips.

263

"Daniel and I have the loft, and you're in the bedroom."

"Well then, I'll just find *myself* a place to stay. You aren't putting him out."

"I forbid you to leave this house."

"You still got your dander up 'bout me, don't you?" Hope asked.

"Why should I be angry with you?" Mike's tone dripped with sarcasm.

Lucas sat at the table and tipped his chair back.

"The fiddle playin'."

"Actually, no. You had no idea that particular bit of music was inappropriate for church."

"Then you found out about the rat shoot."

Mike narrowed his eyes. "Rat shoot? What rat shoot?"

Chapter Eighteen

"I just *knew* someone would tell you why so many people were in church."

Mike's face turned hard. "Shooting rats had something to do with the attendance?"

Hope licked her lips. With Hope, Mike knew silence was definitely not necessarily golden.

"Explain."

Daniel scrambled to the loft. Lucas's chair came down on all four legs.

"I didn't do anything bad. You said yourself folks wagered on who could kill rats."

"You *wagered* people to church? And what was the nature of your wager? A kiss? Some lucky miner would get a kiss? Or was it more?"

"Mike Mulgrew, you think I promised them a romp?"

Forest green eyes clashed with violet.

Neither blinked until Hope whirled and ran into the bedroom. Mike rubbed his face with both hands. Though she'd slammed the door, he could hear her storming around in there, shouting—not in the soft accent she'd developed, but in her husky mountain jargon.

"This is your fault, you know." Mike leveled the accusation at his brother.

Lucas raised both hands and got up from the chair. "Hey, baby brother, you won't get an argument from me. I'm going to the loft to sleep . . . unless you have an objection."

Mike said, "Go anywhere you want."

"Damn it, Hope," he shouted at the door. "I never know what you're going to come up with next!"

Elsewhere in Coldbottom, Otis Savage shivered in a bedroll he'd swiped from a down-and-out miner. Somewhere nearby was a man who resembled Slow. If he found Slow, he'd find No-Account.

The thin bedroll gave little warmth on the cold ground. He cursed his bad luck. She'd been a plague to him from the first. She needed a good whipping for putting him through all this discomfort.

It began to rain. *Dang it*. He got up and rolled the blanket around his few possessions. A drink of whiskey would taste good about now, but he had no liquor. No money either.

Otis had been sleeping in the livery, but he'd been discovered and kicked out this morning. He piled that onto his growing heap of grievances against No-Account.

This was the third time he'd moved tonight. He climbed onto the porch of a darkened boardinghouse to curl up away from suspicious eyes. The rain came more heavily. He went to sleep wondering where he could steal a pair of shoes.

Rain sheeted the window when Hope awoke. She lay in the cozy bed thinking of Mike with his piss-poor notions.

Telling his brother to leave before he'd had a chance to open his traveling satchel was plain unmannerly. You couldn't throw out kin. What Mike Mulgrew needed was a good scolding.

Her plans for Mike and Pearl didn't seem to be such a good idea. They weren't working, anyways, because Mike had a fuzzyheaded idea that she, Hope, needed protection and that he *had* to marry her.

Pearl had put the words to it, and Hope knew the truth of it. No-Account Savage was lovesick. No-Account could no longer separate herself from Hope. She wanted Mike's love. The house no longer mattered at all, as long as she had him.

She sat on the edge of the bed and caught her reflection in the mirror. The near coupling with Mike the day before had her thinking that marrying him wouldn't be the worst thing in the world, and she was willing to consider it—but he seemed to have a man problem. No matter who he married, he had to get past whatever held him back. This was the fourth time he'd been unable to do what they both so badly wanted.

Back in the hills, men came to Granny Tilton for certain medicines when they couldn't get a rise from their manly parts. Hope knew how to fix it if it was "pintle fever," though after feeling the size of him against her, she doubted he had that particular ailment.

Putting her chin in her hand, she wondered what she could do to help Mike leap the fence. He had dandy particulars. There had to be a way. She sat up straight with the obvious answer. Lizzy could teach her, as Pearl had shown her manners and cooking.

True, the rain would make it uncomfortable to hike into town, but she needed instruction on how to pleasure Mike.

She dressed before going to the kitchen, where Mike had coffee brewing.

"Morning," she said, then went into his arms, kissing the dimple at his chin. She put her heart into that hug, knowing he hadn't expected it.

He awkwardly returned the embrace. "Good morning, Hope." He coughed into his hand. "We need to talk."

She filled two coffee cups. *Uh-oh. Now what?* She carried them to the table, where Mike pushed the sugar bowl in her direction. "Where are the others?" she asked.

"They went to check the creek. The snow melted and it's warmer now."

Hope nodded. "I don't think the rain let up all night. If you're going to squawk at me, get it over with. Daniel gets overset when you yell at me."

"I should apologize. I seem to be constantly caught off guard by what you do."

Caught off guard? She held her cup to savor the aroma much longer than usual. "You should know I wouldn't lie down with a man over a brace of rats. Want to know what I put up for my bet?"

"Daniel told me. He says you're the best shot around. They think you have a 'lucky gun.' "

She positively beamed.

"Hope, I think we should marry soon, and not wait for the circulating preacher. Gossip can get vicious in a small town like Coldbottom. Besides, I have my reputation to consider."

"You paid cash money for a wife, and you should have a wife. Before you say something you'll regret, I have a few things to explain. I just don't know how to say them."

Mike came around the table, where he squatted before her to tip her chin. He kissed her, drawing her off the chair and up into his embrace.

Hope put her arms and legs around him. A small turn to the right and Mike rested her bottom on the table. "Ah, Hope." He sighed into her mouth. Lightning shot through her. They exchanged hot kisses while he stroked her everywhere.

She boldly placed her hand against his trouser-covered hardness. It sure felt perky. Maybe this marriage would work out. While that hand rubbed against him, the other found the buttons on his shirt. She opened several so that she could feel the rough texture of his hair.

Mike groaned when his shirt fell from one shoulder, baring it for her tongue and teeth.

Hope slid down his body onto her toes. "Let's go to bed," she whispered, licking his ear for emphasis.

Predictably, Mike left her arms and went outside. He came back to get his shirt and slicker.

"You got a real problem, Mike, and I aim to fix it," she muttered to his retreating figure.

Frustrated, she found comfort in cooking and soon had breakfast ready. When Lucas, Daniel, and Mike returned, the three men were soaked through. She kept their meals warm while they dried themselves.

Mike took his seat. He wouldn't even look at her.

Lucas hooked his arm around her waist to pull her onto his lap. "Where's that sweet smile?"

"Aren't you full of yourself today." Hope laughed, pushing away from him.

Mike knew Lucas wanted to rile him, and stuffed his mouth with a big bite of biscuit.

His eyes followed each dainty bit of egg that passed between Hope's lips.

Lucas remarked, "Mike, I'm in need of a haircut. Do you know where I can get one?"

"I'll cut your hair, Lucas," Hope said.

"He can cut his own hair," Mike snapped.

"You're testy this morning, little brother. That'd be nice Hope. I never get the back straight."

Mike tugged at his ear. "Don't you have anything better to do?"

"What would you suggest in this downpour?"

"You could make travel plans."

Hope turned stormy eyes on Mike. "You should be more welcoming. Don't pay him mind, Lucas; you can stay as long as you want."

"Thanks, Hope. Maybe I'll stay until spring."

Either Mike's food had no taste, or he'd lost his appetite. He scraped the contents onto the tin plate they kept for the animals.

While Hope trimmed his hair, Lucas spouted compliments. "You have the softest hands, Hope. Why, it's almost sinful the way they make me feel."

Hope slapped him on the shoulder. "Sit still. You're a nothing but a sweet-talker."

The dishes clanged against the dishpan. She knew Mike was looking for a reason to lose his temper. Well, let him, she thought.

"I smell roses. Hope, do you use rose soap?" Lucas took one of her hands and put her wrist to his nose.

Mike snorted. "What you smell is something that's getting pretty deep in here."

At Mike's words, Lucas laughed aloud. "Did you say what I think you said? My, my. You wouldn't be jealous, would you?"

"I'm not jealous. But I won't let you charm her into a compromising situation with your flattery."

Hope moved back. "You're finished, Lucas. Daniel, you're next."

"Aw, Si . . . ma'am, I ain't got enough left ta cut."

She indicated the chair with the scissors, and Daniel sat like a martyr.

Mike dried his hands, coming to lean against the dry sink. "Lucas, why not find a room in Coldbottom?"

"In this weather?"

Hope interrupted their squabbling. "I've got an errand in town myself."

"Oh? May I ask what?"

"You can ask all you want, but I have something to take care of."

"You aren't going anywhere today," Mike said.

Hope brushed Daniel's shoulder. "There you are. All spruced up."

Mike took the broom from the corner to sweep the floor. "Daniel, take Lucas to the barn. You could use a little help, and he's very good at shoveling manure. I need to have a little talk with Hope."

"What did you do that for?" Hope challenged once they were alone.

"You have too many 'somethings.' I mean to find out what they are."

Hope folded her arms, her lips set in a firm line. "I am not telling you my personal business."

"Where did you learn those words?"

"In the dictionary."

"Where do you and Daniel go on Sunday?"

"Away from your church. We wouldn't want to bring you down."

"What do the two of you do all day long?"

"That's between him and me."

"You won't tell me?"

"The time isn't right." She didn't look away.

Mike yanked a chair away from the table and straddled it, his arms folded across the top.

"Tell me about the violin. Why did you keep it hidden?"

"It's mine. I thought you'd take it."

"I wouldn't do that."

"Men take things and sell them."

"Your Pa?"

271

She nodded. "I was going to tell you."

"I'd like to know where you got it, and who taught you to play."

"I found it one day when I was hiding from Pa. He was laying a stropping on Ma. I lit out to hide and found it in a hollow log. I knew it was for making music. I didn't steal it, if that's what you're thinking.

"You remember I told you I went anywhere I wanted? After that I went anyplace I could watch a fiddler. Church socials, barn dances, prayer meetings. Then I tried to do what the fiddle players did."

"You taught yourself. I wondered about what you carried in that big sack. Is that the end of your secrets?"

"A gal needs to keep some things to herself."

"So you're not going to tell me about you and Daniel?"

"I can't risk it right now."

"You don't trust me."

"I know you're a good man, Mike, and I do love you, but it takes a heap of time to learn trust."

"I can't let you go into Coldbottom today."

"You can't stop me. I have some business there."

"Where?"

She pressed her lips together.

Mike sank into a chair, hands folded between his legs. "You can go if you let me take you."

"No."

Lucas came in, Daniel behind him. "They didn't kill each other, Danny boy," said Lucas.

"Will you let them accompany you to town?" Mike asked.

"Long as they don't follow me after that."

"You'll come home before dark, or I'll come after you."

"I will." She left him sitting on the bed while she joined Lucas and Daniel. "Let's get to Coldbottom."

* * *

The road was almost washed out. Daniel was worried. "We ought ta turn back." When the mud sucked at Hope's boots, Lucas helped her navigate the wide runnels. Finally they struggled into the mercantile. "We made it," she shouted over the din created by the rain. "I'll see you later."

She turned to leave, but Lucas stayed her with his hand. "Hope, I doubt we'll make it home tonight. Let's wait until tomorrow. Daniel and I can sleep in the hotel lobby, or over at Doc's, and Pearl would keep you for the night."

"I promised Mike I'd be home before dark, but you can stay if you want."

"I might drop in on the widow this afternoon," Lucas said. "Maybe I'll see you there?"

"My business will take a little time, Lucas."

"Can I come with you, ma'am?" asked Daniel.

She and Daniel had no secrets, but this was different. "Not this time."

Thaddeus came from the back of the store. "What are you folks doing here on a day like this? Mike need something?"

Lucas turned to answer while Hope motioned Daniel to the door.

"Where you goin', Sis?"

"I have business with Miss Lizzy. But you have to do me a favor."

Daniel's eyes widened. "I knew it would be bad. You want me ta tell Mike a lie."

"After I see her, I'm going back to the house."

"But Lucas'll be put out. He said he'd look out for you."

"If you don't tell him, he won't know until tomorrow. You can stay wherever he does."

"Mike'll give me a scold if you get hurt or drowned."

"I have my mind set." She went down the steps, then looked up at him. "This is between us now."

He nodded and went back inside.

* * *

Over warmed wine, Hope had plied Lizzy with questions. She found herself blushing over some of the answers. No-Account Savage thought she knew everything. Hope realized she wasn't as worldly-wise as she'd thought.

She found her way home before the winter dark set in. For the last half hour she'd been walking in sleet.

Taking a deep breath, she opened the door.

Mike looked up when she entered. His face relaxed in a smile of relief. "You're back. I thought the weather might keep you."

She hung her dripping slicker on a peg and took off her boots. "I pledged to be back, and here I am."

With a frown Mike looked at the door. "Where are Daniel and Lucas?"

"In Coldbottom." Hope began to pull the pins from her wet hair.

"They stayed there and let you come home on your own?" Mike's voice rose in disapproval.

"Don't get your balls all knotted up. We have to confabulate, but first I have to get sweet cream from the cellar."

"What for?"

"I'm making a salve."

Mike filled plates for them from the warming oven. Sleet pounded at the house while they ate. Mike caught her looking at him several times. Her eyes caressed him. Though there was no physical contact, he felt himself responding.

"You have some gravy at the corner of your mouth," he said.

She licked it off, holding his gaze. "Mike, did anybody ever tell you you're a right handsome man?"

Mike was so surprised he dropped his spoon.

Hope waited. When he didn't reply, she broke off a

piece of bread, took a bite, then reached across the table to feed him the rest.

It was an intimate gesture that had Mike wondering if he should run or wrap his arms around her to taste her lips. He was tired of fighting his feelings.

"You can't go to the creek tonight. It's slippery out there," she remarked.

Mike's heart slammed in his chest. To calm himself he gathered their leavings, taking them to the cellar, where he rearranged bags and checked crocks. When there was nothing left to do, he went back up the ladder.

Hope sat in her rocking chair, absorbed in her book. She had combed her hair, leaving it dry and shining over her right shoulder.

The busywork had calmed him. He felt in control again. "I think I'll go to bed now, Hope. I'm really tired."

She looked up, putting the book aside. "No wonder. Your shoulders are all bunched up. Take your shirt off and get on the bed. I'll rub the knots out with my new sweet-cream-and-honey salve."

His shoulders did ache. In fact, he ached all over. Surely he had enough self-control to keep his hands off her.

"That sounds good." He self-consciously removed his shirt, rolling his shoulders to relax them. The potbelly stove warmed the room.

She moved the lantern aside, on the nightstand replacing it with several candles. He noticed that the room smelled like lilacs in spring.

"Hope, the candles are nice, and I know this is your room, but I really wish you wouldn't move things around."

The ropes creaked when she climbed onto the bed to straddle him. His muscles bulged with tension. To Mike it seemed she wore nothing, though he glimpsed a flannel sleeve when she dipped into the cream. Her hands slid from the base of his spine up into his hair. He sighed. Hope kneaded his shoulders, soothing the tension away.

Mike closed his eyes while she smoothed and stretched every muscle in his back and shoulders, using long, deep strokes. From his shoulders, she worked his upper arms with the sweet cream mixture, occasionally allowing her hands to glide down his chest, where she applied a bit of friction by letting his nipples feel the slight scrape of a fingernail. He flexed under her.

She dipped her fingers again to smooth his lower arms and hands, riding them out flat with open palms, until her fingers interlaced with his.

Her loosened hair moved with her rhythm. He felt its heavy silkiness slide across his skin. "Don't." He forced the word from his dry throat.

"What?" She swept her hands back to his shoulders to apply gentle pressure with the palms of her hands between his shoulder blades.

He didn't reply. The lines between bliss and torture blurred.

She left his back and he felt bereft, but she'd merely moved to take off his shoes and stockings. "What are you doing?"

"Trying to get you to relax," she whispered. She dipped into the sweet-smelling, sultry-feeling cream again. With strong outward strokes she moved from his lower back to his waist in front. "Let the tension go, Mike." With each circling, her hands lowered until she felt his navel. She applied soft pressure there, meeting her hands at his abdomen, sometimes pulling back with her nails.

With his eyes closed, he could feel himself drifting, waiting for each soothing touch down his back and around his waist. He was oblivious to all else but Hope's hands, until he suddenly became aware that his pants had become unbuttoned. He wanted to object, but he wanted what she administered, even as she gave her attention to his buttocks, smoothing, then scratching. He wanted it. His heart beat quickly, and he would not make her stop because he wanted her.

She leaned over to kiss the back of his neck and across one shoulder. That flowing hair of hers followed the trail blazed by her kisses.

Mike became aware of a humming when she drifted to the bottom of the bed, inching his trousers down while stroking along his muscular legs. The sound began in his head, echoing into his veins. She began to massage his toes and stroke the instep of each foot then—sweet agony—she was sucking his toes while she lazily brushed his legs from his calves to his knees.

"Your body is beautiful, Mike," she murmured from right below his ear.

She lay on top of him, using her feet to glide up and down his legs, creating an erotic abrasion against the hair on his legs.

He seemed exquisitely sensitive to everything, so that when she ran her finger from the back of his neck and around to his lips with the cream, he was ready for her. He took the finger into his mouth to extract every bit of flavor from the digit, his lips and tongue molding, rolling, and curling.

"Off," he begged, and Hope gave him what he wanted, rising from his back to lie beside him, where he enfolded her in his arms. When had she removed her nightgown?

They tasted each other, feeling the stickiness that clung to their bodies. Once when she moved away to suck his ear he said, "Ouch."

"Where?" Anxious deep violet eyes probed his.

He touched his chest. "Sticky."

Some of his hair had come off onto her breasts. They laughed together, lapping at each other like cats.

277

The humming became a roar throughout his body—a tension, a need so fierce he forgot propriety . . . and his vow.

Hope wanted him, too. She could feel Mike, heavy and hard against her stomach. He savored her, behind her ears, inside her elbows, in the hollow of her throat, seeking almost wildly for each sensitive spot.

Surprise widened her eyes when he kissed and licked each breast, working his way in ever smaller circles to the hardened center, teasing the breast. When he suckled, Hope gasped. Inside she reached for something that she didn't recognize, yet rushed toward.

Mike became frantic.

"Let me." Her voice thick with passion, she returned what he had given. He trembled with need at the feel of her lips and tongue upon him.

Desperate, she asked, "How?" grasping at his ready shaft.

He clasped her hand. "Not yet."

He dipped into the salve with his tongue, returning to his exploration of her flesh. Each small sound from the back of her throat fed his desire to give her pleasure. Repeating her movements, he licked and kissed his way to where she tingled so exquisitely. He tugged at her downy covering while he tasted her for the first time, a mere flick, and she dragged at his hair, needing to kiss him, yet needing him there, too. Her reaction pleased him and he tasted more of her.

At Hope's cry, he moved up to take her kiss again, letting her taste herself through him before poising himself before her. The mere feel of her wetness and warmth led him home. He sank slowly into her, only to meet a barrier. "What?" he said, drunk with passion, but the roaring in his brain sluiced through him and silenced his questions.

Her eyes were luminous as she wrapped her legs around him, and he gave in to his desire to thrust beyond, sinking into her.

He stilled for a moment, but she began to move. Mike clasped each of her hands so that their fingers interlaced once more. Instinct led them. He retreated, then thrust back deep and slow, and then again, until he was conscious of everything: her eyes, and the lips he wanted to taste forever, and the feel of her, tight and warm, moving with him to . . . where?

He needed to kiss her, and she had anticipated that too. Releasing her hands from his, she ran her fingers through his hair to pull him close. When their lips touched, Mike felt an explosion, a sweet release that went on and on.

Hope saw his aura when he threw his head back with a shout of sheer joy. His dazzling gold light entered her own spirit, filling her until it burst into a million shiny pieces.

They lay like that, drifting. Mike smoothed her hair back away from her face to gain access to her mouth. "You purr," he whispered against her lips.

"You hum," she said when the kiss ended. She cuddled into him.

"Hope, there's something you should know," he whispered into her hair. "I think I'm in love with you."

She smiled. "I think we're in heaven."

They lay facing each other on their sides, still joined. "I love the feel of you." She moved her hips, nuzzling his neck.

Mike was amazed when he felt himself growing within her. They gave to each other once more, then drifted to sleep.

Mike woke first. They had not broken their contact through the night, and he needed her again. What was it about her that drew him?

Everything. She made him human, not the paragon he had tried to be. He kissed her rosy mouth. She had fallen asleep with her lips raised for his kiss. The Hope of his life lay in his arms, and he had ruined her.

He wanted her so badly, one last time, but even as she came awake, ready for him, he withdrew.

"Mike?" She wore only the flush of sleep and satisfied woman. Coming to her knees, she said, "Come back to bed."

"We can't do this. I can't."

With a raised eyebrow, she remarked, "Oh, yes, you can. And very well, too, though I'd like a little more practice, if you're up to it."

He looked at the window. "Damn. Everything is covered with ice."

She left the bed. "Is something wrong?"

He stood at the dresser, buttoning his pants. When he reached for his shirt Hope slipped her arms into it. "Now you will always have me in your arms."

"You don't understand. I have done the unthinkable. I want to marry *you,* Hope. But I never wanted to take advantage of you. Last night was . . . last night. I'll stay away from you until we're married."

She flew at him, his shirt billowing to expose her. "You don't understand. You can't ruin someone who wants to be ruined. And it was a mighty fine coupling. There's no shame in that. Mike, I know love now. You gave me a wondrous gift."

He wrapped his arms around her. "Don't make this harder than it is. What I did was wrong. As soon as some of this ice melts we'll go to Sheriff Stably."

"Why?" Pressing herself against him, she wanted just one more loving before letting the real world intrude. "Come to bed," she said.

Setting her away from himself, he said, "No. I had a personal code of conduct. This is the first time I've broken the rules, and I am so sorry, my Hope."

She jumped into the bed, pulling the quilt around her. "I give up. Just when I think you have all your parts workin', you quit. After last night, I *know* you ain't ailin'."

He had picked another shirt from his drawer and inserted one arm. "Why would you think that?"

"Well, you look healthy enough. God knows your kisses leave me weak. We got that itch folks talk about, but you ain't willin' ta scratch it." She had come to stand close enough that temptation surrounded him. The essence of honey and their coupling filled his senses.

He took a deep gulp of air. It was time for honesty. "Hope, I love you. I've never felt this way about a woman in my life. With my love comes the responsibility of keeping you safe. Even from myself. *Especially* from myself."

"This is a bothering thing to me. I didn't want protection. It's a natural thing, what we done, and I wanted you to be the one to do it. That's why I went to Lizzy. I thought you had a 'man problem.' "

"You told Lizzy *what*?" He had passed through the bedroom doorway and turned back, hoping she'd say she was "funning" him.

Hope ignored him. "I'm going back to bed. Saving me from yourself. Harrumph! I never heard such nonsense. Close the door when you leave. There's a draft blowing at the candles."

Chapter Nineteen

Mike stormed back into the room. What did you tell Lizzy?" He loomed over her. "Lizzy who?"

She stepped up to him so that her nose nearly touched his chin. "She ain't got a last name that I know."

"You mean *Lizzy?* What right did you have to discuss me with her?"

Hope's slender forefinger stabbed into his chest. "I ain't got a ma I can ask about your . . . your . . ." She tried again. "Every time we get going, you go running off. So I asked Lizzy to give me a lesson."

Mike gaped at her, walked out, then turned back.

She slammed the bedroom door in his face. In his face! "You open that door right now. I told you not to go near that place. Then you sneak behind my back to tell that . . . that woman I have a . . . 'man problem?' " Hope didn't answer. This was an outrage; that was what it was. Everyone in Coldbottom would think him impotent. "Hope, open this damn door. I have a few things to say to you."

283

"I don't have to open the door. I expect they can hear you over on the next mountain—even with that storm outside," she shouted back at him. "And stop swearing in the house."

He continued his diatribe with no response from her. Mike stopped pacing. In the face of this disaster, he could hear her in there tuning her fiddle.

He opened the door. Eyes closed, she sat on the floor playing an agitated tune.

"Hope."

She lowered the bow. "Are you going to tell me I can't play my fiddle?"

"Why should I? You seem to do whatever pleases you anyway. I would like to discuss this situation."

"I'll talk to you about it when you stop speaking short with me. For now, playing my fiddle settles me."

Mike went to the main room to stand by the fire. Every nerve in his overly lustful body screamed with unsatisfied tension. He couldn't form a coherent thought.

Hope continued to play. Mike sat on the edge of the rocking chair. After a time, a subtle change in tune and cadence soothed him. The music took another turn and he felt some more of his tension drain away.

He sat back in the chair listening. Her music calmed his soul, leading him to drift into sleep. He awoke later to find she had gone to bed, not bothering to close the door.

The bedroom stove burned low. He stepped across the threshold to add more wood. Before he left the room, he crossed to the bed. She had one arm flung over her head, partially uncovering her. Mike tucked the blankets around her. A wave of tenderness overcame him. He wanted to lie down next to her, wrap his arms around her, protect her. *That's the trouble. I want to treat her like a fine conservatory lily—but she's as strong and lovely as the wildflowers that survive the worst weather to awaken at the first warmth of spring.*

284

* * *

Ice covered the trees when Hope awakened. She dressed, then went to the kitchen, where she found Mike had started the fires. Fresh coffee sat on the warming shelf. "He must have gone to feed the animals," she muttered.

She cooked a light meal. Mike came in, bringing with him a gust of frosty air. "I don't think they'll make it back today," he said.

"It looks like it might be hard traveling weather. Breakfast is ready. What time is it?" She smiled at him. "All that loving has made me hungry." He ignored her comment.

"Past one. I'm pretty hungry myself."

She swept the floor and cleaned a little. Her indoor herbs needed watering. Then she claimed her book, leaving him to work on his lists.

After a while she asked, "Mike, why are you so all-fired overset about last night? I can understand about the Lizzy part, but I didn't have anyone else to ask." She chuckled. "It took a heap of washing to get that stickiness off."

Mike surprised her when he returned her smile. Though he didn't answer, he continued to look at her, his longing obvious.

"I love you," she said. "That's the whole of it, straight and true. But you don't have to marry me. I'm just a back mountain girl."

His eyes turned an almost black shade of green.

"Ah, Hope. Now that I know what real loving is, I couldn't be with anybody but you." He rose from his chair to take her in his arms, all his plans for discipline gone. They made love for hours on a blanket before the fireplace. Mike needed this day; somehow he would make her accept his proposal.

"Hope," he said later. They had spent the day in each other's arms.

"Hmm?"

"I'll help you plant *next to the house* next spring."

"Uh huh."

Doc had gone to Butter Creek. A note tacked to his unlocked door explained that a boardinghouse had collapsed and he was needed there.

Lucas and Daniel knew they couldn't make it home yet, so they built a fire and hunkered down to wait out the weather.

A knock interrupted their dominoes game on the second day. The day had brought rain warm enough to melt some of the ice.

Lucas answered the door. "Good day," he said to the sodden girl. Come out of the rain."

"Lizzy sent me for Doc."

"He's gone," answered Daniel.

The girl began to sob.

"Maybe someone else can help." Lucas turned his hands palms up.

"Scrawny Sal is bad. She's smelling putrid."

"Ma'am was lookin' after her some. We could go get her," offered Daniel. He knew this girl, and patted her shoulder in an effort to calm her. "Don't you cry, Miss Raven. We'll bring ma'am."

Lucas looked at the window. "I don't know. Those roads are washed out, and there's ice underneath."

Raven's tears increased.

Daniel had seen this pretty girl in town. He didn't want her overset. "Hush now, Miss Raven. If he won't go, I will."

"But what if she can't come? Sal might die."

"Ma'am says we're all goin' to die sooner or later," Daniel said. "Miss Sal's been sick for a long time."

He tugged his coat and slicker on. "Are you comin', Lucas?"

286

"I think it might be best if I did. An accident to one man might not be discovered for days. Go see if we can rent a mule."

Raven offered her hand to Daniel. "You're the nicest fella I ever come to know."

Daniel took her hand, not knowing what to do with it. He blushed scarlet.

They were exhausted when they finally arrived at the parsonage. Mike and Hope looked up in surprise when they entered. "I thought you had more sense than to travel in this, Lucas," Mike said grouchily. He hadn't expected them, and resented their intrusion into the idyllic world he had allowed himself to believe in.

Hope dropped her book. "Something's wrong."

"Miss Lizzy sent for Doc. Scrawny Sal took bad."

"I'll get my things."

"You can't chance it, Hope. Let Doc take care of her."

"Ma'am, poor Miss Raven was cryin' her eyes out."

"Please, Hope. I beg you to stay here."

"I'm obliged to help her if I can."

"I can't let you go."

"You got something on your mind. Spit it out."

"Scrawny Sal works for Lizzy. Even I know that."

Hope lifted an eyebrow. "And that means she isn't worth the services of a healing man or woman?"

"Lizzy's a . . . er . . . " He cleared his throat and tried again. "You know what Lizzy is. I don't want you to go back there."

"We'd better settle something right now. If I decide to jump the broom with you, that won't give you the right to order me around. I'll go where I'm needed."

"Jump the broom?"

"Get hitched. You told me you wanted to get married." Hope felt a little stab of fear. Maybe he'd changed his

287

mind. After yesterday, how could she not marry Mike?

"I won't have you consorting with women like that."

His words slammed into her. "Someone needs me. Doesn't make a never mind where she lives."

"I forbid you to go to that . . . that . . . "

"Whorehouse," she supplied, stepping past him to retrieve her sack. Checking the contents, she took out a pouch. "Here. Put a pinch of this in some milk or water. You look like you might take a fit."

Hope tied her sack, then went for her boots.

"I'll bet Doc's drunk again." Mike had turned surly.

"Doc's in Butter Creek. There's been an accident," Lucas offered.

"You're pure mean today, Mike. Scrawny Sal's belly's got a lump in it the size of a punkin. She's wasting away." Hope said, then looked at them. "You two sit and rest. I can go by myself."

Daniel jumped up. "I'll take ya."

Mike shot an angry look in her direction. "You're putting yourself in danger."

"We brought a mule ya can ride back on," Daniel offered.

"I'll take her," Mike said.

"I said I'm goin' with ya," Daniel insisted. "Miss Raven needs someone ta look after her. She be grievin' powerful."

"Hear that, Preacher Perfect? He has more care for the human soul than you've ever had. Come on, Daniel."

That galled him. Mike put on his rain gear, determined to see her safely to Coldbottom.

Hope took the trail without complaint, as she had when Jeb Landry had needed her. The rain had turned frigid again, weighing them down with ice, yet she moved the mule forward.

When they arrived in town, she asked, "I don't suppose you're goin' up the hill with us, Mike?"

"You know I can't. I'll be at Doc's if you need a preacher."

"Will you come if she dies?" Her eyes bored into his.

"I'll arrange for a coffin to be sent up."

"I don't suppose she's worth a blessing before she's planted."

Mike looked away.

"I thought preachering was for saving souls." She turned the mule toward the hill dominated by Miss Lizzy's Establishment for Gentlemen.

Scrawny Sal wouldn't see another day. Hope knew it when she entered the room. She had spent many a night awaiting the angel of death, never tiring of the silver-white glow that suffused the room as the time for passing drew near. Sal's own light had faded.

Hope kept her comfortable with a potion of honey and ground poppy seeds.

During the deathwatch, she thought about her feelings for Mike. She knew that she loved him. In many ways she felt the same toward Mike as she did for her brother. But there was more. Contentment and energy filled her when she was with Mike, even at the angry times. Making love with him had seemed so right.

He'd said he wanted to protect her from himself. She'd never heard of such a thing. Nobody had ever tried to care for her. Hope wanted to be loved and cared for, but she wanted to keep her freedom.

She'd done her best to be accommodating. Heck, she even wore the confounded dresses he bought, *and* she washed every day. The time had come for Mike to make some changes.

She awakened from a light sleep to Sal's weak voice calling for Mrs. Mike. Going to the bed, she took Sal's cold hand and brushed the matted hair from her forehead. "I'm here."

"Look behind the mirror," Sal said softly.

There, held by a drop of candle wax, she found a folded sheet of paper. "Do you want this note?"

Sal nodded, closing her eyes. Her fingers curled around the paper when Hope put it into her hand. "I have a sister—and a younger brother, Jason. He hated me for telling our father about his drinking and gambling. Gloria sided with him. I left home . . . ended up here." A tear ran down her cheek to her neck. She closed her eyes, lips set in a straight line.

Hope waited.

"Mrs. Mike, take it . . . to her."

Hope had to lean in to hear. "I'll put it in the mail for you. I need an address, though."

Sal licked her parched lips. "You take this . . . to her. Sacramento. Look on the back. I was a fool. Tell her I'm so sorry. Love her."

Hope took the paper. "Don't worry yourself none. It's as good as done." She watched as Sal's light was absorbed into the blazing light of peace.

Hope went for Lizzy, then wrote a note for Mike. She was finished here, but she couldn't go home.

"What does she mean, 'Send me some clothes'?" Mike roared at Daniel. He'd not wanted to be seen near Lizzy's, so he'd dropped Hope off a few doors downhill. His anger had intensified when Daniel came back with the message. The note said only that she wasn't coming back right now, and would he please send her some clothes, hairbrushes, and other personal items. She'd even asked him to send her book. She wanted her book. Not him. "Where's she staying?"

"Miss Lizzy let her have Sal's room."

"What?" Mike's nostrils flared. Suspicion wormed its way into his thoughts. "And where are you staying, Daniel?"

"I be there, too."

"Oh, you are? I can't imagine Lizzy giving up two beds. It would cut into the profits," he said bitterly. "You can tell your precious Hope to come get her own clothes."

"Whatcha mad at me fer? I didn't do nothin'."

"Get out." Mike clenched his hands.

"But she needs some duds. She be goin' away."

Mike had gripped Daniel's arm to haul him to the door. He stopped. "Going away? Where?"

"Sacramento."

Furious, Mike stormed to the bedroom. He yanked clothes from the trunk. His voice dripping with sarcasm, he asked, "Will she need underwear?" as he jammed her things into a straw suitcase.

"Travelin' clothes, 'n her workin' pants, she said."

Mike heaved the case at Daniel. "Tell her I said good riddance."

Daniel hurried out, wanting to get as far away from Mike as possible. "He's a real hothead. Just like Sis."

The weather had cleared considerably, and Otis Savage again took up the search for his two ungrateful children. As usual, folks avoided him if they could. Some went out of their way to do so.

Hope had actually come within touching distance of Otis the day of Sal's death. He sat near the bank where she'd purchased two tickets for Sacramento. But she never looked at Otis, and he didn't recognize her.

Otis was an angry man. He liked to pile on the agony, and he had quite a heavy stack of grievances against his elusive children.

He'd finally uncovered the fact that a man answering Slow's description had been seen in Coldbottom. But nobody offered the information that Slow stayed with the parson.

* * *

With the clearer weather, Mike made some repairs on the barn. Bitter at first, he tried to keep himself occupied, but he needed to feel her presence. He found that she'd left a piece of herself everywhere. The fiddle rested on the dresser, and he often ran his hand over its shiny wood, sometimes strumming the strings. When he slept, he did so in the bed where they had loved each other with such hunger.

A week after she'd gone he went to her herb garden. There he found her spirit in the fragrance of her plants.

"I'm going to Coldbottom," he told Lucas when he went back to the house. "Do you want to come along?"

"I'll walk with you." Lucas knew his brother was hurting. He followed Mike, and catching up he said, "I'll be leaving Coldbottom, little brother."

"Praise the Lord" Mike barked. "Not enough women for you?"

"I have my sights set north. Word has it the logging business needs a permanent, reliable shipping line."

Mike's breath came out in a frosty whoosh. "I didn't exactly welcome you, did I? I apologize."

Lucas put a hand on Mike's shoulder. "Accepted. I know why you've been the way you have. She's got your heart. I can see that."

"What about Pearl? I thought you and she were getting along."

"She's not ready for marriage . . . at least not to me."

"Our family?"

"They thought *you* were crazy. I can only imagine what they'll do when they get my letter."

"When are you leaving?"

"After the weather stabilizes."

They traveled the rest of the way in silence.

Mike went to Allgood's to pay for what Hope had bought; then he looked around in town, not knowing what to do next. Many new tents had been erected since he'd arrived in Coldbottom. He could see children playing. A woman, old before her time, came out with a basin to empty. Two men walked by her on their way to the saloon.

A familiar little boy ran past him, rolling a hoop. He recognized him as Ziganya's grandson. Mike didn't even recall the child's name.

That fact decided him on what he must do. He put his aversion aside and walked into the maze of poverty and hopelessness. If they wouldn't come to him, he would minister to them where they lived.

One by one he visited the tents to bring hope to these desolate people. In his heart, he knew this was what his Hope would do.

Another week of balmy weather passed with him going into town every day. He wondered what could be keeping her in Sacramento for so long.

Hope was having the time of her life. Sacramento teemed with people, and she and Daniel took rooms at a respectable hotel. Since she now planned to marry Mike, she had no qualms about directing the bill for her lodging and any other necessities to him. He deserved it, since he'd filled her satchel with everything but what she needed.

In little more than a day she'd located Sal's sister. The wife of a banker, the woman resided with her family in the finest house Hope had ever seen.

Hope took a deep breath before lifting the door knocker. A pretty maid opened the door. "I'll see if Mrs. Winter is at home. What is your business, please?"

"I have a note from her sister."

The servant took her to the parlor.

Moments later Gloria Winter came to her. "You have a message from Sally?"

Hope took a deep breath. "You look like her."

"We're twins. And you are?"

"Hope Savage. She left this note."

Gloria took the news badly, telling Hope she'd tried to contact Sal to make things right between them. When she asked the particulars of her sister's life and death, Hope glossed over the details, knowing that only heartache would come from revealing the truth.

When Hope rose to leave, Gloria Winter said, "Thank you for coming all this way to deliver the letter. It makes her passing easier to bear. Will you be staying in Sacramento?"

"I didn't give it any thought."

"Stay for a while. I'd like to have you meet my husband and younger brother. We're giving a party tomorrow evening. Please say you'll come."

A party invitation! She'd never been to a party.

"I didn't bring anything but traveling clothes."

"I'll come to your hotel tomorrow morning and we'll have a merry time shopping. I'll take you to my dressmaker."

Hope arrived at the party to find the house ablaze with hundreds of gaslights. Self-conscious, she smoothed her gown. It was fine, and made for a fine lady. She felt like an imposter wearing it. After taking her coat, a man in black announced her at the entry of what he called "the ballroom."

The room was filled with elegantly dressed men and women. Music came from a balcony above.

Gloria took her hand. "I'm so glad you came. This is my husband Randall, and my brother Jason.

"This is the young lady I told you about."

Jason bowed before her. "Will you dance with me, Miss Savage?"

"I don't know how to dance." Hope had no intention of

dancing with the man who'd to her way of thinking, had forced his sister out.

"Just follow my lead." He took her hand.

Ah well, it was just a dance, and Jason seemed to want to palaver. Hope didn't listen . . . she just concentrated on keeping her feet straight.

"How long do you plan to stay?"

"I've finished my business with your sister."

"How kind of you to come personally to tell Gloria of Sally's demise."

What in tarnation is a demise?

"I'd consider it an honor to escort you to some of the attractions in Sacramento."

"You would?"

"There's a lecture on Tuesday afternoon I'm particularly interested in. Would you come with me?"

Now what is a lecture? Being naturally curious, Hope accepted. Before the evening ended, she had invitations to several teas, the symphony, the conservatory, and a sharpshooting display followed by a ball.

Hope loved being the center of attention. For once she was sought after rather than being ridiculed. Several eligible gentlemen besides Jason Aldwin clamored for her attention.

Sal's brother, with his sparkling brown eyes, seemed determined to court her. And Gloria took her shopping every afternoon. Gloria decided Hope needed something different for every occasion.

Hope directed that all bills be sent to Rev. Mike Mulgrew in Coldbottom, California.

Chapter Twenty

Mike found life without Hope increasingly empty despite a rigorous schedule he again followed. He went to Coldbottom daily to bring peace to his troubled people. As a result, the little church gained more worshipers each week. The people were beginning to accept him. It was little satisfaction to Mike, who was filled with remorse for his moral lapses, with caring for his people, and with missing Hope.

His lists lay in the drawer untouched, while he harbored an inner rage that Hope had left him.

Lucas returned from Coldbottom one evening with a stack of mail. He placed the stack on the table. "Mail from Boston," he said.

Mike continued to work on his sermon.

"There are several letters from Sacramento," Lucas said as he dipped stew into bowls for them.

Mike looked up. "Sacramento?" He immediately went for the mail. The top envelope bore the crest of the Nottingham Hotel. He thumbed it open. "It's an invoice. "I might have known!" He threw the letter onto the table and opened another. "First she ruins me; now she's trying to bankrupt me."

"She is?"

"Read it." Mike ripped open the next envelope, then threw it down as well. He tossed them one by one onto the stack. He went to the yellow cabinet, returning with a glass and a bottle.

"When did my sanctimonious brother turn to the bottle?" Lucas asked, in surprise.

"By thunder, she's driving me to drink. Read it. Read them all."

Lucas read the letter and began to laugh. As if he couldn't believe his eyes, he read it aloud.

"Dear Reverend Mulgrew:
Thank you for directing the future Mrs. Mulgrew to our establishment. Enclosed is the bill for lodging for one week for Miss Hope Savage and Mr. Daniel Fox."

Lucas howled with laughter.

"I'm glad you think it's funny," Mike snapped.

Lucas tried a sober face, and, holding the letter up, he remarked, "I see Mr. Fox had quite a few meals. Miss Savage required only breakfast and the occasional noon meal." This started him laughing again.

Mike's temper rose in proportion to his brother's merriment. "It's not funny."

"I see they had separate rooms." Lucas tried for composure and neutral ground.

His usually unflappable brother ripped the letter from Lucas's hand. "Nice of her to think of my reputation."

"Are any of these letters from Hope?" Lucas asked.

"Look at them. Not a word from her. They're from

every business in Sacramento. And she's billing me." He ground out the words.

"Here's one from a dress shop." Lucas whistled. "That's a hefty sum."

Mike took another swig of liquor. One by one he opened them, his hands shaking. "Milliner." He slammed it on the table. "Shoes." *Slam.* "Lingerie." *Slam.*

Lucas hadn't seen Mike this angry in years. The time he'd lost his temper and beat the tar out of Howard Spencer for trying to take advantage of one of their sisters came close. He took the bottle back to the cabinet, capping it. "Hey, Mike, don't take it so hard. Finish your sermon. It'll help you put things into perspective."

"What day is it?"

"Saturday, and you haven't written a thing. If it's anything like the last two Sundays, you'd better have a good one prepared."

"People are filling the church because they're wondering when she's coming back. They know she left town, and that we had a blowup. Even Dead-Eye Stiles comes now, and it isn't because of the wager." Mike pushed the bowl of stew away to make room for him to write.

"I don't think that's it. Your parishioners respect you since you came off your pedestal. As for Dead-Eye, you gave him a wool blanket to roll up in, and a rubber one to keep out the cold."

Mike didn't answer.

"You going to be all right, Mike?"

"I'll be fine. I have a sermon to write."

Among the church attendees that December Sunday was Otis Savage. He'd finally heard that a man of Slow's description worked for the preacher. Otis stood in back so he could view everyone who entered. He was running out of patience, but made up for his disappointment by palming a little off the collection plate when it passed him.

* * *

Tuesday, Mike went to tent town, then stopped to mail a letter to his mother. Hettie Elger looked up when he came in. "Parson. There's mail for you . . . from Sacramento." Mike reared back as if the letter she held under his nose contained a snake. He didn't recognize the return address, but the crude handwriting told him Hope had written.

"Parson?" said an expectant Hettie. She had high hopes he'd open it there.

Instead Mike jammed it into his pocket and left. He didn't hear Hettie call to his back, "Wait! There's more mail."

He marched home in a fury. What was she up to now? What business took her to Sacramento? Daniel *Fox?* He'd bet she made that up. There was some connection between those two.

He put the letter on the table, where he sat glaring at it, half-afraid it might deliver the final break. He told himself, *She'll come back. After all, she left her precious fiddle, so she'll have to come back to get it.* It was all bluster, he knew. She could get some rich man to buy her another. Sacramento teemed with millionaires, he had heard.

Lucas came in from the claim two hours later. "No supper?"

"I'm not hungry."

"Another bill?" He gestured at the unopened letter.

"No."

"Aren't you going to open it?"

Without an answer, Mike took it into the bedroom and closed the door, then sat on the edge of the bed. She'd said trust wasn't easy. He found it impossible. He had told her not to come back, but he couldn't bear it if she did not.

Dear Mike:
I never writ a letter before. Don't worry about me and Daniel. We met some fine folks. They are letting us stay with them, so you won't be getting hotel bills. I needed some close bcaws I bin to fine places. We will keep away from you. Maybe stay the winter. I won't buy no more duds. I am sory I put you out. Thank you kindley.

Hope Savage

Mike clutched the letter in his fist. Someone had definitely taken advantage of her. She wouldn't stay in Sacramento on her own. Not with her dislike of crowds and close quarters.

Guilt washed over him. She was sorry to put him out. A tear slid down his cheek and into the beard he had grown.

He threw a few items into a carpetbag. Hope might give him a fight, but he would bring her back—willing or not. He wanted her here, where she would be safe. Where he could take care of her—and love her.

"Sis, when we goin' home?" Daniel asked.

They were having breakfast in the morning room. Hope often wondered about that name. Gloria had given Daniel a room when Hope had revealed that he was her brother. The two ate early and alone.

"I'm plumb worn out myself. These folks are nice, but they sleep late and stay up all night. It's all backward.

I want ta go home 'n marry Miss Raven, if she'll have me."

"Miss Raven? Marry?" Hope dropped her fork with a clatter.

"I ain't a real smart fella, but I'd be good to her. Don't ya think she'd want me?"

"Of course she'll want you. It's just that I never thought . . . well, I thought we'd always be together."

"When you an' the parson get hitched, well, three in a bed'll be kind o' crowded. What was ya expectin' to do with me?"

"I thought you'd want to stay on. Besides, he doesn't want me back."

"You goin' out again today?"

"Today's the sharpshooting contest. Jason's been talking about it all week. You want to come?"

"Sure do. I seen 'bout all I want to o' this place. Yestereve while you was at that lecture place again, I went to see boxing."

"What's that?"

"Two fellas punch each other till one cain't get up. It were dandy!"

"Doesn't sound dandy to me."

"You goin' to shoot?"

"Maybe. Depends if they let me."

"Then can we go home?"

"I'll have to think about it. I'm tired of Jason buzzing around me like a bee on a flower. He's so damn uppity I want to puke. But it don't seem right to hightail it out of town. I like Gloria. I guess she'd understand, though. Maybe we can write to her." Her eyes sparkled. "And it sure would set Jason back."

The December fifteenth sharpshooting exhibition began the social season for the holiday round of parties.

Hope looked at herself in the mirror. No-Account Savage didn't exist in that reflection. "I want to go home. I'm not me anymore," she mumbled.

Later they traveled in a closed coach to the contest grounds. Jason helped her alight. Hope wanted to leap to the ground.

She scanned the crowd for Daniel, but she'd lost him in

the press. Most of the onlookers stood. Gloria took her arm, chattering about what fun they would have today. They stopped at a canopy where Jason held a chair for her; then he excused himself. "I'm in this competition." He looked down his nose at her with a smile.

"Can I shoot, too?"

Taken by surprise, Jason laughed. "Those guns have a pretty good recoil. Not fit for a lady, my dear." He touched her shoulder with a condescending grin.

That did it! No-Account Savage would rescue her. She would set her scheme in motion this afternoon.

One by one the contenders took a turn at shooting bull's-eyes. Jason and several others were declared winners of the first round.

Gloria leaned toward her. "Jason is an excellent shot. The most difficult part is next. Flying pigeons are difficult to hit."

"Who cleans them for supper?"

"Oh, my dear, you are so amusing." Gloria laughed.

Hope tilted her chin. "If you don't eat them, what do you do with them?"

"Why, I don't know."

The first pigeon was loosed. The slaughter had begun. At each round the shooters took down one each. Two birds were released at the next turn. At the end, Jason downed three. No one challenged him.

Daniel had worked his way to the front of the crowd of working-class men who kept to the back. Hope looked at him, winked, then stood. "I'd like to take you on, Jason."

The shock of the situation quickly became amusement. Men stomped and applauded. Some jeered. Gloria tugged at Hope's skirt.

Jason raised his arms to quiet the amused audience. "We have a guest, a young lady who would like to try. Miss Hope Savage."

Some men sneered.

"I can do it, you know," she said.

Coming to her side, Jason escorted her to the mark. A hush fell.

"Mind if I use your rifle?"

He handed it to her.

"Anyone here got a gun?"

Someone offered her one.

"Swing the target." She held the rifle in her left hand, the pistol in her right. In a blinding flash she hit the bull's-eye twice—dead center. Making sure both of the guns were fully loaded, she shouted, "Now I want to shoot four birds."

Jason walked to her side. "Don't make a fool of yourself," he whispered.

"Make that four birds *and* the swing target. If I hit them all, I want those nice people who are standing in back to have the birds for supper." She hadn't missed the signs of poverty that abounded here in the city.

Silence settled on the crowd. Men coughed. Someone in the back began to applaud. The applause rolled forward until it thundered in her ears.

"Go!" Her guns exploded again to hit all targets. Pigeons fell to the ground. The target swung wildly.

Jason went white.

The ladies rose to leave—except Gloria, who beamed at her. While men pushed forward to congratulate her, Jason stood alone.

Mike hadn't liked the way Jason touched Hope. Mike had started the applause. Close to a group of women, he heard the comments they'd made.

"Disgraceful."

"Shameful."

"Not seemly."

Mike's heart lifted. She'd looked so ladylike, but she was still the same.

304

Mike joined two gentlemen who stood nearby. "Well done," he said. "I must ask her to dance at the ball. I seem to have forgotten the location. So many this year," he said.

A few minutes later, having received the information he sought, he mounted his horse. He needed to find a tailor.

Jason's silence on the return trip gave testimony to his disapproval. Hope beamed. She would be on her way to Coldbottom tomorrow.

She dressed carefully in a twice worn evening gown that revealed creamy shoulders in the style of the day.

At a knock she opened the door. "Jason. Ya shouldn't clamp your jaw so hard. Ya could break a tooth. Whatcha want?" She slipped easily into mountain speech . . . just for him.

"I'd like a word with you."

"Come on in 'n set a spell."

"Not in your *room.*"

She accepted her cape but left her gloves on the dresser. "I don't feel like wearin' gloves tonight."

"I thought we might ride together without Mother and Father."

"I ain't wantin' ta cause talk. And ya can bet I won't frolic with ya." She passed before him into the hallway.

"Frolic. What do you mean?"

"I mean, ya try ta feel my teats an' I'll have ta shoot ya."

"You're not carrying your gun."

"Just my little one." She pulled it out of her bodice. As his eyebrows came together over his pretty nose, Hope felt more like herself than she had in a long time. She'd been so easily seduced by society. Acting out like this made her feel right. She and Jason went downstairs.

Gloria joined them in the front hall. "I like your spunk, Hope. That was more excitement than we've had in years."

Randall Winter huffed uneasily. "You look lovely," he said. He bent to kiss her hand, but stopped when he saw she wore no golves. "Are you in need of new gloves? I would gladly provide them."

"Ain't you a caution," she said, her voice echoing from the walls and ceilings. "Jason wants us to ride separate from you. I don't know why, unless you don't want us along."

Gloria pursed her lips. "I don't know, Hope. Jason? Does this have something to do with this afternoon?"

"Gloria, really!"

Hope ran to the coach and scrambled in; then she chattered about the afternoon's entertainment.

Instead of taking Jason's hand at their destination, Hope pushed it away, lifted her skirts well above her knees, and jumped. "That felt mighty fine. Y'all ought ta try it."

"Hope, I really do wish you would, er, restrain yourself." Jason knitted his eyebrows again.

His sister jabbed her elbow into his chest.

The cool night air didn't make its way into the overcrowded supper room and ballroom.

When announced in the receiving line, Hope stepped up to her hosts to pump the matron's hand. In a voice that could have shattered windows, she said "Howdy do. I'm sure pleased ta meet ya."

Several heads turned her way. When the orchestra struck up, Hope danced without discrimination.

During a short interlude, Jason came to her side. "You should pick your dance partners carefully. Some of them aren't acceptable."

"Don't worry 'bout me," she cried as the music began another round. "You ought to loosen up. Here, this should do the trick." She handed him the glass she'd been drinking from.

Jason tipped the glass to his lips. As Hope left him, she

couldn't resist the urge to watch his reaction, and was delighted to see his eyes tear. She'd been holding a glass of Kentucky whiskey. Pretending to sip it, she'd waited for the opportunity to shock Jason.

Her feet were killing her, and she'd never been so hot in her life. She kicked her shoes off to dance, daringly barefoot.

Three gentlemen were clamoring to escort her to supper when the room went quiet. The orchestra continued to play, but voices hushed. Hope noticed that everyone faced the entry. "What's everyone lookin' at?" She turned. A smile split her face, while her heart leaped into her throat. Mike had come for her. *Oh, happy day!*

He looked elegant in evening clothes—dangerous, with his black hair and crooked smile. Several girls flounced their skirts to gain his attention.

Their host walked to where he stood. "Good evening, sir. Have we met?"

"We have not."

"Ah. You've probably gotten the wrong direction."

"Indeed not. I've come for my promised bride."

The musicians stopped as the conductor dropped his baton. Whispers dwindled to silence.

Hope drifted halfway across the floor. Mike covered the rest of the distance. "May I have this dance?" He pulled her into his arms, nodding to the orchestra. The conductor recovered himself and tapped smartly to signal the beginning of a waltz.

They whirled around the floor. Hope felt as light as air in his arms, unlike the awkwardness she had felt with other partners. She looked into his eyes. "You came for me."

"Did you think I wouldn't?"

"Some. We're not quite promised, you know."

He pulled her closer than was considered proper. "I love you, my Hope."

"You do?"

"Mmmm. I missed you."

"Say it again."

He leaned back a little, eyes twinkling, "I missed you."

She brazenly kissed his jaw. "No. The other."

"I love you. Will you come back to Coldbottom and marry me?"

"What if I want to stay here?"

"I saw how you were misbehaving today. You wanted to be asked to leave."

"How'd you know?"

"Because I watched you. You brought No-Account out to shock them."

Someone tapped on Mike's shoulder. "See here. Miss Savage made no mention of a fiancée."

"Nobody asked, Jason. This is Mike Mulgrew. We been livin' together out by Coldbottom." She batted her eyelashes at Mike.

Jason backed away.

Several women, who'd heard, gasped. "One of those women from gold country."

"Will you leave with me?" Mike whispered into her ear.

"Try to leave without me 'n I'll strip naked."

"You're outrageous."

"I know."

He took her arm to lead her to the entrance. Gloria waited at the door. "Hope, why didn't you tell me?"

"I shouldn't have stayed at all. It worried me how to let you down easy."

"I'll have your things sent to you in Coldbottom."

"Are you put out with me?"

"No, you did me a great favor. Thank you."

Jason stood nearby. He muttered, "I can't believe this."

"Jason, shut your mouth," said Gloria. She waved to the departing couple. "Good luck."

* * *

Mike had a coach waiting. As soon as they were inside, he pulled Hope to him for a long, satisfying kiss. Mike kissed and caressed her with deep hunger.

The coach stopped at the Nottingham. Mike rearranged the top of her gown. "Here, let me help you look presentable." He kissed her shoulder before covering it once more.

"Hell, I've never been that anyway." Her hair had tumbled loose. She quickly braided it. There was no way to find her hairpins in the darkened coach.

"Do I look proper?" She giggled while she helped him tuck in his shirt, using the opportunity to touch and caress him. "Mike Mulgrew, you wait till we get inside. We haven't even started yet." Her lips traced his ear.

He touched the tip of her nose, then opened the coach door. He exited first, intending to lift her down in his arms, but she put her hands on his shoulders, letting him take her full weight, sliding down his body.

They walked into the hotel holding hands until he stopped at a door. "This is your room."

She tugged at his hand. He followed her inside, where they shared another round of scorching kisses. He released her with reluctance. She closed her eyes and fell onto her bed.

"Mike?" She opened her eyes when she heard the door open.

He stood in the dim hallway.

"Where are you goin'?"

"My room is next door." He took another key from his pocket. "Lock your door," he said as he closed the door.

"Dadblamed man. He's contrarious. Mike Mulgrew is a low-down tease," she shouted.

A knock on the wall interrupted her tirade. "Hope. Go to bed."

"I ain't got a sleepin' gown."

"I put one on the bed."

She stepped out of her layers of clothing to put the nightgown on.

She couldn't sleep. "Mike?" she called through the wall.

"Hmm?"

"I love you," she said softly.

"I'm glad."

Mike purchased the coach the next day. A married man needed a decent vehicle to carry his wife and family. When he returned, Hope wasn't in her room. He whistled on his way to the dining room. Daniel sat with her. "Howdy, Mike," he called.

"What are you doing here?" He sat opposite Daniel, shaking out his napkin with an angry snap.

"I'm goin' home with ya. Ma'am told me this mornin'."

"You're staying here."

"Ma'am says I can come home."

"Hope?" He looked over at her.

"He needs me."

"What about me?"

"He doesn't have anywhere else to go. Trust me a while longer?" "

Mike sighed. "Hell, Hope, I can't think straight with you around. We'll discuss this later."

She lifted his hand to her lips to plant a kiss on his palm. "I can't wait." Her smile filled him with warmth.

"Before we leave, I want to settle your accounts here in Sacramento."

After breakfast she directed the coachman to one store after another, including a bookseller. It seemed Mike's soon-to-be wife had acquired an appetite for reading. She chose a few more books while there. "Gloria will send the others," she told him.

The warm, sunny day sent them on their way. They spent the night in Placerville, where Mike paid for two rooms. Hope in one, he and Daniel sharing the other. Mike didn't sleep much that night either. His sin of jealousy weighed heavily on his conscience.

The washed-out, frozen roads to Coldbottom weren't easy traveling. When they arrived, Mike paid off the hired coachman; then he took the reins himself.

Hope climbed up to sit next to him. She wanted to let everyone know she had returned, but few people were on the dark, cold streets.

Weary from travel, Mike just wanted to eat and go to bed. As soon as he stopped the rig, Daniel climbed to the roof for their parcels.

"Ain't it purty? There's Lucas. Hey, Lucas. We be back."

Lucas swung Hope off the seat as soon as the coach stopped. "Aren't you a sight for sore eyes."

"Hands off, brother," Mike said as he climbed down.

Lucas clapped him on the back and laughed. "I missed you, too. Supper's ready."

"How'd you know we'd get here today?" asked Hope.

"I made a big pot of stew two days ago. If you hadn't come home today, your forest friends would have dined well."

After dinner Daniel went to the loft.

Mike and Lucas sat at the table, while Hope dozed in the rocker.

"How long did it take to find her?" asked Lucas.

"The first day. I watched her for a couple of days. I still don't know why she went, but she stayed with a prominent family."

"And Daniel?"

"Strange. He kept to the hotel. I can't figure out what's between them."

"Did you ask her?"

"She sidesteps to another subject. I'm going to marry her tomorrow, Lucas. Maybe then she'll tell me about him. I have this feeling that he hasn't forgotten his name at all, and that she knows exactly who he is."

"Mike, there's something you should know. Some rag-tag fellow has been asking around, looking for a man who might be Daniel. I caught him in the woods near the barn the other day."

"Who is he?"

"He didn't say. I escorted him off the property. He said he only wanted what was his. Mean-looking cuss."

"Could he have some claim on Daniel? Let me know if you see him again." Mike went toward Hope. "Thanks for looking after things, Lucas. You're not such a bad brother after all."

Chapter Twenty-one

Hope was not asleep. Lucas's words stupefied her. *Pa's here! I should have listened to Slow.*

Lucas stretched. "I'm for bed, Mike."

"It's been a long week for all of us."

She kept her eyes closed until Mike leaned over to kiss her softly. "Hope. It's time for bed."

"Are you sleeping with me?"

"I'm sleeping upstairs tonight. We can share that bed tomorrow."

She didn't give him an argument. Instead she snuffed the candles and started for the bedroom.

"You didn't disagree."

"Won't do any good. You're stubborn as a mule about some things."

Mike came to where she stood at the bedroom door. Putting his arms around her, he slanted a long, slow kiss on her mouth. "One more night, my Hope; then we'll have the rest of our lives."

"Mike?"

"Yes?"

"If you want me to, I'll learn that damn clock, and if it will make you happy, I'll make a list too."

He held her close. "I just want you to be yourself."

"After the wedding nobody can take me away. I mean, I'm yours for good?"

He pulled her close. "Hope, nobody could take you where you don't want to be. I intend to be such an attentive husband that you won't want to leave the bedroom." He put her away from him. "Sleep well; you'll need it."

She smiled at him and went into the bedroom. Before she slipped into her nightgown she checked her guns. Of course she wouldn't shoot Pa, just scare him.

What could he want? It had to be something important for him to risk his neck. He was the biggest coward ever born.

He couldn't hurt her. Hell, he couldn't *catch* her.

Stop your brain fussin'. My new name may be Hope, but I'm still No-Account Savage, and I'm a heap smarter than Pa.

If she avoided him long enough, he might get gold fever and go up in the hills. That thought cheered her. Maybe he'd come to stake a claim and would leave her alone. Just the same, she'd better warn Daniel.

Before breakfast the next morning, she made for the barn. She didn't have to worry Pa might be watching. The lazy cuss never moved a bone out of bed until he had to.

A cat slipped through her ankles at the barn door. "Daniel?"

"Howdy, Sis. Looks like today's yer weddin' day."

"I sure hope so. Pa's here."

"Naw! You said he wouldn't come. You said he'd be skeered."

"Don't fret yourself. You read the signs right. I'm wondering why he came." Hope sat on the milking stool.

"I cain't force the sight when I want it."

"Go in the corner there and think on it a while. That might do it. We have to know what he wants."

"He wants you, I'm thinkin'." But he went to sit in the hay with his back to her.

She milked the cow and cleaned out the stalls. When he came away he said, "I don't see aught. Could he be comin' ta kill us?"

"He has a lot of bad in him, but he's not the killing kind. Let's go eat." She patted the cow's rump and took the pail.

After breakfast, Mike cleared the table and withdrew his neglected lists from the drawer. He planned the day to the last detail.

"Lucas, you and Daniel go to Coldbottom. Ask Pearl to stand up with Hope as a witness."

"What time do you want us at the church?"

"Two o'clock. Daniel, you take this note to Sheriff Stably. If he can't make it at two, find out when he'll be here."

Mike regretted the lack of fresh flowers, but he intended to gather greens and holly.

"What can I do?" asked Hope.

"It's your day. Do whatever pleases you." He pulled her into his arms and kissed her soundly.

"I always do what pleases me."

Lucas grabbed his hat. "Let's go, Daniel. We want to get these lovebirds married."

"I gotta ask ma'am somethin'." Daniel's fingers worried the brim of his hat. "Ma'am? Can I see ya private?"

"I'll walk along with you a piece. Lucas, would you go ahead?"

Mike glared at Daniel. "What do you have to say to her that's so secret?"

Daniel looked at Hope.

"Don't let him worry you," she said.

Watching them walk arm in arm had Mike biting his lip. He saw her say something, then stand on her toes to kiss him on the cheek.

When she stepped onto the porch, her face shone with joy. "We're getting hitched today, and they're gone for a time." With a leap she had her arms around his neck, legs around his waist, wiggling herself against him. "Let's get an early start."

While she opened his shirt buttons she licked her way along his jaw. His *unyielding* jaw.

She leaned back a little.

His eyes were nearly black with anger.

"Aw, dang blast it. You're still plannin' to wait, ain't ya?"

"How much of a fool do you think I am?" he snapped.

She moved so her feet touched the floor. "What are you talking about?"

"I saw you kiss Daniel. Are you going to continue your affair with the hired hand after we're married?"

"What's an affair? In fact, what's he have to do with you and me? Might be nice if we built him a little place of his own so he doesn't have to live in the loft, though. Tonight I'll tell you a surprise."

Mike spun away from her. "Brazen, aren't you?" he said angrily. "We're on the porch in broad daylight and you conduct yourself like a hussy."

"There you go again. What's 'brazen' mean?"

"Look it up. You can read."

"I don't know what's got your dander up, but you're extra testy of a sudden. It's all this waiting. Your man parts are making your head soft."

"I want to know where Daniel fits in your life."

"I'll tell you tonight. After we say our 'I dos'—so you won't send me back."

"I've a mind to send you back now." Mike's voice carried the edge of self-righteousness.

"Oh, go do your business. You're just being contrarious. I got a good reason to keep quiet for now."

Mike's formidable anger took quite some time to cool. The physical exertion of gathering greens calmed him. When he returned after noon, hauling a makeshift sled filled with fragrant pine, he vowed to trust Hope.

Near the house he thought he saw movement out of the corner of his eye. Could it be the man Lucas had mentioned?

"Hello?" he called. His voice echoed to join the wind creaking through the trees. The weather seemed to be turning. He carried the branches in, glad he and Hope would be married before the next onslaught.

Hope looked up from the book she had been reading. "I baked a cake."

"Chocolate?" His nose gave him the answer. Mike smiled. She loved anything chocolate. Of course, she loved vanilla, too.

"Are you still spoiling?"

"You said you had an explanation. I'll wait for it."

"You will?" She closed the book and put it aside. "The cake didn't slump in the middle this time."

Mike looked at it after piling the evergreens on the floor. "Looks good."

"What's all the trees for?"

"I'm going to decorate the house and the church. I'm sorry there aren't any flowers."

"You don't need flowers to make a wedding. Just two people. Us is all it takes." She ran her fingers over the soft pine. "Thank you for going to the trouble, though."

317

"Why don't you go get dressed while I do this?"

"I am dressed."

"Most women want to wear their prettiest gown for their wedding day."

"Is that so? I brought two with me from Sacramento." She took off her apron and went to the bedroom while Mike began the work of making a wedding.

Daniel lagged behind Lucas, who set a brisk pace on the road to Coldbottom. He constantly looked over his shoulder. He feared Pa. The fact that he could be nearby made Daniel skittish.

Lucas went to Allgood's to find a wedding ring. They agreed to meet an hour later.

Sheriff Stably looked up when Daniel entered. "Mornin' Daniel. Mike got a problem out your way?"

"No, sir. He be wantin' ta marry ma'am today and wants ya to hitch them up."

"I thought they *were* married. We all thought they were married."

"He were waitin' for the ridin' preacher, but he said he cain't wait no more."

Stably let out a loud guffaw. "Is that so? Must be a real problem for a man like Preacher Perfect. Do you have witnesses?"

"Yep. Lucas went ta get Mrs. Pearl. Mike wants the nuptials at two o'clock. Here's a note."

Hettie Elger had found business that needed her attention at a desk close to the corner that housed the jail, so she couldn't help overhearing the conversation. That didn't make her an eavesdropper. The building housed the jail, the post office, and a bank. The men didn't notice her satisfied smile . . . especially at the the word *wedding*.

"Tell Mike I'll be there." The sheriff let out a loud hoot.

Tempted

Hettie asked Fred Barstow to look after things for her. She had an errand to run that took her to the mercantile.

Otis Savage had his foot on the rail at Harry's Saloon when Zeke Poteet came in to spread the news about the parson. "I heard it straight from Hettie. She always gets it right. I'm going to tell the missus." Several men paid for their drinks. This news wouldn't wait. Otis was watching them leave when he saw Slow walk past the window. He gulped down his whiskey to go for the door.

"Pay up, you worthless bag of filth," Harry demanded.

"Aw, crap, I'll pay later."

"Now."

Otis dug in a pocket for a coin and deliberately tossed it in a spittoon.

Furious, Harry brought his gun from under the bar. "Don't come back. Find someone else to cheat." Otis never argued with a shooting iron.

Damn. Slow was gone. He ran up the street hoping to catch a glimpse of his quarry. Slow stood head and shoulders above most men, making him easy to spot. Suddenly his son came out of a house and walked up the hill. Otis followed, ducking behind brush.

When Slow stopped at the whorehouse and knocked on the door, Otis cussed, adding, "I'll be damned. He's goin' fer a jab." It had turned colder but Otis would wait across the street. Where the boy was, the girl would be. He knew he'd find No-Account soon.

While Daniel courted Miss Raven in Lizzy's parlor, a crowd gathered on the east end of town. Preacher Perfect and his lady were tying the knot, and everybody wanted to watch. Word traveled to the mines where men dropped picks, pans, and everything else they were working with at the time. They strode down the mountain.

319

After the ruckus Hope had raised at the earlier weddings, would she be starched up again over the little word *obey?*

Bits of conversation confirmed that most of the townsfolk had thought the pair were already married.

"Ain't she already Mrs. Mike?"

"Guess not."

"By cracky, I want to see this. Might be she'll put him in his place again."

Otis saw the growing crowd. He wondered if there would be a hanging. He didn't like to be foozled 'twixt things. If he followed the crowd, he could pick a few pockets. Turning his brain around the puzzle for a while, he decided to miss the hanging. Slow would bring the better prize.

His feet ached from the cold when he saw Slow emerge from the building, then pass no more than three feet from where he watched.

Scooting from bush to house corner, he followed his son, who took the same path the mob had traveled earlier. Otis had to be careful. Slow looked over his shoulder often. Something had the boy spooked. At an area known as Little Falls, Slow stopped to take a drink from the fresh stream.

There Otis made his move.

Mike had the church decorated when he heard the excited crowd approaching. He had just started down the aisle when the door burst open. People pushed and shoved to get in.

"Afternoon, Parson," said Bart Stoker. "Me and Ada came to see the wedding."

An astonished Mike said, "Surely you didn't all come for that."

Lucas pushed through the crowd. "I'm afraid so, big brother."

"I hope you brought Pearl." Mike pulled at his ear.

"She's with Hope."

"Lucas, come inside."

Mike drew his brother into the storage room. "Why are all these people here? How did they hear about this?"

Sheriff Stably followed them. "I'm here, Parson. What in blasted hell are all those folks out there for?"

The door opened, and Hettie Elger joined the three men. Lucas leaned against the door.

"They found out somehow," said Mike.

"Damn it, Hettie," said Stably. "I'll bet you've been talking again."

Mike spoke with a grin. "You're in church. Watch your language."

Hettie's chin jutted out. "I only told Hester and Alberta. Everyone likes the parson since he lost his uppity ways. I did think it was important for Doc McBride to know, too. After all, he's been courting Mrs. Mike." Hettie got a sly look on her face. "I guess she wasn't Mrs. Mike just then was she?"

"You've got to learn to keep your mouth shut, woman." Stably moved closer to her. "What you need is a husband to keep you busy raising a handful of younguns."

"I don't want a husband."

"Damn right you don't. A man might curb that wagging tongue of yours."

Mike threw up his arms. It seemed he'd lost control of what happened in his own church.

"Oliver Stably, you can't talk to me like that."

"Why not?"

"Because I know where you spend Friday nights."

He stepped back. "Are you threatening me?"

Mike cleared his throat and tugged at his shirt collar.

Lucas spoke into the silence. "Let's get on with this, Mike. It's two o'clock and Pearl wants to be home before dark." He opened the door.

With a sniff, Hettie cast a withering look in Oliver's direction, then made her way to the best seat in the church, the piano bench.

Shy Dahlia Coachman had already taken the bench. Hands poised over the keys, Hettie said, "I was hoping you'd let *me* play piano for your wedding, Parson Mulgrew."

Mike looked at them. "I didn't know either of you could play."

Oliver Stably chortled. "Hettie will play music when she gets her angel wings. Which might never happen. Give her some room, Dahlia."

Hettie sat on the edge of the bench. When Dahlia began a soft melody, Barney shouted, "That's my wife up there."

Mike checked his watch. "Lucas, it's five after. What's taking them so long?"

"Getting anxious, little brother? I think I hear them coming now."

The church was crammed tight as beans in a can. Maybe he should give a sermon to this captive audience. Mike was searching his mind for something uplifting when the door opened. Wind scattered a few leaves inside.

Every head turned.

Hope stood a little behind Pearl, radiant in a gown of rich gold velvet. The gown showed every curve of her petite figure. When had she become so heart-stoppingly beautiful? At least Mike *thought* his heart had stopped, because he couldn't breathe.

He took a slow breath while Dahlia launched into a jubilant processional. Hope smiled and Mike's world shrank. There were only the two of them. He watched her walk toward him.

She wore her hair in a braided coronet twisted with gold ribbon, and in her arms she carried a small bouquet of fragrant herbs from her indoor garden. How had he ever thought her a boy, even in all that dirt?

She put her hand into his, and lightning shot through his body from the contact. *Dear God!* He was aroused in church! It became necessary to move closer to her so that a fold of her gown covered the evidence.

"Your dimple is showing," she whispered.

Sheriff Stably cleared his throat. "Parson wants me to do a reading from the Bible. So you all be quiet. Mrs. Coachman, you can leave off that piano now."

Dahlia's hands fluttered into her lap.

For a change nobody moved or spoke. There was a cough here and there, but Stably read the passages without interruption.

Hope leaned against Mike. "When's the wedding going to commence?"

"Soon," he said in croak. Mike regretted asking for the readings. He wanted to tie this up and get rid of everybody.

"Where's Daniel?" she asked.

"He didn't come with Lucas or Stably."

"I hope he gets here in time."

Mike felt an instant flash of jealousy, but pushed it down. He'd know all tonight. It all came down to trust.

"Hey, Hope, we're all waitin'. Speak up," yelled someone from the back.

Mike smiled. "It's time."

The sheriff waited for her response, but before Hope could reply the door opened once again. "Hope."

She turned. "Matthew. You came. Take a seat."

"Hope, I've been with Ziganya Kalmenos. She's asking for you."

323

"Why? Is she sick?"

"It's that grandson of hers, Christo. Hope, I think it's the whooping cough, and she won't even let me look. It's bad."

Hope started toward where Doc stood at the door. "I'll get my things."

"Don't go." Mike put a hand on her arm.

"I got to go when someone needs me. You know that."

"She's a Gypsy—a fortune-teller, and probably a swindler as well." His blood pounded in his ears.

She stopped at the door. "I'll be back soon as I can."

"I forbid you to go," he whispered. His heart felt as though it had frozen in his chest.

"I'm going."

"If you leave now, I don't ever want to see you again."

She turned to follow Doc.

Chapter Twenty-two

"Well, I'll be." Sheriff Stably rubbed his jaw. The throng sat in silence until someone said, "Parson's lady walked out on him." Suddenly everybody broke for the doors.

Mike stood as if he'd taken root, stone-faced, his jaw like a rock. He wanted to cry . . . howl . . . curse . . . go after her and . . . and what? Apologize? Pride held him immobile.

"That was pretty harsh, don't you think?" Lucas asked.

Hettie slid off the bench. She came to where Mike stood. "She's a good girl, Parson. God doesn't make them any better. You've just bitten off your own nose." Her words, spoken softly, echoed off the walls in her wake. Sheriff Stably left with her.

Mike turned his back to gather holly branches. He clutched them until blood dripped from his hands and Lucas took them away.

"Get out, Lucas."

"Your hands are bleeding. Come home. I'll clean and bandage them."

"Get out!" Mike roared.

Lucas touched Mike's shoulder. "If you need me I'll be at the hotel." His boots clicked on the wooden floor. At the door, he looked back before leaving.

Mike sat on the floor examining his bloody hands. *A fortune-teller. She left with Doc for a fortune-teller.*

A little piece of his heart that still beat reminded him that Hope had always said she had to go where she was needed.

It began to rain, falling like the cold tears he wouldn't allow himself to shed. Mike Mulgrew never wept. Mike Mulgrew would hold his chin up, go about his business, continue with his life. No self-pity for him.

He sat in the church all night while his better judgment gnawed at his stubborn pride. No prayer passed his lips nor entered his heart. What hurt most was what he'd said to her: *Don't come back.* He didn't think he could go on without her.

Hope gathered a nightdress and robe, a change of clothes, her medical sack, and her moccasins. Everything she might possibly need she placed into a "gathering sack," which she'd made from an old sheet. She looked at the bundle, which was far bigger than what she'd brought to Coldbottom.

Matthew stood by the door waiting. He thought he saw the glint of unshed tears.

"I didn't eat, Doc, did you?"

"No."

Hope went down to the cold cellar for cheese and apples.

She wrapped one of the two loaves of bread she'd made earlier.

"I think I'll wear my boots. The weather is turning." She checked to see if the gun in her pocket was loaded, never noticing she was still in her wedding dress.

With her boots on she reached for her parcel. Matthew picked it up. "Hope, I'm sorry. He'll change his mind."

"No, doesn't like to be discommoded. He's too pig-headed for his own good." She grabbed her rifle and led the way to the path.

While Slow drank from the steam, he'd had a powerful vision that Pa watched him from nearby. "Pa?"

Otis had crept up behind him and whacked him on the head with a sturdy branch.

When he regained consciousness, Slow opened his eyes to find two Pas hovering over him. One Pa was bad enough. Two were downright terrifying.

"Wake up, ya ungrateful scalawag." Otis kicked at Daniel's ribs.

His son curled up in a ball, covering his head with his hands. "Nah, Pa. Don't hurt me."

Reprobate that he was, Otis aimed a kick at Slow's private parts. Unfortunately for him, he didn't notice a root near Slow's bottom. His foot slammed against it. With a yell fit to wake the dead, he hopped around holding his injured foot. "Ya made me stove my foot. Yer plain evil ta hurt yer Pa like that," he whined.

Daniel scurried for the shelter of a thornbush. "Why'd ya come fer us? We ain't done nothin' agin' ya."

"I got ya there, boy. You know where that No-Account is, don't ya?" He did a little dance, putting down his injured foot with less force than he would normally have used.

"Cain't tell. Anyhow, ya cain't do a thing 'bout her now 'cause she belongs ta someone else." He looked up at the sky, trying to determine if it was past two. Without the sun to tell him, he used his best guess that Hope and Mike were married.

"What's that ya say?" The rain that had threatened earlier began to fall. "Well, don't this cap it all. Ever'thin's agin' me."

Footsteps slapped along the road and he hobbled to see who was passing. It was a doctor and some uppity lady type.

He scuttled back in time to grab Slow, who was trying to crawl away. "I ain't lettin' ya go so easy, boy. Find us a dry spot."

Daniel decided to go along with him until he could give him the slip. "There be a cave right over here."

It was a small hideout, so that after Pa settled in, there was only room enough left for his large son to crouch with his back exposed to the drumming rain.

"Who has her?"

"She give her hand ta the parson."

Otis leaned forward so that his fetid breath blew in Daniel's face. "Ya mean she's hitched?"

"Yep. Forever 'n ever, amen."

"A parson? That be the parson what lives 'bout a mile yonder?"

Daniel glared at him, refusing to answer.

Otis didn't have enough room to haul off and hit him. "You're butt-deep in a lie, boy. I been watchin' up there."

"I ain't lyin'."

"Then you won't mind moseyin' on over ta give the parson a note."

"A note? You kin write?"

Pa cocked his head.

"I knowed it. Ya cain't. Ha!"

Otis screwed up his face in thought. "Don't get smart with me, boy." He hadn't thought of that. He disliked having to change his plans.

The rain picked up, soaking Daniel. "Can I do my chores whilst you're thinkin'?"

"Trouble is, I cain't cogitate on a empty stomach. Ya bring me some eats, I'll let ya go fer a time."

"I'll bring ya somethin'."

"Liquor too."

"Ain't got no liquor. Got lots o' milk, though."

Otis spit and made a sour face, as if he'd eaten something bad. He squinted his eyes in the failing light. "You come back right soon or I'll go after that preacher with my pigsticker."

Daniel hurried away, anxious to find Hope. She'd know what to do.

The house seemed deserted, with no fire, no lamps lit. "Mike?" He checked the loft. On his way to the barn he noticed the closed, dark church. He lit a lantern, then milked the cow. After he fed the chickens, he spread clean hay.

Finished, he went back to the house for a loaf of bread and some cheese. Daniel changed into dry clothes and put on his boots and slicker.

It would be a long night. Pa and the rain made for some planning. He might as well be as dry as he could.

When he returned to Little Falls, Otis fussed at him. "What took ya so dad blamed long?"

"I told ya. I got chores ta do."

Otis grabbed at the bread as soon as Daniel took it out of its oilcloth wrap. He sank his teeth into it.

"Can I have some? I ain't ate neither."

Pa spoke while he chewed, spewing saliva and bread as he did. "Whyn't ya git yer own?"

"Ya told me ta be quick." Daniel always did as he was told.

"What else ya got?" He took another huge bite.

Holding on to the cheese under his slicker, Daniel made up his mind not to share it. If Pa wouldn't let him have some bread, he'd probably keep everything for himself. "I got milk in a jar."

"Phaw! You can have it."

Daniel slipped the cheese into his pocket for later and lifted the jar to his lips. "I do like milk."

"Well, now I can think proper." Otis leaned back and

closed his eyes. "That bread was pure tasty. Cain't get a handout from a soul in that dang town." He shut his eyes. "Don't go sneakin' off ta your sister like ya did back home. You're my prisoner."

"You thought o' how to write a note yet?"

Daniel got his answer in the form of a snore. He looked around and decided to sleep in the barn. He would be back before Pa woke.

Ziganya Kalmenos's grandson Christo was nearly blue. Hope and Doc passed through the ragged curtain that served as a door. Some of the red letters on the curtain had faded badly, but they still proclaimed FORTUNES TOLD HERE.

Matthew had started a steaming kettle before going in search of Hope.

Ziganya was a true woman of this new country: strong, determined, fearless. But she loved this child. "You have come," she whispered from the bed where she sat next to Christo, running a cool, damp cloth across his forehead.

"Why wouldn't you let Doc tend him?"

"My cards said it must be the woman to fix, or he will die."

"Tsk. You might have waited too long. He needs an opening." Hope used a white handkerchief to pull the boy's tongue flat to view his throat.

Matthew crouched beside the cot. "May I at least assist?"

"Can you not do it alone?" the Gypsy asked Hope.

"Doc will have to hold him. It's the only way."

Ziganya nodded her consent.

"All right Doc, let's do it."

Matthew squatted near the boy's head. He closed his eyes and bit his lip.

"Something troubling you, Doc?"

"I had a baby daughter. She got whooping cough, and I couldn't save her."

Ziganya approached him. You will not fail this time." She took Doc's hands in her own. "You will heal."

Hope took a flexible hollow stick from her bag. "I'm ready." She waited until Christo stopped coughing. The boy started struggling under Matthew's powerful grip as another spasm wracked his body.

His grandmother sat beside him, whispering words in her native tongue into his ear.

Hope said, "Now, Matthew."

He hesitated, then took the stick from her. This he inserted in Christo's nose. He would blow air into the boy's lungs while she removed the heavy membrane. Hope prayed she would do it right. She probed with her finger to find her way through the hole she'd made. "Ah, there 'tis." She pulled and removed the blockage.

Though Christo was now very weak, his color changed immediately. Hope was relieved to see his aura was again strong as well. "He'll be all right, Ziganya."

Doc stood to walk outside. He pressed his thumb and forefinger to the corners of his eyes.

Christo gave a weak cough. Ziganya looked up in alarm.

"He'll have a little sore throat for two or three days." Hope said. "Give him this with broth every few hours, and keep the kettle going."

"Now my grandson will live. And you, Hope. Your heart will be full someday."

"I'm afraid my somedays are lost." She patted the Gypsy's hand and joined Doc outside.

Matthew McBride's jaw worked while he got himself under control. "I couldn't have done that, Hope, and she knew it.

"I'm going away for a time. I need to face my failures. Walk with me to my house."

They talked as they walked along. Hope had to ask, "Have you seen Daniel? I have to tell him we aren't welcome at Mike's anymore."

"I haven't seen him all day. What is he to you, Hope? Why are you always looking out for him?"

She looked into his eyes. "He's my brother."

Doc opened the door to his house for her to pass through. "I think he's with Raven."

"There's been gossip about them. I think everyone in Coldbottom has heard it but Mike."

Hope smiled. "How do you think Mike would have taken the news that Daniel is my brother?"

Matthew blew out a breath. "I don't know. But what happened this afternoon, Hope—his pride took a beating."

"He's got more damn pride than he has a right to."

"Why didn't you tell him?" He put two cups of coffee on the table. He was glad he'd left the pot to keep warm.

"He sent for a bride. And he got one that wasn't exactly what he bargained for. I feared he'd send us back if he knew he had another mouth to feed for good. Maybe I was wrong. Don't much matter now. I guess we'll have to move on anyhow." She examined her fingernails. "Maybe Daniel won't want to go with me. It's hard to think about. We've been a pair longer than I can reckon."

Doc leaned over her chair to kiss the top of her head. "Mike will come around. He's cockeyed in love with you; it's why he's been so jealous. And if he doesn't come around, I'm still available."

"Oh, get along with you. You have enough sweet talk for a dozen men." She slapped at his hard-muscled shoulder. "Stay away from the drink, now. If you need more herbs before you leave, I'll be at Lizzy's until I decide what to do about my life."

"I can fight it on my own now, thanks to you. You're a rare woman, Hope Savage."

* * *

Hope trudged up the hill. Lizzy had a guest room in her private quarters, and Hope knew she would be welcome there. Daniel's absence concerned her, though. Normally he'd have come as soon as he heard she'd left the wedding.

Ziganya's grandson recovered quickly, and no other children came down with the cough. Later in the week she told the Gypsy he was back to normal. "Do you think you can handle getting him to take his medicine?"

"Don't give concern for me. You must seek your destiny."

Hope smiled to cover her aching heart. "My destiny is gone."

"You have not completed your circle." The Gypsy said.

"I don't know where to go from here."

"Your man will come for you. It will take time, but he will soften."

"Not him. He has a heap more starch in his neck than a body needs."

Ziganya chuckled. "He has weakness, but you have a hell of a man there." She cocked an eyebrow. "Ziganya take if you don't want." She batted her dark eyes seductively.

"There won't be any other for me. If you say wait, I'll wait. I can't go back, though."

"You stay where you are for now. That is where he will find you. At Lizzy's."

She left, then, thinking Raven might know where to find Daniel. The thought that Daniel had a lady love brought a smile to her lips. He would be good to Raven.

Daniel didn't know what to do. Pa had an idea, and that meant trouble: he wanted to capture No-Account. With her as hostage, Mike would ante up, according to Pa.

In addition, Daniel hadn't seen Hope. He'd been unable to visit Raven in Coldbottom. Every morning and evening he looked for his sister, but there was no sign of Hope or Mike. On several occasions he went into the house near mealtime, only to find the hearth fire and cookstove cold.

"Where is that ugly sister o' yourn?" Pa demanded. "If she be hitched like ya say, she'd be thar at the house."

"I looked 'n looked. If ya let me go ta Coldbottom, I might hear some news."

"Where ya goin' ta ask?"

"Up at the whorehouse. Them gals like ta jaw 'bout ever' little thing."

"They let you in there, do they? Won't let me set foot over the doorsill."

"I got me some friends, Pa." Daniel beamed.

"Yer too damn softheaded ta have friends." Pa got a glint in his eyes. "Ya know any folks would give ya liquor?"

"Aw, Pa. Ya know I don't like that stuff. It burns like fire."

"Not fer you. Fer me."

Understanding dawned. Daniel knew a chance at freedom when he met one. "If ya let me go ask around, I might be able ta get ya some." He tried to keep the excitement out of his voice.

Pa worried a stick with his fingers. He had the shakes. Daniel knew he'd won, because Pa needed liquor bad.

"Ya hotfoot it in 'n back 'fore dark or I'll come lookin' fer ya." He swished the stick in the air. Unfortunately he slipped in the mud. Cussing a blue streak, he got to his knees. "Whatcha waitin' fer? Skedaddle!"

Mike hadn't been home since the day of his humiliation. He stayed in the old shack he'd erected near his claim, working until he could barely stand. He stayed away from his ministry in Coldbottom. Two Sundays came and went without his notice.

He knew he had to face the future sometime. He woke to a sunny morning. It was the first night he'd slept in the bed he and Hope had shared. After washing and putting on a clean shirt, he checked the animals. The barn appeared tidy. Who had been caring for his stock? Daniel?

He went back to the bedroom. Her fiddle lay on the chest. He picked it up and held it under his chin, wondering why she had left it.

There was no bread in the kitchen, only the folded oilcloth in which he stored it. A busy line of ants made their way inside for crumbs. Obviously he needed supplies.

At the mercantile, Thaddeus forced a smile, but wouldn't look Mike in the eye. The place had become silent the minute he entered.

Mike bought some nails and a new shovel. There were no more honeycombs in his cabinet. He remembered exactly where the honeycombs had gone, and felt himself becoming aroused . . . and blushing.

Thaddeus seemed to want him out of there. He did a poor job of wrapping the parcels.

When Mike took them he asked, "Have you seen Hope or Daniel?"

"No, sir, I haven't."

Mike looked around. "Anyone else?"

Heads turned away. Obviously nobody would enlighten him.

Withdrawing a nugget the size of a glass marble, he said, "Anyone knows where I can find her can have this." He flicked it into the air and caught it.

One of the regulars at the store pushed his chair away from the game of checkers he'd been playing.

Alberta came from the back room. "You sit down," she directed. She looked Mike over from head to toe. "For such a good-looking, educated man, you sure have a boatload of wrongful pride."

Thaddeus accepted payment for the goods. "Sorry, Mike. Folks around here aren't too well disposed to you. You might want to lie low for a time."

Mike took his package to the door. The bell above jingled when he opened it, reminding him of Hope's delight in such a simple thing. His gut roiled. He'd find her himself and take her home.

Across the street at Harry's Saloon, a rowdy crowd had warmed up for the evening. On impulse Mike crossed over. He hadn't been in a pub since he was seventeen.

"Parson?" asked Harry.

Mike put his foot on the rail at the bar. "I'm looking for my reluctant wife. Anyone here seen her?" He looked around. The card game came to a halt.

"You're not welcome here, Parson," said Harry. "Unless you want a drink." Harry wiped the bar where Mike stood.

"I'll have a whiskey."

One of the card players lost his cheroot. Another dropped his cards.

"Afternoon, Parson. Would you mind if I had one of those too?" A short, pretty girl stood at his elbow. "I'm Lulu Mae."

"You're too young to drink." Mike turned back to Harry.

"I'm old enough—and I might be inclined to help you find your missus if you buy me one of them." She pointed to the bottle. Mike nodded to Harry.

She swallowed the whiskey in one gulp.

Mike sipped at his. "You belong at home."

"Don't have one. Mama married someone who didn't want no reminder of my pappy."

"Where is Hope Savage?"

"She's in town."

His eyes bored into hers. "Where is she staying?"

Lulu Mae poured another glass, tossed it back, then smacked her lips. "She's—"

"She's where she doesn't want to be bothered, Parson," declared Harry.

The door opened. Mike felt a draft of cold air hit his back.

Harry's eyes widened. "What's the world coming to? I never thought to see either of you in here. Least of all at the same time."

Mike turned around to see Daniel approaching.

"Mike! You're a sight ta see right now." He threw his arms around Mike, who stood stiff as a cigar store Indian.

"But first I cain't ferget what I come fer. I need a bottle o' liquor." He dug in his pocket for a coin.

Harry looked at the money. "You'll pay more than that if you want a full bottle."

"I didn't know you drank." Mike sipped from his glass again while Lulu Mae motioned for another fill-up. Mike turned her glass upside down. "No more for you."

She stuck her tongue out at him. "I'm glad I didn't tell you." Lulu swished her skirt when she turned away.

Daniel emptied his pockets, allowing Harry to take what he needed. Harry put a bottle in front of him.

"Mike, I got no one ta help me. Somethin' bad is happenin'."

"You want *my* help?" Mike felt the slow burn of anger that had begun at Daniel's entrance. "What have you done with Hope?" His voice rumbled through the room, his look black as a stormy summer sky.

"Don't ya know either? Aw. I gotta hurry." He grabbed for the bottle.

Mike fisted his hand and reared back.

Daniel never saw the punch that smashed into his face.

Chapter Twenty-three

Daniel lay sprawled at his feet. Sickness born of shame began in the pit of Mike's stomach. His eyes burned. *I will not cry.* Breathing hard, he left without his purchases.

Mike now knew himself to be a sinner of the worst kind. He'd harmed Daniel, an innocent. He had slid into a pit of violence.

He skirted the perimeter of the tent town, not stopping to ask if anyone had seen Hope—no, *his wife*. For she was his wife in his heart. Humiliation burned within him. Anger the depth of which he'd never experienced filled his soul—anger directed squarely at himself.

I've got to find her. Hell, I need the peace she brings to me. Mike realized he required her gentleness, her calming ways. Hope soothed him as one of her healing balms did others.

He walked fast, picking up the pace to a jog. Without conscious thought he went into his church, where he tumbled benches and tossed hymnals and prayer books.

Filled with a towering rage, he broke candles over his knee.

"God, where are You?" With each word he hammered his fist on the piano keys.

When his frenzy abated, he looked about him at the chaos, his vision blurred. He swiped at his eyes to clear them. His hands came away wet. Tears? The perfect preacher couldn't control his anger or his grief. For the first time he found himself without a handkerchief.

Like a small boy, he hunched on the floor with his arms wrapped around his knees. His tears soaked his shirt.

Mike Mulgrew wept for a long time, his eyes fixed on the small crucifix on the altar. "Father, help me. Forgive me. I need her." The little church remained hushed and still.

Daniel woke flat on his back. Faces hovered above him. Harry mopped at his face with a towel. Daniel scrambled to his feet. "Where's Mike?"

"Probably going home. Who'd have thought he'd knock you cold?" said Harry.

"Parson never hit nobody." Daniel looked around. "Where's my liquor?"

"All over the floor. Sorry, son; the bottle broke."

"Pa's goin' to beat me now. Aw, what am I goin' do? I got ta find ma'am. Harry, do you know where she is?"

"You mean Hope?" Harry cast a wary glance at him. "Where have you been? She walked out on the wedding. Mike told her not to come back."

"Not Parson," said the loyal Daniel.

"Doc came to the church. That fortune-teller's little boy got a whoop in his cough," said Harry. "Miss Hope said she had to go. Isn't that the way of it, fellows?"

That set off a general babble from the others.

"I'll go find Doc, then."

Harry offered a hand when Daniel tried to stand. "Doc's gone, too."

"Don't none o' ya know where ma'am is?"

His question was met with the silence of disbelief. Harry collected himself first. "She's staying at Lizzy's."

Daniel counted on his fingers. "She been up there a while?"

"She took herself up the hill. Says it'll be a cold day in hell when she marries that 'prideful man.' Them's her very words."

"Uh-oh, that's a bad sign. When she says somethin' like that well, folks pretty much has ta crawl on their bellies 'fore she'll budge."

The men, knowing the nature of a riled woman, nodded agreement.

Daniel brushed bits of glass from his whiskey-stained clothes. "Do ya want me to clean that up 'fore I go? I got some mighty disquietin' news fer her."

Harry raised his eyebrows. "What news?" He was as curious as the next man.

"If I tell ya, I won't hear the end o' it all my days."

"Then you better go, Daniel. There isn't anything in the world worse than having your ear chewed day in and day out."

"Mrs. Mike. Are you awake?"

Hope held her finger in the book she was reading when she opened the door. "Course I'm up, Raven. It's the middle of the day."

"Daniel wants to see you. He seems upset."

"I wondered when he'd be by." She placed a bit of ribbon in the book before putting it on the table.

"Howdy, Daniel," she said, entering the parlor.

"Sis, you gotta help me out. I didn't know where ya was. Pa's gettin' sore peevish at me. 'N now I don't have his liquor."

"Pa?"

"I told ya he was comin'. He's holed up near Little Falls since yer weddin' day. Keepin' me prisoner, he says. Sis, he wants his portion."

"Well, I'm not married, so he won't get two bits. He don't deserve it. Did you give him the slip?"

"Ya know Pa. He sends me ta the house fer food. Today he has the shakes, so he sent me fer liquor. I'm supposed ta find you 'n Mike."

"Has he been hitting you?" She stepped closer to examine the bruise on her brother's jaw. "I'll get my persuader and send him packing. That man has air where his brains belong."

Daniel interrupted her. " 'Twasn't him hit me, Sis. It were Mike."

That stopped her dead. "Parson? You mean Preacher Perfect done hit you?"

"Whacked me good. It do hurt."

"Mike doesn't appear to be a hitting man, that I know. Did you mess up his lists? He does value them lists."

"He asked me where ya was stayin'. He got all short with me 'cause I said I didn't know. Next thing, I was wakin' up on the floor at Harry's, 'n Pa's liquor bottle got busted." He cracked his knuckles. "I don't know what ta do."

"You stay here and visit with Raven. She missed you."

"Where you goin'?"

"I plan to say a few things to Parson Mike Mulgrew about keeping his fists to himself. It isn't right for a preacher man to run around busting folks' jaws."

"Sis, hold back some. I gotta tell ya somethin'."

"Let me have it," she said.

"I asked Miss Raven if she'll have me."

Hope looked at her brother. "Well, she'll be plumb lucky, I think. What about Pa?"

"Pa wanted me ta take a message fer Mike. That's 'cause he cain't write. Don't ferget the liquor."

"Pa doesn't need a drink. And I won't let Mike pay for me even again."

"Sis, ya know Pa might beat on you."

Taking the stairs two at a time, she said, "I'd like to see him try."

Late in the afternoon, Mike went back to the house. Shoulders slumped, he lit a lantern.

"I understand you're looking for me. Even taken to bashing folks who don't have the answer you want."

"Hope!" His heart slammed in his chest. "How? Where?" The words would not come.

Hope leaned forward, squinting. "What do you want from me?" She rocked calmly, her rifle on her lap.

"To tell you I was wrong."

"You saying you're sorry?"

"I have a lot to apologize for, but I don't know where to begin." A half smile softened his face. "Apologies are new to me."

"Well, now *that* puts a whole new light on things." Her words dripped with sarcasm.

"I only know I was desperate to see you. I needed to explain. To ask you to come back."

"There isn't anything to explain. You got all prideful because someone messed up your schedule."

"No. It was Doc. You left with him in the middle of our wedding. You're right about being prideful. I'm ashamed of myself.

Her eyes seemed to shoot purple fire.

"But we were saying our vows in front of the whole territory." His excuse rang shallow in his own ears.

"Mike Mulgrew, you're an unforgiving man."

"I know." He stood there waiting for her to condemn him.

"Why'd you hit Daniel?"

"I thought you ran off with him. He disappeared, too."

"Daniel didn't know where to find me. He came up with trouble of his own."

"What kind of trouble?"

"It's something you can't know about."

Mike didn't care anymore. "Will you forgive me?" He said it so softly she didn't appear to have heard. Clearing his throat he repeated, "Will you marry me?"

"You don't trust me. How can I tie myself to a man who won't take me as I am? Ever since I got here you've been pushing and poking at me like I was too big for the basket you wanted to put me in."

"For a while I lost my way. Jealousy, pride . . . " He groped for a word.

"You can add plain male stubbornness to the list."

He scraped his fingers through his hair. The corner of his mouth lifted, revealing his dimple. "That, too."

"I have some business to take care of; then I'll be heading back to Coldbottom. I have to think on this some." She rose to leave.

"You came armed. Did you think you might have to shoot me?"

"You never know what to expect from a feller what beats on simple folk." She walked to the door.

"Hope?"

When she turned he was standing at the table, lists in hand. "Without you I'm lost." He held each sheet to the flame of the lantern from which he'd removed the chimney. When they caught fire he placed them carefully on a tin bread plate. "My life will be ashes."

A moment later she was gone.

Hope went to the church. There were benches everywhere, some overturned. She sat on one that faced the altar. Her foot bumped something—a broken candle. She picked it up and wiggled the two ends, then looked up.

"Well, ain't this a worrisome mess we're all in." She sighed. "You recollect the first time I come in here? I'm No-Account, lest you don't recognize me. I'm not sure what I should do about Parson. He's a good man when you look past that stiff neck of his. Seemed his eyes was all sunk in."

She sat still, listening. "I do love him, though. We'll both have to give a heap of slack if we hitch up. I know I've got to make up my own mind about that. Can't figure why he hit Daniel, though.

"I reckon he holds a lot in. You know how I can see colors around folks? He didn't have any but a bit of gray today."

Silence echoed in the church.

"I've got to ask you about Pa. You know I never hurt a living soul. Except animals for food. Well . . . there *was* that traveling teacher, but he don't count. It was him or me.

"I always tried to forgive Pa. That's why I kept my distance. I guess it's time for a showdown. Mike paid for me once. Got more than he bargained for, didn't he?" A smile lit her face.

Hope stood up. "I don't want to kill Pa, so I'd be obliged if you'd get him to cooperate. Thank you kindly."

She walked from the church to Little Falls with determined steps. In the clearing she called out, "Pa? You wanted to see me. I'm standing here till you show yourself."

She leaned her rifle against a nearby tree, but palmed the derringer.

Her ears caught a rustle in the bushes behind her. She turned.

"Who the hell be you, gal?" Even in the dark she knew Pa's voice. He was hiding like a scared rabbit, as usual.

"It's your daughter, No-Account. I hear you're looking for me."

Otis swaggered out of his cover, pointing his finger at her. "Ya ain't funnin' at me, gal. That daughter o' mine is ugly as sin."

"Look closer."

He pulled his knife, holding it in a defensive position while he moved closer to walk around her.

She put her hands on her hips. "That knife isn't going to do you a bit of good. It's all rusted."

"Don't ya sass me. That No-Account was always sassin'."

He squinted, then turned as if to walk away. Hope braced herself. He whirled to leap at her. Hope ducked.

Otis found himself on the ground a few feet from where she stood.

Hope lost her temper. "You listen to me, Pa. You aren't getting money for me."

Surprising her, he rolled over, coming up close with the rusty knife. "How ya goin' ta stop me? I'm yer own livin' pa, 'n I come all this way 'cause I was grievin' fer ya."

"You're only sorry because you can't fill your gut with that damn moonshine.

"Now look there, my shoe come undone." She sat on the ground to adjust her footwear, sliding her own knife from its sheath and up her sleeve.

As she straightened, he made a dive for her with a length of rope in his hand. "Gotcha! Now move yerself over ta that tree. I don't want any funny business from ya."

Swearing, she scooted to the spot he pointed to. Lord, give me strength to put up with this, she prayed.

Positively gleeful, Otis forgot that Hope only ever became agreeable when she planned mischief. He tied her ankles first, giving Hope reason to once more wonder about the contents of his head. She even crossed her wrists so that he could tie her hands together. While he'd been tying her ankles she'd tucked the gun in her pocket. "No, ya don't, gal. I aim ta tie ya to that stout tree you're sittin' under."

"If you use all that rope tying my hands, you won't have enough to go around the tree."

346

He looked at the rope, then at the tree. "Turn yerself around ta face the tree. That'll work." He cackled while he finished securing her.

"Now what?" she asked.

"Now I get ahold o' that preacher an' talk turkey." He rubbed his hands together.

"He don't want me no more. We ain't wedded."

"Then I'll take ya somewheres 'n see what you'll bring. But first I'm seein' the man what owns all this land." He looked around. "Where be that Slow? I'm dry."

The early evening silence was broken by the mournful wail of some forest creature.

Daniel had a feeling that Hope faced danger. He took leave of Raven after their brief visit. She'd promised to marry him. Daniel Savage would soon have a family, he mused as he trudged the road to Mike's.

There was a light burning in the barn. Daniel peeked in to find Mike talking to the cow. He wanted to put some distance between himself and Mike until he cleared up what he'd done that had made Mike so doggone mad.

He went to the house and helped himself to the makings of a ham sandwich, which he ate on his way back to Little Falls. Mike must have baked bread. It suited Daniel, who hadn't had a real meal in some time.

Nearing Little Falls, he could hear Pa cackling. Pa always sounded like a chicken when he thought he'd won out. Daniel moved close so he could look the situation over.

"I'm goin' ta be set all my days after he pays fer ya. Damn, if I'd knowed you would clean up so nice, I'd sold ya years ago. Used ta look like a damn boy, and that's a fact."

Observing that Hope was bound to a tree, Daniel made a signal to let her know he was nearby.

"What's that?" Pa feared every sound in the woods, and he dove for cover.

347

"Could be a wildcat. Come to think on it, it might be an Indian. There's some around these parts, you know."

In the growing darkness Daniel saw Pa stiffen up.

"Where's that brother o' yourn? I'm parched, 'n he left fer liquon a long time back. You say it might be a wildcat?"

"Yep."

"I got my pigsticker," he said with false bravado.

"Indians are real good with knives. I understand they're partial to white hair."

Daniel laughed into his hand when Pa backed up.

"I don't know if I should leave you an' go fer Slow or what. Ya think he's in Coldbottom?"

Hope shrugged.

Daniel saw him move close to her, lean into her, and smack her. Hope's head fell to the side.

Daniel scrambled to his feet. He had to tell Mike. Mike would stop Pa.

Hope waited for Pa to leave, having already cut her bonds. Pa went behind a bush, where she heard the rustle of trousers, then a grunting sound. With all the stealth she possessed, she crept up behind him, put her gun to his temple, and whispered, "If you got any smarts at all, Pa, you'll stay still."

He rolled his eyes to the side. When he saw that she held a gun to his head, his lower portions did what he'd been straining for just seconds ago. "What the . . . I done ruined my pants!"

"Take 'em off," she commanded.

"But it's cold. They're wet." Otis whimpered.

"Off, Pa. Now!"

He stumbled when he tried to rise.

"Sit right where you are, 'n take 'em off."

"But there's a big pile there." Hope pressed the gun to

his temple. He plopped down and removed his worn trousers.

"Long johns, too."

"But I'll freeze." This wasn't the first run-in he'd had with his foster daughter, so he knew she wouldn't back down.

Obediently naked, he looked up. "Now whatcha goin' ta do?"

"Less than I'd like to. I've had all I can take from men. You all seem to want to get everything your way. Pa, you aren't getting anything. Not from Mike. Not from anyone else."

"Yer a mean, ungrateful gal."

"No. If I did what I'm inclined to do, now that would be mean and ungrateful. Not to mention I could get strung up for it." She gave him a meaningful look. "I'm going to tie you up. Really tie you up. Then I'm going back to Coldbottom to simmer down and think about my future."

He had relieved himself behind a thorny bush, and that was where she tied him. Every move he made would prick or scratch him. Pa was good at dishing out pain, but she wondered how he'd be on the receiving end. She smiled. Coward that he was, he would probably be buried in his own waste by morning. He complained of the cold, so she piled a few evergreens on him. *That should hold him.*

Mike found Daniel sleeping on the front porch when he left his nightly vigil at the church. He was so tired, he wished he could sleep like that. Squatting, he tapped the man lightly on his forearm. "Daniel. Come into the house. We both need to get warm."

Blue eyes snapped open. "There ya are. Mike, he hit her. He hit ma'am."

349

"Wake up. You're having a nightmare."

"It weren't a dream. I been here all night waitin' fer ya. He got her tied to a tree, 'n he hit her so hard she looked ta be knocked senseless." Daniel came to his feet and followed Mike into the kitchen, where a fire blazed in the stove.

Mike stilled. "*Who* hit her?"

"It were Pa. I didn't know what to do, so I come lookin' fer you. Mike, where ya been?"

"In church. I couldn't sleep. You mean her pa captured Hope and tied her up? You must have been dreaming. My little hellcat can take care of herself."

"Not with Pa."

"You keep saying that like you know the man."

Nervous now, Daniel said, "Mike, there's somethin' ya don't know 'bout us. He wants his portion—the bride price. We have the same Pa. Ma'am is my Sis."

Chapter Twenty-four

The words hit Mike like bullets, backing him up against the wood box. When it hit the backs of his legs he sat down. "Your sister? You're nothing alike."

"She told ya Ma took her in. Pa didn't like ta have her 'round, so Ma give me ta carin' for her an' keepin' her out o' his way."

"Why you?"

"I were six winters." Daniel beamed. "Pa didn't take no notice o' me 'cept ta bash on me. It were her showed me how ta piddle out in the bushes so Pa wouldn't hit me for stinkin' myself."

Mike felt his self-control slipping. "He's here? And he hit her?"

Daniel nodded.

Mike stood. "Hope wouldn't let him hit her."

"He had her tied to a tree. I saw it myself. She knew I were watchin' 'n give me a signal ta hide. When he hit her I lit out o' there to find ya."

Mike shoved his arms into his coat. "Where are they?"

"At Little Falls. Are ya goin' to help me get her away from him?"

"I'll take care of him myself."

"Ya ain't mad at me no more?"

"No, my friend. I'm mad at myself." They set off.

At the clearing they found nothing but churned-up mud.

"Aw, shucks, he took her away. I thought we might catch him," Daniel said.

Mike skirted the perimeter. He heard a groan. Putting a finger to his lips, he motioned for Daniel to follow him. Mike held his gun ready. He said a quick prayer that an animal wasn't feasting on Hope's remains.

What he found instead brought him to a halt. Daniel looked over his shoulder. In the dense overgrowth he smelled the overpowering odor of fear before he saw the naked man. "Is that him?" he asked.

"He's naked as a baby. Where's Sis?" Daniel demanded.

Pa had rolled himself into a ball. Otis's head was between his knees, somewhere under his scrawny elbows—a lily-livered pose if Mike ever saw one. "Where is she?" he grated out through clenched teeth.

Otis opened one eye to peek at this new threat.

"Who's he, Slow?"

"Ya asked for the parson. Ya got him."

"That ungrateful No-Account. Look what she did ta her lovin' daddy."

"Where's yer clothes?" asked Daniel.

"She took 'em. I been out here all night shiverin'. I'll give her the hidin' o' her life when I see her."

"You're never going to see her again."

"You goin' ta kill me? Don't let him kill me, Slow." Otis squealed.

Mike laughed. "Killing isn't what I had in mind."

"Would ya cut me loose?"

"Not until you tell us where you took her."

"Took her! Darn girl got loose and pulled a gun on me. I don't know what got her so riled."

"I think kidnapping her and tying her up might have nettled her a little." Mike took a deep breath of fresh air before bending to cut Otis loose. He backed away while the man tried to find cover. "Mind telling me if you have a name besides Pa?"

"It be Otis Savage. Slow, take off some o' those clothes fer yer freezin' pappy."

Daniel moved to unbutton his shirt, but Mike's hand stayed him. "I think not. Why don't we take him to the sheriff just the way he is?"

"But you're a man o' the church. You're 'posed to clothe the thirsty," said Otis.

Mike raised an eyebrow. "You want water?"

"Water? Hell, no. I never touch water."

"Obviously. Come with us."

"Thank ya. I knowed you'd help me."

A few minutes later Otis found himself standing under an icy waterfall, shivering. "What ya got agin' me?" he wailed.

"Don't push me. You'd drown if I took the time to enumerate. I'm saving the citizens of Coldbottom from your stink. Sheriff won't take kindly to a smelly jail." Mike gestured with the gun. "You can come out now, and walk ahead of us."

"You bested him, Mike. Now that's somethin' I'll never forget," Daniel crowed.

Hope usually took her noon meal with Lizzy and whoever was awake at that time of day. Halfway down the stairs, she heard many voices raised in excited conversation. When she entered the dining room every place had been taken, and all talk ceased. "Is there a new strike?" she asked.

Several heads waggled negatively.

"Something happened. Most of you sleep till three."

They stared at her, wide-eyed. Lizzy moved her chair and indicated that the girl on the other side make room for Hope.

"You'll want to hear this. That preacher of yours came into town with his hireling, Daniel. Parson was aiming a gun at that Otis who's been sneaking around here in Coldbottom."

Raven interrupted. "My Daniel was leading the man with a piece of thick rope. Miss Savage that man was buck naked."

"Get it right, Raven. It wasn't Daniel who was naked," piped up Patricia, who had brought a plate for Hope.

With a brilliant smile, Hope said, "My, that must have been a sight."

At her words, they all wanted to talk at once. Hope took a ladleful of barley soup. "Where did they take him?"

"To jail," said Lizzy. "Where trash like that belongs. He drank our liquor and refused to pay. That man wasn't getting anywhere near my ladies."

"They're staying at Doc's," said Raven. "Daniel says Parson wants to work things out with you. Hope, he's looking everywhere for you, but my Daniel isn't telling him where you are. Nobody in town is telling."

"But I thought they had begun to accept Mike." Hope said, buttering a slice of bread.

"They liked you before they liked him. There's a lot of speculation about you two, Hope," remarked Lizzy.

"Good."

The clink of flatware against delft subsided. All eyes were on Hope.

Patricia asked the question on everyone's mind. "You don't want him to know where to find you?"

"He knows where I am, and he's too damn stubborn to

admit it." Finished, she stood and tossed her napkin on her vacated chair. "I'll be keeping to my room."

"Don't be hasty," said Lizzy. "He's a fine-looking man. I'll bet those shoulders of his are something for a woman to wrap her arms around. Why, I can work up a sweat just thinking of what other parts of him might be like."

Hope stopped in the doorway, a sly smile on her lips. "Lizzy, if I didn't know better, I'd think you were after my preacher." She lifted her skirts and left the room.

Bawdy laughter followed her. From the stairs she called out. "Mike Mulgrew is going to have to come down a peg before I'll take him as husband. Still, consider him spoken for."

For the fourth day in a row, Mike went to every business in Coldbottom, seeking information on Hope. As with the first time he'd searched for her, he got nothing but sidelong glances from her protectors. If he weren't so desperate to find her, he'd have been proud of the loyalty she commanded.

On Friday evening he sat with Daniel and Lucas in Doc's kitchen, listening to the usual uproar that came from saloons and rowdy miners. Mike had forgotten how noisy a town could be in the evening. Gunshots rang out randomly, while drunken fights and accusations came and went.

"Daniel, I can't stand this waiting around. Where is she?"

"How many times has he asked you, Daniel?" said Lucas smugly.

"Often enough that he knows I won't say. Where are ya goin' to look tomorrow, Mike?"

"I've asked all over town."

"She says ya have to come to her."

Mike grabbed his coat and hat. "How can I do that without knowing where she is?"

"Where ya goin'?"

"For some air. Did you check the animals this afternoon?"

"You know he did, Mike. I'll come with you." Lucas followed his brother.

"Tonight I'm checking every house within three miles, and that includes my own. It'd be like her to choose my house because she knows I'm looking for her here."

Later that night, Mike again slept in his own bed. Too tired to go back to town, he sat on the bed holding Hope's pillow against him, her scent drifting around him. Eventually he fell asleep. His last thought gave him his answer. He knew what he had to do next.

He went to tent town. It had been several weeks since he'd last visited. He stopped wherever comfort was needed, promising a blanket here, some salve there. There was misery at every turn, and at each stop he asked about Hope. Here, too, he came away without an answer.

He knew now where his ministry would be. Over the next hour he resolved to try to organize some sort of housing to replace the shabby, infested quarters.

When he stepped out of the twisted pathways he'd been navigating, he found himself near the shack occupied by Ziganya Kalmenos. Mouth dry, he tapped at the wooden frame.

She pulled the curtain aside. "Ah, you are here. Come, I have been expecting you."

"You knew I'd be here?"

"You doubt?" She pushed her hair back with her right hand.

Mike sat on a stool that she indicated. "How is Christo?"

"He is well enough to play with the other children."

"I'm looking for the woman who helped you. I did a terrible thing and lost her."

When she lit a cheroot, she looked at him over the tip. "You want me to tell you where to look. I say you know the answer in your heart."

"You don't understand. I've looked everywhere."

"You think I can give you knowledge?"

Mike closed his eyes. "I need her forgiveness. I need *your* forgiveness."

"You must forgive yourself. Then you will find the healing woman."

Outside, he breathed in the crisp air. He'd lost again. *Forgive yourself. You know the answer in your heart.* He looked over his right shoulder. She couldn't be up there. Not in that den of temptation.

It was the only place he hadn't looked. The sunny winter afternoon sparkled off the windows. She'd taken refuge there before.

Step by step he climbed the hill, keeping his eyes fixed on Lizzy's. Breathing in great gasps, he stopped several times. "Please, God, help me." He repeated the prayer like a litany.

The house overlooked all of Coldbottom. Sweat beaded his brow despite the coolness of the day. Checking his watch, he verified what he already knew. Midafternoon. With a silent prayer, he put his knuckles to the door and rapped several times.

"We don't open until—" Lizzy stopped when she saw him. "Parson?"

"I believe you're harboring my future wife. Could you tell her I'm here?" His heart pounded. Did men faint? He thought he might.

"Come in. Have a seat in the selecting room."

Mike hesitated but his love forced him to go into the opulent bordello parlor. He perched on the edge of a velvet sofa, hat on his lap, waiting for Lizzy to return with Hope's verdict.

357

Lizzy bustled back into the room. "She isn't having visitors today, Parson."

"Tell her I'm not leaving until she hears me out." His heart lightened a little. Progress. At least he'd found her.

"She's pretty determined."

"She calls me stubborn, too. I'll wait."

Lizzy smiled. "You're some pair. Would you like a drink?"

"Thank you. I could use some water."

"Patricia? Parson wants water," she shouted. "Excuse me, Parson. I'm busy with my finances."

Finances? Who would think a brothel kept records? He mulled it over, wondering how many women she had to feed. Patricia brought his water on a tray. "Thanks," he said.

"Just call out if you want more."

Three glasses of water later a knock at the door signaled a visit from a miner from up-country. He joined Mike in the parlor.

"You're new around here," he said. "Where are you from?"

"I'm local."

"Howard. You're back." A woman in a pale pink gown floated into the room. A hint of perfume drifted around her. "Evening, Parson."

"Parson? You mean he's a preacher?" asked the startled Howard.

"Does that trouble you?" Mike's look could have seared meat.

"Nooooo." He grabbed his lady's hand and hurried after her.

Lizzy answered the door regularly after the first caller. Every man who entered kept his eyes averted. Soon business slowed.

Lizzy came into the room. "Parson, she won't see you. Why don't you try again tomorrow?"

"I'm not leaving without her."

"Would you go to the kitchen then? There's a big crowd out front and it's cutting into my business. After all, this is Saturday night."

"A crowd?"

"Word's out that you're here. That's big news in Cold-bottom."

Mike followed her to the kitchen, where a cook worked on meals for the ladies and their guests.

Soon the customers rapped at the back door. Rumor had it that a preacher was in the front room. The men held their hats over their faces. Mike recognized a few anyway.

Raven came in with another message, this in the form of a note.

Dear Sir, I will not come down. Please go away. Yours Truly, Hope

It was written in one line. Beneath it Mike wrote,

My Hope, for you are my only hope, I will wait here until you allow me to apologize for my lack of faith in you. I will leave only if you agree to marry me immediately, here and now.

With deepest love,
Mike

Lizzy came to see him out, thinking things had been settled.

Mike handed the note back to Raven. "I'm not leaving."

"But it's almost suppertime. I have customers to feed, and they won't come down if you're here."

Mike went to look out the windows. He hadn't seen so many people since he'd been in Boston.

"Coldbottom is shut down because of you," Lizzy

359

added.

"What does it have to do with me?"

"I'll give it to you straight. Preacher Perfect has been spotted in the whorehouse. He's been there for hours. Does that open your eyes?"

"I'm staying. Tell me where she is."

"Sorry, betrayal isn't my style. I do have scruples, you know." Lizzy looked offended.

"That does it." He left the kitchen, went down the hall, and took the stairs in long strides.

At the landing he shouted, "Hope Savage. I'm coming to get you." Then he opened the nearest door. A couple engaged in heaven knew what looked up, startled.

Mike marched down the hall, throwing each door open. Lizzy followed, shouting for him to cease.

One door revealed Sheriff Stably trying to hop into his pants. "For God's sake, Mike, can't a man have a few minutes' privacy without you spoiling it?"

"Get ready to perform a wedding."

"Now? Here?"

In the next room a man hid under the bed. All Mike saw were his bare feet.

He looked back into the room, where Oliver tried to dress. "In the parlor, Sheriff."

"But you'll need witnesses."

Mike turned around to look over the hastily dressed crush of people following him. "Looks like we've got more than enough." He shouted, "I love you, Hope Savage. Will you forgive me? Will you marry me right here and now?"

Hope had heard every bit of commotion he caused. She smiled at his shouted proposal. Lordy, even the folks in Sacramento must have heard him. Still, she would not give in so easily. Her eyes found the words on the note again, warming her heart.

The house, shaped like an upside-down *L*, had private

rooms around the corner. In a moment he would turn that corner.

She considered the back stairs. No, she'd meet him halfway. He had put aside his dignity to come for her, she too would put away her pride. After a quick look in the mirror, she opened the door to step into the hall.

Mike stopped. "Hope."

Hope's heart quickened. He'd said he loved her. He knew about everything and still wanted her.

Mike advanced. "Lady, I hope you're prepared to be married right now." He stopped a foot away from her, then wiped a tear that slid from the corner of her eye with the pad of his thumb.

The hallway became silent. Everyone strained to hear her answer.

"Will you let me go where I'm needed?"

He pulled her to him. "Anywhere. I'll even help you move your garden near the house."

"What about the "obey" part?"

"I love you. It's not important."

She threw her arms around him. "You just got yourself a wife, Parson. And I promise to learn the darn clock. I'll even keep a list if you want."

Cheers erupted behind them. Someone opened a window to shout, "She said yes!" inciting another cheer.

Hours later, Hope snuggled in the arms of her new husband in Lizzy's guest bedroom. "It was a beautiful wedding," she remarked, tenderly touching his cheek.

"Uh-huh. It was a beautiful wedding night, too." He ran his fingers through her hair. "Do you think they're still celebrating?" The noise from the street had not lessened.

At that moment someone shouted, "Go to it, Parson!"

"I guess they are. Have you thought about how we're going to tell our children about our wedding?"

"We won't have to tell them. Imagine the stories.

Monica Roberts

Preacher Perfect married his lady and had his wedding night in Miss Lizzy's Establishment for Gentlemen." She offered her lips for a long, passionate kiss.

"You're going to wear me out," Mike said.

Hope had rolled over, so that she straddled him. "It's good to know you don't have a man problem. Course, I could dose you for it." Her fingers trailed down his chest until they found him—ready and willing.

Sinking into her again, Mike whispered, "You're what I've waited for all my life."

"Really?"

"My Hope."

They moved together, touching, giving, taking.

When he pulled her to him in that sweet moment of total union, he whispered, "My Hope, my love."

AN ORIGINAL SIN NINA BANGS

Fortune MacDonald listens to women's fantasies on a daily basis as she takes their orders for customized men. In a time when the male species is extinct, she is a valued man-maker. So when she awakes to find herself sharing a bed with the most lifelike, virile man she has ever laid eyes or hands on, she lets her gaze inventory his assets. From his long dark hair, to his knife-edged cheekbones, to his broad shoulders, to his jutting—well, all in the name of research, right?—it doesn't take an expert any time at all to realize that he is the genuine article, a bona fide man. And when Leith Campbell takes her in his arms, she knows real passion for the first time . . . but has she found true love?

____52324-8 $5.99 US/$6.99 CAN

Dorchester Publishing Co., Inc.
P.O. Box 6640
Wayne, PA 19087-8640

Please add $1.75 for shipping and handling for the first book and $.50 for each book thereafter. NY, NYC, and PA residents, please add appropriate sales tax. No cash, stamps, or C.O.D.s. All orders shipped within 6 weeks via postal service book rate. Canadian orders require $2.00 extra postage and must be paid in U.S. dollars through a U.S. banking facility.

Name_____
Address_____
City_____State_____Zip_____
I have enclosed $_____ in payment for the checked book(s).
Payment <u>must</u> accompany all orders. ❏ Please send a free catalog.
CHECK OUT OUR WEBSITE! www.dorchesterpub.com

BUSHWHACKED BRIDE EUGENIA RILEY

"JUMPING JEHOSHAPHAT! YOU'VE SHANGHAIED THE NEW SCHOOLMARM!"

Ma Reklaw bellows at her sons and wields her broom with a fierceness that has all five outlaw brothers running for cover; it doesn't take a Ph.D. to realize that in the Reklaw household, Ma is the law. Professor Jessica Garret watches dumbstruck as the members of the feared Reklaw Gang turn tail—one up a tree, another under the hay wagon, and one in a barrel. Having been unceremoniously kidnapped by the rowdy brothers, the green-eyed beauty takes great pleasure in their discomfort until Ma Reklaw finds a new way to sweep clean her sons' disreputable behavior—by offering Jessica's hand in marriage to the best behaved. Jessie has heard of shotgun weddings, but a broomstick betrothal is ridiculous! As the dashing but dangerous desperadoes start the wooing there is no telling what will happen with one bride for five brothers.

___52320-5 $5.99 US/$6.99 CAN

Winds & Kiss THE BEWITCHED VIKING SANDRA HILL

'Tis enough to drive a sane Viking mad, the things Tykir Thorksson is forced to do—capturing a red-headed virago, putting up with the flock of sheep that follow her everywhere, chasing off her bumbling brothers. But what can a man expect from the sorceress who put a kink in the King of Norway's most precious body part? If that isn't bad enough, he is beginning to realize he isn't at all immune to the enchantment of brash red hair and freckles. But he is not called Tykir the Great for nothing. Perhaps he can reverse the spell and hold her captive, not with his mighty sword, but with a Viking man's greatest magic: a wink and a smile.

___52311-6 $5.99 US/$6.99 CAN

Family Man
Carol Carson

WANTED. FAMILY MAN. MUST LOVE CHILDREN. PAYMENT NEGOTIABLE.

Rider Magrane knows what "wanted" means; he's spent time running from the law. Those days are over now, and he's come back to Drover to make amends. But the man he's wronged is no longer in town. Instead he finds the most appealing woman he's ever met—Jane Warner—and she thinks that he's come about the ad he now holds in his hand. To be near her is tempting, but what does a cattle rustler know about children—or love? Jane posts the ad to lure a capable male into caring for her nephews—she herself has never been part of the deal. But examining the hunk that appears at her homestead, all she can think of are the good aspects of having a man in her life. The payment is negotiable; she's said so herself. No price is too dear for this handsome stranger's heart.

___4625-3 $4.99 US/$5.99 CAN